MIDNIGHT'S WARRIOR

DONNA GRANT

St. Martin's Paperbacks

This is a work of fiction. All of the characters, organizations, and events portrayed in this novel are either products of the author's imagination or are used fictitiously.

MIDNIGHT'S WARRIOR

For information address St. Martin's Press, 175 Fifth Avenue, New York, NY 10010.

ISBN: 978-0-312-55259-6

Printed in the United States of America

St. Martin's Paperbacks edition / December 2012

St. Martin's Paperbacks are published by St. Martin's Press, 175 Fifth Avenue, New York, NY 10010.

10 9 8 7 6 5 4 3 2 1

ST. MARTIN'S PAPERBACKS TITLES BY
DONNA GRANT

For Lisa Renee Jones, sister of my heart.
Exceptional writer, valued confidante,
and dearest friend.

ACKNOWLEDGMENTS

As always my thanks goes first to my brilliant, fabulous editor, Monique Patterson. I'm so very blessed to be working with such a wonderful person, and talented editor. Thank you. For everything.

To Holly Blanck and everyone at St. Martin's who helped get this book ready, thank you.

To my extraordinary agent, Amy Moore-Benson. Thank you!

A special note to Melissa Bradley, Kim Rocha, Rasit Ra (Maria). Thanks for everything you all do. Y'all make my life easier, and for that, I owe each of you so very much.

To my kiddos, parents, and brother—A writer makes sacrifices when writing, but so does the writer's family. Thanks for picking up the slack, knowing when I'm on deadline that I might not remember conversations, and for not minding having to repeat things.

And to my husband, Steve, my real-life hero. You never mind spending dinners talking about upcoming battle scenes or helping me work through a spot I'm stuck in. Thank you for the love you've given me, for the laughter you brought into my life, our beautiful children, and the happily-ever-after life I always dreamed of. I love you, Sexy!

CHAPTER ONE

Dunnoth Tower
Northern Scotland

Tara tapped her toe beneath her desk as she discreetly listened to her iPod in one ear. She quite enjoyed her job as a booking agent, tour guide, bookkeeper, and anything else they needed at the castle.

She hadn't thought about where she would go when she left Edinburgh after that disastrous run-in with the Warriors and Druids. She'd driven and driven and driven until the road led her to the sea and Dunnoth Tower.

Tara had stopped at the medieval castle to eat and stretch her legs. She'd been instantly taken with the structure and took the tour of it. To her surprise there had been a position open, and she'd applied. She'd started work that very day.

It had only been a few weeks, but she was thoroughly enjoying her time at Dunnoth, which she hadn't expected after teaching. Yet, she found the quiet and peace of the castle and the North Sea helped to settle the turmoil inside her.

It also helped that the owners were pleasant, her coworkers friendly, and the tourists so eager to learn about the castle that they weren't much of a problem to handle.

Although tourism in the middle of January in the far north of Scotland wasn't much to talk about. Most tourists were at the ski resorts, but come summer, the castle was going to be very busy.

Tara looked forward to it. For now, she was reading over the accounting books to make sure everything was in order, and taking bookings for the castle for the summer months.

A door opened to her left and in walked the newest member of the castle employees. Tara's mouth had dropped open the first time she saw the tall, black-headed hunk with the amazing gray eyes that seemed to see right into her soul.

That had been the day before. And now, she found herself staring at him again as he walked across the entryway and began to work on the electrical outlet that had shorted out months ago.

Though this time she did manage to keep her mouth closed and not make a complete fool of herself.

He filled out the navy short-sleeved tee to perfection with his thick shoulders and muscular arms. Yesterday evening they'd been hit with a rain and snow mix, and he'd gotten caught in it. When he'd come rushing into the castle with his shirt plastered to his abs, she'd been able to count each and every muscle in that washboard stomach of his.

The sight of it had made her wish she could see him without his shirt on to get a good glimpse of that tanned skin and ripped body.

Tara smiled. She'd always been a sucker for a man who knew how to take care of himself. But with Ramsey it wasn't just his body.

It was his long, black hair that hung past his shoulders with just a hint of a wave to the shiny locks. He kept it pulled away from his face in a ponytail, but she longed to see him with it down.

Then there was his face. She sighed. And what a face it was. Sculpted jaw with just a small shadow of whiskers, square chin, strong nose, and a high forehead with black brows slashed over his eyes. His lips were full and wide, and he had eyelashes so thick, so black, that any woman would be envious. His steel-gray eyes held a hint of laughter in them, as if he knew far more than anyone around him, and he wasn't going to share.

"Good morn," Ramsey said in his deep baritone voice.

A shiver raced over Tara's skin every time he spoke, as if her body were dialed into his husky voice. "Morning, Ramsey."

"What are you listening to?" he asked. He stopped at the wall and bent to open his toolbox and pulled out a couple of tools.

Tara blinked. "Huh?"

Ramsey glanced at her and smiled. "Your music, lass. What are you listening to?"

"Ah . . . Rihanna," she answered, still baffled that he had known she had her iPod on. She had turned it down low enough so that no one would hear, and the cords to her earplugs were hidden by her hair.

Tara's heart began to pound as her mind raced. Had the Warriors found her again? She scooted her rolling chair back, prepared to grab her purse and keys and run.

Until she spotted the white cord against her black sweater.

She looked at Ramsey to find him staring at her. After a moment, he shrugged and turned his back to her.

Tara released a long sigh and put her elbow on the desk before she dropped her head into her hand. She was so paranoid. She hated living her life this way, but for her, there wasn't another way.

Because she was a Druid. And not just any Druid.

She was a dangerous one.

Tara squeezed her eyes closed and thought over the past ten years of her life. It wasn't that she had had a good or bad childhood. It had been average, just like her grades in school.

Hell, she had been average. Average height, average looks, average clothes, average everything.

She had known since she was a small child that she had magic. It ran strong through her family, and it never worried her. That is, until the day of her eighteenth birthday and she learned far more about the Druids than she had ever been told before.

Her family had lied to her all those years before, telling her that all Druids were the same. Not only were there two different kinds of Druids—*mies,* the good Druids, and *droughs,* the ones who dabbled in black magic and gave their souls to the Devil—her family were all *droughs.*

That wasn't what bothered her. What had made her run from her family was their insistence that she become *drough* as well. They demanded she give her soul to Satan, which would have condemned her to Hell when she died.

For some odd, inexplicable reason, that didn't bother anyone in her family. Just her. And they didn't understand her. Not that they ever had before.

Tara hadn't wanted anything extraordinary out of life. She had just wanted a simple life. A husband who loved her, children surrounding her, and a house filled with lots of laughter.

Instead, she now couldn't stay anywhere too long before she had to leave again. Already she had spent ten years in Scotland, which was most likely ten years too long. She should have left and gone somewhere else when she ran away from her family, but she loved Scotland too much to leave.

However, she knew this was her last stop in her beloved land. She was going to have to leave. And it saddened her.

It was just five days until her birthday. She had always thought by the time she reached twenty-eight she'd have at least two children.

Instead, she was alone.

She didn't even allow herself to make friends, because friends asked questions and became curious about her past. And she hated lying. So, she kept to herself.

There had been one time she made the mistake of thinking someone was a friend. But Declan Wallace had been anything but.

To this day she didn't know how he had found her in that pub in Aberdeen, but his good looks, charm, and silver tongue had done the trick for a scared, confused eighteen-year-old who had run away from home.

Tara should have known what kind of man he was, but she blamed her emotional state for having overlooked it. She had stayed at his mansion for a month before she learned he was a Druid.

When he didn't push her to undergo the ceremony to become *drough,* she worked with him on strengthening her magic for several more months. Tara had been careful about how much she used her magic. No one, least of all her, understood why her magic was so out of control.

But Declan had pressed her to use more of it, to learn to control it. He hadn't understood her reluctance, and she hadn't told him. Nothing had worked, yet he hadn't been upset. He seemed to enjoy the fact that her magic was all over the place. If her emotions were high, she could blow up a lightbulb without even trying.

Then, one night, she hadn't been able to sleep and she'd ventured downstairs to get something to eat when she'd overheard Declan's plans for her.

Once again Tara was on the run.

She knew eventually she would be caught. Would it be by her family? The Warriors hunting her? Or Declan? Who among them would end her life? Would they come in the middle of the night, or in the light of day? Did it even matter anymore?

"Tara?"

She jerked at the feel of Ramsey's hand on her arm. "Yes?" she asked as she tugged the earphone out of her ear.

"Are you all right?" His brow was knit, his gray eyes full of concern.

"Yes," she lied.

He raised a thick black brow and flattened his lips. "I doona believe you're telling me the truth, but I willna press you."

The heat of his body seared her skin through her sweater where his hand was, but it didn't hurt. What it did was cause her blood to heat and made her think of leaning close and pressing her lips against his.

She cleared her throat and looked away from his hypnotic

eyes. "I'm fine. Really," she said, and plastered on a smile as she glanced at him.

He released her and stepped back. Instantly she missed his nearness, his touch, and his heat. How he could walk around in a short-sleeved tee in this frigid January weather, with the snow outside several feet thick, she didn't know. But she wished she could do the same.

"How long have you been at Dunnoth Tower?" he asked as he once more knelt in front of the outlet on the opposite wall.

She hated when people asked her questions, but for some reason she wanted to answer Ramsey's. Which wasn't a good sign for her at all. "A few weeks."

He pulled the outlet from the wall and inspected it before he twisted a few wires. "Hmm," he responded.

"What brought you here?" She licked her lips, refusing to wonder what made her ask her own question. She never did this. It made it appear as if she were interested in him when she needed to keep her distance.

But there was something so alluring, so fascinating about Ramsey that she couldn't help herself.

"Chance, maybe." He shrugged and tightened a wire. "Who knows? How about you?"

"I was driving and the road took me here."

He looked up and met her gaze. "Definitely chance on your part."

She grinned as she leaned her forearms on her desk. She had no idea what had come over her, asking and answering questions. And she even left her answer open so Ramsey could ask something else.

But he didn't.

Because he didn't it gave her the insane urge to inquire about something else. Thankfully, the phone rang, saving her from making an utter fool of herself.

Tara kept glancing at Ramsey as she looked at the calendar to book a company conference. She grew agitated at the woman on the other end of the line because Ramsey was finishing up with the outlet and she was still on the phone.

And then Ramsey closed his toolbox and stood. He gave her a smile and walked away.

Tara sighed. "I beg your pardon, ma'am. I didn't hear that last bit. Could you repeat it?"

As she wrote down the dates in the calendar and calculated the deposit, Tara told herself now wasn't the time to find a man she was interested in.

The problem was there was never a good time for her to get involved with anyone.

CHAPTER
TWO

Ramsey leaned against the wall and dropped his head back. Touching Tara had been a mistake. A drastic mistake.

He looked down at the spread fingers of the hand that had held her. White tendrils of magic floated along his skin like smoke. It made his skin tingle and his own magic burn to be released.

Ramsey fisted his hand and clenched his jaw. In all his immortal years, never had he encountered a Druid who had affected his magic the way Tara did.

He tilted his head slightly and listened to her sweet voice as she spoke on the phone. She laughed, the sound shooting straight to his balls, making them tighten. Need, thick and strong and unyielding, ran through him.

If he had known how being near Tara would affect him, Ramsey might have brought another Warrior with him. But he'd come alone. It was a risky endeavor, but he knew he had to accomplish it by himself.

After all, he was a Warrior, a Highlander with a primeval god locked inside him that gave Ramsey immortality and a host of enhanced senses as well as incredible power. Those same gods were the ones freed by the *droughs* from their prison in Hell to help fight the Romans who had invaded Britain so many centuries before.

He wasn't just a Warrior though. He was also a Druid. A

fact he had kept from his brethren until a few days ago. He hadn't known how they would react to the news, but that wasn't the only reason he hadn't told them. It was a secret he had kept from everyone since the day Deirdre took him and unbound his god.

A smile pulled at Ramsey's lips as he thought of Deirdre. Finally, after centuries of fighting her, they had managed to awaken her twin from a magical sleep. It had been dangerous finding and awakening Laria, but in the end, she was the only one who could kill Deirdre.

None of them had expected that it would claim Laria's life as well.

Deirdre's death should have ended all their misery. Should have, but didn't. Because there was another power-hungry *drough*, a man who had used his magic to pull Deirdre forward four hundred years in time.

Declan Wallace.

He was the reason Ramsey had tracked Tara. Declan was a menace who needed to be killed, but he was devilishly lucky. Too lucky, in fact.

Ramsey covertly leaned around the doorway and looked at Tara. She had her earphones back on and was slowly tapping her left foot to the beat of whatever she was listening to.

She seemed oblivious to his real motives for coming to Dunnoth Tower, and that worked perfectly for Ramsey. He would do everything he could to stop Saffron's vision from coming true.

His mobile phone vibrated in his pocket suddenly. Ramsey hurried away from Tara and reached for the device. He was still getting used to the technology of the age, but he was catching on fast.

Ramsey answered his iPhone with a whispered, "Aye."

There was a sigh, and then Saffron's voice said, "You're supposed to say 'Hello.'"

"Ah. Well then, hello."

The Seer chuckled. "Have you seen Declan yet?"

Ramsey glanced around him as he shouldered his way

through a door that led outside to the cottage given to him as the all-around handyman of the tower. "No' yet. How are things at MacLeod Castle?"

He missed being at the castle. It was the only home he'd had in centuries, and now that most of the Warriors had found their mates with Druids, the castle was more of a home than ever.

"Everyone is anxious to hear from you. Uh. Actually, I was calling to let you know that you're going to have a visitor."

"A visitor?" he repeated as he reached his cottage and set down his toolbox to open the door. As soon as he stepped inside he found the leader of the Warriors, Fallon MacLeod, sitting in the overstuffed chair. "Fallon."

"Yep," Saffron said in her American accent. "He's already there, isn't he?"

Ramsey nodded, then said, "Aye."

"My cue to hang up."

Ramsey returned the mobile to his pocket as Fallon stood. They clasped forearms and nodded their greetings.

"It's good to see you," Ramsey said. "Is something wrong?"

Fallon shook his head. "Nay. I just wanted to see how things were going."

"It's been naught but two days." Ramsey eyed the eldest MacLeod and appointed leader of the Warriors. "What really brings you?"

Fallon ran a hand down his face. "I never liked the idea of you being here alone, not with Declan coming for Tara."

"I can handle him."

"I'm no' saying you cannot. All I'm saying is that I willna lose another friend. It's been four centuries, but I feel the loss of Duncan to this day."

Ramsey rubbed the back of his neck and nodded. "I as well. Who do you want to send here?"

Fallon grinned.

Ramsey rolled his eyes as understanding dawned. "Who's here?"

"Arran and Charon."

He cringed. "No' two I'd have paired after their time in Deirdre's mountain together."

"Arran says he's over it. I think it helps that he now knows Deirdre was forcing Charon to spy for her."

"Where are they?"

"Around. You willna see them unless there's trouble. I still think you're taking a huge risk doing this, Ramsey. Declan could recognize you."

Ramsey shook his head. "He was too preoccupied with Saffron and Camdyn as well as watching Malcolm turn against Deirdre to have noticed me during the battle at the Ring of Brodgar."

"If there's any trouble, take Tara, by force if needed, and get back to MacLeod Castle."

Ramsey gave a brief nod of assent. None of them knew just how powerful he was, and for the moment, that's exactly how Ramsey wanted it. There would be no running for him. He intended to kill Declan before the *drough* had a chance to get to Tara.

Ramsey was descended from a line of male Druids from the Torrachilty Forest who were fabled for their potent magic. They had been the warriors of the Druid world, the ones who had kept the *droughs* and *mies* from massacring each other. Add the power of Ramsey's god and he was a force to be reckoned with.

On only one occasion had he shown some of that power, and that was the first time they had killed Deirdre. With all the Warriors battling her at once, no one realized what Ramsey had done. But for all their power, Deirdre hadn't stayed dead. This time, however, was different. She was well and truly gone.

It had relieved Ramsey for all of a day before Saffron's vision. As a Seer, Saffron didn't always see everything in her visions. What she had seen was Tara. Saffron had been shown that Tara's life was in danger, and that Ramsey was to be the one to save her.

It hadn't taken them long to piece together from Saffron's earlier visions that Declan was the one after Tara. And after

Ramsey paid a little visit to Tara's drunk of a mother, it was confirmed that Declan had called on her looking for Tara.

Ramsey watched as Fallon walked to the window and looked across the snow-covered grounds to the castle. "Have you spoken with Tara?" Fallon asked.

"Aye. She's guarded, as I expected. From your description of the Druid who ran from you in Edinburgh, she's one and the same."

Fallon crossed his arms over his chest. "You seem different, old friend."

Ramsey had never been much of a talker. He liked to formulate his answers and think of every possible outcome or decision before he voiced anything. But there were times, like now, when he didn't have that option.

Fallon was a noble man, a natural leader, and a good friend. He didn't want to lie to Fallon.

"Tara's magic is . . ."

"Different?" Fallon offered as he turned his head to look at him.

Ramsey nodded. He held up his hand where the magical tendrils could still be seen.

"Bloody hell," Fallon murmured as he dropped his arms to his sides and stared at Ramsey's hand.

"I touched her on her arm briefly. Through her sweater. Her magic is unexplainable. I've never felt anything like it. It's strong, but no' as strong as Isla's or Reaghan's. Yet, in some ways it's stronger than all of the Druids at MacLeod Castle combined."

"Is she *drough*?"

Ramsey had looked at Tara's neck for the Demon's Kiss, a small silver vial that held the first drops of a *drough*'s blood after the ceremony where they gave their soul to the Devil. "I've no' seen proof of it. And with the sweaters she wears, I've no' had a chance to look at her wrists for the cut marks."

"Does her magic hurt?"

"Nay." Anything but. Her magic was the most wonderful thing Ramsey had ever felt. He wanted to keep touching her, to keep that feeling close to him. It was like a drug, and after just one touch, he was addicted.

Fallon's green eyes narrowed as if he knew exactly what Ramsey was thinking.

"Get back to your wife," Ramsey said. "I doona want Larena angry at me because you've stayed away too long."

The mention of Fallon's wife and only female Warrior always made Fallon smile. "Aye. She and Isla want to go to Edinburgh Castle to see if they can find the hidden spell that would bind our gods that Laria spoke about. I know it's long gone from Edinburgh, but the girls say they need to start somewhere."

"I want to know the progress of that, so keep me informed."

"Will do. And doona do anything stupid, Ramsey. We need you at the castle."

Ramsey grinned. "Fallon, I'm no' the rash one."

"True, but I wanted to issue the caution just in case. I've seen what my sisters-in-law did to my brothers and the other Warriors. It seems that Druids are paired nicely with us Warriors."

"You have nothing to worry about with me. I've no desire to find a woman."

Fallon slapped him on the shoulder. "Good luck with that. Until later."

And then Fallon teleported back to MacLeod Castle.

Each Warrior had a special power, and Fallon's was jumping places in a blink, but he had to have visited the place before. He couldn't teleport somewhere he'd never been. Which was why he had driven with Ramsey to Dunnoth.

But it did make travel easy with Fallon around.

Ramsey shook his head as he walked to the refrigerator and grabbed a Coke. He unscrewed the cap and tilted it to his lips for a long drink.

There was a huge list of things for him to do around the castle, and with the heavy clouds overhead, there was little doubt that more snow was on the way. Ramsey replaced the bottle of Coke in the fridge and decided to do the outside chores first before it began to snow.

If he waited, they'd start asking why he wasn't wearing a coat. He couldn't exactly tell them that he didn't get cold or hot as mortals did, or that he rather liked the feel of the cold against his skin.

It was just better not to take any unnecessary risks unless it was absolutely essential. He snorted. He'd heard that so many times from his father and uncle that it had stuck. It had been something Ramsey lived by, and only rarely did he take such a risk.

He consulted the list the owners had given him that morning at dawn and searched for the things that needed to be done outside. After making note of the first two, he folded the paper and stuffed it in his back pocket before heading out the door.

Dunnoth Tower sat on the beach, by Sinclair's Bay in the North Sea. The water was darker and choppier than the sea at MacLeod Castle, but no less pretty.

The salt hung in the air, and the brisk breeze coming off the water only added to the stoic beauty of the castle. It hadn't stood as long as MacLeod Castle, but neither did it have its grisly history.

Ramsey inhaled deeply as he finished fixing the lock on the gate leading to the private drive of the owners. He walked toward the shed to get the snow shovel and remove the snow from the path leading down to the beach. There were only two guests in the castle at present, but everything needed to stay spotless at all times.

Ramsey had shoveled half of the path when he felt someone watching him. He paused and leaned against the shovel as his gaze roamed the area.

And came to rest on Tara standing ten feet from him holding a steaming cup of coffee.

His magic swarmed through him as he drank in her beauty. She had a natural look that he liked entirely too much. She wore makeup, but very little, and what she wore only accentuated her large, almond-shaped eyes and full lips.

Her skin was the color of mocha that complemented her long, wavy soft brown hair and golden highlights to perfection. And her blue-green eyes were a shade no color palette could capture.

Her oval face had high cheekbones, a small nose, and gently arching brows. She was of average height, not coming quite to Ramsey's shoulder, but she was all woman.

With her infectious smile that combined seduction and mischievousness, tantalizing eyes that beckoned, and a voice that made his blood heat, Ramsey wanted her.

Desperately.

But he wasn't there to woo a woman, no matter how fine a lass she was. He was there to protect her, and find Declan so he could kill him.

Everything else would have to wait.

She smiled and licked her lips as she walked toward him. Ramsey could see she was nervous. The fact she was coming to him was unexpected. From what he had seen of her, and heard from the owners and few other employees, Tara liked to keep to herself and rarely, if ever, answered any questions about herself.

"I thought you might need this," she said as she handed him the large mug. "Though maybe I was wrong. I don't know anyone who could stand to be out here longer than a few moments without some kind of sweater at least."

Ramsey shrugged as he took a sip of the hot liquid. "I like the cold."

"I can see that," she replied with a chuckle.

Her dark, multicolored scarf was wrapped tightly around her throat, and her black coat disguised the shapely body he had seen when she wore just her jeans and a sweater.

Ramsey noticed the way she tried not to look at him too long, and how her gloved fingers kept fidgeting with her scarf or hair.

"I didn't mean to bother you," she said.

He suddenly realized he'd let the silence between them go on too long. "You didna. I'm sorry. I'm no' much of a talker."

She shrugged and grinned shyly. "Neither am I. Usually. I don't know what's wrong with me."

"Sometimes a person needs to talk. Even if it's about nothing."

Tara nodded. "That must be it. I—"

"Doona stop on my account. Just because I doona like to talk does no' mean I'm no' curious about you."

She tugged a strand of light brown hair behind her ear. "I usually like to keep to myself."

"Usually?"

"Always," she said with a small lift of a shoulder, her eyes glancing down at her feet. "But I saw you out here and . . ." She trailed off, this time folding her hands together in front of her.

"The coffee was just what I needed. I thank you."

Her lips parted as she began to talk, but just then the phone rang. Tara gave Ramsey one more look before she ran into the castle.

"Damn," Ramsey said as he lifted the cup to his lips, his eyes following Tara. "I'm in trouble."

CHAPTER
THREE

Tara replaced the phone on its cradle and ran the credit card number she'd just gotten for the guest who was arriving later that evening.

She smiled as she looked at the list of requests that had been asked for as the credit card machine verified all the information. As soon as the card was approved Tara made a notation on her sheet.

With the instructions in hand, she rose from her chair, but her gaze was quickly snagged by Ramsey once more. She couldn't tear her eyes away from him.

The way his muscles moved beneath the form-fitting tee had her hands itching to touch his tanned skin. Ramsey's muscles weren't huge like a bodybuilder's, but they were visible and very, very pleasing to look at.

"Ripped," she murmured.

Each muscle, even in his arms, was toned and defined so that there wasn't an ounce of fat anywhere on his body. He turned his back to the windows and leaned over, giving Tara a perfect view of his butt.

"What a bum," said a voice behind Tara.

She jerked and turned around to find one of the owners, Liz Maxwell. Liz cut her hazel eyes to Tara and grinned.

"There's no harm in looking," Liz said. "I've certainly done enough of it since Ramsey arrived."

Tara glanced at Ramsey to find he faced the castle once more as he continued to shovel the thick snow. She dragged her eyes away from him and looked at the owner. Liz was in her early forties, but didn't look it. She worked out and ate healthily, and having a lot of money helped to keep her in high-end clothes and her blond hair impeccable.

Tara smiled. "He is rather good-looking."

"Oh, please. He's not good-looking, Tara. He's gorgeous. Swoonworthy even. I can't believe he's not on the telly or in movies. Men like him aren't easy to find. I'd snatch him up if I were you."

Tara shrugged, unsure of what to say. Did she want to run her hands over Ramsey and kiss him until she forgot who she was? Definitely.

Did she want a relationship with him where he knew everything about her past and her family? That would be a huge no.

There were too many things in her past she couldn't outrun, and she didn't want anyone else hurt when those things caught up with her.

"What's in your hand?" Liz asked.

"Ah, instructions," Tara said, reluctantly tearing her thoughts away from Ramsey. "We have a high-profile guest coming tonight to stay through the weekend. He's surprising his girlfriend, so he has some requests he'd like us to take care of."

"And who is this high-profile guest?" Liz asked, a big smile on her lips.

"The name was withheld. I was told it was to make sure the media didn't find out where he was."

"Well, it isn't the British royalty. They have castles of their own in Scotland." Liz tapped her finger on her chin. "I can't wait to find out who it is. Let's begin to get everything in order. We only have a few hours. Which room did they book?"

"They'll be on the fourth floor."

"Oh, the Duke's rooms," Liz said with a satisfied nod.

Tara looked down at the list. "He wants champagne, at least four dozen roses—"

"What color?" Liz interrupted.

"He didn't say."

"Hmm. I'm thinking a mix of red, pink, and white. Go on."

"Chocolate-covered strawberries, rose petals sprinkled over the bed, and lots of candles throughout the room. He's also requested the best meal our chef can prepare so they can dine in the room tonight. The entire thing is supposed to be a surprise."

Liz rubbed her hands together. "I'll talk to Stefan now and also contact the florist about the roses."

Tara made notations by those items and tucked the pencil behind her ear. "I'll get on the rest."

Liz hurried away while Tara removed her scarf and coat. Before she hung them up on the hooks near the door, she grabbed her mittens that were atop her desk and tucked them in the pocket of her jacket.

Unable to resist, Tara took another look at Ramsey. But to her disappointment, he was gone, the path well and truly cleared for anyone who wanted to venture out to the beach.

She sighed and hurried to find the housekeeper.

Ramsey replaced the shovel in the shed before he returned to his small, one-bedroom cottage and called Arran.

"I guess Fallon told you," Arran said by way of hello.

Ramsey chuckled. "Aye, he did. There's little vegetation or buildings to hide you or Charon around the castle. The two of you should come to the cottage and stay."

"And then how would we have a look around the place?"

"At night, obviously. The closer you are, the faster you can help me if I need it."

Arran was quiet so long Ramsey was beginning to wonder if the Warrior realized that he planned to take on Declan himself.

"Charon doesna like the idea," Arran said finally.

"I doona like the fact that either of you are here, but there's nothing I can do about it. Fallon wanted you both in case something happened. It's no' a matter of if Declan will come, it's a matter of when. You've had to go some distance from the castle in order to find cover. If you're here, I wouldna have to wait for you to arrive."

"Doona try to manipulate us," Charon's disembodied voice said over the phone.

Ramsey smiled. "All right. I doona trust Declan. I cannot watch both Tara and the two of you."

"We're Warriors, Ramsey. Immortal. With powers," Arran said, his voice thick with irritation.

"Aye. And in case you've forgotten, Declan has the X90 bullets filled with *drough* blood. One drop. That's all it takes to kill us."

Arran sighed loudly. "We'll be there shortly."

"I'll leave the back window unlocked."

Ramsey ended the call and ran a hand down his face. If need be, he would lock Charon and Arran away somewhere so they couldn't be harmed by Declan.

In their war against Deirdre they had come away with only the loss of Duncan but entirely too many Druids. Ramsey didn't want any more to die.

Declan didn't care who got caught in the middle. He was going to kill anyone who got in his way. Ramsey stood a chance against him, but even he wasn't sure how much of a chance.

During the long centuries of his life Ramsey had tried to call forth his magic while releasing his god only once, and the power of it had frightened him enough not to try it again. Yet, he knew that to battle Declan, he would have to use all of his considerable magic, and the power of his god.

Ramsey turned and looked at the castle through the wide window of his cottage. The tower, which was five floors, rose high above the rest of the castle. The tower had been the original building, and the two additions on either side were built many decades later.

Yet, it flowed well. Dunnoth Tower wasn't nearly the size of MacLeod Castle, but like any castle, it had its own special history that included one of the previous owners running off with his wife's sister and leaving his wife to run the castle.

A sound from his room had Ramsey looking over his shoulder to see Arran and Charon come into view.

Arran smiled as he held out his arm for Ramsey to clasp. "You didna really think we'd leave this to you alone, did you?"

"I had hoped," Ramsey replied with a welcoming smile.

Charon stepped forward when Arran moved aside and clasped Ramsey's forearm in a strong grip. "I didna get away from MacLeod Castle quick enough, it seems."

Ramsey laughed and dropped his arm to his side. "Fallon does have a way of getting what he wants."

Charon shoved aside his dark hair that grazed his shoulders, and narrowed his eyes at the castle. "Does Tara know what you are?"

"Nay. And I doona think she will unless I tell her."

"Or until Declan shows his face," Arran added.

Ramsey hooked his thumbs in the front pockets of his jeans. "Tara hasna been here long, and by the way she acts, I'd bet she has her bags packed, ready to leave at a moment's notice."

"She's a runner," Charon said. "If what her mother said is true, Tara hasna settled anywhere long except Edinburgh."

Arran crossed his arms over his chest. "And that didna turn out well for her."

"She thought she was safe there," Ramsey said. "It's why she stayed so long. A huge city to get lost in."

Charon's lips twisted in a frown. "You can never outrun your past."

Ramsey looked at the Warrior. He knew how Charon had spied upon Quinn, Arran, Ian, and Duncan while they had been imprisoned in Deirdre's mountain. But he had done it because Deirdre threatened to kill his family. That was something to be forgiven, yet it seemed there was much more to Charon's past than he had told anyone.

Charon's head turned and he met Ramsey's gaze. "How many people are staying at the castle?"

"Right now only one couple. Why?"

"It would be easier to move around with more people."

Arran rubbed his chin. "I think we need to have a look around tonight. Inside and out."

"I agree," Charon said.

Ramsey raised a black brow. "I've already done it, but both of you need to know the layout as well as I do. Tara's room is on the main floor, toward the back of the tower on the left. The owners occupy a set of rooms on the fifth floor."

"And the other employees?" Arran asked.

"Also on the bottom floor, and even in the basement."

Charon turned on his heel and walked to the overstuffed chair angled away from the television. He sank into it and put his hands behind his head. "Have you spoken to Tara?"

"Aye."

"About what?"

Ramsey leaned back against the windowsill, his hands braced on the sill. "She's verra closed off. No one knows anything about her past or even much about her other than that she's had various jobs over the past ten years."

"So the owners of the castle would know more," Arran said. "Her employment history."

Ramsey shrugged. "Aye. Unless she lied."

"Which she's likely to do," Charon said.

The crunch of shoes on the snow had Ramsey looking out the window to see Tara coming his way. "Hide. She's coming."

Charon and Arran were in the bedroom out of sight without a sound well before Tara knocked on the door.

Ramsey opened it and welcomed her inside before he closed it, and the cold, behind her. "Something wrong?"

"No," she said with a soft laugh as she loosened her scarf. "Liz wanted me to let you know we're having guests in the Duke's rooms beginning tonight. The last time there had been a problem with the shower, so she wanted to see if you would check it out."

Alarm spiked through Ramsey. "Who is the guest?"

"All I know is that it's a high-profile man who is coming to surprise his girlfriend. Isn't that romantic?"

Ramsey returned her smile. But he couldn't help but suspect that the guest wasn't just anyone. It was certain to be Declan.

"When does the guest arrive?" he asked.

"By six."

That gave him several hours to prepare. Since they couldn't find Declan because his magic blocked even Broc from using his god's power of finding anyone, anywhere, they had to rely on other means.

Tara's hand rested on his arm. "Are you all right?"

Ramsey mentally shook himself. "Aye. Just thinking of all I need to do."

"I better let you get to it." She gave him another soft smile before she left.

Arran whistled long and slow as he leaned against the door frame. "Damn. That's one fine-looking woman."

"You think it's Declan arriving tonight," Charon said as he walked out of the bedroom.

Ramsey nodded, looking from Charon to Arran. "But I pray I'm wrong."

CHAPTER
FOUR

Declan Wallace didn't notice the scenery outside of his window as Robbie, his cousin and first in command, drove the A9 through the Highlands.

No, all Declan could think about was finally tracking down Tara. It had taken far longer than he would have liked. Years in fact. He knew Tara's magic was potent, but it shouldn't have allowed her to elude him for this long.

Not that Declan didn't like a good chase. It had been amusing at first when he found her gone from his home. He hadn't set out right away to catch her because he'd thought he'd find her easily enough.

How wrong he'd been.

And with each year, each hunt that ended in failure, his anger grew. Declan had warned Tara that she was his. She hadn't listened, hadn't taken him seriously. By the time he was through with her, she would know exactly who she was dealing with.

"Just another few hours," Robbie said as he glanced at Declan through the rearview mirror.

Declan didn't bother to answer him. He was relishing the idea of walking into Dunnoth Tower and seeing Tara's surprised face.

Was she still as pretty as she'd been at eighteen? He'd always thought her blue-green eyes unusual, but pleasant to look at. She wasn't what he would call a great beauty, but she would serve her purpose.

Especially since Deirdre had been killed, and Saffron had once again been taken by the Warriors of MacLeod Castle.

Even with Saffron and Deirdre out of the picture, Tara could give him all that he desired because of her magic. All he had to do was convince—or force—her to undergo the ceremony to become *drough*.

Declan let out a long breath. In a matter of hours Tara would be his.

Tara finished scattering the last of the rose petals over the king-sized four-poster bed. She stood back and looked at her work with a smile.

"Whoever this woman is, she's certainly in for a treat," Tara said to herself.

She'd never thought herself a daydreamer. She'd always kept herself firmly planted in reality, but for the first time in her life, she couldn't help wondering what it would be like to be the woman who walked into such a room. To know that the man she was with cared so much, and had gone to such lengths, for her.

No one had ever done such a thing for her. Not that she could be upset about it. She'd never let anyone close enough.

Of course she went out on dates. Occasionally.

Tara rolled her eyes as she turned and walked into the bathroom. She had a few more roses left over, and she wanted to add a special touch there.

Dates. The last time she had gone on a date had been over two years ago. He'd been nice and quite handsome. But he'd wanted another date from her. He'd wanted a relationship, and Tara couldn't allow that.

She'd quickly broken it off. And the nights alone in front of the telly hadn't been so bad. She'd watched almost every movie known to man, and spent hours on her laptop.

Tara shook her head as she thought of her dour life. She knew she needed to go ahead and pack up to leave Scotland. She should do it tomorrow.

Her hands filled with roses slowly lowered to the counter in the bathroom as an image of Ramsey sprang into her mind. She didn't want to leave Dunnoth Tower. She didn't want to leave Ramsey.

Although she couldn't say exactly why.

Tara shook her head to clear it of her thoughts. She needed to concentrate on finishing the room, and decide later that night what to do about leaving.

She opened the cabinet and found the vase Liz always kept in the room for such occasions. Tara rose on the very tips of her toes, but couldn't reach the vase.

With a sigh, she carefully set down the roses and tried again. When that still didn't work, she found the small footstool and stepped on that.

She stretched, her fingers just grazing the crystal vase. "Oh, come on," she muttered in frustration.

Tara licked her lips and scooted a bit more to the left of the stool. She knew she was close to the edge, but she only needed to reach a little bit farther.

Her fingers took hold of the vase the same instant she felt the stool tilt. Instinctively, Tara released the vase as she felt herself falling sideways. Her arms cartwheeled wildly to try and grab on to something so she wouldn't fall, but there was nothing.

And then arms like bands of steel wrapped around her. Her hands gripped muscled arms. For a moment all Tara could do was soak in the feel of the heat and sinew beneath her palms.

She knew without looking up it was Ramsey. Tara kept her eyes locked on the middle of his torso and his T-shirt. Her heart pounded rapidly in her chest and it had nothing to do with the fall and everything to do with the man holding her.

It wasn't like her to act like a silly schoolgirl, but around Ramsey, she could hardly form a coherent thought, much less act rationally.

Slowly, Tara raised her face to find him staring down at her, his amazing ashen eyes locked on her. He said not a word as he gradually shifted her so that she was standing. Yet, he didn't release her.

Tara reveled in the feel of his heat, the same heat that had stolen through her when he'd touched her earlier. It felt amazing, almost as if it went directly into her chest and spread outward.

It did more than warm her, though. It made her body tingle, as if every nerve ending were stimulated and waiting for more.

His fingers tightened for a second, as if he too felt the current between them. Tara wasn't sure what to make of it. No one had ever affected her so strongly.

"Thank you," she finally managed.

"I'm glad I was here," he said and released her. "It could have been a nasty fall."

Tara raised her hand to her temple and the small scar hidden by her hair. A forgotten memory of her mother pushing her down the stairs in an attempt to make Tara use her magic to protect herself filled her mind. She squeezed her eyes shut as a shudder went through her.

"Tara?"

How she loved the sound of her name on Ramsey's lips. She took a deep breath and opened her eyes. "Just a bad memory."

"A recent memory?"

"No. One from long, long ago."

Ramsey gave a small nod of his head before he stepped around her and retrieved the vase. He placed it on the counter with a slight grin.

Tara set about arranging the roses while Ramsey worked on the shower. There was nothing to fill the companionable silence, but then again, there wasn't a need.

She covertly watched Ramsey work in the mirror. And long after she was finished with the roses she found reasons to stay in the bathroom so she could be near him.

Her body still tingled from his touch, and she hated how she wanted more of it. Tara had never been one of those girls who threw themselves at men, but she was certainly thinking of doing just that to Ramsey.

It was ridiculous, but her body craved his touch like her lungs craved oxygen.

Tara rearranged the roses for a third time. She shifted one of the flowers and looked into the mirror to meet Ramsey's gaze.

"Why are you here?" she asked.

A black brow arched. "I already told you."

"No. Really. Look at you. You're smart and good-looking. You're able to fix anything. A man like you shouldn't be doing a job meant for someone who couldn't graduate from school."

Ramsey leaned his forearm against the shower. His chest expanded as he took a deep breath and slowly released it. "I could ask you the same question."

"You could." Tara lowered her eyes, hating that she wanted to tell him what had driven her to the northern fringes of Scotland.

"But you wouldna tell me."

"Just as you won't tell me."

Tara scooted the vase into the corner of the countertop and turned to go. She quickly halted in her tracks when she found Ramsey filling the doorway. And blocking her exit.

"You doona need to be afraid of me," he said.

She lifted her chin. "I'm not afraid of you."

"Good. Why no' tell me the real reason you're here?"

The wall she had erected around herself trembled as it cracked, but she didn't let it crumble. If she did, she wouldn't have the strength to continue. She swallowed and voiced the lie she'd told everyone since arriving at Dunnoth Tower. "I was looking for something different."

Ramsey looked at the ground for a moment. He said nothing as he picked up his toolbox and walked out of the room.

Tara leaned her forehead against the wall of the bathroom and fisted her hands. It was the only show of emotion she could allow, the only evidence that she wanted so much more.

When she collected herself, Tara left the room and made her way back downstairs to her desk. She was scratching the items off the list their mysterious guest had given her when the first drops of rain hit against the window.

She looked out the window at the gray sky and thick, heavy clouds. Before she knew it she had risen and walked to the windows. The rain poured down the glass as rivulets of water made trails of their own before disappearing from sight.

Headlights drew her attention as a car drove up the long drive. She took a startled step back when she saw the black Jaguar and all the blood drained from her face.

Declan had always favored Jaguars. He owned a few other vehicles, but always he used the Jaguar.

Tara was calculating how quickly she could grab her bags and leave without Declan seeing her when the car door opened. She took two more steps back.

There wasn't time for her things. She had to leave. Immediately.

She hurried to her desk and grabbed her keys as the driver opened the rear door of the black Jaguar and a man with white hair stepped out of the car.

Tara nearly collapsed from the relief. She released her keys so they clanked back on the desk, and just as she was turning back to the door she spotted Ramsey on the stairs watching her.

CHAPTER
FIVE

Ramsey had been coming down the stairs to the front entry when he'd felt the tremendous fear in Tara's magic. He jumped from the third floor of the switchback stairs to the landing leading down to the main floor when he'd seen her reach for her keys.

He'd halted, wondering what she would do. It was obvious she thought the Jaguar was Declan's, and she hadn't intended to stay to find out.

Several possible scenarios flashed through Ramsey's mind in those few seconds, and the one theme in all of them was getting Tara away before Declan spotted her.

But as he looked into her cool, clear blue-green eyes, Ramsey could feel her relief. Though he was equally pleased it wasn't Declan, what the episode had proved was that Tara feared Declan above all.

His respect for her grew as she squared her shoulders and looked him full in the eye. She knew he had seen her, but she wasn't going to hide what she had done.

"You can no' run forever," he said as he descended the few remaining steps.

"I know."

"What are you running from?"

"What are *you* running from?"

He inwardly smiled at her bravado. She was scared witless, but she wasn't going to let anyone know it. "I'm no' running from something, lass. I'm running *to* something."

Her brow furrowed, but before she could respond the door opened and the man walked into the castle, a large smile on his face.

"I'm looking for Tara," he said in a friendly voice tinged with an English accent.

Tara returned his smile and held out her hand. "That would be me. I suppose you're our special guest, Lord Huntington?"

Ramsey moved out of sight as Tara showed the gentleman into the front sitting room and fetched him some champagne. He'd had no idea who the man was, but obviously Tara had. Apparently Lord Huntington was well-known.

"Is everything I requested in order?" Lord Huntington asked.

Ramsey didn't need to move closer to hear the conversation. His enhanced hearing could pick it up easily, but he needed to be close to Tara. Especially after touching her again.

The feel of her body against his had been a jolt straight to his soul. There was something remarkably different about Tara, but he had yet to discover what that was.

"Of course," Tara answered. "And if there is anything else you need, you have only to ask me."

"Good. Good," the lord answered.

Ramsey watched from the shadows as Tara poured the champagne into a fluted glass. She kept glancing out the windows, as if she expected Declan at any moment. And Ramsey suspected that's exactly what she felt.

Tara set down the bottle of champagne and said, "Your dinner will be ready at eight as you requested."

"Wonderful. Sara should arrive shortly. I just wish it wasn't raining. She hates to ride in my helicopter in the rain."

Ramsey's mobile vibrated in his pocket, and once he retrieved it to see it was Arran, he hurried away from Tara and answered it.

"Aye?"

Arran said, "How is everything? We saw the car pull up, but once we noticed it wasna Declan, we waited for you to call."

"Tara thought it was Declan as well. She had her keys, ready to run."

"We could have caught her."

"Aye. She's terrified of him."

Arran sighed. "If what Declan did to Saffron is any indication, Tara has every right to be afraid."

"Keep watch on the drive. I doona want a surprise."

"We'll see to it. One of us will stay here and have a look around the grounds while the other goes to the road as look-out."

"Remember Declan's X90 bullets."

Arran snorted. "As if I need reminding."

Ramsey ended the call and replaced the mobile in his pocket. He'd been ready to spring into action when he'd thought it was Declan who had arrived.

What worried him was that he hadn't decided whether he would first protect Tara by taking her away or first battle Declan. If he fought Declan, Ramsey could end it all right then.

But if he got Tara away, he knew she would be safe at MacLeod Castle and not have to run anymore.

He ran a hand down his face. The Druids at MacLeod Castle wanted him to tell Tara who he was and convince her to return with him to the castle.

Ramsey wished it were that easy, but after learning Tara had run away from her home at eighteen, he knew earning her trust would be a slow process. There was no way he could do it in the short amount of time he suspected he had.

Nor would he allow Tara to be brought to the castle against her will unless it was to hide from Declan. And even then it was Fallon's rule that no one be kept against their will at the castle.

So that left Ramsey exactly where he was. Waiting. And watching.

He wouldn't be nearly as concerned if Tara's magic didn't

affect him so. A look down at his hands confirmed the swirling bands of magic had returned.

How long would they stay this time? And that was just from touching her sweater. What if he actually touched her bare skin?

The idea appealed to him entirely too much. Too damned much.

Ramsey stayed on the main floor, and made sure he could hear Tara wherever he was. His advanced hearing made it easier for him to watch over her without her knowing it, but still he found he wanted to be nearer to her.

It wasn't long before the sun began to set and the rain turned into an icy mix. Ramsey had hoped for a snowstorm that would keep everyone off the roads.

He chuckled as he realized he had exactly what he needed at the castle. With a quick dial on his mobile he had Arran on the phone. "I need you to do something."

"What?" Arran asked.

"I need snow. Lots and lots of snow."

Arran laughed heartily. "Ah. You want to keep Declan from reaching the castle."

"Aye."

"For how long?"

Ramsey rubbed the back of his neck. "I'm no' certain. As long as we can manage it."

"I can give you the kind of snow you need for years, my friend."

"Nay. Just a few days. I need to try to get closer to Tara. Maybe I should convince her to get to MacLeod Castle."

"Ah, Cara and Marcail's argument finally got to you, did it? Do you think you can persuade Tara?"

"Nay, but it's worth a try."

"Why now?"

Ramsey recalled how desperately he wanted to battle Declan. "I doona know when Declan will arrive, but I know in my gut that he will. Saffron's visions have no' failed us yet. And in her vision Saffron saw that if Declan comes, he would kill Tara."

"Then I suggest you get close to Tara. And fast. Give me a few moments on the snow."

The phone clicked as the conversation was ended by Arran. Ramsey thought long and hard about how to approach Tara. He didn't like that he was second-guessing himself now.

But how could he have known what his reaction to her magic would be? Or how scared she was of Declan?

Even now, he wasn't sure which course to take. And that wasn't like him at all.

Ramsey heard the soft footfalls of Tara's boots on the carpet and he headed toward the door to see she had gone outside in the rain, which almost instantly turned to snow.

He hurried out to her and reached for the handle of Lord Huntington's suitcase before she could. She jerked back and gasped.

"Bloody hell! You move so silently I never heard you," she said breathlessly.

Ramsey shrugged and hefted the suitcase to the other hand so he could grab the second piece. "At least it isna raining anymore."

"No," she said and glanced at the sky. Snowflakes fell on her eyelashes and she blinked them away. "Odd how it changed so suddenly, isn't it?"

"You never can tell about our weather."

She stepped away and the driver shut the trunk of the car. Together, Ramsey and Tara returned to the castle. He continued on to the stairs to take the luggage to Lord Huntington's chamber while Tara made her way to the kitchen.

Ramsey delivered the luggage in record time. He paused in the Duke's rooms to look out the window. As promised, the snow was falling rapidly, and in no time at all the roads would be so thick with snow no one would venture out.

But until then, Ramsey was going to have to keep an eye on Tara. Declan was as devious as Deirdre had been, so Ramsey wanted to be prepared for anything. And knowing Declan, anything was possible.

Ramsey made the rounds of the castle, checking everything. He spotted Arran a couple of times, but only because of his enhanced eyesight. No mortal would have been able to see Arran in the darkness and snowfall.

It was only when Lord Huntington's female companion, a pretty middle-aged brunette, arrived and both had retired to their suite that Ramsey left the upstairs area.

He stepped off the last stair and heard Tara call his name. Ramsey looked over his shoulder to see her head sticking out of the kitchen door.

"Are you hungry? Chef made some extra for all of us."

Ramsey walked to her with a smile. "I'd be a fool to pass up his excellent dishes."

When he reached the staff table he found only two place settings. And by Tara's wide eyes, he wasn't the only one surprised.

"Where did the others go?" she asked.

Ramsey shrugged and held out her chair. "Maybe they doona like me."

"No. It's probably me."

She sank into the chair as Ramsey took the one opposite her.

"It's no' you. You've a friendly smile and kind eyes," he told her.

She chuckled and took a sip of wine. "And you're entirely too generous with your compliments."

"I never give compliments unless I mean them."

She lifted her glass to him. "Then I thank you. I don't get very many compliments."

"Why is that?" he asked as he cut into the braised chicken.

She dabbed at her lips with her napkin and swallowed her bite. "You seem the kind of guy who has everything figured out. I'm sure you have me figured out."

"No' so. I'd rather you tell me."

Ramsey was surprised at how much he was enjoying their conversation and dinner. It was an unexpected opportunity for him to learn more about Tara. The fact that he wanted to know more made caution swell within him.

Gaining her trust or not, he shouldn't want to know more.

"Hmm." She took another bite as she studied him. "I don't normally tell anyone anything."

"Why?"

"It's not safe."

"For them or you?"

She looked down and swallowed. "Mostly me. It's better if I don't have any friends."

"Everyone needs friends, Tara."

Her blue-green gaze lifted to his. "Even if it isn't safe?"

"Especially when it isna safe."

"Are you offering?"

Ramsey gave a slow nod. "Indeed I am."

CHAPTER
SIX

Tara set down her fork and threaded her fingers together as she studied Ramsey. "Why?"

"Why?" he repeated.

"That's what I asked. Why do you want to be my friend?"

He shrugged and lowered his gaze to his plate to stab his fork into some green beans. "Why no'?"

"I'm serious."

He chewed slowly before he lowered his fork and leaned back in his chair. Once he swallowed, he took a drink of wine to give his thoughts time to settle before he answered. "What are you afraid of?"

"Excuse me?"

"Why are you afraid of having a friend?"

She rolled her eyes and swiped at a strand of hair that fell in her face. "Some people have a problem trusting others. I'm in that category."

"Aye," he said, as if he were unsurprised by her admission. "I've no' given you a reason no' to trust me."

"You've not given me a reason to trust you."

"We could go round and round all night like this."

Tara survived for ten years on the run by learning to read people, and despite Ramsey's efforts, she could tell he was hiding something. But what?

"Do you trust people?" she asked, more curious than she wanted to be.

"Aye. It didna always come easy, but it became a necessity if I wanted to survive."

Now she was really interested. "Survive? Survive what?"

He shrugged. "It was a figure of speech."

"I think you're lying."

One side of his lips lifted in a crooked smile. "Is that right?"

"It is. Just as I know you're hiding something."

"And how is it you can see that, lass?"

Tara leaned her forearms on the table and met Ramsey's silver gaze. "I learned the hard way how to read people. It's how I survive."

"Then tell me what you've read in me."

She knew she shouldn't. Already things had gotten entirely too personal. The fact that she wanted to know more about Ramsey, and that she wanted to trust him, only complicated things.

If she didn't take a step back, she was going to find it difficult to leave when the time came. Which was why she was already thinking of leaving. If only that damned snowstorm hadn't blown in.

"Well?" Ramsey urged.

Tara picked up her wine glass and swirled the golden liquid of the pino grigio. She tilted the glass to her lips and let the wine slide down her throat.

The delicious food forgotten, she leaned back and took a deep breath. "Are you sure you want to know?"

"Do your best."

"All right. You've an old soul. You're cautious, and you have secrets. Not a lot, but I suspect they're dangerous secrets. You know modern tools, but you aren't meant to hold them. You're a warrior, a man who knows how to look after what's his. You have close friends who you consider family, but . . ." She paused as she cocked her head to the side. "But you've left them for something important."

Tara blinked and looked away from Ramsey's gaze and

the confusion she glimpsed there. She took another drink of wine. "I told you I could read people."

"Interesting."

"Am I right?" she asked without looking up.

"And if I said aye?"

Slowly, her gaze lifted to his. "I would ask if your friends know your secrets?"

"They do. Now, I think it's my turn."

Tara's body jerked. "What do you mean?"

"You're no' the only one who can read people, lass. It's only fair I get my turn."

She wanted to bolt from the kitchen, and from the castle. Then she realized Ramsey wouldn't be able to tell anything about her. She was too good at hiding her true self from everyone, including herself.

"Go ahead," she said with a nonchalant shrug.

Ramsey's smile and the way his ashen gaze leveled on her made a shiver race down her spine. What did he think he knew?

"You've been running a long time," Ramsey said softly. "You're a loner, but you're also lonely. I can see it in your eyes when you watch families and friends together. Especially when you see a couple. You have secrets of your own, and you're afraid of everything. You can no' find peace, because you have no' stopped running."

Tara shook her head in dismay. She rose to her feet so quickly her chair fell backward, breaking the silence. Ramsey stood and reached for her, but Tara jerked away.

"Who are you?" she demanded.

"I'm a friend. If you believe nothing else, believe that."

With her hands shaking, she set down the wineglass and took a step back. "I can't afford friends."

She turned and started to walk away. Tara reached the doorway when Ramsey's words halted her.

"Running again?"

For a moment she wavered. She desperately wanted to collapse in the chair and spill all her secrets. She wanted to tell Ramsey everything, and maybe he could even help her.

But Tara knew what kind of magic Declan had. If she involved Ramsey she was sentencing him to death. And she liked him too much to do that.

So, once more she would stand alone.

"Thank you for sharing a meal with me." She glanced over her shoulder at Ramsey.

Before she gave in and told him everything, Tara walked to her room and quietly shut the door. She locked it, and then bolted it. Not because she was afraid of Ramsey, but it was a habit she couldn't let go of.

Her eyes swam with unshed tears as she leaned her forehead against the door. She tried to hold back the tide of emotion, but Ramsey had opened the floodgates when he'd read her so perfectly.

The first tear escaped, and then the others quickly followed. Her shoulders shook with the force of her loneliness and fear. She covered her mouth with her hands to hold back her sobs, but it was too late.

Ramsey laid his palm flat on Tara's door. He hung his head as he heard the sound of her tears. He hadn't wanted to make her cry. He hoped to let her see that he was there for her.

Instead of making progress, he had taken a giant leap backward. And he knew if he hadn't asked Arran for the snow that Tara would have left Dunnoth Tower. How would he explain it if he followed her? At least he hoped he wouldn't have to.

Tara was scared, but she wasn't witless. She wouldn't venture out in such weather.

Ramsey stayed by the door for several more moments listening to the soul-deep sobs from within the room. Only when Tara's tears began to lessen did he return to the kitchen and clean up after their meal.

He couldn't help walking past Tara's room once more before he made his way outside. After he closed the door to the castle and locked it, Ramsey added a quick protection spell.

"Will that keep Declan out?" Arran's voice asked behind him.

Ramsey wasn't surprised to find his friend there. "Nay," he answered as he turned to Arran. "But it will take him a few moments to get through the spell."

"Moments we could use in getting Tara out."

"Aye."

"Good idea," Arran said.

They fell in step as they walked to Ramsey's cottage. The snowfall hadn't stopped, and already it was piled thick on the ground so that they sank to their knees when they stepped through it.

When Ramsey opened the door to his cottage, a fire raged in the hearth, and the smell of coffee filled the air. Charon turned from the stove and set two heavy mugs on the table before reaching for his own.

"Thanks," Ramsey said as he reached for the cup and sank into the chair.

He felt Charon's and Arran's eyes on him as they took their seats and silently waited for him to tell them if anything had happened with Tara.

"The snow will keep away any visitors, but I'll head out in a few hours for another look anyway," Charon said.

Arran chuckled. "There willna be anyone on the roads, at least no' coming here. I've made sure of that."

"It willna keep Declan out for long," Ramsey said. "If he wants Tara as desperately as we think he does, he'll figure out a way to get here."

"Then we need to move things along," Charon said.

Ramsey set down the thick mug. "I think I might have scared Tara off tonight."

"What happened?" Arran asked.

Ramsey raked a hand through his hair and dislodged the strip of leather he used to keep the strands tied back. He tossed the leather on the table and sighed. "She told me she has a gift for reading people, so I told her to read me."

"You didna," Charon said with surprise.

"I did. And she read me."

Arran leaned forward on the table. "Well?"

"She's good. Verra good, actually," Ramsey confessed. "She didna get into specifics, but she obviously can read people."

"What did she say exactly?" Charon asked.

"She said I had an old soul, and that I had a few secrets. That I left friends I considered family for something I deemed important. She said I was a warrior who would protect what was mine."

"Damn," Charon murmured. "She is good."

"I tried to tell her she would need friends, but when that didna work, I asked if I could see if I could read her as well as she did me."

Arran rolled his eyes and sighed. "Well, doona keep us in suspense!"

Ramsey leaned his elbows on the table. "Apparently, I did a good job. I didna give specifics, just general things as she did with me. But I hit a nerve, I think. She bolted to her room."

He didn't tell them about her crying, because he knew Tara would be mortified if he knew. She was a strong person, who he suspected rarely gave in to such emotion.

"What now?" Charon asked.

Ramsey shook his head. "I doona know. I thought to show her she could lean on me, to trust me, but I think I've ruined it. If it wouldna be for the snow, she'd already be gone."

"Shite," Arran said.

Ramsey took a deep breath. He might have lost any chance of gaining Tara's trust, but he wasn't about to give up on protecting her.

"Did both of you learn the layout?" he asked.

Charon nodded as he swallowed a drink of coffee. "Aye. The landscape is easy enough so that we can spot anyone approaching. There are a few spots we could use to our advantage if we need it."

"Ah. On the left side of the castle, about two hundred yards out?" Ramsey asked.

Charon smiled. "That's the one. The land naturally dips,

and with a little help in making the hole larger, then covering it with snow, it could be used."

"I'd rather just use our powers," Arran said.

Ramsey shook his head. "Nay. There could be too many witnesses. If we can get away without calling forth our gods, then that's what we need to do."

"Besides, Ramsey has magic," Charon replied with a sly grin.

Ramsey pushed back from the table and stood. His chest had tightened at their words, but he kept his voice normal when he spoke. "You better hope we can get Tara away so I doona have to use my magic and my power."

Arran rose to his feet. "Why?"

"I'm going to get some rest," Ramsey said.

Charon and Arran exchanged a worried look as they watched Ramsey walk away.

CHAPTER
SEVEN

Declan stared out the window of the inn, his anger growing with every beat of his heart. The weather had changed rapidly. Too rapidly.

"They're saying this is the worst snowfall we've seen in decades," Robbie said from the chair where he listened to the radio.

"Are they now?" Declan saw Robbie's reflection in the mirror as he lifted his head.

Robbie frowned. "What is it?"

"Just a feeling, cousin."

"About Tara?"

"I find it suspicious that we got such a nasty snowstorm as I was on my way to Tara."

Robbie rose and walked to stand beside Declan at the window. "You think the Warriors are involved."

It wasn't a question. "I do."

"I can take care of them with the X90 bullets."

Declan turned his head and smiled at his cousin. "For all the Warriors' strength, the power of their gods, and their immortality, seeing what a bit of *drough* blood does to them is priceless."

"And how much pain."

Declan chuckled. "At least we killed one of them during the last battle."

"The one who was trying to reach Saffron, that huge hulking Warrior the color of brown?"

"Aye. He's the one."

"One down and how many more to go?"

Declan's smile vanished. "That's the problem. We doona know. Deirdre had a suspicion of how many were there, but she would never tell me."

"I still can no' believe Malcolm betrayed her."

Declan fisted his hands. "I'm going to make him suffer for what he's done."

"We'll have to find him first."

"Oh, I've no doubt we'll find him. But first, Tara. Once I have her undergo the ceremony to become *drough*, we'll begin taking out the Warriors one by one."

"It's taken too long to reach Tara. She could have already run again."

Declan tapped his finger on the windowsill. He wanted Tara to know he was coming for her. He wanted her terrified, and he knew Tara well enough to know just how to go about that.

He spun on his heels and knelt in the middle of the room. With his palms held facedown, he leaned back on his heels and closed his eyes. He kept Tara's face in his mind as he began to chant the spell that would allow him to reach her mind if she was close enough.

Declan had tried this many times since Tara had run away, but he'd never gotten close enough to her. They were only about forty miles away from Dunnoth Tower. That was on the fringes of where the spell could reach, but it was worth a try.

Anticipation grew as the spell reached out its fingers and searched for the one he sought. He poured more of his black magic into the spell, urging it to search harder, farther.

And then he smiled as it found her.

"Tara," he whispered.

"Tara."

Tara bolted upright in the bed as Declan's voice echoed

in her mind. Her heart pounded in her ears as her stomach fell to her feet.

She had heard him, as clearly as if he had been standing beside her. Tara, still fully dressed, looked around her room. She must have fallen asleep because the light was still on, and it proved she was alone.

At least in her room.

She swallowed, trying to wet her now-dry mouth as she ran her hands up and down her arms. Declan was close, possibly at the castle somewhere. There was no more time to waste. Tara had to leave.

A glance outside told her she wouldn't be leaving in her car. There was no way she would make it on the road, much less out of the castle's drive.

"Damn," she muttered as she jumped from the bed.

Tara opened her window, thankful she was on the bottom floor. She gasped as the frigid air slammed into her. Her teeth chattered, but her coat and scarf were in the entryway. And she wasn't about to brave the dark corners of the castle to try and reach it if Declan was there.

With her shoulders set, Tara sat on the windowsill and swung her legs over. She slid off the sill and sank into snow that now reached almost to her hips. It took some effort, but she was finally able to close the window.

She was soon shivering as she looked around. The clouds hid the moon, which would thankfully hide her, but it also meant there was no light to help her find her way to the road.

Tara shuddered as the thick snow continued to fall. It clung to her hair and eyelashes, making it even more difficult to see. But she wasn't going to give up. Declan might be hunting her, but she wouldn't ever stop running.

The snow quickly penetrated her jeans, and she wasn't even twenty steps away from the castle. Desperation kicked in. Tara used extra effort to try and walk through the dense, hip-high snow.

She worked her way around the castle to the driveway where the snow shouldn't be nearly as thick. It was a huge chance, because if Declan was there, he might see her. But if she didn't get away from the castle, he'd catch her soon enough.

Tara could see the driveway, but no matter how desperately she wanted to reach it, her body was exhausted. Her knees buckled and she fell face-first in the snow.

As much as she wanted to lie there and catch her breath, Tara pushed herself up and started forward. She heard what sounded like a crunch of a shoe on the snow, so she halted and listened.

For several moments she didn't move. There was no other sound, and even though she looked around she didn't see anything. But she knew something was out there.

Tara continued on until she reached the edge of the castle. Across the drive was Ramsey's cottage. She could go to him, ask him for help, but as soon as the thought entered her mind she dismissed it.

She checked to make sure there were no lights on in the cottage before she made a dash to the driveway. She had taken just two steps when a large form stepped in front of her.

A scream lodged in her throat, and a hand quickly covered her mouth.

"Tara," Ramsey whispered in her ear as he pulled her against him. "It's me."

She nodded her head as she found herself clinging to him.

"Shite, you're shivering."

The adrenaline spike as well as the cold air had her body shaking uncontrollably.

Without asking her permission, he lifted her in his arms and stalked to his cottage.

"Fool of a woman running around in such weather without a coat. Are you trying to kill yourself?" he demanded angrily.

Since her teeth were chattering so badly she couldn't talk, Tara shook her head.

"What were you doing out here?"

She glanced at him, thankful she couldn't speak, because she was liable to tell him everything. It was the first time since leaving Declan's that she felt he was nearly upon her. And it was the scariest thing she had ever felt.

Tara laid her head on Ramsey's shoulder, amazed to find he still didn't have a coat on, nor did he appear to be affected by the cold.

He nudged his door open with his foot and shouldered his way inside before shutting it with his elbow. Nothing else was said as he set her in front of the roaring fire and draped a thick blanket around her.

She snuggled beneath the warmth, grateful to be out of the cold. Beneath her lashes, she watched Ramsey as he took one of her feet in his hands and gently pulled off her boot. He set it beside the fire and repeated the process with the other shoe.

"You're soaked through."

The rough tenor of his voice made a thrill go through Tara. She lifted her eyes to his face. "A little."

"Soaked," he repeated. "You need to get out of your clothes before you catch a chill."

"I will. Just give me a moment to warm up, and I'll go back to the castle and change."

He shook his head, and that's when she saw his hair was loose around his face. It hung black as midnight just past his shoulders.

"No' until you tell me why you risked your life tonight."

Tara looked away and focused on the flames before her.

A moment later Ramsey stood. She heard him in the kitchen, and she took that time to look around the small cottage. The kitchen and living room were one large open room. She did spot a door that she suspected led to his bedroom and bathroom. The cottage was sparsely decorated with just enough to offer the occupant comfort.

"Here."

She jerked when she found Ramsey squatting in front of her holding a cup of steaming coffee. "How do you constantly sneak up on me?"

"Drink," he urged.

Tara eagerly wrapped her numb fingers around the hot

cup. She had to take turns holding it because it hurt her fingers to have the feeling return to them so quickly. But the coffee tasted delicious and helped to warm her.

Ramsey had taken a seat in the chair beside her, and he watched her silently. His look wasn't unkind, but it was disapproving.

She had to admit it wasn't one of her smarter plans, but then again she'd never heard Declan's voice in her head before.

"I didna mean to upset you earlier," Ramsey said.

Tara released a breath and looked into her coffee mug. "I shouldn't have gotten so defensive. I've been alone for so long that I don't always react well to people."

It had been different with the children she taught. They had been young, curious, and full of laughter. They hadn't cared about her past or wanted to know everything about her. All they had wanted was her attention and to have fun. Those were two things she had been able to give.

But being with those kids had made her come to terms with how dearly she wanted a child of her own.

It took a moment for her to realize her fear of Declan had vanished almost as soon as Ramsey had picked her up. How could a man she hardly knew make her feel safe?

"You aren't going to tell me, are you?" Ramsey asked.

Tara thought about returning to the castle and held the blanket tighter. She wanted just a few more moments with Ramsey, just a few more moments where she felt safe.

She set down her mug and looked at him. "There is a man after me."

"What does he want?"

"Me," she answered, and laughed at how absurd it sounded. "I once thought him a friend, but I learned he was anything but."

"That's who you've been running from?"

Tara didn't want to lie, but she wasn't quite ready to tell everything. "Partly."

Ramsey leaned forward so that his elbows were on his knees. A soft smile pulled at his lips. "That wasna so difficult, was it?"

"Actually," she said with a choked laugh, "it was."

His smile slowly melted away and his brow furrowed. "Tara, you could have frozen to death out there."

"I know. I just . . ." She trailed off as words eluded her. She swallowed back another rise of tears and shrugged.

"Stay here tonight. Nothing will harm you here, and you need to rest."

She wanted to tell him no, but she was so damned tired of looking out for herself. Just this once she was going to give in and allow someone else to carry some of her burden for her.

"All right."

CHAPTER
EIGHT

Ramsey had expected a fight. The ease with which Tara relented proved just how terrified she was. What had made her run off in the middle of such a storm without a jacket?

"The man you say is chasing you, you think he's here? At the castle?"

Tara shook her head slowly. "I did, but maybe I was wrong. I don't know anymore."

"What made you think he was here?"

Her blue-green eyes turned to him. "You're going to think I'm daft."

"Nay," Ramsey said with a small smile.

She licked her lips and adjusted the blanket around her. "I heard his voice."

"What did he say?"

"My name. It sounded as if he were right beside me, but I think maybe it was just a dream."

Ramsey let her lie to herself and him, but he knew Declan was anything but a dream. He might have stopped Declan from reaching the castle, but he hadn't prevented Declan from using magic to get to Tara.

"Take my bed," Ramsey said. "I can find you something to wear."

"The couch will be fine."

"But the bed is better," he said as he rose.

Ramsey held out his hand and helped her to her feet. As soon as her skin touched him, magic shot through him like lightning, sizzling his skin until his entire body craved more of her.

He reluctantly released her, and then fisted his hand as the tendrils of magic swarmed over his skin. Ramsey didn't need to look down to see them anymore. He knew the feel of it, of her glorious, exquisite magic.

It took a great amount of effort to walk ahead of Tara into his room instead of letting his fingers skim down her face to her neck.

Ramsey thought turning away from her was difficult, but once in his room with the bed so near, his body hungered for one thing. Tara.

He pulled out the first shirt in the small bag he had yet to unpack and tossed it on the bed. The longer he stayed near her while her magic swam over his skin, the more his control slipped.

Tara might be beautiful, and he might be attracted to her. But keeping her alive was his only duty. Ramsey hadn't thought that would be a problem. Then again, he hadn't felt Tara's magic at the time.

"The bathroom is there," Ramsey said, and pointed to the closed door. In two steps he was at his bedroom door. Just before he closed it behind him he said, "If you need anything, let me know."

"Thank you," Tara said as he shut the door behind him.

Ramsey took a deep breath, then another before he realized his hand was still on the doorknob. It would be so easy to give it a little twist and be back in the room with Tara.

"Nay," Ramsey whispered, and released the doorknob.

He stumbled to the couch and plopped down, his gaze on the hand that had touched Tara. As he expected, the white tendrils were thicker, more solid from touching her skin.

As with any Warrior, he had the ability to sense magic. It allowed a Warrior to find and track Druids. But there was a connection that neither the Druids nor the Warriors had realized when the Druids first called up the gods.

There were instances where a certain Druid's magic would affect a Warrior more deeply. He could feel her emotions in her magic.

The fact a Warrior could do that was magic itself, but what it signified was a strong bond between Warrior and Druid. That bond had formed eight times at MacLeod Castle, and each time the Druid and the Warrior fell in love.

Ramsey had felt the intensity of Tara's magic miles before he arrived at Dunnoth Tower. Then he had grabbed her arm and watched as her magic swirled around his hand.

But what had him in complete shock was that it was the stark fear he had felt in her magic that had led him outside. There hadn't been time to analyze why he had sensed her distress. He had simply reacted and gotten her to his cottage as quickly as possible.

Yet, while she had been with him, he'd tried to discern more of her emotion through her magic. Unfortunately, he'd sensed nothing. It was as if she had somehow cut it off.

Ramsey held up his hand. The magic moved with the grace of white smoke while it danced upon his skin. It moved around and over, swirling slowly.

"Well, fuck me."

Ramsey jerked his head around at the sound of Charon's voice. He found both Charon and Arran staring at him, so he lowered his hand. "I'd rather no'."

Arran chuckled and shoved Charon forward so he could shut the door. "Care to explain what's going on with your hand?"

"No' really."

"Too bad," Charon said. "We want to know."

Ramsey flexed his fingers and watched the tendrils move with him. "I touched Tara's hand."

"Damn," Arran said, his eyes wide.

Ramsey shook his head and held his finger to his lips. "We've a visitor."

"The lovely Tara," Charon murmured with a smile.

Ramsey rose and walked over to them so they could talk.

"She tried to run away. She said she heard Declan's voice in her head."

"Shit," Charon ground out as he ran a hand through his hair. "We covered the entire estate three times. He's no' here."

Arran frowned. "Wait. She told you about Declan?"

"Nay," Ramsey admitted with a sigh. "She did tell me there was a man chasing after her, and that same man is the one she thought she heard."

"Careful you doona slip up then," Charon warned.

"I know. She said he only spoke her name, but it was enough to send her out into the night without a jacket."

"In this weather?" Arran said, his face wide with shock.

Ramsey nodded. "She's verra afraid of him."

"So was Saffron," Charon said.

Arran snorted. "She still is, but Camdyn is there to protect her."

"Tara does no' know about the two of you yet. I wouldna put it past her to leave if she saw both of you."

Charon blew out a long breath and braced his hands on the table. "I'll keep watch on the road. The fact that Tara allowed you to bring her here, and is staying, says you're making progress. We doona want to muck that up."

"Promise me you willna engage Declan if you see him," Ramsey said.

"What is it you are no' telling us, mate?"

Ramsey looked at Charon then at Arran. "It's the X90 bullets I'm worried about."

With a nod, Charon straightened and left the cottage after grabbing a bag of chips from the kitchen counter.

When the door shut behind him, Arran crossed his arms over his chest and stared at Ramsey. "Charon may believe that bullshit you just doled out, but I doona."

"It's the truth," Ramsey replied with a shrug.

"My arse. Have we no' been through enough that I deserve the truth?"

"You want the truth?" Ramsey asked as he stepped closer to Arran. He rarely let anger control him, but it wasn't as easy to control at the moment. And he didn't care. "I'll give you the truth. The truth is that we doona have Sonya here with her healing magic, nor do we have Phelan and his blood that can heal anything. It's just us. It's why I didna want Fallon to bring anyone else here."

"Then who would look after your ugly arse?"

Ramsey blinked, taken aback by Arran's calm reply.

"I'm going to have a look around Tara's room. Maybe we'll find something useful," Arran said.

Ramsey watched his friend leave. He had expected Arran to comment on his lack of control or at least his anger. Instead, Arran had said nothing.

Ever since coming to Dunnoth Tower, Ramsey hadn't been himself. Whether it was because of Tara, or finally admitting to everyone he was half Druid as well as Warrior, and then using his magic, he didn't know.

Nor did it matter. All he wanted was to return to being the man he was. The man who always kept himself in control. The man who didn't make rash decisions. The man who thought things through thoroughly at least six times before making a decision.

The man who didn't let anger rule him.

Ramsey tossed another log on the fire before he leaned his ear against the door to listen for sounds of Tara. When he heard nothing, he feared she might have run away again.

He had the door open before the thought finished in his mind. When he caught sight of Tara asleep beneath covers she had pulled nearly over her head, he quietly closed the door. It wasn't until he was seated on the couch and caught sight of Tara's boots that he realized what kind of fool he'd just made of himself.

"What is wrong with me?" he asked.

His gaze shifted to his arm that rested atop his leg to see the magic still there, still as thick as before.

Though he had been a man of twenty-one years when Deirdre unbound his god, he had been raised as a Druid of Torrachilty Forest.

Since their magic ran powerful and deep, it was only the males who could control it. Any female born with magic in

Torrachilty was killed, because if she were allowed to live she would go insane from the force of the magic.

Ramsey came from a long line of males from Torrachilty. He had learned spells as soon as he could talk, and they were perfected before he learned any more.

His teachers had been brutal, but effective. The Druids of Torrachilty had been known as the Druid warriors. All Druids, even the *droughs,* feared them.

Like all Druids, Ramsey had been taught how the *droughs* had called up the ancient gods from Hell so they could take the host of a man and rid Britain of Rome. Ramsey had also learned how it had taken both *droughs* and *mies* alike to bind the gods inside the men.

Ramsey had learned how difficult it had been to correct something the *droughs* had done. There were consequences to such decisions, and those consequences had fallen to the *mies*. They were the ones who followed the bloodlines the gods would travel through generation after generation.

But Ramsey's teachers hadn't known everything. They hadn't known about Deirdre or what she would do. They hadn't realized the gods could be unbound once more.

And they hadn't known he would be taken by Deirdre and that his god would be released.

Ramsey thought of his father and uncles, and he thought of his family. It wasn't something he allowed himself to do very often, because he had no idea what had happened to them.

All he did know was that the infamous warrior Druids of Torrachilty Forest were no more.

He jumped up and reached for the laptop Saffron had sent with him. Sleep he would not get that night, but maybe he could learn something about his people.

Maybe he could find some clue as to what happened to them, or where they went.

He would never find his family, that he knew. But if there was another out there, Ramsey wanted to find him. He couldn't believe he was the last of the Torrachilty Forest Druids.

It seemed too cruel, too brutal.

But Ramsey had a sinking feeling it was all true.

CHAPTER
NINE

MacLeod Castle

Galen sat at the end of the long table in the great hall, his finger tapping slowly on the wood.

"You look worried."

Galen started and turned his head to find Lucan standing beside him. Galen shrugged. "My thoughts are dark today."

"You're no' the only one." Lucan lowered himself onto the bench and propped his elbows on the table he had made so many centuries ago. "You're thinking about Ramsey."

Galen wasn't surprised at the statement. His power might be to read other's minds, but Lucan wasn't a fool. "Aye. I doona like that he wanted to go alone."

"He's no' alone now."

Galen ran a hand down his face and sighed. "Ramsey was the one Deirdre caught after you and your brothers. He's the eldest next to you three MacLeods."

"Your point?"

"He's cautious for a reason, Lucan. The fact that he wants to face Declan alone doesna sit well with me."

"Nor did it with Fallon, which is why my brother sent Charon and Arran to Dunnoth Tower."

"Will it be enough though?"

Lucan's sea green eyes narrowed. "What are you no' telling me, Galen?"

"Nothing. It's just . . . I've a bad feeling. Ramsey might have admitted to being half Druid, but I'm no' sure that was all of it."

"How so?"

Galen shook his head. "I'm guessing here, but it was something Reaghan said last night before she fell asleep. She wondered what kind of magic Ramsey had."

"Verra powerful if we judge by what we saw in the battle with Deirdre and the awakening of Laria."

"Exactly." Galen leaned forward so that his arms rested on the table. "I did some research on the Druids of Torrachilty Forest."

When Galen didn't immediately continue, Lucan flexed his hands in agitation. "Well?"

"They were considered the warrior Druids, Lucan. They were feared. Greatly. No one messed with them, no' even the *droughs.*"

"Ballocks." Lucan blew out a breath. "I doona know whether to be impressed or worried."

"Me either. Reaghan's question did make me curious. What with Deirdre's death, Camdyn and Saffron's wedding, the search for the missing scroll with the spell to bind our gods, and Declan going after Tara, none of us spoke with Ramsey about his magic."

Lucan rubbed his forehead. "Nay. We should have. I think we were all so relieved to have Deirdre finally dead that we forgot. But I doona think Ramsey would go after Declan himself if he didna believe he could take him."

"And that in itself scares me. I would have expected Hayden or even Camdyn to act in such a way, but no' Ramsey. He's the one who thinks everything through, the one who listens to everyone before he makes a comment."

"I'll go tell Fallon," Lucan said as he stood. "See if you can find out anything else about the Torrachilty Druids."

Galen watched Lucan stride away as he continued to worry about Ramsey. It didn't sit well with any of them that

Ramsey had wanted to go alone. They all wanted to fight Declan, but Ramsey and Saffron convinced them of the need to get Tara to the castle first.

Galen just hoped Ramsey's decision didn't cost him his life.

Tara stretched her arms over her head and yawned. When she opened her eyes to see the grayness of dawn coming through the shutters she knew she wasn't in her room.

A second later the events of the night before rushed through her mind. She slowly sat up, a smile pulling at her lips as she thought of how safe she had felt with Ramsey. It never entered her mind to be afraid of him or of Declan.

Tara couldn't remember the last time she'd felt so free. Maybe that's what allowed her to sleep so deeply, but whatever the cause, she felt like a new woman.

She threw back the covers and slid off the bed. The mirror on the back of the door stopped her cold when she saw her reflection. She hadn't paid much attention to the shirt Ramsey had given her the night before, but now she couldn't look away.

It was flannel, but one that had been washed many times. The plaid was blue, white, and black and smelled like a heady mixture of pine and man. She turned her nose to the collar and inhaled the scent that was all Ramsey.

The cuffs were unbuttoned and hung well past her hands when she lowered her arms. She'd never understood why in movies they always showed a woman walking around in the man's shirt after they'd had sex. Now she knew.

She'd never felt sexier in her life.

Tara snorted at her own thoughts. "I've never felt sexy at all."

She tried to smooth down her sleep-mussed hair with her fingers without any success. Then, she slowly turned the doorknob and opened the door.

Silently she peeked around the doorjamb at the couch, only to find it empty. Her feet walked soundlessly across the wooden floor and rugs to the kitchen, but she found herself alone.

Tara was about to return to her room and see how dry her clothes were when her gaze was caught by the view out of the huge windows that took up a large portion of the wall.

Snow had fallen at an incredible rate the night before, leaving huge mounds of it everywhere. The flurries that continued to fall were large and showing no signs of decreasing anytime soon.

Everywhere Tara looked it was white. Only the gray stones of the castle broke up the white wonderland. If she tried really hard she could almost believe she was in another world, a world where Declan didn't exist and she didn't need to run for her life.

Ramsey nearly dropped his armload of wood when he caught sight of Tara. Every fiber of his being was attuned to her. It wasn't only because Tara leaned over and his shirt hem came up to the top of her shapely thigh, giving him a peek at bright green panties with white lace trim.

It wasn't only because her hair was tousled as if she had just been made love to.

It wasn't only because her smile transformed her face into something that stole his breath away.

He was seeing a side of Tara he suspected few ever had. The sun broke though the thick canopy of clouds and shone directly on Tara, highlighting her light brown hair so that the golden strands in it shone.

To his amazement, she leaned to the side so that he was able to see a white frog on the back of her panties and the word JAMMIN' atop it.

It brought a smile to his lips, because he hadn't expected to see Tara wear panties like that. She was a loner, a runner, so she had expressed herself in ways others wouldn't be able to see.

He could stare at her all day, his imagination running wild over what she was—or wasn't—wearing beneath his shirt. All he could think about was how good it looked on her, but how desperately he wanted to rip it off her body.

His cock thickened and his blood quickened at the

thought. How would her magic affect him if they kissed? Or made love? The fact that he was even thinking about it told him she had already affected him too much.

"Oh," she said as she turned and found him staring. "I thought you had left."

Ramsey finally shut the door behind him and stomped his feet to get the snow off before he walked to the fireplace. "We were running low on wood, and with the temperatures continuing to fall, I needed to stock up."

He stood after putting the wood away and once more he was lost. Tara was a classic beauty, but there was something so compelling, so alluring, about her that Ramsey had been struck by it from the first moment he saw her.

"Did you sleep well?"

She smiled and glanced down at her feet. "It's been a long time since I've slept that well."

"I'm happy to hear it."

"Thank you for the use of your shirt."

Ramsey walked back to the kitchen and leaned against the stove. "It looks much better on you than it ever did on me."

Her slow smile made his balls tighten and his hands itch to touch her. He'd only gotten a small feel of her smooth skin, and he wanted, no, he needed more.

Ramsey mentally shook himself. He wasn't there to seduce her, he was there to protect her. He needed to remember that before he got her killed.

"I was about to make pancakes and sausage. Are you hungry?" he asked.

"Famished. Would you like some help?"

He shook his head as he began to get everything out. "Nay. You sit and talk."

"About what?"

He glanced at her as he opened the refrigerator. "Anything."

"I'm not that interesting."

"I doona believe that. Everyone is interesting in their own way."

"Not me," she said with a laugh.

Ramsey wanted her to get more comfortable with him, to trust him. And that meant she had to start opening up to him. "How about telling me something you did that you weren't supposed to as a child?"

She bit the side of her bottom lip, her blue-green eyes alight with pleasure. "All right. I used to sneak out of my house to swim in the loch."

"That's the best you can do?" he teased as he stirred the mixture in the bowl. "I didna just sneak out. I would take something from my father and put it with one of my cousins so he'd get in trouble. It was a game we had played since we were old enough to walk."

"Did they ever discover you?"

He grinned. "No' once."

They shared a laugh, their eyes locking. Ramsey was the first to look away. He told himself it was because he didn't want the pancake to burn, but the real reason was that he didn't trust himself with Tara.

She was allowing him to see a little bit into her world, and it startled him how much more he wanted to know. She only had herself to lean on to survive, and through it all, she could still smile as if Fate hadn't screwed her.

"What?" she asked, her head cocked to the side so that her wavy, light brown hair hung over her shoulder.

He flipped the pancakes with a twist of his wrist. "How long will you run from this man who is after you?"

She looked down at the table and exhaled. "Either until he catches me or I kill him."

"You doona believe he'll give up?"

"No."

The firm note in her voice made him nod. "What if I said I could help?"

"Why would you want to? You don't know me, Ramsey. I'm not going to hand my problems off to you or anyone else."

He got out a plate and put the first pancake on it before handing it to her. "Why did you stay here last night?"

"What?" she asked as she slowly lowered her plate to the table.

"Why did you stay?"

Tara pushed herself up from the table. "I shouldn't have."

"But you did, and there's a reason. Say it."

She shook her head.

Ramsey closed the distance between them and lifted a lock of her golden-brown hair with his fingers. "You felt safe."

Already Ramsey could feel her magic moving from her hair onto his fingers. His god all but purred at the unique and heady sensation that was becoming all too familiar.

He found himself leaning closer to her, drowning in her beautiful blue-green depths. The tendrils of magic were once more swirling around his hand and were working their way up his arm the longer he touched her hair.

"Yes," she finally admitted. "Thank you for that."

She rose up on tiptoes and kissed his cheek. Her lips on his skin was his undoing. He turned his head slightly so that their mouths brushed, which halted her retreat.

Her lids lifted so that she looked into his eyes, and the need he saw there was all it took for him to shift his head a little more until their lips brushed.

Ramsey's breath locked in his lungs at that first, hesitant touch of their mouths. He tilted his head and kissed her again, longer, deeper.

His body roared to life, demanding and needy. The ends of her hair tickled his hands as he placed them on her back. He coaxed, he seduced. Anything to get closer to her, to feel more of her.

To know more of her.

To have her.

Tara's soft moan had his blood burning through his veins like quicksilver, and when she softly laid her hand upon his chest, Ramsey wanted to crush her to him. The urge to pin her against the wall and ravage her lips was overwhelming.

His chest constricted, his heart pounding inside him as if he'd run for days. He heard her soft intake of breath that was part gasp, part pant.

And it drove him wild.

Ramsey fisted his hands in her shirt as he swept his tongue inside her mouth and she eagerly returned his kiss. For a moment he couldn't breathe, couldn't move, the passion and pleasure was so intense.

She leaned into him, her breasts pressed against his chest. Ramsey bit back a groan as her magic joined in the frenzy that surrounded him. It became too much to govern, too much to resist.

Just before he lost all control and kissed her as he'd been dreaming about, he heard footsteps approaching. Grudgingly, reluctantly, he pulled back.

It took a moment before Tara opened her eyes. They were dilated and her breathing was rapid, proving she was just as affected as he from the kiss.

"We're about to have guests," he said a moment before the door opened and Charon and Arran stepped inside.

Ramsey met their surprised gazes, but when Charon's eyes lowered, Ramsey knew he had seen the magic that was once more swirling around him.

CHAPTER
TEN

Tara looked at the two men filling the doorway. They were tall, brawny, and there was something about them that reminded her of Ramsey but had nothing to do with looks.

It was something to do with the men, something that set them apart from other guys. Almost as if Ramsey and these other two were in a class by themselves. A class where coiled violence, tangible danger, and dark seduction were part of their DNA.

Despite their similarities, Tara wasn't attracted to the newcomers as she was to Ramsey. She met the dark gaze of the one nearest the door, the one who had narrowed his eyes on Ramsey before shifting to her.

"Tara, these are my friends," Ramsey said as he moved so that he stood behind her. "The one with the goofy grin is Arran MacCarrick, and the one behind him is Charon Bruce. And this is Tara Kincaid."

"A pleasure to meet you," Arran said as he held out his hand.

Tara looked into his pale brown eyes and returned his smile as she briefly grasped his hand. "Likewise."

Charon moved around Arran and held out his hand. "Tara."

"Charon," she said as they shook hands.

He was studying her, of that Tara was certain. The why,

however, was what she didn't know. Charon wasn't rude, but he was reserved, almost as if he didn't trust her.

That made Tara smile, which in turn had Charon's dark brows rising.

"Something amusing?" he asked.

She looked at their still clasped hands and pulled hers from him. "You don't trust me."

"Ramsey said you were able to read people. Does it bother you that I'm . . . reserved?"

She glanced at Arran to find him watching her intently. "Not at all," she answered Charon. "I'll leave you lads to breakfast."

"Will you no' stay?" Arran asked.

Tara shook her head, wishing it had been Ramsey who asked. "I must return to the castle and my duties."

As she walked to the bedroom, she felt three pairs of eyes watching her, and it was everything she could do not to look over her shoulder at Ramsey.

She shut the door behind her and leaned back against it before she closed her eyes. A sigh escaped her lips as she thought of the all-too-brief kiss.

He had been about to deepen the kiss, but pulled back to announce that they had visitors. How could he have known that? Charon and Arran hadn't knocked.

Tara frowned, but realized she was most likely overreacting. She did it constantly and it had kept her on the run. Maybe it was time she relaxed a little.

She pushed away from the door and began to unbutton Ramsey's shirt. Her clothes were still damp when she put them back on, but she wouldn't be in them very long.

After making the bed and trying once more to fix her hair, Tara walked out of the bedroom to find all three men sitting at the table. They looked up at her arrival, but she focused on Ramsey.

"I cleared a path to the castle," he said as he stood.

She smiled, hating to leave. Not only did she enjoy Ramsey's company, but she liked how she felt around him. And then there was the attraction.

"You can stay. Eat your pancakes," he offered.

Tara took a deep breath and grabbed her boots. She shook her head slowly while she put on her shoes. "I appreciate everything, but I need to get back."

"Of course."

"I hope you are no' leaving on our account," Charon said, his hand around a large mug of coffee.

She met his probing stare. "Not at all. I do have a job to do." With one last look at Ramsey, Tara left before she did decide to stay.

The cold hit her instantly, and she crossed her arms over her chest and walked as fast as she could back to the castle. The first thing she was going to do was take a long, hot shower to warm up. Though thinking of Ramsey's kiss was definitely helping her to withstand the cold.

Ramsey stood by the window and followed Tara with his eyes until she was inside the castle. He licked his lips, still tasting her upon them. He'd never tasted anything so wonderful, and he craved another kiss.

One that would allow him to explore Tara at his leisure with his mouth and his hands. It had been a mistake to kiss her, but a mistake he wouldn't reverse if he could.

He looked down at his right arm where the tendrils of magic swarmed up to his shoulder. Somehow he'd managed to keep it hidden from Tara, but the longer he touched her, the more her magic would show.

"She's a damned fine-looking woman," Charon said. "If we'd known we were interrupting, we wouldna have returned."

Ramsey shook his head and turned to his friends. "I'm glad you did. It doesna need to go further than it already did, which was much further than I ever intended."

Arran leaned back in the chair and regarded Ramsey. "Why no'? We've all had a hell of a life thanks to Deirdre. Why no' take a sliver of happiness and enjoy it?"

Ramsey held up his arm. "This is why. This is from touching her hair and briefly kissing her."

"What does it mean?" Charon asked.

"Hell if I know. I know if I touch her skin, the magic is stronger and lasts far longer. Other than that, I have no answers."

Arran rose and gripped Ramsey's arm where the white tendrils of magic swarmed. He pulled back almost instantly. "Shite! That is strong magic."

"This may have something to do with you being part Druid," Charon said.

Ramsey nodded. "Or the fact that one moment Tara's magic is the strongest I've ever felt, and then the next, some of the weakest."

"When we walked in earlier, it felt strong to me," Arran said.

Charon scratched his neck, his brow furrowed deeply. "Aye, but when she came to see Ramsey yesterday and we hid in the bedroom, I could barely feel it."

"I've touched plenty of other Druids at MacLeod Castle and even before, and no' one of them has made me have such a reaction," Ramsey said.

Arran shrugged and stabbed his fork into the stack of pancakes before dumping them on his plate. He straddled his chair and sank down in it as he reached for the syrup. "Maybe that's why Declan wants her so badly."

"Maybe. But if her magic comes and goes so quickly, it'll be a great risk he's taking." Ramsey speared four pancakes for himself before Charon and Arran ate them all.

Charon stuffed a huge bite into his mouth and shrugged. "Maybe Declan knows something we do no'," he said around his food.

"I've already considered that," Ramsey said as he turned the syrup upside down and coated his pancakes thoroughly before Arran snagged it out of his grip. "Tara is opening up to me, but it's going slower than I'd like. We doona have the kind of time it will take to earn her trust."

Charon set down his fork. "You do realize whatever trust you earn from her will be shattered the moment she discovers what you are? She'll think you tricked her, mate."

"I'm aware of that," Ramsey said with a deep sigh. It was something that had bothered him since he'd first come to Dunnoth Tower. "I doona know another way."

"Tell her what you are, what we are," Arran said.

Ramsey halted his fork midway to his mouth and just stared at Arran. "She'd run."

"Run where? Have you looked outside? I'm making sure Declan doesna get here, remember?"

Charon chuckled and said, "Arran does have a point. Tell her, and if she runs, then we catch her."

"You doona understand how skittish she is," Ramsey said.

Charon snorted. "Oh, but, mate, I do. I was once verra much like her. I might no' have liked the truth, but being lied to, even by omission, was much harder to take."

Ramsey, his appetite suddenly gone, lowered his fork to the plate and looked out the window at the castle. "If I doona tell her, she may open up more to me and give me information about her family and who she is. If I do tell her, we can forget about learning anything from her."

"No' so," Arran said. "It's no' as if she'd tell you, who she thinks is just an ordinary man, about magic or that her family are Druids. That's a secret she'd only share with someone who understood."

It was a no-win situation Ramsey was in, and one he couldn't find a way out of without incurring Tara's hatred.

He ran a hand through his hair and rose from the table. "Arran, call Broc. See if he can try to locate Declan. I know Declan has been using his magic to block him, but I suspect Declan is verra close."

"All right," Arran said.

Charon finished the last of his coffee and set aside the mug. "What are you going to do?"

"First, I'm going to take a shower. Then, I'm going to talk to Tara."

"The only place for her to run if she tries is either to the road or across land. I'll be at the road watching," Charon said.

Arran threw one arm over the back of his chair and flattened his lips. "I know we suggested telling her, but do you think you should do it today?"

"Putting it off will only be worse for everyone involved," Ramsey said.

"Doing it in the middle of the day at the castle is no' such a grand idea either," Charon added.

Ramsey inhaled deeply and wondered why it was so difficult for him to make a decision about anything involving Tara. He'd never had a problem before.

He closed his eyes and thought of her, searching for her magic. It took less than half a heartbeat for him to feel her magic. She was in her bedroom. She seemed content, but before he could get a decent read on her magic, it vanished. As if there had never been any.

Ramsey looked at his right arm and knew she did indeed have magic. But what was turning it on and off? The only way to learn that was to tell her he was a Warrior and half Druid.

He prayed she didn't run, because he would catch her and she'd never forgive him for that. With his decision made he looked at Charon and Arran.

"It's being done today," Ramsey told his friends before he stalked into his room.

CHAPTER
ELEVEN

Declan stood in the snow uncaring that it quickly coated his uncovered head. It wasn't as if he feared getting sick. The Devil had invested too much in him for a little cold to do him in.

"I looked at the weather report as you asked," Robbie said, his breathing heavy after tracking through the dense snow.

"And?"

"They're as stumped as everyone as to where this weather came from."

"As I suspected. It's magical," Declan said.

"By who?"

"Someone who doesna want me to reach Tara."

"Could it be Tara?"

Declan chuckled at the absurdity of such a notion. "I'd bet my entire fortune she hasn't learned to control her magic any more than when she was with me."

"Then who?"

"That is the question, is it no'?"

Robbie shrugged. "It doesna matter, cousin. We cannot go anywhere with the snow coming down so heavily."

"I doona have all this black magic for nothing." Declan turned to his cousin and smiled. "I think it's time we move onward. I've waited too long to have Tara back in my control."

"When do you want to start?"

"Now. By tonight I expect to have Tara and be on my way back home."

Robbie smiled and rubbed his hands together. "I'll start shoveling around the car."

Tara couldn't remember the last time she'd been so happy and almost carefree. Because of the weather, the guests had decided to spend some quiet time in their respective rooms, which suited Tara perfectly.

She couldn't stop daydreaming about Ramsey and their kiss. When she'd given him the light peck on the cheek, she hadn't envisioned it turning into a kiss. But she was so glad it had.

It had been just a little over an hour since she'd walked out of Ramsey's cottage, but when he appeared in front of her, Tara's stomach did a somersault.

"I need to talk to you," he said.

Tara licked her lips nervously as she noted the seriousness of his expression. "Of course."

"Somewhere privately if you have time."

"Yes. All right. I've . . . I've caught up on everything for the moment, so do you want to talk now?"

"I do."

Tara rose, but as she did he released a harsh sigh as his phone vibrated.

He glanced at the phone and said, "Give me just a moment."

She nodded and he answered it in front of her.

"Aye?" he said.

Tara could hear the deep timbre of a male voice, but she couldn't make out the words. Ramsey's frown deepened the longer the conversation continued, however.

"Are you certain? Is there anything Arran can do to stop whatever is interfering?"

Tara had eavesdropped on conversations before when she thought Declan might have found her, and though she knew it was wrong to do it, she was too eager to learn what had upset Ramsey so drastically.

"Shite. You know what this means?" he asked the caller.

There was a one-word response that Tara took to mean the caller did understand.

"I was about to talk to Tara."

The mention of her name had her lifting her gaze to Ramsey to find him watching her. Whatever he had to tell her wasn't going to be pleasant.

She swallowed the lump of dread in her throat and wished she could have enjoyed her day a bit longer, a day that had begun wondrously, but that she suspected was going to end badly.

"I will," Ramsey said, and ended the call.

"I suppose that isn't good news," Tara said.

Ramsey shook his head. "Nay."

"I'm not going to like this little talk of ours, am I?"

Again he shook his head.

"Can it wait?"

Ramsey's gaze briefly shifted to the floor before he said, "Nay."

"Then let's get on with it. The back room behind Liz's office should do well enough for privacy."

"Actually," Ramsey said, halting her, "I was thinking my cottage."

"Let's go then."

Tara watched Ramsey walk to the coat rack and lift hers. He wore faded jeans, thick black boots, and a dark green T-shirt with a silver Celtic trinity knot that covered his entire left shoulder and ran onto the sleeve.

She allowed him to help her into her coat and then she walked through the door he held open for her. The path that had been cleared wasn't wide enough for them to walk side by side, so she stayed behind him.

Her gaze soaked up his nice bum and the way his hair, loose again, moved around his face and shoulders as snow tangled in its inky strands.

Tara was excited to be alone with Ramsey again, but he'd warned her she wasn't going to like what he had to say. As usual her mind ran the gambit of what it could be. Anything from her family to Declan, and even to the Warriors who had found her in Edinburgh.

Though she tended to think of the worst possible outcome, she also liked to speculate on what she hoped would happen. Which had her thinking that maybe Ramsey wanted to apologize for the kiss and tell her they could never let it happen again.

If that were the case, she'd be mortified, but the anxiety that twisted her stomach in knots would loosen and she could stay at Dunnoth a few more days at least.

All too soon they reached the cottage. She stepped inside, quickly enveloped in warmth. Ramsey held out his hand for her coat, but if she had to make a quick exit she didn't want to be caught out in the cold without it again.

"I'll keep it on," she said.

He nodded and then motioned to the couch. "Would you care to sit?"

"I like to take my bad news standing."

She didn't mean it to sound so harsh, but the longer she watched Ramsey the more that knot in her stomach tightened until she thought she was going to be sick.

"Tara—"

"Just tell me," she interrupted him.

He raked a hand through his hair, grim lines bracketing his mouth. "You asked me why I came to Dunnoth Tower. I told you I was looking for something."

Tara tried to swallow, but her throat wouldn't work. She knew in that instant he had been looking for her. And she had felt safe with him, she had let him shelter her the night before.

"You found it," she said.

He gave a quick nod. "I'm . . . Tara, I'm . . ."

She rolled her eyes and slapped her hands on her legs. "Just spit it out."

Tara wasn't sure why she hadn't already run for the door. Maybe it was because she wanted to know who had hired

Ramsey or why he hadn't tied her up and locked her in his room until the snowstorm passed.

Maybe she just wanted to know why he had kissed her.

Instead of telling her what he'd been about to say, he held out his arm, palm out toward the hearth. A second later a blast of magic erupted from his hand and shattered the glass candleholder on the mantel.

Tara stumbled backward until she collided with the wall behind her. Her eyes looked from the broken bits of glass to Ramsey.

"I've wanted to tell you," he said.

She tried to calm her racing heart. Her only recourse was to lie, because she couldn't admit the truth. Not to Ramsey. Not to anyone. "I don't know what you're talking about."

The sadness on his face evaporated, replaced by cold rage. He stalked toward her, causing her to press against the wall.

"Really? You want to lie?"

She shrugged.

Ramsey leaned close until his face was inches from hers and she could see the dark silver band around his irises. "I know you have magic, Tara. I know you're a Druid."

And then he placed a finger atop her hand.

Confused, she looked down and gasped as wisps of white smoke curled around Ramsey's thick index finger to his hand, around his wrist, and up his arm.

"This is what happens when I touch you," he whispered.

Tara was mesmerized by the ribbons of white that continued to circle Ramsey. They originated from her, but when she moved her hand away, the wisps remained with Ramsey.

"Try to lie to me now."

Her eyes jerked to his. "Is this why you think I've magic?"

She could have sworn she heard a growl as he pressed both of his palms on either side of her head. "I can sense your magic, Druid. It was the fear in your magic that sent me outside looking for you last night."

"Sense?"

Her heart plummeted to her feet. There was only one

kind of being who could sense Druids—Warriors. With her blood now icy in her veins, Tara looked longingly at the door. If she could reach it she might be able to get away.

"Aye," he said softly. "I see you've pieced it together, Tara. I'm a Warrior, but I'm also a Druid."

"That's not possible."

"Oh, but it is."

Tara shook her head. "I don't care what you are, just tell me who sent you."

He blinked and looked at her strangely as if just realizing he had her pinned to the wall. Ramsey dropped his hands and took several steps back.

Tara took in a deep breath. She might feel a little better without Ramsey's body so close to hers, but she wouldn't feel remotely safe until she was as far from Ramsey as she could get.

"Did Declan send you?" she demanded.

Ramsey shook his head and slowly lowered himself into a chair. "There is much you doona know. I should have begun at the beginning."

"I know what a Warrior is. Several attacked me in Edinburgh."

"Nay," he said, his gaze intense. "The maroon one had been sent by Deirdre to bring you to her to kill. The others are my friends. We have a Seer at MacLeod Castle, and she saw what was going to happen. The others were there to stop Malcolm, no' to harm you."

"You expect me to believe you?"

"I hope you'll listen to what I have to say before you start running again. Declan is close, Tara. Verra close. Our Seer, Sonya, saw a vision of Declan finding you, and somehow I was involved. I was sent here to protect you from Declan."

Tara looked down to hide the tears that had gathered in her eyes. She wanted to believe him, because it would mean she wasn't alone in the world anymore. But to believe him she would have to trust him, and he'd already proven he was a liar.

"Arran created the snowstorm to keep Declan away," Ramsey continued.

"Arran?" she asked, her head jerking up. "Oh, God. Arran and Charon are Warriors as well?"

Ramsey rubbed his chin and sheepishly nodded. "The leader of us, Fallon MacLeod, didna like me coming here alone. So he sent Arran and Charon to help me keep an eye on things."

Tara slid down the wall until she was sitting on the floor, her knees to her chest. Her stomach roiled with nausea after all she had heard.

She didn't know what to believe or what to do.

"I'm here to keep you safe from Declan, Tara."

She lifted her gaze to find him staring at her, a silent plea upon his face. He was so damned gorgeous. It hurt to think she had put such faith in him.

Tara held her stomach and crawled to her feet. She rushed to the door, but in a blur Ramsey was suddenly standing in front of it, blocking her exit.

"If you believe nothing else, believe that I doona wish you harm. I had plenty of opportunities in which to take you if that had been my intention. But I didna."

"Move," she demanded.

To her surprise he did, but hesitantly. Tara didn't waste a second getting away from him. Her mind was too jumbled to think straight.

She needed to be alone, to think over all that she learned and all that she knew. A glance at the sky showed the snow had lessened, but it was still falling.

Arran had created the snow at Ramsey's request. If Arran could control the weather, then what could Ramsey and Charon do? And did she even want to find out?

Tara walked into the castle and straight to her room. She sank wearily onto the bed, her mind going between Ramsey's kiss and discovering he was a Warrior.

And a Druid.

She fell back on her bed and covered her eyes with her arm. How did she always manage to get herself into such awful situations?

CHAPTER
TWELVE

Ramsey fought the urge to go after Tara. He needed her to understand why he was there and that he wasn't a bad man. Yet he had seen the anger in her eyes, the fury and distrust.

Her beautiful blue-green eyes would never look at him with passion and desire again, of that he was sure.

With a resigned sigh, Ramsey sat on the couch as he stared straight ahead, going over his conversation with Tara again and again.

He had no idea how long he'd been sitting there when the door opened and Arran stepped inside the cottage.

"Is it odd that Tara is doing almost the same thing in her room?" Arran asked.

Ramsey leaned forward and scrubbed a hand down his face. "She didna take it well."

"I've deduced that much already," Arran stated flatly. He took the chair near Ramsey and shook his head. "I'm sorry, but I still believe it was the right thing to do."

"It was." Ramsey didn't like to admit it, but it was the truth. "Trying to continue to lie to her and keep her from discovering I'm a Warrior would only have grown more difficult."

"Especially after that kiss."

Ramsey glanced down at his hand where the ribbons of magic were slowly vanishing. "Aye."

"That doesna mean you cannot woo her, my friend."

"That's exactly what it means. How are you managing with the snow?" Ramsey asked, deliberately changing the subject.

Arran shrugged. "It's increasingly more difficult. It's Declan. I know it. His black magic is strong, but he willna be able to halt the snow altogether."

"Ah, but if it lessens, they'll clear the roads and he'll be on his way here," Ramsey said.

"Unfortunately, you're exactly right. Do you think you could add your magic to my power?"

Ramsey was so surprised at the request he could only stare at Arran. Finally he shook his head. "Nay. And doona ask again."

"Why?"

"It doesna matter why. It can no' be done." Ramsey rose, but Arran quickly stood to block his retreat.

Arran narrowed his eyes as he crossed his arms over his chest. "You tell us just days ago that you're half Warrior, half Druid, and then doona bother to explain why you can no' add your magic to my power when Declan is after the very lass we're here to protect."

"Arran . . ." Ramsey was going to try and convince his friend to let it drop, but he realized it would be a futile attempt. Arran wouldn't give up trying to discover what he was hiding.

"How bad can it be?"

Ramsey snorted. "What do you know of the Torrachilty Druids?"

"Only what you told us, which was that they were verra powerful and kept to themselves."

"We were the warrior Druids, Arran. It wasna just our magic that was strong. We were set apart from other Druids because only the men could harness the potent magic that ran through us."

Arran dropped his arms to his side, realization dawning. "That magic aided in your battle abilities."

"Aye. Only once have I tried to use the full extent of my magic with my powers. The outcome was . . . horrendous."

"I doona understand. You used your magic to help awaken Laria, and then again to destroy Deirdre in that final battle."

"At great cost to myself. I only used a portion of my magic each time, and it took all of my concentration to keep it from expanding as it wanted to do."

"As long as you doona call forth your god, you should be all right."

Ramsey shook his head. "It isna that easy. The blood of the Torrachilty runs through my veins, but so does the blood of the god. It is mixed."

"Oh, hell." Arran rubbed the back of his neck as he began to pace. "Do any of the others know?"

"Nay. No one needed to know as long as I kept it in check."

Arran stopped pacing and glared at Ramsey. "This mix you have, it's the reason you wanted to come fight Declan by yourself."

Ramsey didn't deny it. There wasn't a need. "I did. I'm the best advantage we have in taking him, but I couldna chance doing it and allowing anyone else to get harmed."

"And Tara?"

"I knew that after one look at Declan and me, she would run. It didna matter if she returned to MacLeod Castle with me, only that Declan no' apprehend her."

"Shite," Arran said, and turned his head to the side to look out the windows. "You might be able to take Declan on your own, Ramsey, but you'll need someone to watch your back because Declan willna be alone." He turned back to Ramsey. "Besides, Charon and I are no' exactly easy to kill."

"You know as well as I that magic can harm a Warrior. We saw what happened with Galen and Broc. And Duncan."

Ramsey hated to bring up their long-dead friend, but he had a point to make and the quicker Arran comprehended it, the better.

"Declan could kill you," Arran said.

"He might. But you and Charon will get Tara safely away."

Arran looked at the floor and slowly shook his head, a wry smile on his face. "You have this all planned out."

"I do. We doona know why Tara is so important or why she continues to appear in Saffron's visions, but she's the one who needs to be saved."

"And no' you?"

Ramsey shrugged. "Declan is a scourge upon this land, Arran. I would willingly give my life if it meant he would die."

"What the hell is going on?" Charon demanded from the kitchen entrance.

Ramsey blew out a breath and met Charon's furious gaze. "I'm explaining my plan to Arran."

"What he's doing is trying to convince me he can take Declan by himself," Arran said.

Charon's dark brow rose slowly. "You cannot be that daft, Ramsey."

"Oh, but he is," Arran hurried to say.

Ramsey lifted a shoulder to answer Charon.

"Is it because of your magic?" Charon asked.

As quickly as possible, Ramsey repeated all he had told Arran. By the time he finished, Charon was seated at the table with a surprised expression on his face.

"Shite. This is good and bad. Obviously, I agree with Arran. I'm no' about to allow you to fight Declan on your own."

"You have to," Ramsey said. "He has the X90 bullets that can kill each of you instantly."

Arran smiled as he popped the top of a Coke. "If his gang of mercenaries are quick enough, maybe. I doona intend to be that slow."

Charon chuckled and nodded at Arran. "I like your thinking. Those mercenaries are just mortals. They have no magic, no power. Just guns that these," he said as he held out his hands and his copper claws extended from his fingertips, "can easily slice through."

"I would rather you both take Tara as far from here as you can," Ramsey said.

"We'll try to talk her into it before Declan gets here, but I'm all for a fight with that bastard."

Arran nodded in agreement, a sly smile pulling at his lips. "I didna get my turn at Declan in the last battle. I'm eager to take out his mortals."

Ramsey knew it was pointless to try and talk his brethren into what he wanted. They were Warriors, Highlanders who didn't know the meaning of running.

They were Warriors because they were the strongest, the best, the undefeated of their bloodline.

Ramsey glanced at the window to see the snow was nothing but a light sprinkle of flurries now. "Declan's magic is winning, but he willna be able to halt Arran's snow. Enough fell that it will take him maybe another day to get here, two if we're lucky."

"We're never that lucky," Charon added.

"At any rate, Tara doesna trust me now. I doubt she'll even allow me near enough to speak to her, but we all have to keep watch on her and the castle. I want as much advance warning of Declan's approach as I can get."

Arran leaned against the counter and shrugged. "We'll sense his magic early enough. No' even his ability to cloak himself will stop that."

"Then we use it to our advantage." Ramsey leaned on the back of the chair with his hands. "Arran, since you can control the snow and ice, stay out of sight from Declan, but use your power against him and his men. Charon—"

"I'll do my thing."

Ramsey nodded. "And I'll do mine."

"What is yours exactly?" Charon asked.

"My power is to manipulate mass, but I have to touch it first. Which means I can transform the mercs' rifles into baby rattles if I want."

Charon threw back his head and laughed. "I can no' wait to see this. But you have to touch the weapon?"

"Aye. No way around that."

"What of your magic?" Arran asked.

Ramsey didn't have an answer for them, at least not one they would like. "We'll have to wait and see."

"I wish you had learned just what this mix of magic and power could do," Charon said. "No' knowing could be detrimental."

Ramsey had learned firsthand how harmful his mix of magic and power could be. "A Torrachilty Druid learns from the moment he can talk about his magic. It's difficult to control from the verra beginning, but eventually we master it."

"Unless you have a primeval god inside you that amplifies your emotions and anything else," Arran said quietly.

"Aye. It's why I doona use my power or my magic verra much. Either one can easily get out of control if I doona concentrate."

"Tell me," Charon said, "why did only the males get the magic?"

"Because we were the only ones able to withstand the force of it. A few females were born with our magic, but they were no' allowed to live."

Arran's face was a mask of horror. "Why?"

"Because they went insane from the magic."

"Damn," Charon muttered. "So you are the most powerful Druid we have at MacLeod Castle?"

Ramsey wasn't about to point out that Charon had said "we." This came from a Warrior who had kept clear of the MacLeods until this final battle with Deirdre.

"I am. Despite Deirdre's magic, I believe the Torrachilty Druids could have ended her centuries ago."

"Why did they no'?"

"That's what I'd like to know."

Arran tossed the empty Coke can in the garbage. "I say we begin to look. I'm as curious as you to know what happened to such a powerful group of Druids. My first thought is Deirdre, but you never know."

Ramsey shifted from foot to foot and looked at the castle. "First, let's focus on Tara and Declan."

The sound of a chair scooting back on the floor drew Ramsey's attention. Charon stood and met his gaze for several long moments.

"Let me talk to Tara," Charon said.

The idea of a man, any man, whether mortal or Warrior, alone with Tara made Ramsey's hackles rise. But they needed to convince Tara not to fight them, and if Charon or Arran was able to do so, then Ramsey wasn't going to object.

"All right."

Charon gave a nod before he stalked from the house.

Arran moved up beside Ramsey and said, "If he fails, I'll try talking to Tara. She may no' like us, but in the end, we just need her to be cooperative."

The problem was, Ramsey wanted her much more than cooperative. He wanted her as she had been the day before—flirting and looking at him as if she couldn't stop staring.

But that was long gone.

CHAPTER THIRTEEN

MacLeod Castle

Galen faced the people that were now his family as they stared at him around the long table in the great hall. Ten Warriors, including the lone female Warrior and Fallon's wife, Larena, as well as eleven Druids waited for him to speak.

It was Reaghan who touched his hand and gave him an encouraging smile. His wife had helped him do the research on the Torrachilty Druids and compile the information.

"We're not nearly done with looking through the information on the Torrachilty Druids," Reaghan said. "However, we thought it important to share with everyone what we have learned so far."

Quinn, the youngest MacLeod brother, leaned a forearm on the table and asked, "Is there that much information?"

"Surprisingly, aye," Galen answered. "Thanks to Saffron's connections we were able to look over scanned pages from ancient texts that many doona even know exist."

Saffron looked around the table. "In other words, these books are highly prized and once bought are never sold again. They don't see a museum, and are kept in controlled environments where no one touches a page with their bare hands. They wouldn't even allow me to see the books myself, but they did offer to scan some pages to help us."

"Thank them for us," Fallon said.

"They've been well thanked," Camdyn, Saffron's husband, muttered.

There was a chorus of chuckles because everyone knew Saffron had sent over a case of Cristal champagne and a box of Macanudo cigars to the owners of the book.

Galen was thankful that someone like Saffron, a multimillionaire, had the connections and the wherewithal to get them the information they otherwise would have had to steal.

"What did you discover?" Hayden asked.

Galen looked at his fellow Warrior and shifted in his seat. "The Torrachilty Druids were wiped out by Deirdre."

"Damn," Broc swore, and shook his head.

Logan raised hazel eyes to Galen and asked, "All at once as Deirdre did the MacLeod clan?"

"No," Reaghan answered. "It appears as if the males left Torrachilty Forest a few at a time in order to kill Deirdre."

"Wait," Ian interjected before she could continue. "Was this before or after Ramsey was taken?"

Galen glanced at the table and released a sigh. "After. From what we've gathered they knew exactly what happened to Ramsey, and they intended to get him back from Deirdre."

"Does Ramsey's name appear in any of the scanned pages?" Larena asked.

Reaghan shook her head of curly auburn hair. "Unfortunately no. What's mentioned over and over is the word *mac*."

"Which means son," Isla said.

Galen nodded slowly. "There's also mention in there that they no' only knew their line had a god through it, but they knew exactly who the god would choose."

"Ramsey," Marcail said.

Lucan leaned forward and said, "You said these Druids were warrior Druids. That they were greatly feared. How did they lose against Deirdre?"

Galen shrugged and spread his hands wide. "I've no idea. All it says is that they went out to fight. When those warriors didna return, more went. It continued that way until the group went from several hundred to a few dozen. When all that remained was a handful of the Druids, females, and children, Deirdre attacked and wiped them out."

"Does Ramsey know all of this?" Cara asked.

Saffron shook her head, her gaze moving from Camdyn's to Cara's. "He doesn't. When he woke Laria he said he wanted to know what happened to his people."

"That's right. He did," Camdyn said.

Sonya tucked a strand of her curly red hair behind her ear. "I think we should continue to find out more. Ramsey deserves to know about his people and his family."

"I agree," Gwynn said softly, her Texas accent thick. "But like Saffron, I've had a personal run-in with Declan. Can Ramsey really take him on by himself?"

"I wouldna chance it," Fallon answered. "Charon and Arran are there, and they'll call me if there's trouble. I can have all of them back here in a blink."

Dani cleared her throat to gain everyone's attention. "That's all well and good, Fallon, and we all love how you can teleport, but it takes time to make that call. If they're fighting Declan they won't have that time."

Lucan turned his head to look at Fallon who sat next to him. "When is the last time you spoke with Ramsey or the others?"

"Arran called early this morn," Fallon responded. "It appears Declan had somehow spoken in Tara's mind, so Ramsey had Arran bring on the snow."

"I knew it was Arran who did the snow," Ian said with a chuckle.

Hayden rubbed his chin thoughtfully. "With the amount of snow coming down, no one is moving around up there. It was a wise choice, but then Ramsey always makes good decisions."

"That he does," Logan agreed.

Broc laid his hands flat on the table and asked, "So what now? We continue to wait?"

"I've got a good lead on the hidden scroll we're searching

for," Larena said. "While Galen and Reaghan continue their research, we're still looking for this scroll."

Hayden rose and leaned his hands on the table. "As much as I love spending time with Isla, I doona feel right leaving Ramsey, Charon, and Arran to face whatever is coming at them alone. I'm going after them."

"As am I," Logan said, after kissing Gwynn on the cheek.

Ian gave a nod. "Include me in that."

"And me," Quinn said.

Fallon rubbed his eyes with his thumb and forefinger before he looked at each of the men and nodded. "I doona want Charon or Arran to know you're there, but most especially Ramsey. You four will only be there as backup."

"Understood," Hayden said.

"But I think it's an excellent idea," Fallon said with a smile. "I'd like to be with you."

"But you're needed here, my love," Larena said as she smiled at him. "Who else would jump us from one location to another?"

After a quick kiss to Larena, Fallon yelled out, "Be ready in half an hour!"

Tara told Liz she was ill in order to be alone, and it hadn't been a lie. She was sick. Not just from all she had discovered about Ramsey, but because she couldn't leave. She was essentially trapped.

A light tap on her window had her jerking her head up from her pillow to find Charon standing outside looking at her. She knew what Warriors were and how they had come into being. She knew they were immortal and had powers individual to each god.

She also knew—and had seen—that their skin changed the preferred color of whatever god was inside them. Along with fangs and claws.

Tara didn't know what Charon was up to. If he wanted to, he could force his way in. For all she knew his power was the ability to walk through walls.

But she wasn't in the mood to listen to anything anyone

had to say, especially a Warrior. She laid her head back down and shut her eyes.

A second later there was a louder, more forceful tap.

Tara slammed her hands on the bed and growled as she jumped from the bed to stand in front of the window. "What?" she demanded.

"I would talk with you. Let me in."

She shook her head at Charon.

"Fine," he said calmly. "We can talk through the window."

"Oh, for goodness sake," Tara muttered as she threw open the window. She leaned her hands on the sill. "I really don't care to hear anything you have to say."

"Actually, I think you do."

He didn't try to sweet-talk his way in, or lie. His simple statement did what it was supposed to do—draw her curiosity.

"Did Ramsey send you?"

Charon shook his head, his dark eyes meeting hers. "Nay."

With her ability to read people, Tara saw another soul who didn't trust easily, someone who might not have run as she had, but who had closed himself off to everyone.

She stepped away from the window, and he promptly climbed through. Once inside he closed the window and leaned against it. He didn't crowd her, almost as if he were going out of his way to make her feel safe.

"I know you doona trust us," he said. "And you have every right no' to. All that Ramsey told you was the truth. For centuries the Warriors at MacLeod Castle have been fighting Deirdre, and more recently Declan."

"Why?"

He gave her a flat look. "Why do you think, lass? Because Deirdre and Declan are evil, and they must be stopped. The Warriors fight because it is what they believe in, and it won us the day with Deirdre's death once and for all."

"You keep saying 'they.' Are you not one of the MacLeod Warriors?"

She watched how all expression left his face. His eyes became shuttered, and his entire body stiffened slightly. She had hit a nerve without meaning to.

"Nay, I'm no'."

"The fact that you are here with two of those Warriors makes me think that you are one of them."

Charon shook his head, his long dark hair damp from the snow moving with him. "You'd be wrong. After getting free of Deirdre, I spent the last four hundred years in my village, protecting my people. I didna help the MacLeods, and if it wasna for an overwhelming urge to go to the Orkney Isles, I doubt I'd have taken a stand against Deirdre this last time."

His confession stunned her, almost as much as the knowledge that he was telling her the truth even though it didn't exactly put him in a good light.

"Why?" she asked again.

"Things happened in Cairn Toul, Tara. Things I didna have control over because of my god. I must live with what I did. I didna believe I had the right to find a home or a place with the others at MacLeod Castle. I still doona, but Fallon asked me to help. How could I refuse when I knew what we were up against? Most of the Warriors there are married. I couldna walk away and let one of them take my place."

Tara lowered herself onto her bed and rubbed her hands on her thighs. "Why are you telling me all of this?"

"Because you need to know who we are."

Tara slowly let out a breath and ignored the pounding headache that was growing worse by the moment.

"Ramsey didna lie when he said he was sent here by our Seer, Saffron. She saw Declan find your mother and question her about you. She also saw Declan coming for you and Ramsey being there to help. You've been raised as a Druid, you know the importance of Seers."

"How do you know I was raised as a Druid?"

He shrugged nonchalantly. "Ramsey and a few others paid your family a visit."

Tara's eyes grew wide as she covered her mouth with her hand. She couldn't believe all she was hearing. It had been ten years since she had seen or spoken with her mother, yet Declan and Ramsey had both seen her.

"Did my family know Ramsey was a Warrior?"

Charon gave a single shake of his head. "We try to reserve that information for a select few."

She looked down at the carpet, her mind even more confused than before.

"You can keep running," Charon said into the silence. "Eventually Declan will find you, but you're aware of that. Or, you can take a chance and put a small measure of your trust in us. Ramsey will die before he allows Declan to harm a single hair on your head."

"He doesn't even know me," she said as she raised her eyes to Charon. "Why would Ramsey risk so much?"

"Because whether you like it or no', your destiny is tied with Ramsey's."

CHAPTER
FOURTEEN

Ramsey stared up at the sky. He was doing as Arran had asked and was going to combine his magic with Arran's power. It was a tricky thing they were about to do, and Ramsey would have preferred not to do it.

But he needed more time with Tara, and the snow would keep Declan away.

"Ready?" Arran asked as he walked up.

Ramsey rubbed the few flakes of snow from his eyelashes. "Nay."

"We're as far from the castle as you'd let us get, my friend, and still be close enough to Tara. Either we get farther away to keep everyone safe in case you go nuclear, or we stay close to Tara."

"Nuclear?" Ramsey repeated as he turned his head to Arran.

Arran smiled and shrugged. "I love the new words I've learned since leaping forward to this time. People in this time have such colorful ways of expressing themselves."

"You've been watching too many movies with Dani and Ian."

Arran's smile broadened. "They're fascinating. So. Do you think you can contain that mix of magic and power of yours?"

"It's no' like I have much of a choice, do I?"

Ramsey rubbed his hands together and focused on his

magic. It had been so long since he had tried to call forth just his magic.

He'd spent his immortal years controlling his god and tamping down his magic and power in order to keep those around him alive. He'd known then he should have been learning his limits on just what he could do with such a mix inside him.

Now, he'd have days, if not hours, to learn what he could. He should have known better than to make such an idiotic mistake. He should have known there was a reason he had survived Deirdre's torture and her mountain.

"Ramsey?"

He blinked and nodded to Arran. "I'm here."

"Nay, you're no', no' that I doona blame you for worrying. Tell me, how great was your magic before you became a Warrior?"

A memory flashed in Ramsey's mind of standing in the forest surrounded by his family as he passed yet another test with his magic. He'd been lauded as one of the greatest Torrachilty Druids ever, his magic had been so vast.

But that was in the past.

"I was as good as any of my people."

Arran's lips flattened as he grunted. "That wasna an answer, but I suspect that's all I'm going to get."

"Come, Arran, before I change my mind."

In the next heartbeat Arran released the god within him. His skin turned white and long white claws extended from his fingers. His eyes, now milky white from corner to corner, turned to Ramsey, and he smiled, showing his fangs.

"I'm ready. Are you?" Arran asked.

Ramsey wanted to just call forth his magic, but every time his magic answered him, so did his god. There was no way around it. In order to use one, he had to use the other.

With barely a thought Ramsey called forth his god, Ethexia. He looked down to find his skin had turned the bronze of his god and his claws a shade darker. Ramsey ran his tongue over his fangs as his entire body vibrated with the force of the magic he had called up.

Normally when he released his god he ignored his magic as best he could, but this time was wholly different. Ramsey could practically feel the magic stretch from fingertip to fingertip and from the top of his head to the bottom of his feet.

It filled him, merging with the power of his god until Ramsey could no longer tell where one ended and the other began. It was a heady feeling, but one that also filled him with trepidation.

"Bloody hell," Arran muttered beside him. "I can feel your magic as I would a Druid's."

Ramsey opened his eyes and found himself smiling. When he looked at Arran it was to see how the Warrior blended in with the snow while he stood out like a beacon.

"How come I never felt your magic before?" Arran asked.

"Because I tamped it down. No' to mention there were always other Druids around us, so you assumed what magic you did feel came from them."

"No one ever knew?"

Ramsey remembered the time Larena had questioned him. "Larena suspected."

Arran shook his head in bewilderment. His gaze shifted away from Ramsey and focused on the sky. Flurries of snow began to swirl around him. The clouds bulged as if wanting to spill the snow, but they were held back.

Magic, potent and fierce, flowed down Ramsey's arm to his hand as he placed it onto Arran's shoulder.

"Fuck," Arran muttered as the magic and power shifted from Ramsey into him.

The snowflakes increased as they fell from the sky, but it wasn't enough. Ramsey knew he was going to have to use more of his magic, and if he did, it would put him past the safe limit he knew he could use.

"I can handle it," Arran said, as if reading his mind.

Ramsey was about to refuse, then he thought of Tara, of what he knew Declan to be capable of, and his decision was made. He released more magic.

His god bellowed with approval, and euphoria filled

Ramsey at the feel of his magic rushing through him. It had been so long. He'd forgotten how good it felt, how wonderful it was to have such a potent ability.

Ramsey closed his eyes as memories assaulted him from his childhood. Memories of his family, of training to be one of the powerful Torrachilty Druids. Of facing his people, knowing his magic exceeded those around him, and that was saying something.

Suddenly, Ramsey was hit from behind and taken down into the densely packed snow.

"I said enough, dammit," Charon bellowed in his ear.

Ramsey pushed up on his hands and tried to dislodge Charon from his back. "Get off me."

"No' until I know you've reined in that magic of yours."

"Aye."

"I can still feel it, Ramsey."

Ramsey paused, and realized it had gotten away from him as he'd feared. He tried to pull his magic back in, and to his fury it took three different tries before he was able to.

Charon rose off him, and Ramsey jumped to his feet. He noticed two things at once. One, the snow was once more coming down thick and fast, and two, Arran was lying in the snow unmoving.

"Shite," Ramsey said as he rushed to his friend. He shook his shoulders. "Arran?"

"He's no' moved since I took you down," Charon said.

Ramsey ran a hand down his face, wishing he hadn't sent more magic into Arran. "This is my fault."

"Aye, it is," Arran said, his eyes still closed as his white skin and claws faded. "I feel like horse shite."

Charon leaned his hands on his knees and he bent over Arran. "Are you hurt?"

"Nothing that can no' be mended." Arran's eyes opened to stare at Ramsey. "You nearly went nuclear. You couldna hear."

Ramsey gave a quick shake of his head. "Now you both know why I doona like to use my magic."

Charon helped Arran to his feet. "You did what had to be done, and as Arran said, he's immortal. He'll be fine."

Ramsey climbed to his feet and followed them back to his cottage. They were nearly there when something stirred in the air. He halted in his tracks and softly called to the other two.

Charon and Arran turned, silent questions on their faces.

"Did you feel that?" Ramsey asked.

"You mean something besides the snow?" Charon asked, sarcasm dripping from his words.

Arran shook his head. "I'm sorry, Ramsey, I didna feel anything."

When Ramsey didn't respond, Charon gazed over Ramsey's shoulder and looked around.

"Where did you feel it?" Charon asked.

"Behind me."

Arran moved the shoulder where Ramsey had held him and frowned. "Was it Declan?"

"Nay," Ramsey said with a slight shake of his head. "It was no' Druids I felt. It was different. I can no' put my finger on it."

Charon's hands fisted by his sides. "Do you still feel it?"

"Slightly. I doona think it's dangerous."

"But you felt it," Arran stated.

Charon loosened his hands and snorted. "It looks as though your mix of magic and power is going to be useful. As soon as we all figure out what it is you just felt."

"I swear he knows we're here," Hayden whispered to his friends.

Fallon shook his head. "There's no way. Warriors sense Druids, no' other Warriors."

"Aye, but Ramsey isna just a Warrior," Logan pointed out.

Ian sighed. "At any rate, we're going to have to keep hidden. I doona want them to know we're here."

"Good idea," Quinn said. He turned to Fallon and said, "I thought Charon and Arran were supposed to keep their distance from Ramsey?"

"Apparently Ramsey had other ideas," Fallon said. "See if

you can determine what they were doing out here so far from the castle."

"Of course."

"I'll return tomorrow, but if you need me before then, call."

Quinn rolled his eyes and shoved his brother. "Get out of here."

Once Fallon had jumped back to the castle, Quinn turned to the others. "Hayden, I think you're right. I think Ramsey knows we're here."

"Or at least that something happened," Logan said.

Ian nodded. "Just moments after we arrive he stops, and then Charon and Arran are looking behind him to the exact place we are."

"Ramsey didna believe whatever it was he felt was dangerous or all three would have investigated," Hayden added.

Quinn glanced at the sky and the rate of the falling snow. "It looks as if we're in for a cold one, mates. Let's split into two groups. Ian, come with me. We're going to have a look around here as well as the road. Ramsey said he thought Declan was close."

"Let's find the bastard," Ian said with an excited gleam in his eyes.

"Logan and I will get closer to the castle," Hayden said.

Logan smiled and said, "We willna get too close. We promise."

Quinn grinned as they all clasped forearms. They had been in enough battles together to know anything could happen at any time. They were always prepared, and not once did they head into battle without saying farewell to those they cared about.

Which included everyone at the castle. They had become one huge family, and like all families they had their disagreements, but the evil they had been fighting for centuries bonded them deeply.

Though Fallon and Lucan were Quinn's brothers by blood, he considered every Warrior at the castle his brother and every Druid his sister.

"Hayden. Logan," he called before they could move away. "There is a reason Ramsey wanted to take this mission alone. If he discovers we're here after sending Charon and Arran, he'll likely try to take Declan out by himself at a later date."

"I ken," Hayden said, his black eyes somber. "At least here we can keep an eye on him and help if needed."

Quinn nodded. "Exactly."

"We're all worried about Ramsey," Logan said. "He willna know we're here."

Quinn watched them move away, a nagging feeling of doubt in his mind.

"What is it?" Ian asked.

"I doona know. Ramsey shouldna have been able to sense our arrival."

"Maybe there's more to his mix of magic and powers than we know."

"I suspect that's the case. Let's just hope Ramsey doesna do anything stupid."

Ian's face scrunched up. "Ramsey? Nay. He's the last one to do something reckless."

CHAPTER
FIFTEEN

Ramsey was going to do something stupid, of that Tara was certain. It was probably the talk Charon had given her, or maybe it was the way Ramsey's silver eyes had held hers, but she knew it as certainly as she knew the world of magic existed.

Though she was afraid and distrustful of the Warriors, there was no doubt Charon hadn't been lying to her. Neither had Ramsey if she were honest with herself.

She hadn't wanted to see that at the time he'd been trying to tell her, but she'd reflected on it since then.

Still, could she trust a Warrior? Did she dare?

"How can I not when I know Declan is coming?" she muttered.

Tara rose from the bed and reached for the coat she'd discarded earlier. A glance out the window showed the snow was once more falling rapidly. She tied her scarf snugly around her neck and tugged on her gloves before she walked out of her room and then left the castle.

With each step that brought her closer to the cottage all she could think about was the kiss Ramsey had given her. It wasn't as if it had been her first kiss. She'd been kissed before. Not often, or even in the past year, but there was no reason for it to hold her attention the way it did.

Especially after learning about Ramsey. It shouldn't matter that someone wanted to help her against Declan, though it was wonderful not to feel as if she were alone in the world.

But that didn't erase the lies and omissions of the truth. Trust was how she survived. Without trust, there was nothing.

There was the kiss.

Tara kicked at the snow, hating herself for coming back to the kiss time and again. And it wasn't as if the kiss knocked her off her feet.

It had been soft, sensual. But she had sensed his hunger and his passion in his firm lips. Just thinking about it made her stomach flip.

If Ramsey could make her feel like this with just a brief meeting of their lips and tongue, what would it be like if he really kissed her? If their tongues mated and she tasted him as she longed to do?

And God help her, she desperately wanted to find out.

"I'm so pathetic," she said to herself. "Pathetic and lonely."

She neared the cottage and heard the sound of all three male voices within. Tara paused outside the door for a moment as she tried to distinguish what they were saying. She had to press her ear closer to the door to hear.

"Stop being so dramatic, Ramsey," Arran said. "I'm fine."

"You are no' fine. I almost killed you."

"You know it takes a lot more than that to kill a Warrior. Decapitation works best, as you know."

"Stop kidding around, Arran," Charon said gruffly. "I happen to agree with Ramsey. I didna understand what he was saying until I saw it with my own eyes."

"And I was the one who urged him to use his magic," Arran said, his voice rising. "I'm the one who sat there and had that jolt of magic and power go through me."

"Maybe so, but I saw it," Charon argued. "I saw Ramsey standing there, his magic blasting into me even from that distance. I saw you yelling at him and the pain on your face from his magic. I saw that he didna hear you."

"Enough!" Ramsey bellowed. "It's over and done with. Arran suggested it, and I did it knowing the consequences. It was the only way to ensure that Declan stay away so we could have a few more hours with Tara to try and earn some of her trust back. I apologize to both of you for what happened today."

"There's nothing to apologize for," Arran said, his voice deep with emotion.

Tara's heart ached for the pain she heard in Ramsey's voice.

"There is," Ramsey said. "Fortunately, it willna happen again. I've a favor to ask of both of you."

"Name it," Charon said.

"I need one of you to stay at the road, and the other to return to MacLeod Castle."

The sound of a chair scraping over the floor filled Tara's ears. She could just imagine one of them jerking to his feet at Ramsey's statement.

"I'm no' leaving you here alone," Arran said.

Another chair scraped back and then Charon's voice said, "Me either."

"I willna be alone for long."

Tara frowned, not understanding Ramsey's words. Of course he wasn't alone. Though the guests had departed the castle, there were still the owners and staff.

"Why do you want one of us to return to MacLeod Castle?" Arran asked.

Ramsey sighed. "To take Tara away from here, away from Declan."

"So you can fight Declan yourself," Charon said at the same instant Tara grasped it.

She opened the door and stepped inside the cottage without any of them realizing she was there.

Ramsey stared at his two friends, wondering how he could make them understand how important it was that he fight Declan alone.

"No one is dying for me."

Ramsey's body jerked as if he'd been struck. He slowly turned to see Tara's form filling the doorway, her blue-green eyes filled with fury.

"Tara," he said, and took a step toward her.

She held up a hand and said, "No." She turned to glare at Arran and Charon as she softly closed the door behind her, belying the fury he saw coursing through her.

"No," she repeated. "No one is dying for me. I want you all to leave."

"I can no' do that," Ramsey said.

She leaned back against the door and shrugged. "I always knew Declan would catch me one day. I'm tired of running and looking over my shoulder. I'm tired of distrusting everyone. And I'm tired of the lies."

"You can give all that up but no' give yourself to Declan." Ramsey swallowed and took a small step toward her. He had to convince her, and he knew he had just one shot. "You'll be safe at MacLeod Castle. Declan can no' reach you there."

"Oh, but he can, Ramsey." Her smile was sad. "He can reach me anywhere."

"There will be Druids there to help you," Charon said.

Arran nodded. "And other Warriors who would die before they allowed harm to come to any Druid."

Ramsey watched Tara carefully, hoping for some sign that they were getting through to her. Her eyes moved back to him, where she held his gaze.

"If I go, will you?"

Ramsey wanted nothing more than to go back with her and the others, but he couldn't. If he did, it would mean a battle with Declan at a later date that would involve the others. At Dunnoth Tower, he could take care of Declan once and for all.

"I'll come," Ramsey said. "When I'm finished with Declan."

Tara pushed off the door and strode across the floor until she stood before him. "You don't go, I don't go."

"You are no' safe here."

"I can hold my own against Declan."

Ramsey saw Charon and Arran exchange a look out of the corner of his eye. He swallowed and said, "You are no' safe here with me."

His admission cost him more than he had realized. It felt as if he'd plunged a dagger into his own stomach and turned the handle. But the truth of what he was, what he was capable of, had been proven earlier with Arran.

Ramsey wouldn't endanger innocents again. Ever.

And Tara was most certainly an innocent. He hadn't even felt her magic when she'd walked to the cottage. She was a Druid. He should have known the instant she left the castle, but then again her magic had always come and gone.

He knew she was a Druid, but what kind exactly was what confounded him. He wanted to know. For himself and for her.

"I'm not safe with you?" she repeated.

Ramsey shook his head, hoping this would end the disagreement.

Instead, she walked to Arran and placed her hand atop his on the back of the chair. When she lifted her hand, she looked from it to Ramsey. Then she moved to Charon where she placed her hand on his neck and repeated the same process.

Ramsey dragged in a ragged breath when she stood in front of him once more and placed her hand on his face. He didn't need a mirror to know the white tendrils of magic were moving from her to him.

He felt them, heard her magic's call to his own. But it wasn't just his magic that answered her. It was his god and his passion. He wanted to drag her against him, to lock his arms around her so that her curves pressed against him and he could kiss her.

"What are you trying to prove?" he asked.

She raised a brow and cocked her head. "What am I trying to . . . ? I feel it, Ramsey. I feel the magic inside you. How is that possible?"

"I doona know."

She lowered her arm, and for a few moments the tendrils of magic could be seen around her hand before they faded. But Ramsey's wouldn't fade for a while.

Ramsey searched for something to tell her, something that would ease her mind and allow her to go with Arran back to MacLeod Castle.

"I may not trust you. I may not agree with how you went about telling me who and what you all are, but something happened over these past few days. I . . ." She paused and swallowed. "I am who I am, and I'm not hiding anymore. I will face my family, Declan, and whatever else comes for me."

Ramsey was shaking his head before she was finished. "Be smart about this, Tara. Declan has searched for you for nearly ten years. You've stayed ahead of him somehow, but he's found you."

"I know."

"Nay, you doona," Arran said. "I doona think you know what kind of man Declan is."

Her blue-green eyes never left Ramsey's when she answered Arran. "I may not. Declan never hurt me. He never treated me unkindly."

"Then why did you run from him?" Ramsey asked.

"Because he wanted what my family wanted. He wanted to force me to become *drough*. The night I left him, I overheard him tell Robbie about his elaborate plan to seduce me and trick me into the *drough* ceremony. He said it would be done before I knew what had happened. And as scary as that was, it was nothing to what he had planned next."

Charon asked, "Which was what?"

"He said the magic within me would be his to control. That I would help him in his quest to—"

"Take over the world," Ramsey finished for her.

He ran a hand down his face and sighed. He'd thought Declan might want her for something like that, and Tara's words confirmed it.

"Every time he had me use my magic I could feel myself grow stronger. It wasn't until that night I heard his plans that

I realized I wasn't growing strong. The magic he was having me perform was black magic. He was dragging me farther and farther into evil. I left before it took me completely, but I'm too afraid of my magic now."

"Shite." This was far worse than what Ramsey could have imagined.

"If your magic is so great, how come we didna feel you walk up?" Arran asked.

She shrugged. "My magic has always been so volatile. No matter what I've done I've never been able to control it properly."

"That's all the more reason you should go with Arran to MacLeod Castle," Ramsey said.

Tara smiled softly. "I know about Deirdre and all that she did. The stories my grandmother told me mentioned Warriors who stood against her, but I never believed that part until today. You stood against her, even when the possibility meant death or falling under her control once more. You didn't run."

"There was more than just one of us," Ramsey hastened to tell her. "There was a group of us, and we did it in part to kill Deirdre, but also to protect Druids. You only had yourself, and you did the one thing that ensured your survival."

"I was a coward."

"You were smart."

The doubt in her eyes made him want to comfort her. He wouldn't allow himself to hold her, but he could offer a little comfort.

Ramsey softly tucked a strand of her golden-brown hair behind her ear. Her head leaned against his hand slightly, but it was enough.

As he lowered his arm, more wisps of magic wound around his hand while his gaze was caught by Tara's. Trapped. Ensnared.

And well and truly held.

CHAPTER
SIXTEEN

"I'm really beginning to grow angry," Declan said from the front passenger seat of his Jaguar.

Robbie leaned forward and looked at the sky through the windshield. "I doona understand, cousin. Your magic should have halted the snow."

"Should have, but didna. I suspect this is more than just Warriors' work."

"Druids?"

Declan nodded.

"But surely no' Tara. Her magic was much too volatile."

"Was. It's been a decade since I last worked with her. She was progressing nicely too. In a matter of months she would have been *drough*."

"You'll have her back under your roof soon enough. I'd like to know why she ran from you though."

"I as well. I still doona think it's Tara's magic involved in this. This would take verra potent magic. My kind of magic."

Robbie's brows shot up in his forehead. "Another *drough* then?"

"That's the only explanation."

"A *drough* working with the Warriors?"

Declan shrugged. "Anything is possible. Call for my helicopter. I'm tired of playing around."

As he listened to Robbie put in the call for the chopper, Declan's gaze was on the horizon to the north where he knew Tara was.

It wouldn't be long now. She would have nowhere to run, and with his added magic, Tara wouldn't be able to refuse him when he demanded she turn *drough*.

"Verra soon now, sweet Tara," Declan said with a smile.

Tara sat on the couch in the cottage and tried not to show how anxious she was. It hadn't mattered why she had come to the Warriors to begin with, especially once she learned Ramsey's plan.

She hadn't lied when she said she didn't want anyone dying for her. Especially not someone like Ramsey. She wasn't worth that.

From what she'd gathered by the looks they'd exchanged and their unspoken comments, Ramsey was unique among his brethren by being part Druid. What that meant exactly, Tara didn't know.

Ramsey walked into the cottage from outside and gave a small smile. "The castle is empty. No one stayed behind, just as we asked."

"You're still sticking with your plan?" Charon asked.

Ramsey's gaze shifted to Tara for a moment. "I am."

"It's not going to work then," Tara said. "Because I'm not leaving. Or weren't you listening to me?"

"I heard you," Ramsey replied. "I just hoped you'd changed your mind."

"I'm stubborn like that."

"So I've noticed."

Arran cleared his throat. "I have an alternative plan."

The way Ramsey didn't immediately dismiss Arran proved how close the men were. "Does it involve me staying?" she asked.

"It does, but only because I doona want to force you to leave," Arran said.

Charon leaned against the wall, a bored expression on his

handsome face. "Unless things get too dangerous, lass. There are too few Druids for us to allow even one to be harmed or killed if we can do something about it."

"Well said," Ramsey replied softly.

Tara rubbed her hands on her thighs. "It's not in me to just hand you my life and allow you to do with it what you will."

"Taking you to the MacLeods isna handing us your life," Ramsey said as he walked toward her. He stopped when he reached the overstuffed chair and placed his hands on its back. "The Warriors and Druids would protect you there. You can come and go as you wish. Think of it as a sanctuary."

He made it sound like the heaven she had been dreaming of since first running from her family. But places like that didn't really exist. She should know since she'd been looking for one for a decade.

"I stay," she declared.

Ramsey's gaze lowered as he shook his head. He looked to his comrades. "I doona like this."

"Our only other choice is to force her," Arran said.

Tara rolled her eyes and got to her feet, indignation boiling within her. "Ugh. I'm right here. I can hear you."

Charon merely smiled at her. "We know."

"What's your plan?" Ramsey asked Arran.

Arran grinned wickedly and clapped his hands together as he rubbed them eagerly. "Though I like a battle as well as the next Warrior, since Tara will be with us, I say we handle this differently. Charon will alert us when Declan arrives. I'll be in the castle waiting for the bastard."

"Because that's the first place he'll look," Charon said with a nod.

"Exactly. I'll take out as many of his mercs as I can while Charon does the same."

Charon's smile was wide, his eyes gleaming. "I'm liking this plan."

Tara looked at Ramsey to find him with his arms crossed over his muscular chest and his gaze intense as he listened.

She noticed that about him. He listened, observed, and took everything in.

"I'll be here with Tara," Ramsey said.

Arran nodded. "Correct. He'll never expect what you'll deliver to him."

Tara's heart jumped in her throat when Ramsey's silver gaze shifted to her. He stared at her for one heartbeat, two before he looked back at the men.

"On one condition will this work. While you and Charon take out the mercenaries, I'll attack Declan and touch as many of the rifles as I can. When it comes time for me to face Declan—"

Charon nodded. "We take Tara."

"No," she interrupted. "I want to see Declan's death."

Ramsey blew out a breath and lowered his arms to his sides. "If you stay, there's a chance that what I unleash on Declan will kill you. I can no' have that happen."

A thread of fear wound around her heart. Ramsey wasn't joking, and the way neither Arran nor Charon would meet her gaze told her how serious the situation was.

"We cannot just leave you to face Declan on your own," she said.

Ramsey shrugged. "I'm the only one capable of defeating him."

"If you can."

"I will."

He sounded so sure of himself that Tara began to believe him as well. But she knew what Declan was capable of. For now, because she didn't have any other choice, she nodded her assent to the plan.

"Good," Ramsey said. "Since we have the entire place to ourselves, let's get set up."

Charon pulled out his mobile from his pocket as he walked to the door. "I'll phone Fallon and fill him in."

Arran bowed his head to her before he spun on his heels and walked out of the cottage. Leaving Tara and Ramsey alone. The cottage had gone suddenly quiet with only the howling of the storm outside to break the silence.

"Are you hungry?" Ramsey asked.

Tara shook her head. "Not really."

"There's plenty of food, so help yourself."

She slowly sank onto the couch as he took up a spot in the shadows beside the window so he could keep a lookout. Tara studied him silently for several moments.

He continued to keep his long hair loose, which she loved. It was damp from the snow, as was his short-sleeved tee. Ramsey was unlike any man she'd ever come across. He didn't boast of his accomplishments or his money. He said very little, but when he did speak it was because he had something to say.

While anyone could see Arran and Charon were not men you wanted to tangle with, Ramsey was different. You didn't see what you had coming at you until it was too late. His violence was hidden, the danger was not tangible until he wanted it to be.

"Is this what you do?" she asked.

Ramsey glanced at her. "What do you mean?"

"Do you save people?"

"Sometimes," he said with a small shrug. "Mostly we've spent our lives battling Deirdre. With her gone, our attention is on Declan."

"So you came because of him."

This time Ramsey turned his head to her. "I came for you."

Tara shouldn't have felt the small thrill his comment gave her. She didn't want to feel anything toward Ramsey, but she had learned long ago she couldn't control her emotions. "There are other Druids out there to be saved."

"But none that Declan wants more than anything."

"Have you saved many Druids?"

He shook his black head slowly. "No' as many as we should have. Deirdre wiped out so many, and then when Declan pulled her forward in time, during those four centuries the Druids that did survive lost their way."

"Not all of them. My family is steeped in its magic. It's just the wrong kind of magic."

"Magic is magic. Although I wish more *mie* magic had survived than *drough*, at least there is magic. Each Druid has a choice whether to become *drough* or no'. You made that decision."

She leaned back and let her head rest on the cushions so she looked at the ceiling. "In my family there isn't a choice, Ramsey. We were born into a *drough* family, and we will be *drough*. If we refuse, they force us."

"How? I thought you had to be willing? One of the Druids at MacLeod Castle was forced to become *drough* by Deirdre. Isla's magic was strong, and the evil never took over as Deirdre had planned. Isla is one of our strongest Druids."

Her head shifted so she could look at him. "My family is very . . . persuasive. The ones before me might not have wanted to be *drough*, but my family is relentless. None have ever refused."

"Until you."

"Until me," she said with a smile. "I think my grandmother was impressed with my stubbornness. She even tried to talk my mother into allowing me to remain as I was."

Ramsey turned so that his back was against the wall and he faced her fully. "What happened?"

"If you spoke with my mother I suspect you know what happened."

"Your grandmother was never brought up."

Tara leaned forward and dropped her face in her hands. Images of her grandmother laughing and teaching her magic rolled through her mind.

"My grandmother was *drough*, like all the rest of my family. Yet she was different." Tara lifted her head and released a long breath. "Grandmother always had time for me, teaching me, or just laughing with me. From the time I was a wee child she told me over and over again to follow my heart even if it meant going against the ones I loved."

"Do you think she knew what you were going to do?"

Tara shrugged. "I have no idea. When I first refused and Grandmother stood up for me, my mother—" She had to stop as the wave of pain slammed into her. "My mother's fury was legendary in our family as was her affinity for whisky. She turned on my grandmother in her drunken rage. I didn't realize her intent until it was too late. Until Grandmother lay dead on the floor."

"I'm sorry, Tara."

She swallowed, determined not to cry. "My mother turned on me next. She wouldn't listen to me, just kept yelling and throwing magic at me. I dodged many of them because she was so clumsy, but not all of them."

Tara lifted her eyes to Ramsey. "She intended to kill me. I got away with my life that night, with my mother's promise to find me ringing in my ears."

CHAPTER
SEVENTEEN

Ramsey was glad he hadn't known this when he spoke to Tara's mother or he might have killed her.

After hesitating just a moment, Ramsey walked to Tara. He could feel her pain and her loneliness in her magic and it called to him.

He knelt before her and looked into her blue-green eyes. "I'm sorry, Tara."

"I've never told anyone that story before."

"If it helps, I doubt your mother will be looking for you. Her liver is failing, and she's no' expected to live out the year."

A tear dropped on the back of Ramsey's hand. He'd never really known what to do with a crying woman, but this time was different. This time he knew what to do.

Ramsey wiped the second tear from Tara's cheek before it fell. To his surprise, she took his hand and closed her eyes as she held it against her cheek.

He remained still, torn between giving her the time she needed and the urge to pull her into his arms. But if he gave in to the need surging through him, Ramsey knew it wouldn't stop at just holding her.

His gaze moved from her face to the wisps of magic that began to float around their hands. He still didn't know what it meant, and though it could be something dangerous, all he knew was that it felt wonderful to touch her.

She drew in a deep, shuddering breath and to his disappointment released his hand. With no other reason to touch her, Ramsey let it fall to the cushion, but the tendrils of magic continued to grow stronger as they wound around him.

"You aren't what I expected in a Warrior," Tara said.

"What did you expect?"

She shook her head, staring at the fire. "I don't know, but not you. You must make some lucky woman very happy."

"I doona have a woman."

Her brows knit as her gaze swung to him. "I find that difficult to believe."

"It's the truth."

"No. You're too handsome, too dangerous, too amazing not to have some gorgeous woman on your arm."

There was only one woman he wanted, and she was sitting before him. Tara's face was so close to his. He could lean up slightly and brush his lips over hers.

As if reading his thoughts, she lowered her eyes to his mouth, and Ramsey bit back the groan that rose swift and true within him.

"Why are you alone?" she whispered.

"Because of what I am."

"A Warrior?"

"A Druid and a Warrior. I have to stay in control always, lest something bad happen."

Tara looked down at his hand where the magic swirled around him and placed the tip of one finger on the back of his hand. As she lifted her finger, a white line of magic stretched between them until it moved like smoke around her before joining the others that surrounded his hand and arm.

"Something bad has happened, hasn't it?" she asked.

He gave a single nod.

Her blue-green eyes met his. "Innocents were killed."

Ramsey wanted to look away, to hide his guilt, but he couldn't. "They did."

"I'm not an innocent, Ramsey."

He could hardly breathe from the passion that overtook him. Tara was too close, her magic too alluring. And with the wisps from touching her, he was a powder keg waiting to ignite. He had to get away from her, to put some distance between them. But the very thought kept him rooted where he was.

"You are an innocent," he insisted.

She shook her head, leaning toward him a fraction. "In all my years of running and hiding, I've only ever felt at peace and free one time. The night I spent here."

Ramsey dug his fingers into the cushions, only vaguely aware that his claws punctured the fabric. The hunger, the need tearing at him was overwhelming. He had to have another taste of her, one that went deeper, longer.

Her hands covered his, and one of her fingers touched a claw. She jerked slightly but didn't pull away.

"You fear me."

She shook her head, her golden-brown waves moving with her. "No. I've only seen Warriors once, while I was in Edinburgh. I've heard what you are, but I've never been this close."

Ramsey found himself leaning closer, closer. He rested his forehead on hers as he tried desperately to find the will to pull away. But when it came to Tara, he had none. All he wanted was her.

He tilted his head, their mouths breaths apart. No more waiting, no more wanting. He was going to kiss Tara until neither of them could remember their own name.

Her eyes fluttered closed, and just before his lips touched hers his mobile rang.

Ramsey pulled back, muttering, "Fuck," beneath his breath so Tara wouldn't hear. He got to his feet, his claws sheathed, as he hurried to the phone atop the kitchen table.

He wasn't surprised to see Fallon's name appear. Ramsey answered it with a curt, "Aye?"

"Charon has filled me in on what's going on."

"All of it, I assume?" Meaning what had happened with Arran earlier.

Fallon sighed. "Aye, my friend. All of it. There's nothing to be upset about. Arran is fine."

Ramsey didn't bother to reply, because he knew if it had been anyone but a Warrior, they'd be dead.

"I'm no' comfortable with just you three handling this alone. And I'm told Tara refuses to leave unless you do."

Ramsey glanced at Tara who watched him from the couch. "That's right."

"Damn," Fallon said with a long sigh. "I'd feel better if I could send others to help you out."

"As it is I'm worried Arran, Charon, and Tara willna get out in time. I can no' worry about any others as well."

"Just what do you have planned?"

"I'm going to kill him."

There was a pause before Fallon asked, "Will this kill you?"

"I doona know the answer to that."

There was a bang on the other end of the line that Ramsey could guess was Fallon's fist hitting the table. "That's unacceptable, Ramsey. I willna loose another friend."

"And you have no idea what's going to happen when I face Declan. Trust me, Fallon. You doona want anyone else around."

"If they're Warriors they'll survive."

"Possibly. Do you want to take that chance?"

As expected, Fallon didn't have an immediate answer. Ramsey didn't like putting his friend in such a tight spot, but as leader, Fallon needed to know all the details. As ugly as those details were.

But Ramsey also knew Fallon well enough to know he'd already sent men ahead. "Who did you bring?"

"It wasna my decision. They were going with or without my help. I figured I'd get them there earlier in case they could help."

"Who, Fallon?" Ramsey demanded, raising his voice. He needed to know how many were here so he could ensure they were gone. Soon.

"Hayden, Logan, Ian, and Quinn."

Ramsey turned and punched the cabinet door, shattering the wood as his fist went through it. "Come and get them. Now."

"They're your friends, Ramsey. They want to help."

"Then they can help by no' being here."

There was a string of curses from Fallon before he said, "I'll do my best to get them out of there. How much time do I have?"

"No' much."

Ramsey ended the call and tossed the phone on the table. He didn't even look at the mess he'd made with the cabinet. Rarely did he lose control of his anger in such a fashion, but it was bad enough Charon, Arran, and Tara were staying behind.

The only way Ramsey could face Declan as he needed to was knowing his friends would get Tara out in time. If others were here and refused to leave, then it complicated everything.

He turned to Tara to find she stood just a few paces away from him.

"Are you all right?" she asked.

"Nay, I'm no'. You're here. Arran and Charon are here. And now Fallon tells me four of my other friends are here as well."

"Warriors are immortal, Ramsey. Whatever you have planned for Declan can be survived by all of you."

There was no use trying to tell her exactly what he had planned. If nothing else, Tara would endure after this battle.

"We've a few hours of daylight left. Is there anything you need from the castle?"

She shook her head.

"Then I suggest you rest while you can. I doona expect this storm to hold Declan much longer."

"How else can he get here? No cars can travel these roads."

"Aye, but he has another option. His helicopter."

She turned away but Ramsey wasn't ready to be parted from her just yet. He stopped her and turned her back around to him. Her gaze searched his as he slowly backed her against the refrigerator.

He caressed his fingers down her smooth cheek to her neck before plunging his fingers into the cool strands of her hair to wrap around the back of her head.

Her lips parted and her breath quickened, showing him she wanted the kiss as much as he did. He moved his other hand under her sweater to her waist.

The impact of skin upon skin only fueled the magic wisps flowing between them. Ramsey moaned deep in his throat when her hands rested on his chest before moving to his back as she tugged him closer.

"Tara," he whispered just before his mouth descended upon hers.

The first contact of their lips was like an explosion of magic between them. His skin sizzled, his body burned in pleasure so wild and fierce he thought he would explode with it.

And it was nothing compared to the hunger within him.

Ramsey slid his tongue between her full lips and plundered her mouth. He gave no quarter as he kissed her as he'd been dreaming of doing from the first time he saw her.

He deepened the kiss, holding her lithe body tightly against him. Her fingers dug into his back, her moans filling his ears.

Still it wasn't enough.

The yearning, the longing had taken him. He had only one thought—Tara.

With each heartbeat, each pleasurable moan, the kiss grew in intensity. Ramsey ground his aching cock against Tara, and her answering gasp only increased his desire.

He wasted no time in tugging her sweater over her head. The sight of her dark orange bra and her passion-filled gaze made his balls tighten.

Tara rose up on her toes and wound her hands around his neck, her fingers delving into his hair and her nails skimming his skin.

Ramsey turned so that he was the one against the refrigerator as he crushed her body to him. He used both hands to roam over her back and shapely behind while he kissed her again and again.

The kiss consumed them. It was passion and desire and need. And it swept them along on a tide neither wanted to fight.

Ramsey bent so that his hands moved over her behind to the back of her thighs. He lifted her, spreading her legs at the same time.

She wrapped her legs around his waist as he walked them to the couch. With a flick of his fingers, he'd unclasped her bra. It fell to the floor as he sank back on the couch, his arms full of Tara.

CHAPTER
EIGHTEEN

Tara's body was not her own. Every touch of Ramsey's hands and mouth sent her blood heating and her heart pounding. She eagerly, anxiously, awaited Ramsey's next caress.

Her lips ached from his kisses, yet she wanted more. So very much more.

It never entered her mind to tell him to stop when he had taken off her sweater, nor when he had unclasped her bra. She was the one who had let it fall to the floor.

And through all the passion and heated desire, her body throbbed from need.

Her lips parted and her body arched toward Ramsey as he ran a finger slowly, softly, down her spine and past the waist of her jeans.

He whispered her name and nuzzled her neck, sending goose bumps over her body in anticipation of more. She slid her hands into his soft midnight locks and let the silky strands glide through her fingers.

His hands were on her back while he kissed her neck to keep her head back and her body arched. Never had Tara felt so sexy or like a woman desired.

She sucked in a breath when one of Ramsey's large, callused hands cupped her breast and kissed the inside of it. Her breasts swelled, the nipples tightened in expectation of his touch.

Tara shuddered, waiting for his mouth on her lips. But that wait stretched on and on. She lifted her head to find Ramsey staring at the door with narrowed eyes.

"We've got company," he whispered.

In a blink he had her on her feet as he smoothly rose. Tara grabbed her bra and sweater and rushed into the bedroom as a knock sounded on the door.

She closed the bedroom door and hurried to get dressed while wondering if she'd ever get used to Ramsey's enhanced senses.

The male voice she heard on the other side of the bedroom door was not one she recognized. She put her hand on the doorknob, but hesitated.

"It's all right, Tara," Ramsey called. "Come on out."

She pulled the door open to find a man with cropped dark brown hair and deep green eyes smiling at her. He wore a red sweater and jeans, but he held himself as if he were used to being in charge. He was handsome in his own right, but in her mind he couldn't compare to Ramsey.

"Tara Kincaid, this is Fallon MacLeod, my leader."

"Your friend," Fallon corrected with a glance at Ramsey. Fallon then held out his hand to Tara. "It's good to finally meet you. I apologize if we frightened you in Edinburgh. It wasna our intent. We were trying to reach you before Malcolm did."

She blinked, unsure of what to say. Finally, she remembered her manners and replied, "It's good to meet you as well."

Fallon turned to Ramsey then, his smile gone. "First, that seems to have gotten worse," he said, and pointed to the wisps of magic swirling around both of Ramsey's arms.

"I touched her skin."

"I see," Fallon said. "We'll go into that later. What I really came to tell you is that I can no' find them."

"My arse," Ramsey said without much heat. "You can find them."

"You know if a Warrior doesna want to be found he willna be."

Ramsey sighed and shook his head. "Then take Tara with you back to the castle."

"No," Tara said and took a step back. "We've been through this, Ramsey."

"That was before I had to worry about three additional friends out there. I can no' do it all!"

"Then don't," she argued.

He rubbed the back of his neck and gave a snort. "You all make it sound so easy."

"That's because you are no' telling us everything," Fallon said.

Tara watched the way Ramsey's body subtly stiffened.

"Aye," Fallon said with a nod. "I'm no' dim-witted, old friend."

"I never thought you were," Ramsey said.

Tara walked to the coffeepot and poured three mugs' worth. She handed one to Fallon and another to Ramsey. It wasn't until she was back in the kitchen leaning against the counter with her own mug in her hand that she said, "It appears, Ramsey, that your friends are going to help you whether you want it or not. Either tell them the truth, or allow them to help you defeat Declan."

"This is my chance against him," Ramsey said. "I can end Declan. I have the advantage here. He doesna know me or what I can do. If I show him, if he gets a hint then I've lost what small advantage I have and . . . I may never be able to defeat him."

Tara wasn't used to battle strategy. She was the run-and-hide type, so she had never considered planning for Declan's arrival and the subsequent battle.

"I understand now, but I still won't allow you, or anyone, to die for me."

"No one is dying," Fallon said in a stern voice. "We can still hold the advantage, Ramsey. Declan has no idea there are Warriors here. If we outnumber him, we could win."

Ramsey ran a hand down his face and sighed. He'd wanted to keep the truth from Fallon, but he had a suspicion his friend already knew.

"If we do this, when I face Declan, I need you to get everyone out of here. And I mean everyone, Fallon."

Fallon met his gaze squarely. "You willna tell me why?"

"Because the mixture of my magic and my power is so great and terrible that I can no' control it. It takes me, and when it does, people get hurt."

Out of the corner of his eye, Ramsey saw Tara flinch at his words. He'd been a fool to think he could keep what he was a secret, to keep what he could do a secret. But more than that, he'd been a fool to think he would have a chance with someone like Tara.

"All right," Fallon said. "I've already called the others, and they refused to pick up their mobiles. I'll give it another try while I go looking for them. Then I'm bringing the other Warriors here. We're going to end Declan."

Ramsey turned his head to Tara so he could see her expression when Fallon teleported out of the cottage.

"Oh, my God," she mumbled, her hand over her mouth. Her gaze swung to Ramsey. "Can all Warriors do that?"

"Nay. Each god has its own power."

"I knew each of you had a special power, I just didn't realize that was Fallon's. Why do you all turn different colors?"

He shrugged. "Partly because each god favors a color. The MacLeod brothers share a god because each are equal warriors to the other. Fallon teleports, Lucan controls shadows and darkness, and Quinn can communicate with animals."

"What can you do?"

He rubbed his thumb over his fingers. "I can manipulate mass."

"How exactly?"

Ramsey walked to the brass statue of an elk on the end table and touched it. With just a thought he turned it into first a picture frame, then a candle, and then back to the statue.

"Oh, hell. That's amazing," Tara said, eyes wide with disbelief.

He shrugged. "I doona use my power like the others."

"Because of your mix with magic?"

"Aye. It costs me too much to try and control what little I do."

Tara walked to the couch and tucked her legs under her as she sat. "Tell me about your god."

Ramsey set his mug on the end table and lowered himself into the chair. "His name is Ethexia, and he's the god of thieves."

"Thieves? Wouldn't that make you good at stealing things?"

"Why do you think I can manipulate mass?"

She laughed, the sound shooting straight into his gut and making him grin in return. She seemed so at ease sitting with him talking of magic and gods, yet Ramsey knew at any moment this reprieve could be shattered with the arrival of Declan.

"What color does your god favor?"

Ramsey glanced down at his hands and said, "Bronze."

"Can I see?"

"Why? You admitted you've only seen the Warriors once before. I doona want to scare you."

"You won't."

"Believe me, Tara, it will frighten you. We're meant to frighten. And if we unleash our gods in battle, it's because we mean to protect what is ours and kill what's coming for us."

She shrugged. "Like any Highlander."

"I suppose so." He'd never thought of it like that. When had he stopped thinking of himself as a Highlander and started thinking of himself as a Warrior only?

Probably about the time he stopped thinking and practicing his magic.

"What are you thinking?" she asked.

Ramsey scratched his chin. "About my magic. For so long I refused to acknowledge it was there. Now, when I need it, I'm no' going to be able to control it."

"Was your magic powerful before?"

"Aye."

She smiled and said, "Then you shouldn't have a problem now. As my grandmother used to tell me, once we learn magic it never leaves us. It's always there, waiting for us to call to it."

"Your grandmother was very wise."

"Yes, she was. I think you would have liked her, even though she was *drough*."

Ramsey shifted in his chair and took a drink of the coffee. "Tara, I didna kill your mother when I went to see her. I may no' like *droughs,* but I doona kill them."

"They're evil. They bring evil into the world. They do evil's bidding."

"Aye, and they answer for it all when they die."

"And if I was *drough*, would you still be trying to save me?"

Ramsey looked into her blue-green eyes and answered honestly. "Without a doubt."

Her smile, warm and sincere, filled the room. He was about to ask her about her childhood when his advanced hearing caught the sound of something above the din of the snowstorm.

Ramsey was on his feet instantly. Almost immediately Ramsey's mobile rang.

"He's here!" Charon shouted over the snow.

Ramsey hung up and looked at Tara. Her face had lost all its color and the coffee mug fell from her hands. He had little choice but to protect her until Fallon could get her out.

He went to her and grabbed her arms. "Stay with me. Do you understand? You have to stay with me until it's time for you to leave. I'll keep you safe."

When she didn't answer he gave her a little shake.

"Yes, yes!" she shouted.

"Get your coat," Ramsey ordered.

He wished like hell Fallon was here so he could take Tara away. Ramsey put his hand on the door and looked at the magic tendrils swirling around him.

The sound of Declan's helicopter grew louder as it neared

the castle. Ramsey doused all the lights in the cottage and watched as the chopper set down behind the castle.

The helicopter door opened and four mercenaries clad in all black with black masks covering their faces rushed out, their rifles up and ready to use. A moment later Declan climbed out of the chopper and waved it away.

"The chopper willna be far. Declan will want it close enough to take you away," Ramsey told Tara as she came up behind him.

"I won't go with him."

"Nay, you willna."

The mercs split up. Two went with Declan toward the castle while two fanned out. Ramsey smiled as he saw Charon's copper skin rise out of the snow and snap the head of one of the guards.

"Was that Charon?" Tara asked breathlessly.

Ramsey nodded, a smile on his face as he realized they did outnumber Declan. Ending the bastard was going to be easier than Ramsey thought.

But Ramsey's smile died when Charon whirled around to face ten more mercenaries.

A roar rent through Ramsey when the first X90 bullet ripped through Charon.

CHAPTER
NINETEEN

Tara stumbled backward at the fierce roar that made her ears ring. She stared wide-eyed with her mouth hanging open as Ramsey transformed before her eyes.

His skin darkened to a deep bronze. Claws, long and wickedly sharp, formed from his fingertips. When he pulled his lips back and growled, Tara saw Ramsey's fangs.

But it was his eyes that held her spellbound. Gone were his beautiful silver eyes. In their place the same bronze color as his skin filled his eyes from corner to corner.

It was disturbing and beautiful at the same time. His fury came off him in waves, and she barely had time to take it all in before he jumped through the window.

Tara scrambled to her feet, tripping over her coat and her scarf. She reached the windowsill and put her hands on it to lean out and see where Ramsey had gone.

"Damn," she muttered when something poked her palms.

She looked down to see shards of glass sticking out of both hands. Tara took a moment and pulled out the biggest pieces as she tried to decide what to do.

Ramsey had told her to stay with him, but there was no way she could keep up with him. He had practically flown across the snow toward Charon.

And he wasn't alone.

Warriors were suddenly everywhere. There were three

black-skinned Warriors who fought side by side working their way through the mercenaries. A red Warrior who hurled fire, a brown Warrior who made the earth open up, and a silver Warrior who was using the water from the sea as his weapon.

And they weren't the only ones. There was a green Warrior, a pale blue Warrior, and one with skin the color of indigo. Where Arran was Tara had no idea.

Yet for every mercenary they took down, ten times as many bullets filled the air. Tara didn't understand what these bullets were or why they affected the immortal Warriors the way they did.

She wanted to help somehow, but how could she? The melee was mind-boggling. The Warriors moved with speed and ferocity that left her reeling.

Tara's gaze found Ramsey as he used his claws to slash any merc who got close to him. He would also take the time to touch the rifles the mercs used and turn them into something else.

But the damage had already been done.

Several of the Warriors were injured, blood oozing from bullet wounds. Tara waited for Charon to rise, but the Warrior hadn't moved since being struck multiple times by the bullets.

Suddenly Fallon was there, and with a touch of his hand both he and Charon disappeared. A heartbeat later he returned and took other wounded Warriors with him.

There was a loud, gurgling scream that came from within the castle. Tara's head jerked in its direction as she squinted through the snow. A smile pulled at her lips as she realized Arran had remained inside, waiting for the mercenaries.

Tara took a deep breath and began to relax. Ramsey had been right. They would win against Declan. She should never have worried, and she would never again doubt the abilities of the Warriors.

"Well, well, well," said a deep voice near her. A voice she'd hoped never to hear again.

Tara turned around to see Declan leaning against the

outside of the cottage, oblivious to the thick snow that continued to fall.

"Hello, Tara. You've given me a merry chase these last ten years, lass. I think you owe me an apology."

"Kiss my ass, Declan." She said it with more force than she felt. In fact, she was terrified. So terrified she couldn't even call up a meager amount of magic to help her.

Declan tsked and shook his finger at her. "Now that's no way to treat a friend, love."

"You were never my friend. You were using me."

He shrugged. "So you're a means to an end. You could still benefit from being associated with me. Most would love to be in your position."

"I'm not most, you arrogant ass. I want no part of your plan."

"That's too bad, because you really have no choice. I came here for you, and I've no intention of leaving without you."

Men she hadn't heard enter the cottage grabbed each of her arms and dragged her out the door. She fought against them, kicking and screaming in her fury.

When the mercs brought her close enough to Declan, she kicked out with her foot and connected with his balls. It was a glancing blow though, not the one she'd hoped would have him writhing on the ground.

Declan grabbed himself and bent over, a low moan of pain falling from his lips. Tara watched with glee at what she had caused.

"You bitch!" Declan bellowed as he looked up at her, his face red and mottled.

"I'll fight you every step of the way."

Still hunched over, Declan took a step toward her and backhanded her with enough force that Tara blacked out for a moment. Agony radiated from the right side of her face, and she tasted blood where her cheek had split open on her teeth.

Declan's hand gripped her jaw painfully as he squeezed. "Go ahead and fight, Tara. My magic has grown significantly since we were together last. I can do things to you now that will make you go insane."

She lost what little bravado she had at his words. Her first thought was of Ramsey. She wished he were there the same instant she was glad he wasn't. If he was, there was no telling what Declan would do to him. And Tara couldn't imagine that.

"Stop your men," she said.

Declan's blond brow rose. "Excuse me?"

"Stop your men attacking the Warriors, and I'll come with you."

His laughter wasn't what she expected.

"Why would I call my men off?" Declan asked. "They are taking down the Warriors as no one else ever could."

Tara's blood froze in her veins. "What do you mean?"

"Did they no' tell you, love?" he asked mockingly. "Those bullets are filled with *drough* blood. One drop of *drough* blood kills Warriors."

Tara heard a roar she knew was Ramsey's. Her gaze swung to him, and all thought fled as she saw the blood running down his chest from one of the bullets.

Now she understood what had made him so angry when Charon fell. Now she understood why Fallon had hastened to get the wounded out.

She understood all too well that Declan had the upper hand. And she was well and truly screwed.

"I see you get my point," Declan said as he rubbed his hands together eagerly.

Tara hadn't paid any attention to the two men holding her. They wore masks to protect their faces from the cold, so it wasn't as if she'd be able to identify them.

Then something sharp bit through her coat and sweater to pierce her skin. She lowered her head to give Declan the impression she was defeated and saw a white claw before it quickly disappeared.

Hope sprang up in her chest. She wasn't alone. Somehow Arran was there, and Declan didn't even realize he had a Warrior so close to him.

Tara lifted her head and glared at Declan. "I'll die before I turn *drough*."

"You say that now," Declan said as he clasped his hands behind his back and took another step closer to her. "Soon you'll be begging me for mercy, begging me to do anything to stop the pain. Shall I give you a taste?"

She didn't have time to prepare herself as she doubled over in agony so fierce, so terrible, she couldn't breathe. The pain came from everywhere as it racked her entire body, leaving her sagging in the arms of her captors, a silent scream locked in her throat.

"You are no' what I call beautiful," Declan whispered in her ear as Arran and the other merc continued to hold her up. "But you are passable, and my men would like a turn at you. I'll give you to them, Tara. I'll let them have you again and again until you withdraw so far into yourself that you willna be able to stand against me. Your magic will be mine to command."

"Does your conceit know no bounds?" said a deep, growling voice filled with rage.

Tara managed to glance up and see Ramsey in all his Warrior glory behind Declan despite the agony running rampant through her. Ramsey's shirt was gone and blood coated his chest, but he still stood despite the bullet wounds that marked his chest and arms.

"Thank you for holding him, Arran," Ramsey said.

Declan looked at the men on either side of Tara. Arran released his hold on her and ripped off his mask and smiled, showing Declan his fangs.

The pain hadn't lessened within Tara, and without Arran to hold her, she toppled to the ground. She caught a glimpse of the merc grabbing for his rifle and kicked out with her foot. Since he was already off balance with her fall, it didn't take much to bring him down with her.

"I doona think so," Ramsey said as he touched the merc's rifle and turned it into a toy gun.

"You willna stop me from having what is mine!" Declan bellowed and threw up his hands.

Arran went flying backward, landing with a bone-crushing sound against the cottage. But Ramsey didn't budge.

"You will fail, Declan," Ramsey said.

Tara wanted to watch them, she wanted to see Ramsey tear Declan apart, but the pain was too much. She wrapped her arms around her middle and curled into herself.

"Tara," a female whispered in her ear.

Tara briefly opened her eyes, but didn't see anyone besides Ramsey and Declan.

"I'm Larena," the disembodied voice said. "I'm Fallon's wife, and a Warrior. My power is invisibility. I need you to hang on a moment longer. Fallon will be here in just a second."

"No," Tara whispered. Despite the pain, she didn't want to leave Ramsey.

A hand was placed on Tara's shoulder. "Ramsey will be fine. He cannot do what needs to be done until you are gone."

Less than a second later she was lifted off the ground by Fallon who said, "Declan is all yours, Ramsey."

In the next instant all the pain left her body. All Tara could do was let out a long breath, her body exhausted from the ordeal. When she opened her eyes again, she found herself in the middle of a great hall surrounded by men.

"Are you all right now?" Fallon asked her.

Tara swallowed and gave a slight shake of her head. That's when she noticed a beautiful woman with short red curls leaning over Charon, her hands above him and her eyes closed.

"He willna answer the damned phone," said a giant of a man with blond hair as he stalked from one end of the hall to the other.

A petite woman in jeans and a gray sweater with long black hair joined her hands with the redhead's and said, "Hayden, please keep trying."

"I've found him," said another man who stood away from the rest with indigo skin and leather wings folded behind his back.

Fallon put Tara down on a bench near the long wooden table. "How far away is he, Broc?"

"Too far for me to take the time to fly," Broc said.

"Where?" Fallon repeated.

Broc fisted his hands. "A pub in Edinburgh. Somewhere you have no' been, Fallon."

Tara watched Fallon's expression harden. So he could teleport, but obviously he couldn't go somewhere he'd never been before.

Another man with dark blond hair and cobalt eyes lifted his head. Beside him was a woman with mass of curly auburn hair who frantically tried to see to the wound in his leg.

"I can help," the man said.

Fallon slammed his hand against the wall. "Galen, you're wounded."

Galen waved Broc and Fallon over. "Come. I doona have much left in me."

Tears filled Tara's eyes as she realized all the Warriors there were slowly dying, and Charon, who hadn't moved on the table, might already have died.

Everyone there was injured because of her. Because she'd been too stubborn to leave when Ramsey had asked.

"Broc?" Galen said between clenched teeth as he placed his hand on Broc's head.

"I've got the pub in my head," Broc answered.

A second later Fallon put a hand on both men's shoulders and they were gone. Almost immediately Fallon returned with Galen, who slumped to the ground.

"Go!" bellowed another Warrior to Fallon.

Fallon's gaze met Tara's before he disappeared.

As worried as she was for all the ones injured in the hall, her mind was on one Warrior in particular—Ramsey.

CHAPTER
TWENTY

Ramsey would have preferred that Fallon had gotten Arran out with the rest, but Ramsey would ensure that his friend wouldn't get hurt when he unleashed everything on Declan.

He waited, amused, as Declan looked around to find all his men down and Tara gone.

"What have you done?" Declan screamed as spittle flew from his lips.

The snow and wind had stopped, making everything eerily quiet. Ramsey lifted one shoulder in a shrug. He couldn't lift both because of the bullet in one.

It hurt like hell, but the *drough* blood wasn't having the same effect on him as it did with the other Warriors. He suspected it was because he was a Druid, but none of that mattered now.

"I've ensured that you'll never have Tara," Ramsey answered.

Declan took a deep breath and slowly released it, using that time to get his anger under control. "You've no idea what you've done, Warrior."

"You call me that as if it's derogatory."

"It is," Declan said with a sneer.

Ramsey walked slowly around him. "You've your *drough* ancestors to thank for that."

"I'm going to end all of you Warriors. The gods may still

live on in the bloodline, but there will be no scroll or spell known to unbind them. And there will be no Warriors to attempt to stand in my way."

"You underestimate us if you think we're so easy to get rid of."

Declan threw back his head and laughed. "My X90 bullets seem to do the trick." His gaze narrowed on Ramsey then. "Except with you. What makes you so special?"

A slow, deadly smile tilted Ramsey's lips. "You're about to find out."

Ramsey's magic had bubbled beneath the surface since he'd released his god after seeing Charon fall. He'd barely kept it at bay during the battle, and it was only thoughts of Tara that had allowed him to do so.

But now he was free to do as he wanted.

He took a deep breath and let his magic fill him and mix with the power of his god. With a flick of his wrist Ramsey sent Declan flying over the cottage and far away from the castle.

Ramsey used his speed and caught up with Declan before he could raise himself off the ground. Ramsey thought of all Declan had done to Saffron and all Declan had wanted to do to Tara. He embraced the fury rising within him. Embraced it, and welcomed it.

He kicked Declan in the ribs, tossing him in the air once more. Declan landed with a grunt and lifted his hand palm out.

Ramsey anticipated his move and stepped to the side as a blast of magic went past him.

"Who are you?" Declan demanded angrily.

"The one you should have stayed away from. The one you should be terrified of. The one who will end you."

Declan lunged to his feet unsteadily as he held an arm against his broken ribs. "You are nothing more than a Warrior who's had the aid of magic from some Druid to keep you standing."

"You think you know so much about Druids, but in fact, you know very little."

"I know as much as I need to know. I know that as a *drough,* there is no Druid more powerful than me."

Ramsey took a step toward the weasel and lifted his lips to show his fangs again. "There used to be."

"You're wrong," Declan snapped before he turned his head and spat.

Ramsey threw his arms wide as his magic began to swirl around him. He was tired of Declan's inane babble, tired of seeing such an evil face. Declan's time was at an end. He just didn't know it yet.

The sheer power that swam through Ramsey was amazing. He'd never felt so dominant, never felt so powerful. At that moment, he knew he could do anything, conquer anyone.

"It's time you die," Ramsey told Declan.

Declan's eyes widened as understanding dawned. "Wait," he pleaded.

But Ramsey wasn't interested in anything Declan had to say. He gathered his potent mix of power and magic, letting it grow and grow so that in one blast Declan would be ended.

He was about to release a shot of magic when something slammed into his back three times in quick succession. The added *drough* blood from the X90s sent Ramsey onto one knee.

There were so many of the bullets inside him that he'd lost count, but these last three were apparently too much for even him to take without feeling the effects. He clenched his teeth as his blood began to burn in his veins.

"It hurts, does it no'?" Declan said with a smile.

Ramsey's lungs seized, and he put one hand on the ground to keep his balance as the sound of a chopper neared. He had this one chance to end Declan. He had to do it now before he lost consciousness.

He focused on Declan as he ignored the pain in his body. His magic was ready and waiting for him.

"Doona even try it," said a man as he put the end of the rifle against Ramsey's heart.

Ramsey looked up at the man and smiled. There was no

need for him to touch the rifle since it was already pushing against him. With just a thought, his power transformed the rifle into a rubber chicken.

As the man looked at what used to be his weapon, Ramsey sent a blast of magic into him, hurtling him backward. With the helicopter landing not far from him, he had little time to get to Declan.

Ramsey pushed to his feet and took a few awkward steps toward Declan. His body wasn't working properly, and Ramsey knew his time was running out.

"Robbie!" Declan shouted.

Out of the corner of Ramsey's eye he saw the man he had sent flying rushing to the chopper. Ramsey held up his hands and sent magic toward Declan at the same instant Declan fired a pistol.

The bullet slammed into Ramsey's chest, missing his heart by millimeters. He toppled backward into the snow. The last thing he heard before he lost consciousness was Declan's scream of pain.

Phelan saw Fallon and Broc come storming into the small pub. He didn't bother to move from his position at the bar. Phelan wasn't surprised they had found him. After all, Broc's power was to find anyone, anywhere. The reason they were looking was what mattered. He'd left the castle because he wanted no part in their quest.

Phelan waited for them to speak as they walked up, but then Fallon put a hand on his shoulder and in the next instant he once more stood inside MacLeod Castle.

"Fuck me!" he said as his glass full of beer crashed to the floor. "What the hell is this about?"

"You wouldn't answer your mobile," Hayden ground out.

Phelan pulled the phone out of his pocket and shrugged. "I never heard it ring."

"You were needed," Fallon said. "Please."

Phelan looked around at the Warriors to find most of them wounded. "Shit," he murmured.

"Here first," Isla called.

Though Phelan was curious as to what had happened, he wasted no time in rushing to the table. As he neared and recognized Charon though, he paused for a heartbeat as he looked at the numerous holes in his friend's chest.

"Phelan," Isla urged.

He cut open his wrist. There were too many wounds and by the way Charon's chest barely moved, Phelan had just one way to heal him. "Open his mouth," he told Isla.

The Druid complied, and he let several drops of his blood fill Charon's mouth.

Without a word he moved from Warrior to Warrior until all the wounded had his blood inside them. Phelan ran his finger over the now-sealed cut on his wrist and did a quick count.

"You're missing two."

"And we need to go get them. Now," said a woman with golden-brown hair and clear blue-green eyes.

Phelan shrugged and released his god as he faced Fallon. "Let's go then."

Just as Fallon put a hand on him, Phelan saw the woman rush to Fallon and grab his hand.

"Dammit, Tara," Fallon shouted after he had teleported them into the middle of nowhere.

Tara looked from Fallon to Phelan. "I won't apologize. I've a bad feeling. I need to find Ramsey."

Phelan liked her spunk, but women who were stubborn like Tara tended to get into trouble. And trouble wasn't what Phelan was looking for.

"Where are they?" Tara asked softly.

Phelan didn't like the quiet that surrounded them. They were at the sea, the wind should be blowing. But there was nothing. Only a stillness that unsettled him.

"Fallon?"

"We had Declan cornered," Fallon answered Phelan. "Ramsey wanted to take him out himself."

Phelan shook his head as he started for the castle. "By the looks of those I just healed, things didna go as planned."

"We were supposed to be a step ahead of him," Tara said.

"Fallon!" shouted a woman.

All three jerked to a stop.

"I've heard that voice before," Tara said. "She said her name was Larena."

Phelan frowned as he looked at Fallon. "You left your wife here?"

"No' on purpose. She stayed invisible, and I'm guessing to see what happened with Ramsey and Declan."

Something moved in the growing darkness near the castle, and Fallon took off toward it.

Phelan stayed behind with Tara as they made their way at a much slower pace. They had gotten only halfway there when Fallon teleported to them.

Except he wasn't alone. He had Larena and Arran.

Tara rushed to Arran. "What happened? Where's Ramsey?"

Arran couldn't look her in the eye. "I'm sorry, Tara. I doona know. Declan knocked me against the cottage wall."

Phelan watched curiously as Tara started calling Ramsey's name while she did her best to move through the thick snow.

"Larena, where is Ramsey?" Fallon asked.

The golden-haired Warrior looked at her husband and shook her head. "I saw him toss Declan away from the castle, and I went to Arran to make sure he was all right. The next thing I knew I heard the helicopter, and then it too was gone."

"Did they take Ramsey?" Phelan asked.

Larena shrugged. "It's my guess."

Fallon looked around. "Where were they fighting?"

"There." Larena pointed in the direction Tara had already headed.

Tara's shout had them all running to her as she fell to her knees.

Phelan was the first to reach her, and he wasn't prepared to see Ramsey on the ground, the snow turned red with his blood.

"Someone do something," Tara pleaded as she moved her hands over him, trying desperately to see if he was alive while at the same time trying to stop the bleeding.

"Nay," Fallon said as he knelt on the other side of Ramsey. "Nay, this can no' happen. I willna let another friend die."

"Ramsey, damn you," Arran muttered, his voice heavy with emotion.

Phelan noticed that Ramsey's chest didn't move, but instead of saying anything, he squatted by Ramsey's head and held his wrist over his mouth.

"Hold his mouth open," Phelan said softly to Tara.

She looked up at him, her eyelashes frozen from her tears. With a nod she did as he requested.

Phelan lengthened a claw and once more cut his wrist. He gave Ramsey three times as much of his blood as he had the others, but even then he didn't hold out much hope.

And then the oddest thing happened. Phelan saw what looked like white smoke rise from Tara's hand and loop around Ramsey's head.

Except it wasn't smoke. It was magic, and many more joined the first smoky ribbon until Ramsey's entire body was covered with them.

"What the hell?" Phelan murmured.

CHAPTER
TWENTY-ONE

Tara held her breath, waiting expectantly for Ramsey to open his eyes and tell her everything was going to be all right.

Yet, as the minutes ticked by, nothing happened.

She didn't understand. Back at MacLeod Castle in the few moments she was there she had seen Phelan heal everyone, including Charon, with just a few drops of his blood. Phelan had given Ramsey much more than that, but Ramsey hadn't moved.

"Maybe it's because of his mix of Druid and Warrior," Arran said into the silence.

Phelan gave a shake of his head. "It shouldna matter what he is. My blood heals everything."

"Does it bring them back from the dead?" Fallon asked.

"No."

That one word seemed to extinguish whatever hope Tara had held in her heart. She laid her hand over Ramsey's heart where the bullet had nearly struck.

The ribbons of magic still wound around him, growing thicker the longer she touched him. From what she knew of magic, she was sure that it would help him, not harm him, or she wouldn't still be touching him.

"He was so sure of winning against Declan. He even convinced me," Tara said to no one in particular.

"I felt some of his mix of power and magic," Arran said. "He should have been able to best Declan."

Fallon ran a hand through his hair. "Then what happened? How did Declan know to bring so many men?"

Tara lifted a handful of snow. "Because of this."

"Ah," Larena said with a sigh.

Phelan flattened his lips. "Someone care to fill me in?"

"I caused the snow," Arran said. "It was Ramsey's idea to help keep Declan away and give us more time with Tara to convince her she could trust us."

Tara glanced at Arran. "Except Declan used his magic to slow the snow. Ramsey's mistake was having Arran create another, stronger storm."

"And Declan realized a Warrior was here," Phelan finished with a nod.

Larena put her hand on Fallon's shoulder. "We cannot stay here. We need to bring Ramsey home."

Everyone stood but Tara. She wasn't yet ready to give up on Ramsey, but neither could she keep him in the snow. Tara took Ramsey's hand in hers as Phelan put a hand on one of her shoulders and Arran took the other.

The cold instantly melted away to the warmth that was MacLeod Castle. As soon as they appeared, everyone surrounded them, the silence deafening as they stared at Ramsey.

"Nay," the blond giant, Hayden, said in a disbelieving whisper.

Phelan spoke to the group, but he caught Tara's gaze as he said, "Ramsey isna dead yet. He lives, but hangs on by a thread."

"What the hell is that winding around him?" someone asked.

Arran squeezed Tara's shoulder as he said, "It's Tara. Whenever she and Ramsey touch, those ribbons of magic appear around him."

"And only him," Charon added.

Charon helped Tara to her feet as several Warriors lifted Ramsey and walked with him up the stairs. Tara watched them, silently praying that Ramsey would wake.

She looked down at her hands and coat covered in Ramsey's blood. Every instinct cried out for her to go to him, but it was Fallon's gaze that kept her in the hall.

When the group disappeared Phelan sank onto a bench and propped his elbow atop the table. "I did all I could."

"We know," Arran said. "I saw how many of those *drough* bullets he had in him. He shouldna have remained standing."

Tara looked at the floor, unsure of what to do or say. Then, there was a soft hand on her arm. She looked up to find herself surrounded by women.

"You are welcome here. Please make yourself at home," Larena said.

A woman with chestnut hair that came to her shoulders and framed her face with curls told Larena, "Go change." When Larena walked away, the woman turned her mahogany gaze to Tara. "I'm Cara, Lucan's wife. I'm sure you haven't met everyone yet, and we're a large brood so it'll probably take time to learn everyone's name."

"Come," said another woman as she pulled Tara to the roaring fire in the huge hearth. "I'm Marcail, Quinn's wife."

Tara had never seen such lovely turquoise eyes before, and on the crown of Marcail's head was an array of small braids banded with gold.

"I'm Isla," said the petite black-haired woman she'd noticed earlier. "The giant is my husband, Hayden."

Tara's head began to swim with all the faces so far. Reaghan, who was Galen's wife, took her jacket, and the redhead she'd seen trying to heal Charon was Sonya, who was married to Broc—the one with wings.

Then there was Gwynn, an American from Texas by her drawl, who was married to Logan, Dani who had the most stunning silver-blond hair and was married to Ian, and Saffron, the Seer, who was married to Camdyn.

Tara put her hand to her head that was now pounding. She'd met all the Druids, but remembering each of them was going to take some time.

"And that's not all of us," Dani said.

Cara laughed. "That's right. Fiona is gone with Bráden and Aiden into town."

"Aiden is mine and Quinn's son," Marcail said proudly.

Reaghan nodded. "And Fiona is Braden's mother. They traveled with me from Loch Awe when I first came here."

"Which was when?" Tara asked.

They acted as if all of them had been together for decades and not years.

Gwynn was the one who laid a comforting hand on Tara's knees. "There is much you need to be caught up on. Suffice it to say most have been living in this castle for over four centuries."

"What?" Tara asked with a choked laugh. "But only the Warriors are immortal, not Druids."

Isla with her ice-blue eyes smiled knowingly. "You're correct, of course. That is, unless you have a Druid who is powerful enough to not only hide the castle from view, but also make it so that mortals who stay within my shield aren't touched by the passing of time."

"So you're the one Ramsey spoke about. The one Deirdre forced to become *drough*."

"That's me," Isla said with only a hint of sadness. "I survived five hundred years with Deirdre as my captor. It was being brought to MacLeod Castle that helped me become strong enough to break from her."

"I hope it was more than that," said a deep voice at the top of the stairs.

Tara turned to see Hayden descend the steps and walk to Isla. He placed a kiss atop her head and nodded to Tara.

"We didna get an introduction earlier, though we've heard a lot about you, Tara Kincaid. In case my beautiful wife didna tell you, I'm Hayden Campbell."

Isla elbowed him in the ribs. "Where was Ramsey put?"

"In the south tower."

Sonya rose. "I better see if any of my healing magic can help."

Tara wanted to go with her. It was nice to meet everyone,

but she felt useless in the hall. Not that she would be of any help in the tower. But at least she'd be with Ramsey.

Charon was suddenly beside her. "Come. I'll take you to him."

Tara smiled gratefully and jumped up to follow him. She reached the second-floor landing before she realized she'd not said anything to the others. Charon's strides were long, and Tara had to practically jog to keep up with him.

They climbed numerous other stairs before they reached the tower and ascended the curving steps to the top.

"I doona know what else to do," she heard someone say.

"He should have woken by now," said another.

Tara heard something behind her and looked over her shoulder to see Phelan there. He gave her a small shrug at her questioning look.

By the time they reached the top of the tower, a chill had settled deep within Tara. No one said a word as they watched her walk to the bed. They parted so she could see Ramsey.

The wisps of magic were still around him, but they were beginning to fade. She wanted to touch him again, but she hesitated. What if she were making things worse?

"I never asked what it was that Declan did to you at Dunnoth," Fallon said.

Tara glanced at him and shrugged. "I don't really know. With just a wave of his hand my entire body hurt. I couldn't take a breath. The pain came from everywhere, so I don't know where it derived from."

"He's a soulless monster, so it doesn't really matter," Saffron said as she went to stand next to Sonya on the other side of the bed. "I spent over three years with Declan locked in his prison and tortured. He doesn't have to have a reason for anything. He just does it."

Tara shuddered. "He said his magic had grown."

"As much as I want to get that bastard, right now I'm more concerned with Ramsey," said a man with light brown hair and hazel eyes. He looked at Tara and gave an apologetic half grin. "Forgive me. I'm Logan Hamilton."

One by one the Warriors came forward and introduced themselves. Tara was able to put a couple of them together with their wives. She easily recognized the MacLeod brothers not only by their similar dark hair and green eyes, but also by the torcs around their necks.

"What now?" Ian asked.

Lucan MacLeod shrugged. "We see what Sonya can do, and we wait."

"My blood has never failed to heal," Phelan said, his gaze locked on Ramsey.

"It's no' failed yet," Camdyn said. "Give it time."

"Let's give Sonya room to use her healing magic," Quinn MacLeod said.

Tara began to turn to leave with the others when Saffron caught her hand.

"Stay," Saffron urged.

Sonya smiled and nodded. "Yes, please. We could use your magic to help."

"No," Tara said hastily, then cleared her throat when they looked at her strangely. "That didn't come out right. What I meant to say is that my magic isn't . . . well, I can't control it. Sometimes none comes at all, and at other times it's so powerful I can't contain it."

"Interesting," Saffron said. "I never saw any of that in my visions of you."

Sonya held her hands palm down over Ramsey and closed her eyes. "With Phelan's blood in him, it shouldn't take much of my magic to heal Ramsey."

A few minutes later Tara felt an odd pulse in the room, and realized it was Sonya's magic. She'd never felt any magic before. Odd that she would feel it with *mies* and not the more powerful *droughs* of her family.

Sonya stayed as she was for over fifteen minutes before she released a breath and lowered her hands. "He's not re-sisting my healing, but he's not accepting it either."

Tara couldn't stand it anymore. She placed her hand over Ramsey's and felt a jolt run through her.

"What was that?" Saffron asked breathlessly.

Tara could only stare in shock as Ramsey's chest rose sharply and slowly lowered as he began to breathe normally. The ribbons of magic that were all but gone a few moments before strengthened.

"How very odd," Sonya said.

Saffron shrugged slightly. "That I didn't see coming."

"What just happened?" Tara asked.

Sonya lifted her hands in front of her in a gesture of confusion. "I have no idea. All I do know is that Ramsey is breathing regularly now, and that's good enough for me."

"Maybe Phelan's blood finally kicked in," Saffron said.

Tara watched one of the tendrils of magic wind around her wrist before swirling around Ramsey's. Something had occurred between her and Ramsey when she'd touched him. She didn't know what or how, but it had.

CHAPTER
TWENTY-TWO

Declan reached for the glass of whisky on the coffee table and raised it to his lips with a shaky hand. He looked at his left hand, unable to believe the black marks that ran across his skin like lightning.

He'd never seen anything like it before, but there was no mistaking it was magic. Somehow, some way, the Warrior had used magic on him.

Declan downed the whisky in one swallow and set the glass aside with a thud. He shook his head at the absurdity of his thoughts. Warriors couldn't do magic. There had to have been a Druid nearby that was helping the Warrior.

It certainly hadn't been Tara. She'd not even put up half a fight against him. That thought helped to ease the pain in his arm, but not by much.

"How is it?" Robbie asked as he strode into Declan's office, another bottle of whisky in his hand.

"It bloody well hurts, you imbecile."

Robbie lowered the whisky near Declan's glass and looked anywhere but at Declan's injured arm.

Anger spiked in Declan. "Are you afraid to look at it?"

"No," Robbie replied quickly. Too quickly.

"Do you think I'm no' capable anymore?"

This time Robbie's eyes shifted to meet his. "Never, cousin."

"Then what is it?"

Robbie shrugged and glanced down at his feet. "You were almost killed. That Warrior, a single Warrior, nearly killed you."

"He had help. There was a Druid nearby. It's the only explanation. You know as well as I that no Warrior could have magic."

"How do we know that?"

Declan unscrewed the whisky bottle and poured a double shot into his glass. "It's the way it is. Besides, whoever that Warrior was, he's dead now. The X90 I put in him went into his heart."

"You missed," Robbie muttered.

With his glass halfway to his mouth Declan narrowed his eyes on his cousin. "What did you say?"

Robbie cleared his throat, but held his stance. "You missed his heart. It was just to the left."

"Regardless, the bastard is dead. No Warrior can survive an X90 bullet." He once more tilted the glass to his lips and drained the contents.

Soon, with the help of the whisky, the pain in his arm would numb so he could think straight again. At the moment he couldn't even move the fingers of his left hand. The blast of magic had hit him in the upper arm, and the agony had been instantaneous.

Though Robbie could only see what Declan's rolled-up sleeve revealed, the truth was that the black spiderlike vines began at his shoulder and spread down his arm to the tips of his fingers and were working their way across his chest.

A wave of anguish slammed into Declan as the vines spread even more. The glass dropped from his fingers, saved by the rug from shattering.

Robbie hastened to him, but Declan lifted his head and glared at his cousin. "Get out. Now."

"Declan—"

"Now! And close the door. I'm no' to be disturbed. No matter what you hear, doona come in here!"

The room began to spin around Declan, and at first he

didn't think Robbie would do as he'd asked. Then, with a grim set of his features, Robbie turned on his heel and stalked to the door. With one final look at Declan Robbie firmly shut the door behind him.

Declan slumped over, his throat dry and his body covered in sweat. The whisky was having no effect whatsoever. And the pain was doubling with each beat of his heart.

He pushed to his feet with his right hand and the arm of the couch, only to have his legs give out. It took three more tries before Declan could remain on his feet.

If it wasn't for the couch which he leaned upon, Declan would never have made it to the fire. His legs gave out and he crumpled before the hearth. With sweat running into his eyes, Declan made himself focus on the flames.

There was no doubt that whatever had been done to him was slowly eating away at him. He was dying. And there was only one entity that could save him.

The chant began to fall from his lips. Softly at first, but with each recitation it grew stronger as desperation set in. If the Devil didn't respond, Declan knew he wouldn't last the night.

Then, finally, the flames of the fire jumped and sparks flew.

"Why do you call me?" demanded the deep, sinister voice.

"I've been injured."

There was a pregnant pause before the voice asked, "How?"

"I found Tara. When I went to get her, there were Warriors."

The voice chuckled dryly. "Your special bullets should have taken care of them."

"They did. To an extent. But there was one that the bullets didna seem to bother."

"How so?"

Declan swallowed and pushed past the pain. He wouldn't receive any help until the Devil had all his information. "He barely flinched when they impacted his body."

Black smoke suddenly filled Declan's office from the

flames. He held still as it surrounded him, fencing him in and touching every inch of him.

"Magic was used," the voice said near Declan's ear.

"Aye."

"Strong magic."

Declan bit the side of his mouth to keep his cry of pain silent as the vines worked farther down his chest to his stomach.

"You are in much pain," the Devil said.

"I've never heard of any kind of magic that could do this."

The Devil laughed again. "Ah, but then I've taught you spells that have never been known before. Yet, this isn't black magic upon you. If it was, you'd already be dead."

Nothing Declan was being told made him feel any better. So, he tried again. "Is there a cure? Point me in the right direction, Master, so that I may heal myself."

"You don't want me to do it for you?"

There was nothing Declan wanted more, but he had learned early on not to ask for something like that. "If that is your wish."

"With Deirdre gone, I've put all my faith in you, Declan. Don't let me down."

"Never."

The smoke began to swirl about him. "I will stop the progress of this magic, but in order for you to heal this yourself, you will have to learn who did this to you."

"Do you know?" Declan hurried to ask.

There was no answer as the smoke returned to the fireplace and disappeared.

Declan fisted his right hand on his leg. He'd hoped for more aid than just stopping the magic. The pain had yet to lessen, and he began to suspect that it wouldn't.

This was his punishment for not besting the Warrior and capturing Tara. He still couldn't believe after all the work, all the time, he'd had Tara in his grasp.

Only to be outwitted by a damned Warrior.

It had never occurred to Declan that a Warrior would

replace one of his men, but with the masks the mercenaries wore, it had been an easy switch.

And a lesson learned the hard way.

Declan half crawled, half dragged himself to the coffee table where he poured more whisky and drank it in one gulp.

"Robbie!" he bellowed.

Instantly his cousin was beside him. "What is it?"

"I need you to help me into the library. We've work to do."

Ramsey opened his eyes gradually. It took a full minute for him to realize where he was and to take stock of his body.

"It's about bloody time," Phelan's deep voice said quietly as he leaned against the foot of the bed.

Ramsey lifted his head and looked around the tower. Light flooded in through the windows. Tara slept awkwardly in the chair while Phelan continued to glare at him.

"What did I do to you?" Ramsey asked.

Phelan rolled his eyes. "You nearly died."

Ramsey slowly sat up and swung his legs over the bed as he held the sheet around his middle. He was naked, which meant they had brought him back to the castle to be healed.

Healed? Near death? He pushed through his jumbled thoughts to determine what was going on.

Then it all came back to him in a rush. His jaw clenched as his gaze swung back to Phelan. "Is Declan dead?"

"Nay."

So Ramsey had failed. "How long have I been unconscious?"

"Two days. Tara hasna left your side, and the entire castle is worried."

Ramsey scrubbed a hand down his face, feeling the thick whiskers, and leaned forward so that his elbows rested on his thighs. He turned to Phelan and asked, "Why are you here?"

"I was brought here to heal Charon and the others that were wounded. Then we went to find you. You didna respond to my blood."

Ramsey had seen what Phelan's blood could do, so it made little sense to him that he hadn't healed like the others. "I'm as baffled as you are about the reasons why."

He looked at Tara and drank in her beauty. Her hair was tangled and her clothes rumpled, proving that she had indeed stayed by his side.

"Is she all right? The last time I saw her Declan had done some spell or something."

Phelan nodded. "She's fine. She's a stubborn one though."

"I know," he said with a small smile.

"The others are going to want to talk to you."

"And I them." Ramsey rose and gently lifted Tara in his arms before he turned and placed her in the bed. After removing her shoes, he covered her with the blankets.

She didn't awaken as she snuggled beneath the covers and sighed contentedly.

Ramsey straightened. "Where are my clothes?"

"They were ruined, but Galen brought more for you," Phelan said, and pointed to another chair sitting off to the side.

Ramsey hurried to put the clothes on, his gaze going again and again to Tara.

"If you doona wake her, she's going to be angry," Phelan said.

Ramsey took a deep breath and looked at his hands that once more held the white ribbons of magic. "She's been running too long. She needs to rest."

"Yeah. Tell her that when she comes looking for you later."

Ramsey knew Phelan was right, but he wanted to talk to the others without Tara first.

"By the way, what does that feel like?" Phelan asked, and jerked his chin to Ramsey's hands.

He lifted his hands before him. "It feels incredible."

"We've all touched her. You're the only one who has that reaction to her."

Ramsey sighed as he dropped his arms. "I know. It must have something to do with my own magic."

"Yet none of the Druids are affected either."

This Ramsey hadn't anticipated.

"Whatever this is, it's between you and her," Phelan said. "I have to admit, I'm more than curious. That magic has been swirling about you since we brought you back to the castle."

Ramsey frowned as he recalled the sound of the drums and chanting of the ancients deep in his mind. He'd thought it a dream because it had been centuries since he'd heard them. But maybe it hadn't been a dream. Maybe they had been there.

What did it mean though? Ramsey hadn't sought out the ancients, and the ancients didna come to a Druid unless they wanted to.

Ramsey frowned and glanced down at his hands. The white ribbons of magic were quickly becoming something he wanted to see.

And needed to feel.

CHAPTER
TWENTY-THREE

Ramsey flinched inwardly when he descended the stairs and the conversation in the great hall ground to a halt. He'd tried to fool himself into thinking he was the same as the other Warriors sitting around the long table, but he knew differently now.

And so did they.

Ramsey didn't look at anyone as he started to make his way to his seat. He shouldn't have been surprised when Fallon, followed by his brothers, Lucan and Quinn, rose from their seats at the head of the table and blocked his way.

"You gave us all quite a scare, most especially Tara," Fallon said.

Ramsey stared at the leader of their group, a man he considered a close friend. "It wasna my intention."

"Nothing has changed, you know," Lucan said. "You are still part of our family. You are still my brother, by fate if no' by blood."

Ramsey swallowed to dislodge the lump of emotion forming in his throat.

Quinn raised a dark brow. "No more secrets, Ramsey. We've all had something to hide over the years, but as Lucan said, we are family. We are here for you."

"All right," Ramsey said after a moment.

It seemed to mollify the MacLeod brothers since they

resumed their seats and let him find his own. Ramsey had no sooner sat than a plate piled high with food was placed in front of him.

"It's good to have you back," Cara said with a small squeeze of his shoulder.

Ramsey stared at the plate, not seeing the food. He released a long breath as his shoulders relaxed. This hall, this castle, was his home. It was the one place he felt he could be himself.

Twice now he'd found his way back to the castle and his family. Would he have another chance?

"What happened, Ramsey?" Hayden asked.

Ramsey lifted his gaze to find Hayden's black eyes trained on him. Ramsey shrugged and said, "Declan got away, though I was sure I had struck him with my magic."

Galen cleared his throat and leaned forward over the table. Ramsey's gaze narrowed as he watched his friend. It wasn't like Galen to be nervous. Galen was the antithesis of nervousness, which didn't bode well.

"It wasna until after you left for Dunnoth Tower that I realized we hadna spoken to you about you also being a Druid. I should have."

Ramsey waved away Galen's words. "We were celebrating, as we should have been. And truth be told, I didna want to talk about it."

"But we should have," Galen insisted.

Ramsey saw Reaghan entwine her fingers with Galen's, and Ramsey instantly thought of Tara. A glance down at his hands showed the tendrils of magic had faded to almost nothing now.

"Get to the point," Ramsey said.

Fallon said, "Galen became curious about the Torrachilty Druids, and he also recalled you saying you didna know what happened to them."

Ramsey clenched his hands into fists, trying desperately to stay calm. "What did you learn?" he asked Galen.

"No' much, unfortunately. What I did learn you probably already know."

"That we were warrior Druids, the ones feared by all. Even the *droughs*."

Galen gave a short nod.

"Which is damned impressive," Camdyn said from Ramsey's right.

Logan smiled. "Verra. It's no wonder you've a god inside you."

"What else did you learn?" Ramsey asked Galen.

Galen glanced at the table. "They knew who had taken you."

It was like a dagger to Ramsey's heart. He'd hoped, prayed, that his family had merely thought he'd run away so they wouldn't go looking for him.

Ramsey struggled to keep his breathing even, desperately tried to hold back the anguish over Galen's words. Ramsey kept perfectly still, his gaze focused on a spot on the table just above his plate.

Gradually, the vise around his chest began to lessen so that he could breathe again.

"There had been talk of Deirdre," he said. "It was just talk. We'd heard the rumors of the MacLeod massacre. I was dispatched to discover if it was true. I saw the truth of the attack, and I knew it would mean war between my people and Deirdre. I was on my way back when I was taken."

Lucan caught his gaze, his nostrils flaring. "You saw . . . our clan?"

"There was nothing left by the time I got here. But I saw the evidence in the castle and on the land."

"When was this?" Quinn asked in a whisper. "How long after Deirdre murdered our clan?"

Ramsey looked at each MacLeod brother. "Three years."

He rubbed his forehead with his hand as his father's face flashed in his mind. Deirdre had never used his family against him as she had the others. He thought he'd been spared that, but now he began to worry that something horrible had happened to them.

"What of my people?" he asked.

Galen's blue eyes were sad as he said, "As a warrior clan

what did you think they did? They went out in small groups to try and end Deirdre."

"They should have been able to do it."

"From the text I read that was their second mission. Their first was to find you."

Pain ripped through Ramsey's chest as he rose to his feet and stalked from the hall. He needed air, and some time alone.

Ramsey threw open the castle door as he strode into the bailey. The rush of cold winter air did nothing to calm his heated skin.

His boots crunched through the snow in the bailey as his mind whirled with thoughts and questions. Why had they looked for him? He might have had the greatest magic of any Torrachilty Druid, but he was just one man. His entire people shouldn't have been sacrificed for him.

He walked beneath the gatehouse and away from the castle. On and on he went until he reached the edge of the cliffs. They dropped steeply to the crashing water below.

With a hand over his chest, he rubbed where the ache continued to grow. One of the reasons he'd never delved into finding his people was that he'd been afraid of what he'd discover.

He'd hoped they had survived. Somehow, some way. Though he'd known Deirdre wouldn't allow all of them to live. The Torrachilty Druids had held incredible magic, magic that had rivaled even Deirdre's black magic.

But Deirdre hadn't known he was a Druid. Of that Ramsey was certain. She would have used whatever means necessary to find his clan and destroy them. And there was no telling what she would have done to turn him into a *drough*.

So how did she find him? How did she know he had a god bound inside him? These were questions he'd never know the answers to, questions that would haunt him for eternity.

And knowing he had failed to kill Declan only made him feel even worse.

Ramsey turned his anger to Declan. There he could focus

all his attention on the bastard who had taken Deirdre's place. It was Ramsey's only choice, because if he continued to think of his family and his people, he would lose the last shred of his control. And that couldn't happen.

There was a crunch of snow as footfalls grew closer. He should have known they wouldn't leave him alone. They were family, so they worried.

"Ramsey," Logan said from behind him.

He slowly turned to find not just Logan but Hayden and Galen as well. The four had often traveled together over the centuries. They had been his first friends. And for a very long time they had been the only ones Ramsey trusted.

"You know we're here for you," Hayden said.

Galen nodded. "Always."

Ramsey drew the crisp, cold air into his lungs and slowly released it. "I know. I appreciate you finding out what you did, Galen. It's just . . ."

"Too much," Logan answered.

Hayden crossed his arms over his chest. "And Deirdre never knew you were a Druid."

"Never," Ramsey answered.

Galen stuck his hands in the front pockets of his jeans, his long hair whipping in the sea breeze. "That part of our lives is over with. It doesna matter what she did or didna know. What we need to discover is if any of the Torrachilty Druids survived."

"Besides me."

Logan kicked at the thick snow. "You must have been verra important to your people, Ramsey."

"They would have gone after anyone that was taken," he said. "We were a large clan, but we were close. Our magic brought us together. It bound us."

"As we are bound together," Hayden said.

Ramsey gave a nod to Hayden before he looked at Galen. "How many went looking for me?"

"Over the decades? Nearly all."

The knife in Ramsey's chest turned at the news.

"The rest," Galen continued, "were wiped out by Deirdre."

Ramsey dropped his head back and closed his eyes. The news kept getting worse and worse. If all the warriors had gone to find him, there had been no one in the forest to protect the women and children.

It would have been a slaughter. Just as the MacLeod clan had been.

"Surely the women and children there had magic to defend themselves," Logan said.

Ramsey shook his head as he looked at his friends. "No. The magic stayed with the men only. It was too potent for a female to control. They would go daft with the sheer power of our magic."

"Doona tell my wife that," Hayden said with a grin.

Ramsey found the corners of his lips tilting a fraction as he thought of Isla. She might be the smallest of the Druids, but her magic was a force to be reckoned with.

"I know this is a lot to take in, but we want to help you," Galen said.

Ramsey raked a hand through his hair and looked at the sea where it met the horizon. "There is no way to help me now, my friends."

"We can learn more," Hayden offered.

Logan grunted. "Nay, we will learn more. Gwynn is amazing with what she can do on a computer. There has to be more than that one book we found with information about the Torrachilty Druids."

But Ramsey wasn't so sure. His people had kept to themselves for a reason. Their magic had been guarded against outsiders because everyone wanted to know what it was that made them so powerful.

Only his people had known that the very first man to step forward to offer himself as a vessel for the gods had been a Torrachilty Druid.

As far back as time went his people had been revered and feared. Their prowess in battle had been legendary. They had given their allegiance to no one, yet every king and clan leader had sought them out for help.

The Torrachilty Druids didn't just fight to fight. They

entered battle only after hearing both sides and determining who they believed was the one in the right.

So many battles had been decided by his people. He'd been proud to be one of them, proud to carry the sword of his ancestors.

They kept records of their people first through their historians and by storytelling. Then, later by recording it all on scrolls.

"You willna find anything," Ramsey finally said. "My people were distrustful of outsiders. We kept our history safely guarded. If they were attacked, it was the first thing they would have burned."

"Just what was in your history that they were trying to protect?" Hayden asked.

Ramsey looked into his black eyes. "The source of who we were."

CHAPTER
TWENTY-FOUR

Tara's eyes flew open as she came awake. She sat up and blinked. A frown tugged at her face as she looked down at the blankets surrounding her.

The fact that she was in the bed Ramsey had occupied for days was the next thought that flitted through her mind.

Tara threw back the covers and found her shoes lying beside the bed. She knew Ramsey must be all right. Otherwise they would have woken her. Wouldn't they?

She rubbed her forehead as her confusion mounted. But if Ramsey was fine, why hadn't he woken her?

"Because he doesn't want to talk to you," Tara mumbled to herself.

That realization made her feel like the biggest fool. She'd only thrown herself at one guy before Ramsey, and it had been disastrous. And yet, here she was doing it again.

She grabbed her boots and rose to walk to the door. Something made her pause as she neared the window tower. Slowly, she approached one of the four windows and glanced outside.

At first all she saw was the wide expanse of the sea. Her gaze drifted to the left and she took in the majestic cliffs. And then she saw the four men.

Ramsey with his black hair was the first she spotted. Next she recognized Hayden, then Galen and Logan. Whatever the four were talking about it was a deep conversation based on the stance of their bodies.

Tara was glad to see Ramsey not only up, but seemingly unaffected by the dozen X90 bullets they had pulled from him. She had sat by his side waiting and hoping for him to open his eyes.

And when he had, he hadn't even bothered to wake her.

Tara stepped away from the window. She didn't glance back at the bed as she squared her shoulders and walked from the tower to the chamber Cara had shown her to the day before.

What few belongings that had fit into the two bags she carried were waiting for her. Tara shut the door and stripped out of her jeans and sweater and into her workout gear. If there was one way to help clear her head, it was with a run.

Tara had just finished tying her running shoes and was pulling her hair back into a haphazard ponytail when there was a knock on the door.

Her stomach jumped into her throat as she thought that it might be Ramsey. She forced a calming breath through her body before she opened the door. To find Gwynn.

"Hi," Gwynn said with a smile.

Tara somehow managed a smile.

Gwynn glanced down at the jogging pants and thick zippered hoodie Tara wore. "Is everything all right?"

"Peachy. I'm just going for a run."

"It's, ah . . . Well, there's snow on the ground. Lots of it."

Tara shrugged. "It'll make my workout even better."

"Fallon isn't going to like this."

"Fallon is the one that told me this castle was protected. I'll stay within the confines of Isla's shield."

Gwynn licked her lips. "It's nearly lunch. Are you hungry?"

"Not right now," Tara said, and moved past Gwynn into the hall. "Thank you though."

"Tara," Gwynn called before she could walk away. "I know you don't know us yet, but we're here to help you."

Tara looked over her shoulder at Gwynn. "And I appreciate

it. I've been alone for ten years, Gwynn. I'm used to being on my own, doing my own thing. I don't like answering to anyone."

"We aren't asking you to," Gwynn hurried to say, her violet eyes beseeching her.

"I like you, Gwynn. I'm glad you and the other Druids found a place here."

"But it's not for you, right?" Gwynn finished.

Tara noted the way Gwynn's expression had become flat, as if she had expected exactly this from her. Tara wanted to agree, but instead she found herself shrugging.

"Actually, I don't know what's for me anymore. I thought I knew what Warriors were and what they would want from me. So much has changed over the last days. I need to find myself again."

Gwynn's smile was kind. "I hope you find it here. Come. I'll walk with you to the great hall."

Tara was grateful for Gwynn's kindness. She hadn't known what she expected from Ramsey, but after his kisses, she had wanted more than waking up alone in the tower.

Gwynn spoke of the castle and inane things as they made their way to the hall. The only ones in the hall were Larena and Fallon who were playing chess, and Arran who was on a laptop.

As soon as they entered Fallon's head snapped up, his eyes locking with Tara's.

She didn't give him a chance to say anything as she declared, "I'm going for a run."

"In the snow?" Fallon asked.

Larena laid her hand atop Fallon's. "Leave her alone, love. She looks very capable."

"I'll not leave Isla's shield," Tara said. "I just need to get out. I normally train every day, and it's been almost a week."

Fallon's brow furrowed. "You train?"

"Aye. How else do you think I eluded capture from Declan for a decade?"

He gave a quick nod. "Stay within sight of the castle."

"Please," Larena added as she squeezed Fallon's hand.

Fallon sighed and grudgingly said, "Please."

Tara held in a smile as she walked out the door. Once on the steps, she tightened her ponytail and stretched her legs as she looked around the snow-covered bailey.

A Range Rover, a Mercedes G-class SUV, and an Audi R8 all sat in the bailey. Tara walked between the Mercedes and the Audi slowly so she could look through the windows.

After ogling the vehicles, she continued to stretch her arms until she was through the gatehouse. She spotted Ramsey and the others quickly and kept close to the stone wall around the castle. The last thing she wanted was for Ramsey to see her. The point of her getting out of the castle was to clear her head of him.

Tara waited until she could no longer see the Warriors before she started running. The snow was thicker than she had expected, but it added an extra element to her workout. It wasn't long before her thighs were burning.

With a smile on her face, she ran along the cliffs, the spot Isla had shown her where the shield ended in her sights. As soon as she got there, Tara turned right and ran along the shield.

With her breath billowing in front of her and sweat running down her back, Tara welcomed the pain that came with such a workout. It wasn't so much that she enjoyed hurting herself, but it helped her to know how far she could push her body when the need arose.

By the time Tara ran around the village Ramsey and the others were gone. She sighed, glad that she had this time to herself.

In some spots the snow was so thick that she had to slow to a jog, but she never stopped. She'd let herself go soft once she had reached Dunnoth Tower, and she was paying the price now.

Though Tara couldn't see Isla's shield, she could feel the buzz of the magic. It made it easy to follow as she continued her run. By her estimate, by the time she reached the gatehouse, she had run almost three miles. Which wasn't long enough.

Tara wiped the sweat dripping into her eyes and started on another lap.

With each pump of her legs, the emotions that had built in her chest concerning Ramsey, the Druids at the castle, and even Declan's finding her began to ease.

With each mile she ran her head cleared a little more. And she was going to need a clear mind in order to keep her wits about her.

Ramsey watched the ease with which Tara ran. It was obviously something she did often. She didn't look up at the castle, but even if she had she wouldn't have seen him. Ramsey kept out of sight.

After her second lap around the area, she jogged into the bailey and walked to cool down. To his surprise, she ventured into the stables.

More curious than ever about her, Ramsey quietly followed her. He found a spot at the top of the stables where he could watch her.

She moved from stall to stall testing boards. Then she walked to the center and began doing push-ups. She was at fifty when Ramsey felt a presence beside him.

He glanced over and saw that it was Quinn.

"Damn," Quinn whispered.

Ramsey nodded, unable to find the words. Despite all the time he'd spent watching Tara and learning about her past, he'd not known about her strenuous workout.

She finished with her push-ups and removed her jacket to reveal a black tank. She discarded the jacket and flipped onto her back and began doing crunches and full-body sit-ups.

Ramsey wasn't sure what else she could do when she rose from the ground and looked around the stable with a smile on her face.

In a flash she ran to the first stall, and with her hand atop the tallest board, threw herself over it. She dropped to the ground, legs bent, and rolled sideways before she was on her feet again leaping over the next stall.

The routine continued from stall to stall, and every time Tara would drop to the ground in a different way.

"Impressive," Ramsey said.

"Verra," Quinn agreed. "It's no wonder she evaded Fallon and the others when they tried to reach her in Edinburgh."

Ramsey watched the way her sleek body moved effortlessly. Her muscles were toned, tight. He'd felt along those limbs and knew firsthand what a wonderful body she had.

But he'd never seen it like this. He'd never witnessed how limber she was, or how flexible. He'd never seen such a smile on her face as she pushed her body harder and harder.

And Ramsey had never yearned for a woman like he did her.

He wanted to drop from his hiding place and join her. He wanted to pull her into his arms and kiss her, touch her. And God help him, he wanted to strip off her clothes and see every inch of her body for himself.

"Does she know?"

Ramsey jerked his gaze to Quinn. "What?"

"How badly you desire her."

Ramsey looked away from the keen green eyes of his friend. "Nay. It's best if she doesna know."

"Why?"

"Why?" Ramsey repeated. "Are you daft, Quinn? You heard everything in the great hall. I'm no' a man fit to even think of having a woman such as Tara."

Quinn gave a half smile and said, "Neither was I. But it didna matter how much I tried to resist Marcail. My need for her was too strong."

"I doona need a woman complicating my life. I need answers about my people. About my family."

"Maybe she can help."

Ramsey looked back at Tara to find her leaning against the stable wall, her eyes closed and her chest heaving with exertion. Her golden-brown hair was plastered to the side of her face from her sweat, but there was a contented look upon her face Ramsey had never seen before.

"Nay," he said. "I've saved Tara from Declan. The connection between us is severed."

"And the kisses you shared?"

Ramsey frowned.

"Aye. Charon told us."

Ramsey ran a hand down his face. "I . . ."

"I'm no' asking for an explanation, old friend. I just doona want you to walk away from something that you clearly want."

"Oh, I want her," Ramsey admitted aloud. "I want her badly, but I willna drag her into my life. She deserves more than that."

"We'll see," Quinn said cryptically.

CHAPTER
TWENTY-FIVE

Tara didn't know why she took so much care with her appearance after her workout and shower. She took extra long blow-drying her hair, though there wasn't much that could be done with it.

She hated her hair. It wasn't curly, but it wasn't straight. It had a mind of its own, and did whatever it wanted to do no matter how much hair product she put in it or how many times she tried to flatiron it.

Tara looked at her reflection in the mirror and sighed. She'd parted her hair to the side where the waves of her light brown hair fell down the side of her face. It didn't look too bad, though how long it would look this good was anyone's guess.

She'd even applied a little extra makeup. She normally didn't wear much, but this time she added eye shadow and a hint of color to her cheeks. And before she'd changed her mind, she had applied mascara.

"Why?" she asked her reflection. "Why are you doing this? To attract Ramsey?"

Tara shook her head. "No. I'm doing this to prove to the others I can actually look decent. They've only seen me damp from the snow and sleep deprived with my hair sticking out everywhere."

She wanted to look good, and there was nothing wrong with that.

"And I'm not doing this to impress Ramsey," she told herself for the tenth time.

She just wasn't sure how true that was.

Tara ran her hand down her hot-pink form-fitting sweater to her black jeans. When she was on the move as much as she was, there wasn't a lot of room for too many clothes. She had mostly jeans with one pair of khaki cargoes. And a few tops.

Not a lot, but it had never mattered to her before. Then again, she'd never known a time when she wouldn't have to leave at a moment's notice, unlike here at MacLeod Castle.

She'd been given the chamber and asked if she needed anything. Tara had said no, but it had been stocked with hair products and a blow-dryer.

Tara leaned her hands on the sink and looked into her eyes. "I could get used to this. All of this."

But did she dare?

If there was one thing she'd learned while being on the run it was to never let her guard down. Declan had found her. He had to know she was with the MacLeods now. It was only a matter of time before he came for her.

Tara pushed away from the mirror and reached for the small diamond studs her grandmother had passed down to her on her sixteenth birthday.

After a glance at the clock showing her it was well past six in the evening, Tara decided she'd stayed in her chamber as long as she could.

As soon as she opened the door she smelled the delicious aroma of food. Her stomach rumbled loudly, and Tara wasted no more time walking to the great hall.

No one noticed her as she descended the stairs. The hall was chaotic, but in a good way. A quick glance told her everyone was there except Ramsey, as they all readied the table for the evening meal.

She was on her way to the kitchen when Saffron walked out with two large plates piled high with meat. Tara quickly took one as she and Saffron shared a smile.

"Thank you," Saffron said. "I was about to drop it."

"It smells so good."

"We've plenty. Well, as long as you fill your plate before Galen eats it all."

"Hey!" Galen shouted in mock outrage.

Tara found her smile growing as the teasing of poor Galen continued. It seemed he had a stomach that was never full and had a penchant for taking other's food when they weren't looking.

"Doona worry," Arran said. "I'll make sure he doesna touch your plate, Tara."

Galen put his hand over his heart and sighed.

Reaghan rolled her eyes as she playfully punched Galen in the arm. "I warned you that you'll be eating outside if you keep stealing food."

"It's no' stealing if it's right there, love," Galen argued with a smile.

Tara watched as Galen pulled Reaghan into his arms and kissed her soundly. She'd seen open affection before, but nothing like what she observed at the castle.

The couples well and truly loved each other. They had all suffered greatly because of Deirdre, but together they had survived.

Tara wondered how her life would have been had her family not turned against her. Would she have been married by now? Maybe had a few children? Would her husband have loved her as the Warriors at MacLeod Castle loved their wives?

"Does it bother you?" Arran whispered from behind her.

Tara turned to him and frowned. "Does what bother me?"

"The affection between the couples?"

"No," she said and looked down at her hands. "I was thinking how good it was to see that love really does exist. You can see it in the way they look at each other."

"And talk to each other," he added.

She looked up at him and smiled into his pale brown eyes. "Yes. Does it bother you?"

"No' at all. I find it . . . odd sometimes. The first time I saw such love was between Quinn and Marcail."

"Ah, while they were in Cairn Toul, trapped there by Deirdre." Tara had heard everyone's story during the two days she'd stayed beside Ramsey's bed.

Arran chuckled. "We could all see it grow day by day. There is nothing the two of them willna do for each other. It was no surprise to come here and see Warrior after Warrior fall to love."

"But not you?"

He scrunched up his face and laughed. "Oh, I doona think much about it. I am free of Deirdre, which is enough for me after all these centuries. Now, I do what I must to end the next evil."

"Declan," she said flatly.

"After that, I doona know what awaits me. Maybe a woman, maybe more adventure. I try no' to look too far ahead."

She looked down the table to find Charon and Phelan talking together. "What of those two? They don't have women?"

Arran laughed, the corners of his eyes crinkling. "Phelan likes women. All of them. I doona think there is a woman out there who could hold his interest for long."

"And Charon?"

Arran's smile died. "Like most of us, Charon's past holds him. He keeps a lot secret, so he may verra well have a women and none of us know it."

Tara wanted to ask about Ramsey, but somehow she managed to keep her questions to herself. It was difficult since she was desperate to know more about him, but for her own sake, she refrained from asking.

"What about you?" Arran asked.

"I don't prefer women, actually," Tara said with a playful smile.

Arran threw back his head and laughed heartily. It had been a while since Tara had joked with someone and it felt good.

She soon joined in Arran's laughter, and only belatedly realized everyone was looking at them.

"Oh, that was good, lass," Arran said, still chuckling. "But seriously. There has to be a man out there somewhere."

"Somewhere," she said wistfully. "I like to think I won't be alone all my life. I don't allow myself to get close to people, Arran, not when I have to leave days, or sometimes hours, after meeting them."

"You've had a hard life."

"No more difficult than others, and I'd say a lot less difficult than any of you Warriors. This is my fate, and I accept that. But I won't give up easily."

Arran nodded approvingly. "Good for you, Tara."

She found herself seated between Gwynn and Saffron in the middle of one side of the huge table. Tara found it unusual that the couples sat closest to Fallon while the single men and Fiona sat toward the other end.

The conversation during dinner never lagged though it was hard not to notice Ramsey's absence. There were lots of laughter and jokes, and even stories. No one asked Tara to share a story, and she was eternally grateful. Not that she felt left out. In fact, she'd never felt so included in anything before.

All too soon the meal was over. When she rose to help clean, it was Isla who stopped her.

"We'll handle this tonight."

"It's all right," Tara said. "I don't mind helping."

Isla leaned close, her ice-blue eyes looking deep within Tara's. "Ramsey is in the tower."

"Why are you telling me this?"

"Why did you stay by his side while he healed?"

Tara glanced away, unsure how to respond.

"Ramsey has always kept his thoughts to himself," Isla said. "He is one of us, yet he isn't. He's learned news of his past today, and he's hurting."

"He didn't wake me." Tara couldn't believe she blurted that out.

Isla laid a comforting hand on her shoulder. "But Phelan told me it was Ramsey who put you in the bed, removed your shoes, and covered you so you could rest."

Tara searched Isla's eyes for any lies, but all she saw was truth.

"I don't claim to know what is in Ramsey's head, but he's the one who analyzes everything before he gives an opinion. He's careful. Always."

Tara let Isla take the plate from her hand. She looked to the stairs.

"Go," Isla urged.

Even though Tara knew it was a bad idea, she found herself at the stairs. She ascended them and made her way to the tower. Step by step she climbed the winding stairs until she stood before the door.

A light shone from beneath the door, but no sounds came from within. For several minutes Tara battled with herself over whether to proceed or leave before she could make a fool of herself.

But Isla's words came back to her about Ramsey discovering news of his past.

Tara gave a quick knock before she changed her mind. To her disappointment there was no response. She tried the handle and found it unlocked, so she opened the door and poked her head inside.

Ramsey sat on a stool facing one of the windows, his feet braced on the sill as he stared outside.

He looked so forlorn that Tara was walking toward him before she realized it. She had a view of his profile, and the stark desolation she saw tugged at her heart.

"I'm no' fit company." His voice suddenly rang out in the tower.

"Maybe that's when you need someone the most."

"Nay, Tara. No' this time."

She licked her lips. "I—"

"I need to be alone," he interrupted her.

Tara's blood pounded in her ears as her embarrassment increased. She should have known better, but she'd listened to Isla. Isla knew Ramsey better than she did, which was the only reason she was here.

But she'd done the one thing she hadn't wanted to do—make a fool of herself.

Tara turned on her heels without another word and left the tower as quietly as she had entered it. If she needed proof that Ramsey wasn't interested, she'd just gotten a huge dose of it.

Her feet flew down the steps as she hurried to her room. She wasn't used to feeling so idiotic. She wasn't used to having so many people around worried about her.

Maybe it was a mistake to think of staying at the castle. And with Declan thinking she would stay there for safety, maybe it was the right time to leave Scotland altogether.

CHAPTER
TWENTY-SIX

Ramsey heard the door close and squeezed his eyes shut. He'd hurt Tara. He knew it as surely as he knew her touch would have soothed him.

But he didn't want to be soothed.

He needed to feel the pain welling within him. Because if he didn't, he was going to go insane with the rage he was barely keeping under control.

His advanced hearing allowed him to hear Tara's feet as they retreated down the stairs. He gripped the stool so he wouldn't go after her.

All it took was thinking of Tara and he could taste her kisses, feel her silky skin beneath his palms. With just a thought he had her bare breast in his hand as she straddled his lap.

Ramsey had wanted to be alone, to go over the scanned pages from the book Galen had studied. Ramsey had wanted to delve into his memories of his childhood and recall his parents' faces.

But Tara had changed all of that just by coming to him.

In a blink Ramsey was off the stool and out of the tower.

Tara reached her chamber to find the door not quite closed. For a moment she hesitated, fear spiking through her.

Then she remembered where she was. It would take a lot for Declan to get past all the Warriors and Druids.

She shoved aside the lingering fear and walked into her room. The door was yanked out of her hand before she could close it. Strong fingers spun her so that she was against the wall.

And she found herself staring into amazing silver eyes.

"You shouldna have come to me," Ramsey whispered, his face breaths from hers. "You shouldna have cared."

Tara, still shaken from his sudden appearance, lifted a trembling hand to his arm.

Before she could utter a word his mouth was upon hers. The kiss was long and slow, seductive and erotic. She tasted his desire, the hunger burning bright inside him. That passion grabbed her, took her. Seized her. And she was powerless to do anything but succumb.

Tara tried to get closer to him, but he held her still and ended the kiss. She searched his gaze, trying to determine what he was thinking. Ramsey was such an enigma. Every time she thought she knew who he was, he revealed something else.

"It was a mistake to kiss you that first time," he said as he rubbed his smooth cheek against hers. "The second kiss only made me hunger for you more. And this third kiss was my undoing. I'm holding on by a thread, Tara. If you doona want this, then you need to leave now. Because I can no'."

Leave? Did he really think she wanted to? All she'd thought about was him and his kisses. All she wanted was to be in his arms.

"I'm not going anywhere," she said.

Satisfaction filled his eyes before he was kissing her again. Tara wrapped her arms around Ramsey's neck as he swept his tongue into her mouth. This kiss was fast and fierce.

The kiss stole her breath away. It took her, swept her along a tide of desire so intense she knew she'd never be the same. It was Ramsey's kiss, his touch. He was the reason she could already feel herself changing.

She gave a frustrated moan when he pulled away from her long enough to yank off her sweater. The ribbons of magic she saw winding around them when she opened her eyes shocked her.

"I'm drowning in your magic," Ramsey whispered before he took her mouth again.

Item by item, they left a trail of clothes and shoes to her bed. By the time they reached it, both were completely naked and standing toe to toe, hip to hip.

The passion was high, the need urgent. His arousal, thick and hard, stood between them, but it was the hunger she saw in his eyes that made her stomach flip.

"My God, you're beautiful," he said as he tucked a strand of hair behind her ear.

Tara rose up on her tiptoes and threaded her fingers in his hair. She couldn't get enough of his body. She'd never seen muscles so toned or a body as cut as his. Though she'd seen him without his shirt before, seeing him without clothes only made her want to touch him even more.

She ran her hand over his thick shoulders, down his back to his buttocks and trim hips. Her fingers skimmed the dark hair on his legs before his hands captured hers.

His lips moved over hers skillfully, slowly. Each nip and lick only added to the desire pumping through her veins.

"You make me feel beautiful," she said.

"And I'm just getting started."

A shiver of anticipation raced through her. The promise in Ramsey's eyes made her stomach feel as if it were filled with thousands of butterflies.

With the back of her knees against the bed, Tara gave herself over to Ramsey as he slowly lowered her to the bed kissing her all the while.

The kiss grew, deepened as if a dam had broken inside Ramsey. He moaned deep in his throat as he angled his head and kissed her as if there were no tomorrow. As if they only had this one night.

Tara lost all train of thought when his hands began to

roam over her body. Her back, her hips, her buttocks. Everywhere he touched burned for more.

She felt his arousal against her stomach and yearned to touch him. Her breasts swelled and ached for his touch, and when his hand reached between them and cupped her breast, her entire body trembled.

As much as she loved his hands on her, she couldn't stop touching Ramsey. Her hands roamed over his thick shoulders and arms, and the contours of his back down to his firm buttocks.

"I cannot think with you touching me," Ramsey said before he rolled them to the side and scooted her up.

Whatever Tara had been about to say evaporated from her mind when his hot mouth fastened onto her breast. She gripped his head, her hips rocking against his chest in time with his tongue that laved her nipple.

Tara was floating, her body swimming with pleasure, as magic wound around them. She'd never felt such bliss, never known a touch as seductive as Ramsey's.

Her legs parted on their own when his hand skimmed over her curls. The desire throbbing within Tara surged when his finger slid inside her.

Ramsey smiled against Tara's breast when she whispered his name. He switched to the other breast and laved her nipple as he moved his finger in and out of her.

He was fast losing control. He wanted inside her right then, but he could feel how tight she was and he didn't want to hurt her. But he needed inside. And soon.

Her sheath was wet and scalding hot. And suddenly, he couldn't wait any longer. He'd wanted to make love to her for hours, but he hadn't counted on his craving for her.

Ramsey rolled her onto her back and knelt between her legs. With his arms on either side of her head he looked into her blue-green eyes darkened by desire.

He let his gaze wander over her full breasts and pink nipples to the indent of her waist and her softly flared hips. Between them was a triangle of golden-brown curls that hid her sex. His fingers itched to hold her buttocks again, to run his hands over her sleek legs.

"Don't make me wait," she said as she took his aching cock in hand and guided him to her entrance.

He clenched his jaw when the head of his rod slid inside her. Ramsey made himself enter her slowly, but when she wrapped her legs around his waist, his control snapped.

With a groan, he gave a hard thrust and seated himself fully inside her. Her nails dug into his shoulders as she arched her head back and cried out.

It was all he needed to see. Ramsey began to move with slow, hard strokes and then fast, short ones. He found himself looking into Tara's eyes, found himself falling into her depths.

She met him thrust for thrust. Gone was any illusion Ramsey had of seducing Tara. Gone was any intention he had of taking control.

Desire had them in its grip, and it wasn't letting go until both had given themselves over to it.

Tara held on to Ramsey as if her life depended upon it. Never had anyone touched her as he did. And now, he was taking her to another level she hadn't known existed.

With her ankles locked at his back she could feel his hips shift as he plunged inside her again and again, harder and deeper.

Tara felt the magic sharpen around them as her body began to tighten within. Ramsey caught her gaze and held it.

And then the climax struck. It was powerful and consuming as it devoured her. She screamed as she was taken away on a wave of pleasure that hurled her over a precipice of unending bliss.

He continued to move within her, prolonging her orgasm until the second hit before the first finished. Ramsey's thrusts grew quicker as he pumped furiously inside her.

She opened her eyes and locked with his silver ones.

"Tara," he whispered before he threw back his head and gave a final plunge.

With his body straining from the force of his climax,

Tara could do nothing but hold on to him. As his body relaxed and he looked down at her, they both noticed the threads of magic not just floating around them, but through them.

She smiled against his lips as he kissed her long and slow, the power of their lovemaking still holding them in its grip.

In the next moment Tara found herself lying upon his chest when he rolled onto his back and pulled her over him. He had one arm thrown over his head and the other he moved lazily up and down her back.

"Do you feel the magic?" he asked.

Tara nodded her head. "I do."

"Has this ever happened with anyone before?"

She lifted her head to look at him. "No. Only you. Are you worried?"

"I just wish I knew what it was. I want to make sure this is no' harming you in some way."

"Harming me?" she repeated. "I feel . . . different, yes, but stronger. I feel my magic even more."

Ramsey smiled at her. "Does nothing worry you?"

"Everything worries me. But this," she said as a ribbon of magic went through her hand into Ramsey, "is beautiful."

"And if what we've just done endangers you somehow?"

"Then I'll deal with it." She ran her finger over his furrowed forehead. "I'm not worried, Ramsey."

"I'm supposed to protect you."

"You did, remember."

"I knew the moment I first saw you that I wanted you."

Tara couldn't hold back the smile. "Is that so bad?"

"In a way."

This time she was the one with a furrowed brow. "What's that supposed to mean?"

"I learned things today about my past."

"Will you tell me?" she asked.

His silver eyes slid away from her. "There are things about me no one knows, Tara."

"Then tell me what you can."

Ramsey sighed as his arm gripped her tighter. "You know I'm part Druid, but what you doona know is I'm from Torrachilty Forest."

Tara's brows shot up. "I've heard those were powerful Druids."

"Powerful male Druids. The magic couldna be held by a female. It passed only to the males."

"Only? I find that hard to believe."

"Occasionally it would pass to a female. We learned the hard way that women couldna hold the magic. It drove them daft, so any female born with the magic was killed."

She winced. "That's a bit harsh, isn't it?"

"No' when those females went on a killing spree that would begin with their family. No' when they would leave the forest and go into any village they found and kill everyone."

Tara looked away and laid her hand upon Ramsey's heart. "Only the men, huh?"

"Even then it wasna easy to hold back the magic. Especially for me."

Her gaze shot to his. "What do you mean?"

"If my people were known for how powerful their magic was, mine exceeded theirs ten times over. I was supposed to be their next leader, the one who a Seer foretold could never be defeated by magic."

CHAPTER
TWENTY-SEVEN

Ramsey wasn't sure why he'd told Tara his biggest secret. It seemed right though. As if she needed to know.

He looked away from her steady gaze to the wisps of magic floating around them. Except they weren't really moving around them more than through each of them now.

Almost as if the magic were connecting them.

Ramsey couldn't feel the magic as it entered and left his body, but his magic sensed it. And the longer he touched Tara the stronger the ribbons became.

"I don't think I understand," Tara said into the silence after his statement.

Ramsey smiled wryly. "What? That I'm supposed to have all this magic and yet I couldna defeat Declan?"

"No. If you have that kind of magic why didn't you fight Deirdre? Why didn't you destroy her when you could have?"

Ramsey raised his gaze to the ceiling. "It is a question I asked myself every hour of every day I was held in Cairn Toul mountain. But I doubted myself. I doubted the prophecy of the Seer. Magic has to be certain, and if it's not, only catastrophe awaits."

"Why would you doubt what was foretold? Seers don't give voice to their visions casually."

"I might have learned spells easily. I might have gained unique control over my magic earlier than any Torrachilty

Druid before me, but that didna make me the man foretold. That Seer never saw my face, never spoke my name. It could have been anyone."

Her hand caressed his chest as she laid her cheek over his heart. "True, but the rest of your people must have thought you were the one."

"Actually, no one knew." When her head jerked up Ramsey chuckled as he glanced at her. "I surprised you?"

"Yes. If this foretelling took place how could no one know?"

"It was told only to the elders who passed it down to the next elders. They didna want our people putting thoughts into the head of someone that couldna be the one."

"Then how did you know?"

Ramsey released a long breath. "My uncle was one of the elders. They told my father when it seemed that I could be the one. I was then pushed harder than any others. I never failed a single mission they gave me."

"I gather they were difficult," she said.

"More than difficult. Some nearly killed me, yet I never gave up. I kept going. I had no idea why they were pushing me so hard. For years they kept it to themselves. And then the MacLeod clan was wiped out in a single day."

Tara shivered. "I know that story. My mother thought it was a great show of Deirdre's power to lure the MacLeod brothers away, then come in and destroy the clan. Every last man, woman, and child."

"Deirdre didna even leave an animal alive," Ramsey said. "The horses, the chickens, the sheep. All were slaughtered without thought. Then she set fire to the castle. Time has weathered the burn marks, but they can still be seen."

"You say this as if you saw the destruction yourself," Tara whispered.

Ramsey looked into her blue-green eyes. "Because I did. I was sent here to see if the rumors were true, to see if the MacLeods had been murdered."

"Why? I mean, why you? If you were so important to your people, why did they send you?"

Ramsey shrugged one shoulder and played with the ends of Tara's hair. "Because of what I could do. You know if a Druid's magic is strong enough they are given a gift."

"Like Sonya can heal."

"Exactly."

"Then I suppose if your magic was as strong as they said, you could do something wondrous."

"Wondrous," Ramsey repeated softly. "No' really. I can determine if magic was used and what kind of magic."

Tara whistled low and turned so that she rested her chin on the hand atop his chest. "No wonder they sent you."

"I didna even have to reach the MacLeod lands to feel Deirdre's black magic. By the time I ventured to the castle, the brothers had already been tricked into going to Deirdre's mountain a few years before. I quickly began my journey back to Torrachilty Forest."

His voice died as he recalled the night he was taken. The shrieks, the screams.

"Ramsey?" Tara whispered.

He mentally shook himself and forced a smile. "Just remembering."

"You don't have to tell me."

But he did want to tell her. He didn't understand why he had such a fierce need to have her know about this critical part of him that his friends had only just learned.

"I know," he said.

She smiled, her blue-green eyes soft and patient as she looked at him.

Ramsey licked his lips and said, "The journey took nearly two weeks on foot. I was days from reaching the forest when they came upon me one night."

"Who?"

"The wyrran. They were created by Deirdre using her black magic. They were no taller than a child with pale, hairless yellow skin."

"Large yellow eyes and a mouthful of teeth that their lips couldn't close over," Tara finished with a shudder. "I saw pictures of those creatures recently."

"They are all dead now. We killed them when we killed Deirdre. She had thousands of them before Declan pulled her into the future. She used them to track and find whoever she was looking for. That night, they came for me."

"Did you not fight them off?"

"I killed several, but I knew what they were. I knew if I used magic they would tell Deirdre. So, I used my blade instead. Even without calling forth my magic I was quicker than a mere mortal. Because I knew what the wyrran were, I hid my magic so they couldna sense it. I held them off longer than they anticipated. By the time dawn came, however, they had me. They wasted no time in carting me to Deirdre."

"And then what?"

"I was the first one she captured after the MacLeods. As soon as I was dumped in front of her, she unbound my god. I didna have time to even try to use my magic. And then with my god trying to gain control, I didna dare turn my attention from him for fear he would take over."

Ramsey stopped as memories he'd long kept buried resurfaced with a vengeance. He recalled the pain of his god stretching inside him as bones popped out of joint and broke all through his body before melding back together in a process so painful Ramsey thought he would die.

And then the voice of his god, loud and demanding, echoing in his head as it ordered blood and death to all.

"Was it hard?" Tara asked. "To hold off your god?"

Ramsey chuckled dryly. "There were times I wanted to give in just to have some relief. I couldna sleep, because if I did, he would take over. The lack of sleep combined with the constant assault of my god nearly broke me. He was so insistent, Tara. I know how easy it is to give in, to stop fighting. I doona blame any of the Warriors who can no' hold the gods at bay."

"And your god. What's his name?"

"Ethexia. He's the god of thieves."

She made a sound in the back of her throat. "And his preferred color is bronze?"

"Aye."

"When did you finally gain control over him?"

Ramsey rubbed the locks of her pale brown hair with its golden strands between his fingers. "I have no idea how long it took. It was a constant fight that seemed to last an eternity. Then one day it didna take so long to battle him and win. The next was even less. Day after day it got easier and easier to control him until I had the upper hand."

"Does he not try to take over anymore?"

"Of course. He is a god, after all. But I'm in control."

It was the way her blue-green eyes watched him that told him he wouldn't like her next question.

"Are you always in control?"

Ramsey stared at her for several long minutes before he gave a quick shake of his head. "When Deirdre unbound my god it mixed with my magic. I can no' do major magic without calling forth Ethexia. Even the small bits of magic I've done lately have taken a toll."

"Wouldn't it be the case that the more you use your magic the more control you'd have? Just as when you fought your god?" she asked.

He smiled as he ran his hands through her hair. "Most likely."

"Except you've hurt innocents when you did."

"Aye. I've rarely used my magic in the centuries I've been a Warrior. I can call forth my god without using my magic, but no' the other way around."

Tara's lips twisted in a frown. "That doesn't seem very fair. Is that why you never attacked Deirdre yourself?"

"That and the fact that once I did get control of Ethexia, I no longer had the confidence in my magic I had before. I tried doing a few small spells, and the power I felt left me reeling. Several times Deirdre nearly caught me. I'd seen what she did to Druids."

"Which was? I want to know since most of my family thought she should've ruled the world."

"They might no' have been so quick to admire her if they

had known she hunted Druids, *mies* and *droughs* alike. She brought them to her mountain where she drained them of blood to take their magic and then killed them."

"Oh, God," Tara said as she sat up and covered her mouth with her hand.

Ramsey watched her as all he'd told her sank in.

"If my family knew all about Deirdre, why didn't they know this?" she asked.

"Maybe they chose no' to believe it."

Tara turned so that she faced him. "You won against Deirdre. Dani told me how you and Laria helped to end Deirdre."

"It felt so good," Ramsey said with a smile. "Just like when I tricked her into thinking I would do whatever she wanted, and I escaped."

"I bet that did feel good."

"For a few moments. Then, I remembered all the other Warriors still inside. Broc and I had grown close. I wanted him to escape while I stayed and spied on Deirdre. Somehow, he talked me into letting him be the one who did the spying."

Tara leaned down and kissed him. "It all worked out in the end."

"For the most part. I wish it were all over with. I'm sorry I didna kill Declan, Tara. I promised you I would, and I failed."

She put her finger over his lips. "Shh. We'll get Declan."

Ramsey wanted to argue, but she straddled him and all thoughts save for making love to Tara vanished. His cock swelled instantly, and the hunger for her that had never vanished roared to the surface.

He smiled as he shifted her so he could take one of her luscious breasts in hand and lick her nipple. Her answering moan was just what he needed.

Though he might have hurried through the first time they made love, he wasn't going to make the same mistake twice. He wanted time with her body, time to savor her and love her as she deserved.

But before he could, she moved her hand between their bodies. Her slim fingers wrapped around his aching rod firmly before she began to slowly move her hand up and down his length.

"Tara," Ramsey ground out. "I want to take my time, and I can no' with your hand on me."

She leaned forward and nipped at the lobe of his ear. "You can take your time later. Now it's my turn."

Ramsey groaned from the wonderful feel of her hand on him as well as the realization that this time she was the one in command.

He looked up at her to see her smiling down at him. This time was hers, but next time would be all his.

All thought fled as she lowered herself atop him, her slick heat enveloping him slowly. And then she sat up. Ramsey gripped her hips, his gaze feasting on the beautiful sight before him.

Tara's bare breasts, her nipples hard and gleaming from his kisses. Her hair was wild about her and falling over her shoulders to end above her beautiful breasts. The amazing white tendrils of magic that had grown longer and thicker as they touched swirled about them. But it was the triumphant smile on her face that made his heart beat double time.

Then she began to move. Back and forth, slow then fast. Her head dropped back as she rode him hard.

Ramsey teased her nipples until Tara's soft cries filled the chamber. He could feel her body tightening around his cock. With his fingers splayed on her stomach, he used his thumb to find her clitoris.

He circled the tiny, swollen nub, and with each stroke Tara's hips jerked faster.

The first clench of her tight sheath around his cock sent him spiraling into his own climax. Tara screamed his name and fell upon his chest as her body milked him.

Ramsey held her tightly as his seed spilled inside her. He'd never felt so complete, so content, as he did with her in his arms.

He didn't let go of her, even when his eyes drifted shut.

CHAPTER TWENTY-EIGHT

Declan stared at his face in the mirror of his lavish bathroom. Gone were his polished good looks. Now, the left side of his face was marred by the same ugly black streaks beneath his skin. They radiated out from his hairline onto his cheek and fanned out to his chin and up his forehead.

He'd never seen anything so atrocious. He could barely stand to look at himself now. His looks had been an asset he hadn't had to use his magic for.

And no amount of magic could conceal what marked him now. Because it was magic inside him that was doing it.

Why his potent black magic couldn't win against whatever was inside him Declan didn't know. He'd tried everything, exhausted every spell he knew. And even went looking for other spells that might help.

They'd been risky, but in the end nothing had succeeded.

Declan put his hands on either side of the sink and looked down. It wasn't just that the black forks marked his skin and left him writhing in pain. It was the fact that he couldn't win against it.

And that's what bothered him the most.

That allowed his men, even his cousin, to think his magic wasn't as strong as he'd claimed it to be. They questioned him now. Which he couldn't allow.

Declan lifted his head when there was a rap on his door and Robbie poked his head into the room.

"Cousin?"

Declan turned away from the hated mirror and made his way to Robbie. "Did you call the men as I requested?"

"Aye. They're waiting for you below as you asked."

"Good." Declan didn't bother to roll down the sleeves of his French-cuffed shirt. He let the black marks be seen not just on his face, but on his left arm and hand.

"What's this about?" Robbie asked.

Declan glanced at his cousin to see that Robbie wouldn't look him in the eye. "I'm making a point."

"About what?"

"That neither I nor my magic should be questioned."

"No one is questioning you," Robbie hastened to say.

Declan snorted. How he wanted a glass of whisky, anything to dull the pain raging inside him. But again, nothing worked. He could only suffer through it. "We'll see," he said through clenched teeth.

Robbie didn't utter another word as they descended the stairs. Declan caught sight of the fifteen mercenaries Robbie had been able to recruit.

The fact that so many men had died in his battle with the Warriors was making it harder and harder to find more. The money he was paying them had increased, and even that wasn't always enough to convince them to work for him.

Declan paused at the landing so that he looked down at the men and forced them to look up at him. They were in three rows of five, their feet braced apart, and heavily armed. The men needed to get used to looking up at him since he would rule them one day. If they lived long enough.

Robbie walked halfway down the last set of steps and turned to lean against the wall. He positioned himself not with Declan, but not with the men either.

It was an intelligent move, one that surprised Declan as well as impressed him.

He took a deep breath and slowly released it. "It seems

that my power and magic have come into question. I can no' allow that to continue."

The men stared silently up at him. Some with blank expressions, others not looking quite at him but over his shoulder, and still others who obviously didn't want to be near him.

"You were told I needed an army," Declan continued. "For many, that was enough to sign onto my payroll. Others among you wanted to know who you were fighting and why there was blood inside your bullets."

Declan let his gaze touch each of them in turn before he said, "You've all also seen what kind of magic I can do. Whether you believe it or no', there is good magic and evil magic. In case you didna understand before, I have black magic. In order to have that kind of magic I had to give my soul to the Devil. So I doona care if I kill one of you or all of you. You can be replaced.

"Men like you are found all over the world. I'd rather keep my money with other Scotsmen, but at this point I'm no' choosy. I need men who are no' going to be afraid to look at me. This is war, and there are casualties of all kinds."

Not a single man had moved during his speech. It was a testament to their military training, but Declan didn't care. His gaze landed on one of the men in the back row who wouldn't meet his gaze.

Declan smiled as he drew his magic and with a single finger pointing at the man had him on the floor screaming and thrashing with pain. The other mercenaries took a step away from the man, their faces impassive, but their eyes glued to their comrade.

With just a thought Declan increased the pain. What no one saw was that the man's insides were turning to mush, slowly and with more agony than any of them could imagine.

Pain and death always brought a smile to Declan. It was how he knew he was meant to be *drough,* how he knew he could take over the world and rule it as it should be.

There were too many wars, too many people saying they

were right. He would bring the peace everyone said they wanted. And he would also bring the darkness. But it was that darkness, that evil which would set everything to rights.

Belatedly, Declan realized the mercenary was dead and the others looked at him with fear in their gazes. Just as he wanted.

"I think we understand each other now," Declan said. "You doona just work for me. I own each of you. You're mine to command and to end at my will. If you want to live, doona give me a reason to kill you."

The mercenaries fell into line, their shoulders back as they ignored their dead comrade.

"I willna hesitate to kill more of you," Declan continued, "if I think my magic is being questioned. Am I understood?"

"Aye, sir," the remaining fourteen answered in unison.

Declan glanced at Robbie before turning and ascending the stairs back to his room. Declan didn't care if Robbie recruited more mercs or not. He didn't need them to guard the house. Not only were there several spells preventing anyone from getting inside that he didn't want, there were also spells keeping his whereabouts hidden from anyone looking.

Only once Declan was safely back in his room and the door shut and bolted did he hold his left arm against him and peel back his lips in pain.

Every time he did magic it burned. As if his magic and the one blackening his skin weren't mixing well. It didn't bode well for him, but it was something Declan was going to have to deal with since he needed to use his magic to get to Tara.

Because of all the Warriors at Dunnoth Tower there was no doubt in Declan's mind she was now at MacLeod Castle. But that wouldn't keep her safe from him.

Fallon hastily pulled Larena into the shadows as he jumped them to Edinburgh Castle. Hayden and Isla were quick to follow them into the shadows.

The four stayed silent as a man walked quickly down the

hall, a clipboard in hand. Only once he was out of sight did they sigh in relief.

"That was bloody close," Hayden murmured.

Fallon cut his gaze to the Warrior. "I got the girls as close to the library as I could."

"Hidden library," Larena corrected with a smile at Isla.

Isla flipped the end of her long ponytail over her shoulder. "Regardless of whether it's hidden or not, I want in and out quickly."

Fallon took the lead as they ran quietly down the hall. Hayden, who pulled up the rear, grabbed Isla's hand.

"Tell me again, wife, how you discovered this hidden library?"

Isla rolled her eyes at her husband's protectiveness and waited for him to pull even with her before she whispered, "The last time Larena and I were here, we found some old documents that spoke about a few hidden chambers throughout the castle."

"And since I spent some months here, I had an idea of where to look," Larena replied.

"You spent time here over four hundred years ago," Fallon amended.

Larena shrugged. "It's not as if the castle has changed much."

"Nay, but they do change the rooms," Hayden pointed out.

Isla nodded as they pulled to a halt and plastered themselves against the wall. "We took that into account. And didn't we explain this to you back at our castle?"

"Aye," Hayden whispered and gave her a quick kiss. "I just wanted to hear it again."

"We'll be fine," she said, and took his hand in hers.

"You better be."

Once Fallon and Hayden gave the all clear, Larena and Isla began to look for the secret entrance to the library. They pushed stone after stone, but found nothing.

"Only an idiot would put an entrance right in the middle of the main corridor," Fallon said. "I think we're looking in the wrong place."

Larena shook her head. "Trust me, Fallon. I know this is the spot."

Another fifteen minutes passed and still they'd found nothing. Isla knew the men were getting restless. Dawn had already come, and with it more people roaming the castle. They had to get into the secret room today or who knew when they'd be able to return.

"We've spent enough time here. We need to get back," Fallon said.

"A few more moments, my love," Larena begged.

Isla glanced over her shoulder to find Hayden staring at her with his lips pressed flat. His patience was already gone. She heard Hayden walk up behind her.

"I know how much you want to find this library, but we're out of time."

Isla pressed her head against one of the stones and let out a sigh. "It's here."

"And we'll find it next time." He leaned a hand above her head.

Fallon turned from looking out the window nearest him. "Hayden's right. We have to go."

"Wait," Larena said when Fallon went to grab her hand. "There's one more place."

"Where?" Fallon demanded.

"The birthing chamber."

For several moments Fallon stared at his wife. "I can no' jump us there. I never ventured to that area of the castle."

"Then we better move quickly," Hayden said.

They fell into line once more, moving like ghosts through the castle. Isla could hear people talking and knew that more and more workers were coming into the castle. It was a huge tourist attraction, and it took hundreds of people to keep the castle ready each and every day.

She tightened her grip on Hayden's hand, and his answering glance told her he knew just how anxious she was. If it wasn't so important to find the library, Isla would have agreed with the men and returned to the castle.

But she knew how crucial it was to find the spell. Larena

desperately wanted to have a family, and she wasn't the only one. While she and Fallon were both immortal since they were Warriors, the same couldn't be said for the other women.

Even Isla had no idea if she was still immortal or not, and she didn't want to tempt fate to find out.

They wound their way through the castle, managing to avoid being detected by anyone, even the security equipment located everywhere.

Isla was out of breath by the time they reached the birthing chamber. The room was allowed to be seen by visitors, so they'd have to hurry.

"Just get us inside," Fallon said as he kept watch at the door.

Isla exchanged a look with Larena as they went to opposite sides of the dark wood-paneled room. Their search began all over again as they knocked and pushed upon the wood.

"Dammit," Larena muttered. "I just knew it was here."

Hayden had stayed near Isla and reached up to straighten a picture when the panel before her popped open.

"You did it," Isla said as she gave him a smile.

Hayden shrugged. "That's why you brought me along."

"Get inside," Fallon said as he rushed to them. "Someone is coming."

Tara came awake slowly as memories of the night before filled her mind. She was lying on Ramsey's chest just as she had fallen asleep, and the sound of his heart beating steadily filled her ears.

His arms were around her, as if he had held her against him all night. The thought made her grin like a giddy schoolgirl. She might have been on the run for a decade, and though she wasn't promiscuous, she'd had a couple of lovers. No one, however, compared to Ramsey.

Maybe it was the magic that flowed between them, or the attraction that seemed to connect them so solidly. But all Tara knew was that Ramsey was the type of man she'd always dreamed of finding.

She lifted her head and found him still asleep. Her fingers itched to trace over every line of his face and body as she hadn't been able to do the night before.

In sleep, the frown that had marked his brow since returning to the castle was gone. His lips were slack, and all too kissable.

Tara bit her lip as she remembered what his mouth had done to her, how he'd made her scream.

"I've always been told it isna nice to stare," Ramsey murmured.

Tara chuckled and folded her hands on his chest so she could rest her chin on them. "How can I resist looking at such a fine specimen of a man?"

One eye cracked open to look at her. "Careful, lass. You'll make me conceited."

"Impossible."

He turned his head and opened both eyes. "Did you sleep well?"

"Exceptionally well, actually. And I believe that was all because of you."

"Oh, now I know my conceit is growing," he said with a smile.

"Did you sleep well?"

"I slept," he replied softly.

She frowned. "Do you not normally?"

"No' always."

"Is it good that you did then?"

One side of his mouth tilted in a smile. "Oh, aye."

Not knowing what else to say to such a wicked, seductive smile, Tara glanced down and just then noticed that no more of the tendrils of magic wound about them.

"What is it?" Ramsey asked.

"The magic around us is gone."

He rolled her onto her back and kissed the tip of her nose. "I think no'."

Before she could ask what he was doing, he ran a finger slowly down her stomach. Trailing behind him was a thread of white. It didn't float around them as it had before, but appeared to be beneath her skin. And glowing.

She blinked up at him. Unable to keep from trying herself, Tara trailed a finger over his shoulder and down his arm. The same glowing white thread appeared beneath his skin.

"I don't understand," she said.

"Neither do I, but I feel your magic more. Before it would come and go."

"I'm not sure that's a good thing, Ramsey. My magic is too volatile for it to be with me constantly. I could kill someone."

"Have faith, Tara. All will be well."

As she looked into his silver eyes, she found herself believing him. It wasn't that she wanted to, but that she did. There was no doubt in her mind.

"I stayed in Edinburgh those few years because I enjoyed teaching the children, but I never stayed in one place for longer than a month. And when the school let out, I would leave Edinburgh. I don't know what it means to stay in one place."

"Then you'll get to try it out here," he said with a grin. "You are no' a prisoner. You can leave whenever."

"Not if I want to remain a *mie*. Declan will find me if I leave."

Ramsey nodded. "He knows you're with us. We've strength in numbers here. Isla and Reaghan have verra powerful magic. He willna be stupid enough to attack us."

A sick feeling began in her stomach as she thought of Declan. "No, he wouldn't attack as I heard Deirdre used to. Declan will use different tactics."

"He's already tried to gain information by controlling someone's mind. The poor lass was devastated when she discovered what Declan had done. She threw herself out the tower window into the sea below. But Declan has no' gotten into your mind. What other way can he harm you?"

"I'm afraid to even think about it." A shudder of foreboding rolled down her back. "But I need to be prepared for anything. Because I cannot help but think that when it happens, he'll come directly at me."

Ramsey's silver gaze bored into hers. "Nay. I willna allow it."

And somehow Tara believed him.

CHAPTER
TWENTY-NINE

Ramsey didn't want to let go of Tara, but dawn had come and another day was in progress. He needed to shower and get downstairs, though he hated to wash her scent off his body.

The smile she gave him as she looked over her shoulder, her naked ass tempting him to follow, made him hard in an instant. The only thing that stopped him from going after her were the words she'd spoken about Declan.

They'd left him cold. Because he knew she was right.

Ramsey kept the smile on his face until he heard her turn on the water. Only then did he let the smile slip as he swung his legs over the bed and rested his elbows on his knees.

Once more he realized things had been made worse by him not killing Declan when he'd had the chance. Ramsey couldn't believe he'd failed so miserably.

With a curse, he jerked on his jeans, grabbed his shirt and shoes, and made his way to the tower. He should take up residence in the cottages, but he wanted to be close to Tara.

"Morning," Reaghan said as she passed him.

Ramsey didn't miss the way she looked at his hand where he held his shirt and shoes. "Morning."

"How is Tara?"

Ramsey paused and slowly turned to Reaghan to find her

watching him intently. Her small grin told him that regardless of his answer, she knew where he'd been.

"She's taking a shower. She should be down in a bit."

Reaghan smiled. "Good. I'll make sure Galen leaves food for both of you."

"You had best do so. I wouldna want to blacken his eyes," Ramsey said as he continued to the tower.

Reaghan's laugh followed him down the corridor.

He wasn't the kind who did a lot of joking, so he wasn't sure why he had jested with her. But it felt good. Maybe he was too cautious. Maybe he needed to . . . what were the words Gwynn used? Oh, mellow out more.

The smile was still on his face when he entered the tower and tossed his dirty shirt on the bed before heading to the shower.

It was while he was shaving that he thought again about the magic between him and Tara. Why had the tendrils stopped? He hadn't stopped feeling her magic. If anything, the feel of her magic had increased.

He had no idea why the tendrils of magic had begun either. Did it have something to do with his magic? Or the Druids he descended from?

Ramsey knew how the Torrachilty Druids had gotten their magic. He knew why only the men could handle it, but he had a feeling that despite all the history lessons he'd had, there was something missing. As if he might have learned the part they had kept from him had he not been captured by Deirdre.

As he washed his hair and body, remembered conversations with his father filled his mind. Many times his father had warned him to be choosy when picking a wife. Many times even his uncle had told him to tread carefully when dallying with a woman.

He'd questioned them, of course. Their answers had been that he would know everything in due course. Well, he hadn't learned everything. Instead he'd had his god unbound and now lived as an immortal.

Ramsey wiped the water from his face after rinsing and

turned the shower off. He reached for the towel he'd flung over the glass shower door and began to dry off.

Just as he stepped out of the shower he heard someone come into his room. He wrapped the towel about him and held it together at his waist as he walked from the bathroom.

Arran was leaning against the opposite wall, his arms crossed over his chest. "So much for staying away from her, aye?"

Ramsey rolled his eyes and pulled out clothes from the bureau.

"No' that I blame you," Arran continued while he gazed out the window. "She's a beauty, and there's no reason we can no' have some fun. We've killed one evil. And if we can take down Deirdre, we can take down Declan."

Ramsey glanced up at Arran as he tugged on his jeans. "Did you come here just to annoy me?"

"Nay. I came to tell you Fallon has left with Larena, Isla, and Hayden to look for the hidden spell in Edinburgh."

"The spell that would once more bind our gods?" Ramsey pulled on a solid black tee and frowned. "Do you really believe they'll be able to do that?"

Arran turned with a shrug. "I'd like to think they can. Laria said there was such a spell."

Deirdre's twin had told them that bit of news right before the great battle. Laria had known she wouldn't survive if Deirdre was to die, but Ramsey wished she had told them more about the spell than just that it had once been housed in Edinburgh Castle, hidden within the scrolls and books in its library.

"Laria wouldna lie about something like that," Ramsey said.

"But?" Arran urged.

Ramsey chuckled. "But . . . anything could have happened to that spell. Aye, it was hidden in Edinburgh Castle amid other scrolls, but someone could have taken it or destroyed it without knowing what it was."

"And we doona even know when it left Edinburgh."

"Precisely."

Arran shifted from one foot to another, his gaze on the floor. "Ramsey, do you want your god bound?"

For several moments Ramsey thought over Arran's question. "In a way, aye. I'd like to be able to do my magic without fear of harming someone. Yet, at the same time, if we were no' Warriors, no one would have been able to defeat Deirdre or to fight against Declan."

"The MacLeods want the spell."

"Aye. As I'm sure every Warrior with a wife does. They want to live normal lives, to have children, and to grow old with their women. I understand that."

Arran rubbed his palm along his whiskered cheek. "Phelan told me he wouldna ever bind his god."

"It is his choice. If the spell is ever found, I know the MacLeods would keep it safe so that anytime those who chose no' to bind their gods could change their mind."

"There's a certain advantage to being immortal," Arran said. "To no' having to worry about disease or anything. And if we do get wounded, we heal."

Ramsey didn't bother to mention *drough* blood. He knew his fellow Warrior hadn't forgotten that important bit.

"You doona need to ask anyone's permission if you wish to stay a Warrior," Ramsey told him.

Arran's pale brown eyes met his. "It willna be the same if everyone binds their gods but me and Phelan."

"You'll always have Phelan as a friend," Ramsey said with a grin.

Arran laughed and shook his head. "I doona think I'd last an hour alone with him. He . . . what's that expression Dani uses? Ah, he carries quite the chip on his shoulder."

"We all do to an extent. But think how much Phelan suffered while growing up imprisoned in Cairn Toul. Then, when he reached manhood, to have his god unbound."

"It's why I give him so much slack for his attitude," Arran said softly. "I'm amazed he came out of there with his mind intact."

Ramsey recalled how he and Broc watched Warrior after

Warrior succumbing to Deirdre because their minds weren't strong enough to withstand her and their god.

"Phelan has come through for us on a couple of occasions. He didna have to help us with Deirdre, nor did he have to heal everyone from Declan's last attack."

Arran suddenly smiled widely. "Aye, I know. Listen, I'm up for a workout. Care to spar?"

"Sounds perfect."

Arran let out a laugh and flung open one of the tower windows. His skin turned the white of his god as he leaped onto the sill. "I'll see you below," he said before he jumped.

Ramsey smiled as he rushed to the window and watched Arran land near the cliffs. In a heartbeat Ramsey called up Ethexia. Fangs filled his mouth and claws lengthened from his fingers.

He caught his reflection in the glass from the window and stared for a moment at the bronze skin that covered him, and the bronze eyes blinking back at him.

And then he jumped out the window, the air whooshing by him as he fell. He landed with his legs bent in the snow, and a huge smile on his face.

Arran called out to him a second later. Ramsey watched him jump over the cliffs to the beach below and quickly followed.

The spray of the sea as he landed on the beach hit his face and body, but he didn't care. He was searching for Arran who had disappeared, but then again that was their game. How long would it take him to find his friend?

Ramsey chuckled as he picked up Arran's trail amid the rocks and hurried after him. He spotted the Warrior just as he was about to leap back up the cliffs to a cave.

With a low growl Ramsey raced after him and tackled Arran to the ground. The two came up smiling, ready to spar as only Warriors could.

"My God," Hayden muttered as he looked around the small room and the floor-to-ceiling bookshelves stacked with not just books but weapons and small chests and other things that Hayden couldn't begin to know what they were.

"This room hasn't been disturbed in decades," Isla said.

"Centuries," Fallon corrected as he peered at something on one of the shelves.

Larena blew out a breath. "All right. We need to look for a scroll, or maybe even a book. Anything that might be what we need. If we have to, we'll take it back to MacLeod Castle to look it over."

Hayden gave a nod and began to search through the shelves nearest him. It wasn't long before he began to hear the sound of voices outside that told him the city hadn't just awoken, but that people were about to flood the castle.

They worked quietly and quickly looking at every item on the shelves and every page of the books. Hayden closed a huge tome and was about to replace it when something caught his eye.

"What's this," he murmured, and reached into the bookshelf to find a small book with its black leather binding coming undone.

He opened it and read aloud, "A listing of items taken from Edinburgh Castle to London the year of our Lord 1132."

"What?" Isla asked.

Hayden didn't answer her right away as he ran his finger down the pages looking for mention of a scroll. Soon, the other three were beside him as they all looked over the pages.

"These are things that the crown wanted to be secreted away," Larena said.

Fallon shrugged. "But why? No one has been in this chamber for a verra long time. Those items could have been kept here."

"True enough," Isla said. "But take a look at what's listed. Most are items that some people thought could hold magic."

"Bloody hell," Hayden said.

Fallon ran a hand down his face. "That means the crown knew of Druids and magic for far longer than I had expected them to."

"If they know about us, do they know about the Warriors?" Isla asked.

Hayden softly closed the book and shook his head. "We better assume they do. And we better make plans to get to London for the scroll."

"You found a listing?" Larena asked.

He nodded and handed her the book. "It's on the verra last page of the book. All it says is 'Scroll,' but noted beneath it is a small message that says the words to the spell were deciphered and the scroll burned."

"Damn," Fallon said.

"Wait," Isla said. "There's a final notation here. The contents were split into three wagons, each taking a different route to London. Two by land, and one by sea. Two of the three made their destination, but one by land went missing."

Larena ran her finger over the spine of the book after she closed it. "We can't know until we look in London whether the spell is still missing or not."

"We need to get back to the castle and discuss this with the others," Fallon said.

They joined hands, and in a blink they were once more in MacLeod Castle's great hall.

CHAPTER
THIRTY

Tara was more than a little disappointed to walk out of the bathroom to find Ramsey gone. But then again he did have other responsibilities besides her.

Spending a day with Ramsey pretending they were a normal couple going to a movie and maybe out to dinner was just ridiculous for her to even think about.

She was a Druid, hunted not just by her family but by a maniac intent on evil so great it made her ill to think about it. And Ramsey . . .

He was half Warrior, half Druid. That concept still baffled her. And the magic that flowed between them for everyone to see left her speechless.

Tara knew the women were waiting for her downstairs. They had accepted her easily into their fold and made her feel welcome. Yet, she was used to being on her own.

She was used to answering to no one.

She was used to making her own decisions without conferring with anyone.

And she was used to doing things her way.

At first she hadn't thought much about being at the castle since her concern had been for Ramsey when he lay unmoving atop his bed.

Then he'd woken, and she'd felt such hurt. How could she

go from feeling so lost and hurt one moment to such scorching desire the next?

She smiled as she pulled on a pair of sweats. Over her bra she wore a tank, and then over that she grabbed her favorite sweatshirt. It was light gray with ST. ANDREWS UNIVERSITY written in a pretty black-and-red tartan.

The sweatshirt had been given to her by her grandmother on her sixteenth birthday. Tara had longed to attend the prestigious university, but two years later, her only thought had been to stay alive.

Tara ran her hands down the front of the sweatshirt as she thought of her grandmother. With a smile, she pulled back her hair and twisted a ponytail holder around the thick strands.

After putting on her running shoes, Tara did fifty push-ups and a hundred crunches, then twenty full-body sit-ups. With her body now warmed up, she took another thirty minutes to stretch before she left her chamber.

She decided to do a different round. She jogged through the corridor and down a set of stairs before she found the hallway that led to the battlements.

When she opened the door, a blast of cold air slammed into her, but Tara inhaled it deeply within her lungs and let the door close behind her. With patches of ice all along the battlements, it would be a wonderful way for her to get a workout.

It was after she had leaped over her third patch of ice that she noticed two Warriors who seemed to be locked in a fierce battle.

As she looked more closely, she realized it was Ramsey and Arran. And they appeared to be sparring. Blood dripped from scratch marks on their bare chests. She didn't know where their shirts had gone, but after a look at Ramsey's muscles she didn't care.

Tara continued on, a smile now on her face. She liked the fact that Ramsey also enjoyed a good workout. Though she wasn't a Warrior, she had to learn how to stay alive and keep ahead of those chasing her.

She'd learned self-defense classes first. That had progressed to martial arts instruction of all kinds. Every chance she got she would train with a new instructor, because each of them taught her something different, something that had benefited her in her struggle to survive.

With her trip along the battlements done, Tara carefully descended the stairs into the bailey and ran to the stables. She liked the obstacles she'd found there. It wasn't every day she found things she could jump over.

She gave herself a moment to catch her breath, and then she began the course starting from one side of the stable and around to the other.

Twice she slammed her shin into the boards, and once her hand slipped on the board she was trying to throw herself over which caused her to hit her ribs against it.

But she kept going.

She didn't like hurting herself, but it was realistic. If she could continue despite being injured, then she was training herself well.

The air in the stables suddenly changed, becoming charged with desire and danger. Tara paused and looked up into the rafters, but couldn't see anything. But she wasn't frightened. She knew who was watching her.

"Ramsey," she whispered.

"I think you might move a wee bit faster if you had someone chasing you."

His voice drifted down to her from above, and though she searched the shadows she couldn't find him.

"Is that so? I thought you were otherwise engaged? With Arran? You both seemed intent on your battle."

A board creaked overhead just before Ramsey landed in front of her, a gleam in his silver eyes. "I grew tired of what Arran offered after I spotted you."

Excitement raced through Tara. "Is that so? What makes you think I want you here?"

"The way your eyes darken when you look at me."

She didn't know if he lied or not, but having him near did make her passion rise.

"You've no witty remark, lass?"

"No," she said as she let her gaze roam over him.

His shirt was still missing, but the blood she'd seen had been cleaned away. A fine sheen of sweat glistened on his skin, and his black hair was damp from the snow.

All in all, Tara had never seen a man look so tempting.

"I'll give you a proper challenge. If you're up for it," he offered.

Tara grinned. She wasn't one to back down from a challenge, especially one coming from Ramsey. "It'll be a little one-sided since you can move four times as fast as I can."

"I'll hold myself back."

His lopsided grin made her knees grow weak. "I wouldn't pass this up for the world."

"Whenever you're ready, lass."

Tara's hands itched to run over his chest, but as much as she wanted to touch him again, she also wanted this challenge that he offered her. There was no way she could best him, but he would push her harder than she pushed herself.

She winked at Ramsey and feinted to the right before rushing to the left around him and heading to the first stall. She used her arms to flip herself over the boards and landed on her feet before running to the next wall.

Ramsey couldn't stop smiling. Ever since he'd spotted Tara on the battlements he'd fought the urge to go to her. Then he'd stopped fighting it and watched her as she trained.

Every time she bent or rolled, her sweatpants would mold against her perfect behind until all he could think about was cupping her arse in his hands.

That's when he had spoken to her. The twinkle in her eye as they bantered had sent his blood boiling for her.

To his delight she'd accepted his challenge and had already run around him. Ramsey stood there for a moment just watching her and how easily she flipped over the first wall.

When she started for the second, the need to chase her and claim her took over. Ramsey took off after her, though he was careful to slow himself so he didn't catch her too easily.

Nevertheless, he gained on her quickly. He was taller, so he bounded over the stall walls easier than she did. Even so, Ramsey was impressed with how quickly she moved.

They were on the opposite side of the stables when he finally caught her. Ramsey grabbed her arm and pushed her against the back of the stall.

Their eyes locked as their breaths came in huffs from their exertion. The sweatshirt she wore had the neck cut out of it so that it fell over one shoulder and bared the strap of her red tank beneath.

Her blue-green eyes were bright from the chase. The way her hands clutched his arms told him she was glad to have been caught.

Ramsey lowered his head, unable to keep from tasting her wonderful lips another moment. She lifted up on her toes and met his kiss halfway. As soon as their lips met, the passion exploded.

The kiss was frantic and fiery, intense and blazing. Her fingers threaded through his hair as he slid his tongue past her lips. Her answering moan only drove him to seek more.

More of her nectar, more of her touch. More, always more.

He wanted her desperately, a fire burning through his veins hotter and brighter than anything he'd felt in his very long life.

She whispered his name as he kissed down her neck and across her shoulder. His body shook from the need to be inside her, to feel her slick heat clutching around him.

Before he could cut off her sweatshirt, she had managed to pull it over her head and toss it aside. Ramsey smiled down at her.

"If you doona hurry out of those clothes, I'll cut them off you," he threatened.

She laughed, her eyes roaming over him and leaving a trail of heat in their wake. "That only makes me want you more."

"God's teeth, woman," he ground out. "I'll spill if you keep that up."

Tara looked at him innocently as she kicked off her shoes. "What? Did I do something?"

Ramsey laughed as he slipped his fingers into the waist of her sweats and panties and jerked them down her legs. He squatted before her and kissed her stomach as he removed the pants from her legs.

"I don't think I can wait," she said breathlessly.

He slowly stood, kissing through her tank. "You've still got too many clothes on."

"And you have your pants on."

He began to unfasten his jeans while she jerked off the red tank and unclasped her bra.

Ramsey bent and suckled a rosy nipple deep in his mouth and tugged his jeans farther down his legs. Then he straightened and looked into Tara's eyes.

"Don't make me beg," she pleaded.

"What do you want?"

"You. I want you," she whispered.

It was all Ramsey needed to hear. He lifted her, and her legs wrapped around his waist so that his cock brushed against her sex.

He hissed in a breath when he felt how wet she was. The hunger to seat himself inside her, to plunge deep into her heat, was overwhelming, crushing.

Irresistible.

Ramsey held her over his aching cock, and slowly lowered her. Her hips rocked against him, seeking more until she had taken all of him.

For a moment Ramsey simply held her, reveling in the feel of being inside her, of having her once more. She had become an addiction, an obsession. And he never wanted it to stop.

Ramsey held her hips and slowly pulled out of her, before he plunged hard and fast. She cried out, her nails sinking into his back.

Her slick hotness as it wrapped around his arousal sent him into a fever pitch of need only she could quench. Again and again he plunged within her, driving them both higher and higher.

Tara pulled his face down for a kiss, their tongues matching the rhythm he'd set as he drove inside her. Harder. Faster.

Relentlessly.

The tide of desire had already swept over him. Taking him. Drowning him in all that was Tara.

She suddenly wrenched her mouth from his and cried out. Ramsey continued to move within her, even when her tight walls greedily clutched him, urging him to his own climax.

But he held on to his control. He was unyielding as he pumped inside her. Then when Tara's lips began to kiss and lick his neck while her hips rocked against his, Ramsey's control began to slip.

He pressed her against the wood and gripped her hips to keep her still. Ramsey had always been in control. Always. Except with Tara.

With her, it was as if his mind didn't know the meaning of the word "control." And it didn't bother him, not when such blinding passion thrummed through his body.

"Ramsey," she whispered.

He could feel her body tightening once more, could sense she was about to peak for a second time. He drove his cock powerfully inside her, filling her as deeply as he could.

Her legs tightened around him at the same time his orgasm took him. They climaxed together, their bodies and eyes locked together.

And Ramsey felt the world melt away as he drowned in the blue-green depths of a siren that had stolen his soul.

Peace enveloped them, swathed them. Cloaked them.

Tara smiled and wrapped her arms around him and held him tight.

Ramsey squeezed his eyes shut, and simply gave in to the serenity he'd found with Tara.

CHAPTER
THIRTY-ONE

"One of these days I'm actually going to take my time loving you," Ramsey murmured in her ear as he kissed her neck.

Tara shivered, not from the cold, but from his words. It was true it had been explosive the few times they had made love, but it had been amazing.

"I'm not complaining." She smiled into his silver eyes while she ran her fingers through his long black locks.

His answering smile would have shattered the stoutest heart.

"Tell me again why you don't have a woman?" she asked.

Ramsey squeezed her buttocks. "Is there a rule that says I should?"

"Based on my experience, and it is extensive, men like you aren't ever alone for long."

A black brow cocked at her words. "Men like me?" he repeated. "What's that supposed to mean?"

"Handsome, charming, a bit of a loner. And let's not forget dangerous."

"So that's appealing to women, is it?"

Tara swallowed and ran her thumb over his lips. "More than you could know."

"Hmm."

"You still haven't answered my question."

He shrugged and pressed his lips to hers. "Maybe I have no' found the right woman."

For the briefest moment Tara allowed herself to hope that she might be that woman. But just for a moment. After that, she let reality back in.

A shiver shook her again.

"I'm sorry, Tara. I tend to forget how cold it is when it doesna affect me," Ramsey said as he pulled out of her.

Tara's feet landed on the ground as he gently set her on her feet. Until then she hadn't noticed just how cold she was, but now she couldn't get back into her clothes fast enough.

It wasn't until she slid her sweatshirt on that she realized she'd had sex with him three times now, and not once used protection of any kind.

Tara licked her lips and turned to Ramsey.

"What is it?" he asked when he saw her staring at him. His smile faded and he gripped her arms. "Tara? Tell me?"

"We didn't use any protection."

Tara didn't know what to make of Ramsey's sigh and slight smile.

"You had me worried for a moment," he said.

"Well, how about sharing your little secret so I can feel as relieved?" She didn't mean for her words to have such a bite, but the last thing she wanted or needed was a baby or some disease.

She'd never been so careless before.

"First," he said, "I doona carry any type of disease, so you are safe from that. As for becoming with child, the Druids here take a spell every month that prevents them from becoming pregnant. If I know them, and I do, you were given that spell the first night you were here."

"Really?" Tara had never stopped to think that magic could help prevent her from getting pregnant, but it explained why Ramsey had never worried about it. "And it works?"

"For over four hundred years, aye."

"Oh. Why didn't they tell me?"

Ramsey shrugged and held out his hand. "Because the Druids here like to look after others."

At least that was one worry Tara didn't have to concern herself with anymore. Just as long as she took the spell or potion or whatever it was every month.

She didn't bother to tie her shoes before they walked out of the stable both now fully dressed. Ramsey's arm was wrapped around her as he guided her through the bailey and up the steps to the castle door.

As soon as they were inside warmth began to spread through her. But Ramsey didn't release her until he had her sitting before the bright blaze in the hearth.

"What happened?" Dani asked as she hurried to them.

Tara glanced at Ramsey before she issued a short laugh. "I stayed outside a bit too long."

"You and your workouts," Dani said with a frown. "I'll get you some coffee."

"Two sugars please," Tara called out.

Ramsey squatted in front of her chair. "I shouldna have kept you outside."

"I wasn't complaining. I'll be fine, Ramsey, so stop worrying."

He looked away briefly, a frown wrinkling his forehead. "I've often heard the other Warriors lamenting the fact their women are mortal. Now I understand."

"I'm fine," Tara repeated, and put her hand on his arm.

Ramsey nodded. "I willna make the same mistake again."

"I don't want to be treated like some porcelain doll. I'm hardier than that."

"Aye, you are."

Their gazes locked, and Tara couldn't help but think there was more Ramsey wanted to say. She was about to ask him when Dani returned with the coffee.

"I'll see you later," he said before he stood and walked away.

It took everything Tara had not to follow him with her eyes. Instead, she accepted the mug from Dani and stared into the flames.

"I haven't been here long, but it's obvious even to me that Ramsey likes you."

Tara jerked her gaze to Dani. "I don't know about that."

Dani took the chair beside her and grinned slyly. "I've never seen him pay another woman the attention he pays you."

"He feels responsible for me."

"And you? Is it responsibility that kept you at his side those two days he lay unconscious?"

Tara looked into her mug and shook her head. "No."

"Ramsey is a good man. All the Warriors have suffered so. I don't know all of their stories or how they became Warriors, but I know Ian's. I think they all deserve happiness."

"When I think about what they went through, I'm not surprised so many fell to Deirdre's evil," Tara said and looked up at Dani.

Dani's eyes widened slightly. "So Ramsey told you his story?"

"Yes." She was hesitant to answer because of the way Dani asked the question, as if she knew some secret Tara didn't.

"That's good." Dani smiled and looked over Tara's shoulder, her smile growing wider. "Even now he watches you."

Tara turned to look before she could stop herself. Her gaze clashed with gray ones, and they shared a secret smile.

She was the first to look away. "Have you ever had your heart broken, Dani?"

"Of course. Have you?" the Druid answered.

Tara shook her head. "No. I kept whatever sort of relationships I had very brief, and I was always the one to leave."

"You're afraid you're going to get your heart broken."

She nodded and looked into Dani's emerald green eyes. "I've never met anyone like Ramsey. He's larger than life."

"Yes," Dani said with a chuckle, and crossed one jean-clad leg over the other. "I thought the same thing of Ian when I met him. I didn't think a man like him could exist, at least not in my world. Since he came from the past, I was right."

Tara shared a laugh with her. "That might have something to do with it."

"My advice, though you aren't asking for it, is to just go with whatever is happening between you and Ramsey. If you get your heart broken, then you do. But I don't think that will happen. There is obviously a strong connection between the two of you. Just don't hold back from him."

"So give him everything I have and hope for the best?"

Dani smiled and nodded. "Precisely. It's what each of us women did with our Warriors. I'm not saying it's easy, and it's scary as hell, but you never know what will come of it."

"Thank you. For the coffee and the advice."

Tara wasn't sure she'd ever stop being afraid of giving herself to someone, but Dani was right. If there was ever a time she was going to take that chance, it was with Ramsey.

Ramsey tried to be discreet as he watched Tara from the table where he sat, but Arran's sly grin told him he'd been caught.

"I worry she might become ill," Ramsey said.

Arran laughed heartily and shook his head. "Do you forget we have Sonya? Do you forget Phelan is still here? And Isla has made everyone within her shield immortal."

"Phelan is here for the moment," Ramsey corrected. "And we cannot always count on him. He's the one who chose to leave after Deirdre's death instead of staying with us as Charon did."

Arran shrugged. "I doona think Phelan wants to stay, but Charon has talked him into it for the moment."

"In other words, he'll leave the first chance he gets."

"Still," Arran said with a shrug. "We have Sonya if anyone does become ill or gets hurt."

Ramsey knew Arran was right, but he'd been so caught up in Tara and her body that he'd forgotten she felt the cold much more than he did. Her skin had been ice-cold, and she'd been shivering, though she'd tried to hide it from him.

His gaze went to her again. She was deep in conversation with Dani. It wasn't long after that Gwynn, Saffron, and Reaghan joined them.

A glass was set forcefully on the table, causing Ramsey

to turn his head. He silently watched while Phelan took the spot beside Arran.

"The next time the two of you want to spar, let me know," Phelan said.

Ramsey didn't bother to answer.

"You plan on staying that long?" Arran asked.

Phelan lifted one shoulder casually. "I doona know what my plans are. I go where the wind takes me. For now, I'm here."

"Why?" Ramsey asked. "Doona think I'm no' grateful that you were able to help Charon and the others, but you were so quick to leave last time. Why stay now?"

Phelan glanced away, but not before Ramsey saw a flash of pain in his blue-gray eyes. "Charon thinks if I spend more time with Druids that I'll trust them."

"Ah," Arran said. "You think all Druids are like Deirdre."

"It was Isla that took me when I was but a lad," Phelan pointed out.

Ramsey braced his forearms on the table. "Aye, but she did it for her family. And she is the one who freed you."

"I know," Phelan answered softly.

Arran frowned, his lips twisted in confusion. "So you really equate all Druids with Deirdre?"

"I do. I did."

"Which is it?" Arran asked.

Phelan looked at Ramsey and shrugged. "Hard to say."

Ramsey linked his fingers together. "I would think after witnessing our Druids fighting against Deirdre you would know the difference."

"How do I know they didna do it just to gain her power?"

Ramsey understood Phelan's point. Phelan had never come in contact with any Druids other than Deirdre and Isla the century he'd been in Cairn Toul.

It was going to take a lot more than just being around the *mies* to change his opinion. He was going to have to work closely with one, to see how their magic differed from a *drough*'s.

"We can try to convince you, but you'll have to learn it on

your own," Ramsey said. "The *mies* are different. Their magic is good."

Phelan's gaze narrowed. "You mean your magic is good."

"You heard what I told everyone else about my people. We were *mies,* if that's what you're asking."

Phelan was quiet for a few minutes before he asked, "How different does it feel to be a Warrior and a Druid?"

There was such sincerity in Phelan's gaze that Ramsey decided to answer him. There was none of the sarcasm, none of the bitter hatred he was used to seeing on Phelan's face.

"You'd have to understand what it was to be a Torrachilty Druid first," Ramsey said. "Our skill with weapons came as easily as breathing. But then again, so did our negotiation skills. If we had to fight, we would. Yet it wasna always the first thing we did."

"How is it that more didna know of your people?"

Ramsey licked his lips, an image of his village flashing in his mind. "We kept to ourselves in the forest. We were well hidden so that no' just anyone could come upon us. Our skills made us valuable to others, but we didna want to constantly be sought out for such things."

"I see," Phelan said softly.

"Do you trust me as a Warrior?"

Phelan's gaze sharpened on Ramsey. "I do."

"Do you trust me as a Druid?"

There was a moment's hesitation before Phelan said, "I do."

"Then trust me when I tell you the Druids here are good people."

Phelan suddenly smiled. "I see what you mean about your negotiation skills."

Charon slapped a hand on Phelan's shoulder as he sat at the table. "I've been telling Phelan the same thing you have, Ramsey, but finally he listens. I'm just glad he heard one of us."

"Who said I ever listened to you?" Phelan joked with Charon.

Ramsey watched the two interact with a grin. Though he hadn't been in Cairn Toul when Quinn, Ian, Duncan, and Arran had, Ramsey knew the stories of how Charon had been blackmailed by Deirdre.

Charon had his own pain that he hid well, but it was good that he and Phelan seemed to have bonded. No one needed to be alone, least of all a Warrior who tended to bury his bad memories. And those memories didn't always stay buried.

"No one ever listens to Charon," Arran said.

Ramsey looked at Arran to see him smiling. At one time, Arran and Charon wouldn't even have sat at the same table together.

The killing of Deirdre as well as Charon telling Ian what Deirdre had done to him had gone a long way toward mending old wounds.

Charon rolled his eyes. "They listen to me more than you. You are the baby of the Warriors, no?"

"I'll have you know Larena is younger than me. And Malcolm, he's the newest Warrior."

At the mention of Malcolm, they fell silent.

"He should have stayed," Ramsey said.

Phelan's lips flattened with his sigh. "Where did he go?"

"He didna say."

"Sometimes the time alone is the only thing that will make life bearable," Phelan said, his blue-gray eyes meeting Ramsey's and saying much more than his words ever could.

CHAPTER
THIRTY-TWO

Abernathy Forest

Malcolm squatted beside Loch Garten and looked across the still water to the mountains beyond. Though there were people who lived in the forest, it was a quiet place. A place where he could be alone, a place where only the animals watched him.

He'd had no destination in mind when he'd left MacLeod Castle. His only thought had been to get away from the laughter and peace that filled the stones.

It reminded him too much of a life before he'd been scarred, a life before he'd become a Warrior.

But with every day that passed that life was fading from his memories.

His anger at what Deirdre had done to him hadn't faded with her death. Instead, Malcolm had transferred that rage to Declan since it had been Declan who had pulled Deirdre, and Malcolm along with her, to the future.

That fury was the only emotion Malcolm felt. There was no happiness, no sadness, no contentment. Nothing.

His mind and body were empty.

Malcolm dipped his fingers into the freezing water of the loch before he stood straight. He wanted to stay in the forest, to fade into the nature around him.

He turned and looked at the snow and his footprints that led to the water.

"Yet I can no'," he muttered.

He hadn't been able to stand against Deirdre because he'd wanted Larena kept safe. She was the only true family he had left, and he'd have done anything to protect her.

He *had* done anything and everything.

Even now the memories of the atrocities he'd committed left him emptier than before.

But nothing held him back from going after Declan. Everyone had a weakness, and Malcolm knew Declan better than any of the other Warriors.

If there was some way to get to Declan, Malcolm was going to find it.

Maybe after he killed the *drough,* then he might be able to look at his own reflection.

Before Tara knew it, it was noon and everyone was getting worried because Isla, Hayden, Larena, and Fallon hadn't returned yet.

Though Tara had gone to her room for a second shower, once she'd come back down to the great hall, she hadn't been alone.

The Druids kept her surrounded and talking. She laughed with them, joked with them, and found herself bonding with them. Even when they argued, and they did argue, though never heatedly, it was fun to watch.

"It's black," Dani said while cutting up potatoes for later that evening.

Gwynn rolled her eyes from the opposite side of the large worktable in the middle of the kitchen. "No. It's like a bluish bronze."

"That's not even a color," Cara said with a laugh.

Saffron walked from the counter to the table and set a stainless steel bowl full of olive oil and rosemary in between Dani and Gwynn. "Actually, you're both right. It is a shade of black, mixed with bronze."

"What is it again we're talking about?" Sonya asked.

Tara couldn't hold back the laugh. "It's a Coach purse Dani wants."

"It's pretty," Saffron said. "But I'd rather have the Kate Spade shoes."

Cara sighed wistfully. "Those were gorgeous shoes. I've been dying for Lucan and me to go back to Paris to see a ballet. Those heels would look gorgeous with the gold dress I have."

Tara took her time cutting up the fresh rosemary she'd been tasked with. She enjoyed cooking, though she didn't do much of it. But it was the conversation that kept her attention.

"We need another shopping trip," Saffron said.

Sonya nodded vigorously. "Especially since I missed the last one."

"I want to return to the salon you took us to, Saffron. The stylist worked wonders with my hair. I felt like a new woman," Gwynn said.

Marcail lifted her booted foot out to the side. "I want another pedicure."

"You fell asleep during the first one," Reaghan said.

Marcail put her hand to her chest, a mock look of surprise on her face. "If you had someone massaging your feet so diligently, you would have to. Plus, the color I picked was fabulous!"

"What about you, Tara?" Dani asked. "Do you have any favorites?"

The smile slipped from Tara's face. "I love to shop, but I've never really had time for it."

"That's it then," Saffron said as she leaned her hands on the table. "We're all going shopping as soon as we can. A full day at the salon with manicures and pedicures, and then shopping until we can't stand any more."

Gwynn bit her lip as she smiled. "I can last a long time."

"So can I," Saffron challenged.

Tara couldn't wait to go with them. Even while they ate sandwiches all Tara could think about was shopping with the girls.

She'd never had that. Ever.

She'd been so lost in her thoughts that she'd finished her sandwich without even knowing it. Then she looked around the table and found Ramsey watching her.

They shared another smile. She glanced at his hands, remembering how well they moved over her body, knowing just where to touch to bring her ultimate pleasure.

His gray eyes darkened, and a moment later he said something to Broc who sat beside him, and left the hall.

Tara followed Ramsey up the stairs with her eyes. Excitement drummed through her when he reached the top and looked back at her.

A heartbeat later she excused herself and followed him up the stairs to his tower. She walked the circular steps toward the top of the tower, her breaths coming faster and faster at the urgency to have Ramsey's arms around her again.

When she reached the top and found the door slightly ajar, her stomach flip-flopped. Gently, she put her hand on the door and pushed it open.

Ramsey stood with his back to her as he looked out the window. "I didna think you'd ever get here," he said and turned to face her.

"I practically ran here."

"I know. You took too long. I almost threw you over my shoulder and carried you."

She grinned. "Now that would have been something."

"You've no idea."

Tara stepped into the tower and closed the door behind her. She leaned back against it, content to let her gaze roam over Ramsey for the moment.

"If you continue to look at me like that, we'll have another episode like the last two, and frankly, I want to take my time with you."

Tara bent and unzipped first one boot and then the other, dropping them to the floor as she tugged them off her feet along with her socks. "Is that so?"

"Aye," Ramsey said with a nod. He jerked off his shirt and tossed it aside, his silver eyes blazing with need.

Her jeans were next, and her blood heated when she saw how his eyes watched the denim slide off her legs. "What do you have in mind?"

"Hours of me touching every inch of your body. Slowly. I want my touch branded upon you."

His voice, warm and deep and husky with need, caused her to shiver in anticipation while he removed his jeans. She licked her lips and grabbed the hem of her sweater. She had to force herself to take her time in removing it. Because though she didn't care how they came together, she knew it meant a lot to Ramsey for them to go slow.

Their passion, already simmering, grew with each garment that fell to the floor.

"You've already branded me."

He growled deep within his throat when she stood in nothing but her bra and panties before him. "Nay. No' like I will this time."

Tara fumbled with the clasp of her bra. Not from nervousness, but from the desire spreading through her swift and sure. Finally she unhooked it and let the straps fall over her shoulders.

With a little shake of her arms, the bra tumbled to the floor amid the rest of her clothing.

"You seem to have forgotten something," Ramsey said.

The smile was slow as it pulled at Tara's lips. There was no doubt Ramsey wanted her, no doubt his desire for her exceeded anything she'd ever experienced before.

It was there for her to see in his silver gaze, the way his hands fisted and flexed with each piece of clothing she pulled off. In the way his arousal stood thick and engorged.

Tara had never felt more confident or beautiful in her life. And Ramsey was the one who gave that to her. She'd give him anything in return.

With deliberate leisure, Tara hooked her thumbs in the waist of her peach cotton and lace panties and moved them down her hips and over her thighs. Then, she let them drop around her feet before she stepped out of them and walked to Ramsey.

She'd taken two steps before he closed the distance and crushed her against the hard, lean lines of his body.

"You've no idea what you do to me," he whispered.

Tara's gaze was locked with his silver ones. "Oh, I think I do."

Their words faded away as passion and desire swirled around them. Tara glanced down to see wherever she touched Ramsey that the white ribbons of magic seemed to glow beneath his skin.

Being with him scared her. It frightened her how much she needed him, how much she yearned for him. He was everything she knew she should stay away from, but she couldn't.

All thoughts fled when his hand moved seductively down her back to rest upon her buttocks. She sucked in a breath when he pressed her against the hard length of his cock.

She knew what it felt like to have him inside her, to feel him sliding in and out of her.

The stones beneath her feet were ice-cold, but the blood in her veins was boiling from the passion.

She didn't protest when Ramsey tugged her hair off her shoulder, then gently moved her head to the side. A sigh left her lips when he lowered his head and placed his lips on the sensitive skin of her neck.

Ramsey's hot mouth left a trail from her shoulder up to the spot behind her ear. "I've never felt such beautiful magic, or held such a stunning woman in my arms."

Tara had no words in answer to such a compliment. Instead, she wrapped her arms around him and held him against her. With him she felt as if she'd found the other part of herself, a part she hadn't even known was missing.

He slowly maneuvered them until they were at the bed. With a movement so quick, so smooth, Tara found herself atop the bed and Ramsey next to her. Limbs tangling, hands searching, they rolled skin to skin.

"No rushing this time," he warned her.

She started to shake her head in answer, but his finger

circling her nipple scattered her thoughts. Tara moaned and arched into his hand, silently begging for more.

Her breasts swelled, her nipples tightened. Tara fisted her hands in the covers while Ramsey's fingers played with one turgid peak and his mouth claimed the other.

Liquid heat rushed through Tara's body. She gasped at the intense desire, but that gasp turned into a cry of pleasure when he pinched her nipple.

The pleasure-pain only intensified the need pulsing through her and centering at her sex. Her hips lifted, seeking Ramsey. And suddenly he was between her legs, his rock-hard body atop hers.

Tara was on fire. Each flick of his fingers, each tug of his lips upon her breasts, only fanned the flames.

And then his hands were on her thighs. He held them apart and stared at her sex before he licked her.

Tara sucked in a breath that quickly locked in her lungs when he parted the soft folds of her sex and put his mouth to her curls.

Ramsey licked and laved, he probed and explored. His assault upon her senses and her body was devastating.

She was helpless to do anything but ride the waves of pleasure as he took her higher, wound her body tighter with each stroke of his tongue.

Tara could feel her body constricting, knew she was close to peaking. Just when she was about to go over the edge, Ramsey drew back.

She reached for him as fiery need filled her. Her hands stroked the muscled expanse of his chest.

Silver eyes met hers, his lips softened into a crooked smile as he rubbed the head of his engorged arousal against her sensitive sex.

Tara looked between them to his cock. No one had touched her as he had, both body and soul. This was different. Not just the way they were making love or the magic between them.

It was more. Something she couldn't put into words.

Something she didn't dare put into words.

She reached between them for his rod. It was hot and hard and so flagrantly male. Her other hand joined the first, and together they stroked and lightly squeezed.

He stilled, his entire body going taut. His chest expanded with a breath that he held within him as her hands continued their exploration.

With a nudge he wasn't expecting, Tara had him on his back and turned the tables on him.

"Tara," he whispered, his hands fisting in her hair.

She waited for him to stop her, to pull her away. When he didn't, she wrapped her lips around his smooth flesh and took him deep in her mouth.

She sucked, she licked, she laved.

The sound of his ragged breathing, the way his hands clutched at her only drove her to push him closer and closer to the edge. She sensed the tension in him tighten.

His hips bucked beneath her in time to her mouth moving up and down his thick length.

In a fluid motion, he had her on her back as he knelt between her legs. His gaze never left hers as he gripped her hips and lifted them.

Tara drew in a shaky breath filled with need and urgency as she looked at his cock poised at her entrance. The broad head of his member pressed in.

Seeing him fill her, watching the way her body stretched to accommodate him only sent her need, her desire, spiraling higher.

He steadily pressed deeper to fill her. Her spine arched, her body tingling with sensations.

Ramsey looked down at her, at her blue-green eyes filled with blatant desire, her luscious curves beneath him, her long legs wrapped around him.

And his cock buried deep within her.

His fingers tightened on her arse as he drew out of her only to plunge deep and hard. She moaned, her lids closing over her incredible eyes.

But Ramsey wasn't close to being done with her. He had tasted her, touched her, learned her. Yet it wasn't enough.

The hunger for her inside him was only growing, consuming him.

With her ankles locked around him, he released her hips and cupped her breasts. He rolled her nipples until they were tiny hard buds, throbbing and straining.

She gasped and squirmed, shifting along his arousal with simple movements that caused sweat to break out over his skin.

His mouth replaced his hands as he paid homage to first one breast then the other. Until she was a wordless pleading mass, until her body was damp and dewy.

Ramsey rose and gripped her hips once more. When he glanced up, he found her eyes glossed over with desire, her skin flushed with burning need.

Just as he wanted her.

He rotated his hips and heard her low moan. Keeping her hips still, he began to thrust slowly at first, then gradually set up a driving, gripping rhythm.

With his jaw clenched he watched as she cried out from the pleasure, her head thrashing from side to side, her hands fisted in the covers.

He lifted her higher, sliding deeper. And pounded into her.

Tara cried out Ramsey's name, her back arching as the climax claimed her by surprise. It took her, swept her. Racked her.

The pleasure touched every part of her, but more than that, there was something special, something singularly different that filled her as well.

She grasped ahold of Ramsey as he released her hips and fell atop her, his breathing harsh and ragged. Yet still he pumped his hips faster, harder.

Tara wrapped her arms and legs around him, rocking her body to meet each of his thrusts until she felt his release take him—and her—on a glorious tide of bliss that left them reeling.

Together. As one.

CHAPTER
THIRTY-THREE

Ramsey stared at the moon through the window as he held Tara cradled against him. Her breath had evened into sleep, with her head resting on his shoulder.

In all his life, he'd never been more content than he was at that moment. If everything stayed the way it was, he could be happy. He could be . . . satisfied.

If there was one thing he'd learned from Deirdre, it was that nothing ever stayed the same. Declan was out there, and he wouldn't stop until he had Tara.

Why Tara was so important to Declan, Ramsey didn't know. But Ramsey wouldn't stop until he discovered what it was. He wouldn't stop searching for Declan until the bastard was as dead and gone as Deirdre.

Yet, for the first time in a long time, Ramsey didn't want to see battle. He wanted nights with Tara in bed beside him, to face the morning sun and see her bright smile. To share meals with her.

To share the future with her.

Ramsey glanced down at the top of Tara's head and ran his fingers through the thick, cool strands of her golden-brown hair, marveling at the golden locks within.

He wasn't sure how he felt about wanting Tara with him always. It seemed right, yet . . . he'd never had that feeling with any other woman before. Was it just that he was lonely?

Was it just that his fight with Deirdre was over and he wanted someone to protect?

Or was it something much more?

His thoughts ground to a halt then. He wasn't prepared to go further. Not yet, at least.

The sound of Tara's stomach rumbled into the silence, causing him to smile. They had missed supper, and he was more than hungry himself.

Ramsey gently rolled Tara onto her other side and quietly left the bed. He pulled on his jeans without buttoning them and left the tower barefoot to wander down to the kitchen.

The castle was quiet in the dead of the night, but Ramsey knew that there were Warriors on guard. Until Declan was gone, they would remain guarding the castle and the Druids within.

Ramsey walked into the kitchen and flipped on the light to find Galen leaning against the counter eating a sandwich.

"Hungry?" Galen asked around his mouthful of food.

Ramsey grabbed a plate from the cupboard and set it next to the refrigerator. "Aye."

"You and Tara missed a fine supper."

Ramsey glanced at his friend before he opened the fridge door and began to pile the plate with cold meats and cheese. "That we did."

"Is it serious?"

Ramsey paused while reaching for a bottle of water and turned his head to look at Galen. "I'm no' sure."

"There's time," Galen said. He wiped his mouth with a napkin before he wadded it up and tossed it in the bin.

Time. Ramsey certainly had an abundance of it. But Tara didn't. She was mortal, just like all the other Druids in the castle.

"Do you think about what will happen if the spell to bind our gods is never found?" Ramsey asked.

Galen's blue eyes darkened. "I prefer no' to, however, Reaghan is a realist. She likes to think ahead. She says she's all right with the way things are."

"But you are no'." It wasn't a question.

"Nay."

Ramsey grabbed the water and closed the fridge door. "As long as the Druids stay at the castle they'll no' age. Isla's magic is strong. The spell survived four centuries. It can survive as long as it takes to find the spell to bind our gods."

"I know. We all know. But we've all had our lives on hold for so long. I know Larena and Fallon desperately wish to have a family."

"And you and Reaghan?"

Galen ran a hand down his face. "Reaghan longs for a child. I too want children, but only if we can raise them without the threat of evil that is Declan."

"I'm sorry. Had I killed Declan at Dunnoth Tower, that is one more evil that would be gone."

Galen grinned and slapped Ramsey on the shoulder. "You always try to do too much by yourself, my friend. For whatever reason, fate has decreed you and Declan will have another face-off. And frankly, I'm looking forward to such a battle. I want to give the son of a bitch a few swipes of my claws."

Before Ramsey could respond, Galen walked from the kitchen. With a shake of his head, Ramsey gathered up the plate and water and made his way back to the tower.

When he shouldered open the door he found a small light on beside the bed and Tara sitting up in bed.

"I wondered where you'd gone," she said.

He shut the door and grinned. "Your stomach was growling alongside mine, so I thought food was in order."

"You thought right," she said, and grabbed for the plate as he reached the bed.

Ramsey chuckled and settled beside her on the bed, both of them leaning against the headboard. With the plate and water between them, they each began to eat.

"I didn't realize how hungry I was until I saw the food," Tara said with a grin.

Ramsey popped a bit of cheese into her mouth. "I figured the least I could do for you was feed you."

"The least," she repeated with a laugh.

He watched her eat for a moment before he asked, "Are you happy here?"

"Yes," she said without hesitation. "Why do you ask?"

"Just wondering if you'll take off soon or no'."

Tara ran her fingers through the condensation on the outside of the bottle. "It's odd here, I'll admit. I'm not used to being so included in everything. Usually I have to hide my magic and everything about myself. Here I feel . . ."

"Free," Ramsey supplied for her.

Her eyes widened and she nodded. "Yes. 'Free' is the perfect word. Maybe it's this castle, or the people. All I know is that I like it here."

"Good."

"Why?"

Ramsey broke a piece of cheese in half and stared at the plate. "I'd worry about you out in the world."

"Because of Declan?"

"Nay." He turned his head to her. "I'd just worry."

"No one has ever worried about me before."

Ramsey put the cheese in his mouth before he said more about his feelings. Already he'd told her much more than he'd wanted to. Not that he was trying to keep anything from her, but he wasn't ready to share what he hadn't thought through enough yet.

He needed more time to think about what was developing between them, to consider how it would affect both of them.

Thankfully, she didn't ask any more questions either. As famished as they both were, the food was devoured quickly. Ramsey wanted Tara to stay, and he was prepared to ask her. But as he took the plate, she slid down the pillow and smiled at him.

Ramsey set the plate and empty water bottle on the floor and rose to remove his jeans. He climbed back under the covers and shut off the light, only to find Tara waiting to cuddle next to him.

He closed his eyes, a smile on his face. And the next thing he knew he opened his eyes to find the sky lightening to gray. Tara had her back to him, though she was still pressed along his side. Ramsey leaned over to look at her. He couldn't ever remembering watching anyone sleep before, and he found it fascinating.

Or maybe it was just that he found Tara fascinating.

Her thick, dark lashes lay against her pale cheek, and her lips were parted slightly. Her bare arm was outside the covers, and her feet tangled with his.

It was so intimate, yet so effortless.

Suddenly, Tara's lips pulled up at the corners. "Tell me I don't have drool sliding down my face."

Ramsey chuckled and kissed her cheek. "No' that I see."

"Oh, that doesn't help," she said as her eyes opened and she swiped at her mouth. "I don't. Thank God."

"Why would it matter if you did?"

Her blue-green eyes widened as she turned onto her back. "Ramsey, I realize you've come forward in time, but I don't think it matters what century a woman is in, she always wants to look her best."

"Then you've nothing to worry about."

"How do you always know what to say?" she asked as her eyes briefly lowered.

Ramsey shrugged. "I say what feels right."

"I have a confession."

He looked down at her hand that rested on his chest. "And what would that be?"

"I've never spent the entire night with a man before you. This makes the second time."

"You're the first woman I've wanted to keep in my bed the entire night."

"Really?"

"Aye," he answered, and pressed his lips to hers. "I wouldna lie about that."

She wound her arms around his neck and sighed as he kissed across her jaw. "I want nothing more than to stay in this bed with you."

"But?" Ramsey asked, and lifted his head to look at her.

"I'm supposed to make breakfast with Sonya and Cara this morning."

He groaned and rolled onto his back, his arms out to his sides. "I know how hungry we Warriors get, so I suppose I must let you go."

Tara leaned over him, her curtain of wavy brown locks falling on either side of his face. "Breakfast doesn't last very long."

"Are you suggesting we return to the tower afterward?" he asked with a grin.

"Definitely."

"I like the way you think."

He reached for her, but she scooted from the bed and raced to get her clothes. "No. If I let you touch me again, I'll never leave."

"And that's a bad thing?"

"That's just it." She glanced up after fastening her bra and reaching for her panties. "I don't want to leave."

Her words reverberated in his head long after she departed for her own chamber. Ramsey remained in the bed a little longer.

He ran his hands over her side of the bed, the sheets still warm from her body. When he inhaled, he could smell her sweet scent not just on himself, but on his bed as well.

To his surprise, his thoughts turned to wondering what she was doing to get ready. And he wanted to find out. The next thing he knew, he was wondering how she'd feel if he broached the subject of her moving into the tower with him.

That way, she wouldn't have to rush away from him. She could be getting ready just steps away, and he could watch her, learn more about her.

Ramsey sat up and raked both hands through his hair, his mind in a whirlwind. It wasn't that he'd never wanted a woman by his side, it's that he'd never found the right one.

But all that had changed with Tara.

Was it the magic between them, that even now sizzled in his veins? It couldn't be seen anymore, but Ramsey felt it just the same.

Was it because she needed protecting from Declan?

Though she'd done a fine job of keeping ahead of him for a decade.

Ramsey didn't know what the reason was, only that she now occupied his thoughts constantly. The more he made love to her, the deeper she went in his psyche.

The more he touched her, the deeper she touched his soul.

The more he was around her, the more she was etched into his mind.

Ramsey took a deep breath and swung his legs over the side of the bed. He didn't know what the next step with Tara should be, or if there would even be one.

She said she was happy at MacLeod Castle, but how long would that last for a woman who was used to following the call of the wind when it took her?

He rose and walked to the bathroom. He rubbed his hand over his jaw, heavy with whiskers, and turned on the shower.

It was impulsive of him to want to ask Tara to move her things into the tower with him. And Ramsey wasn't impulsive. He needed time to think things over, time to consider all sides of what was developing with Tara.

He stepped into the hot water of the shower. For several minutes he simply stood there, letting the water wash over him as memories of the night before replayed in his mind.

Tara's sweet body. Her soft sounds of pleasure, and her screams of release. Her hot mouth on his cock as she sucked and licked him until he nearly came.

Ramsey smiled. Tara was much more than he'd ever thought. And he wanted to continue to peel back the layers and discover the rest of her.

After a quick wash and shave, Ramsey turned off the water and reached for the towel. He stepped out of the shower and began to dry off.

Just as he was about to walk out of the bathroom, he heard his door open and close. There was no feel of Tara's magic, or any magic period, so he knew it wasn't one of the Druids.

But Ramsey wrapped the towel around his hips nonetheless. He stepped into his room to find Arran. Again.

"This is becoming a habit," he said with a grin as Arran stared at him. "Do you always know when I'm in the shower?"

Arran leaned back against the wall and shrugged. "My entrances have always been excellent."

Despite the slight smile, Ramsey wasn't fooled. Arran was in the tower for a reason. "What brings you here this morning?"

"Fallon wants to see you."

"About?" Ramsey prompted.

Arran glanced at the ground, giving Ramsey an idea that he wasn't going to like what he heard.

"Arran," he urged.

"Fallon wants to take you to Torrachilty Forest."

Ramsey's mind went blank. His chest felt tight and it was difficult to breathe. Not once in all his immortal centuries had he gone back there.

"I knew you wouldna like the idea," Arran said as his arms fell to his sides. "I tried to tell Fallon that last night when they returned, but he thinks if you go there you might learn more about what happened to your people."

Ramsey ran a hand through his wet hair that dripped down his back and onto the floor. Many responses came to mind, but as he was known to do, Ramsey let the idea sink in before he made any decisions.

Yet inside his mind he was screaming, "Nay!"

"Give me a moment to change," Ramsey said.

Arran frowned before he gave a nod and left the tower.

Ramsey didn't move as fast as he normally did while he dressed. He kept going back and forth in his mind about returning to the forest. He might find answers, but then again, it could only bring him more pain as well.

Was it better to not know? To speculate? Or to have the answers and wonder how he could have changed everything if he'd only been there.

Galen might have discovered that his people had gone out to kill Deirdre, but it never said what had become of those who had left the forest.

Ramsey could well imagine though. He'd not only been

put through many of Deirdre's tortures, he'd seen—and heard—most of them. She had been ruthless and merciless.

He grabbed his chest as he realized she could very well have taken their magic as she had done with countless other Druids. The thought left him ill, with an ache in his chest that threatened to devour him whole.

After pulling on a silver short-sleeved tee that had a dragon on the front mixed with a Celtic design, he raked a hand through his still-damp hair and left the tower.

As he walked into the great hall his gaze sought out Tara, but she hadn't made it down yet. Before he could reach the table Fallon and Galen stepped in front of him.

"A word, please," Fallon said as he held his hand out toward the hearth and the chairs there.

Ramsey walked to the hearth and stood before the roaring fire. The heat licked at his skin while he watched the flames devour the wood.

Behind him he heard a chair squeak as Fallon sat. Ramsey knew Galen well enough to know his old friend remained standing, probably behind one of the other chairs.

"Arran told me," Ramsey said before Fallon could speak.

"And?" Galen asked.

Ramsey didn't immediately answer since he hadn't decided how he felt.

"You want answers to your people's disappearance," Fallon said. "This could give it to you. Frankly, I'm surprised you have no' returned before now."

"Did you want to come back here after the massacre?" Ramsey asked as he turned his head to look at Fallon.

Fallon's dark green eyes clouded for a moment. Then he gave a single shake of his head. "But I knew what happened."

"Ramsey, all we know is what is written in some book. You know as well as I it could all be wrong," Galen said.

It could be, but Ramsey doubted it.

"Galen thinks you might find something there, and I'm inclined to agree," Fallon said.

He understood Fallon's and Galen's arguments. They

were the same ones he'd used on himself. But the thought of returning to his beloved forest, to walk upon the ground he had trod as a lad seemed inconceivable.

A warm wave of magic washed over him then, compelling him, luring him. Ramsey lifted his gaze to the stairs to find Tara descending, her eyes locked on his.

He wanted to go to her, to wrap her in his arms so she could make him forget what Fallon asked. He never had the chance, because as soon as she stepped off the stairs, she headed straight to him.

"What is it?" she asked when she reached him.

Ramsey turned to her, unable to do anything else. "Fallon wishes me to return to Torrachilty Forest."

"Ah," she muttered, her face reflecting the understanding that filled her voice. Tara looked at Fallon. "You really think it will help him? Despite how much it'll hurt him?"

Fallon looked from Tara to Ramsey and back to Tara. "I do, or I wouldna have asked it. Ramsey, as is every Warrior here, is my brethren. I want to help him."

"Ramsey has suppressed his magic for too long," Galen said. "Magic is a part of who he is. He needs to find it again."

Ramsey looked at his friend with new eyes. "You doona think I know who I am?"

"I think you've become someone you think you should be," Galen responded. "But I doona think you're the man you were supposed to be."

Fallon snorted derisively. "None of us are, Galen. That's the curse of being a Warrior. I was supposed to lead my clan."

"You are leading a clan. Just no' the MacLeods," Galen said with a wry smile.

Ramsey had to admit Galen had a point. But he still wasn't sure about any of it.

Tara's hand rested upon his arm. "I've not been back to my family in ten years. I long to go, but I know I can never return. You can go back, Ramsey."

Ramsey looked into her clear blue-green eyes, amazed

that she was able to look at the world so neatly, and despite everything, find a way to make it suit.

Ramsey turned to Fallon. "All right."

"Good," Galen said with a smile as he leaned on the back of the chair in front of him.

Fallon stood. "We need to leave soon. I doona want to be out there too long. I still doona trust Declan. And I willna be able to stay the entire time. I'm taking Larena, Gwynn, and Logan to London to search for the scroll."

Ramsey looked about the great hall, a sudden feeling of dread coming over him. "Fallon, I doona think we should all go at once."

"Why?" he asked, concern flattening his lips.

"I doona know. Just a feeling."

Galen turned and called out, "Saffron, have you had any visions recently?"

Saffron shook her head of long, silver-blond hair. "None. Why?"

"Ramsey has a bad feeling about these trips everyone is taking," Fallon answered.

"I just doona think we should all go at once," Ramsey stated. "If we stagger, then if Declan does strike, we can answer quickly."

Fallon shrugged. "I think it's a good idea. Consider it done."

Ramsey felt a little better, but it still didn't dispel his worry. He looked down at Tara. "I'll be back soon."

"I'll be here," she said with a smile.

Ramsey walked to Galen and Fallon.

"Fallon hasna been to Torrachilty, and neither have I. So, think of it," Galen said.

With Galen's ability to read someone's mind, he could see what Ramsey saw, then put that image into Fallon's mind so Fallon could teleport them. Ramsey let the forest fill his mind as Galen laid his hand upon his head.

The sounds, the smells.

And suddenly Ramsey was standing in Torrachilty Forest.

CHAPTER THIRTY-FOUR

Ramsey didn't move, didn't breathe as he listened to the lively sounds of the forest. Even in the coldest, darkest winter the forest had always been alive with sounds.

In the distance he could hear the Black Water River full of salmon as it thundered off the Falls of Rogie. Wind whispered through the trees. Pine and spruce were most prevalent in the forest, but there were also pockets of ash, oak, and birch.

Ramsey smiled as he heard the claws of a pine marten as it clambered along a tree limb. He could well imagine the dark, silky coat of the sleek animal.

He couldn't believe he was back in the forest. His home.

"Ramsey?" Galen asked.

Ramsey opened his eyes and drank in the sight of the trees reaching toward the sky, their limbs heavy with snow.

"I'm all right," he answered. Though, in truth, he wasn't sure if he'd just lied to his friends or not.

Fallon glanced around the area. "How far are we from your village?"

"No' far," Ramsey said. He didn't say anything more as he turned left and started walking.

Even after all the centuries he still knew his way blindfolded through the dense forest. So much had changed, yet so much had stayed the same.

The closer he walked toward the river, the louder the water became. Ramsey paused as he passed a tree and looked down to find a wildcat.

The animal stared at Ramsey with its pale green eyes. Its coat was of a medium brown color with black stripes, and a small piece was missing off the top of the cat's left ear.

Ramsey used to track these cats, which were believed to be the descendants of house cats. They were stealthy creatures, and did remarkably well in any climate and terrain.

"He's a fighter," Galen said with a grin. "You can see it in his eyes."

Fallon chuckled. "He's a Scot. Of course he's a fighter."

Ramsey lifted his gaze before him. Just through the grove of trees ahead and over a small rise was where his village had been located. But he didn't immediately continue on.

He'd been too content while looking around the forest and remembering his childhood that it took him a moment to notice the forest.

"It's quiet here. Too quiet," he whispered.

Fallon's black claws lengthened from his fingers. "Declan?"

"Nay," Galen said with a single shake of his head. "The magic is older."

And then Ramsey knew. They were feeling the residual magic from when Deirdre had destroyed his village.

He didn't say another word to his friends as he ran through the snow. He needed to reach his village to see it first.

His heart pounded in his chest as he leaped over a fallen tree and slowed as his village came into view. Ramsey put his hand against a tree and took in the emptiness around him.

Gone were the cottages, the well-tended gardens, and the pens for the sheep and goats. Nothing remained but the echo of laughter that only he heard.

"I'm so sorry," Fallon said softly from behind him.

Ramsey had expected to find exactly this, but expecting it and actually seeing it were two different things. "I'm tempted to bring Deirdre back from the dead so I can kill her again."

Galen snorted. "She's burning in Hell, but I agree. It doesna seem enough after everything she's done."

Ramsey pushed off the tree and walked to where the middle of the village had been. "This is where I stood, where each male Druid stood, as we were put through test after test. All around," he said as he pointed in every direction, "were cottages."

"What clan claimed these lands?" Fallon asked.

Ramsey looked at him and smiled. "We did. None dared to cross us."

Galen chuckled. "I can well imagine what neighboring clans thought of you. But I'm having a hard time picturing warrior Druids. You trained with swords?"

"And spears and bows," Ramsey answered. "Anything that could be used as a weapon. Our magic would penetrate the weapons and make them doubly effective."

Fallon whistled. "I'd have loved to have seen your people in battle."

Ramsey squatted and shoved aside the snow. He used his claws to dig through the hard ground until they scraped against stone. For the next few moments he moved aside the dirt until one stone showed.

Ten minutes later and all twenty stones were visible. Each held a carving of a Celtic symbol.

"I feel their magic," Galen said, his voice filled with awe.

Ramsey ran his finger over one of the stones. "These stones tested us, and protected us. They hold powerful magic."

"They look ancient," Fallon commented as he bent and ran a finger over one.

"They are. Though I have no idea how old, they've been passed down through my people for generations too far back to count."

"Amazing," Galen mumbled.

Ramsey took a deep breath and raised his head. "We shouldna have been defeated. They should have survived."

"Anything left would be buried under seven hundred years of soil." Fallon caught his gaze. "Tell us where to look, Ramsey. Tell us where they might have left something behind for someone to find."

Ramsey stood and thought of each elder. "None of the elders would have dared leave anything just anyone could stumble upon. It would have been put somewhere safe, somewhere secluded . . ."

He trailed off as his gaze lifted to the hill to his right. "Only once did I wake and follow my father as he went to join the elders. They met at midnight once or twice a year. One time I followed them."

"Where?" Fallon asked.

Ramsey pointed to the hill. "There. Hidden there is an entrance into a cave."

Galen started forward. "Let's get moving then."

It took no time to climb the hill as they followed the path that Ramsey remembered. Finding the entrance was another matter entirely.

"Do you recall where it was?" Fallon asked.

Ramsey shrugged. "My father later told me that the entrance moved each time."

Galen rolled his eyes and said, "Let me guess. The entrance is hidden by magic."

"Of course."

"Of course," Galen mimicked sarcastically.

Fallon let out a sigh. "Can you use your magic, Ramsey?"

Without a doubt Ramsey knew he could. But did he dare? "I'd rather you both got far enough away from me so I didna harm you."

Galen turned on his heel and retreated back down the hill. "Fair enough."

Ramsey shook his head at his friend. Only when Fallon had joined Galen did Ramsey look at the steep hill before him. He couldn't climb any higher. Ramsey would have to work his magic from where he stood.

He drew in a deep breath and sought out his magic. It

swelled within him, filling, flooding him from each fingertip to each toe. He felt alive with the magic inside him.

Ramsey placed his hand on the slope before him as words from a spell summoning a door fell from his lips. He couldn't believe he remembered the spell, or why he knew it would work.

The hill seemed to inhale as his magic passed through his hand into the earth. And then a section of earth slid away to reveal the entrance to the cave.

His god bellowed excitedly inside him as his magic called him, beckoned him to surrender to it. It would be so easy for Ramsey to give in, to let his magic take him as he'd done when he was younger.

But he hadn't had a primeval god inside him then. Ramsey ignored the call of his magic and concentrated on reining it back. Slowly but surely he got command.

With a sigh, he looked at the opening of the cave and into the darkness within.

"That was easy," Galen called from below.

Ramsey held out his hand, stopping them from venturing forward. "That was too easy," he muttered to himself.

He reached out his other hand and was thrown backward as a blast of magic slammed into him. Ramsey caught hold of a tree before he rolled too far down the hill.

"Ramsey?" Fallon called.

He glanced at them. "I'm unhurt. Stay there."

Ramsey climbed his way back to the cave entrance and glared at it. The spell to get in would cost him much more. Possibly too much more.

He turned to Fallon and Galen and said, "I need a promise from both of you that if I can no' get myself under control you'll do what needs to be done to stop me."

The men both nodded, their faces a mixture of concern and dread.

"If they only knew what could happen they wouldna ask this of me," Ramsey whispered to himself as he turned back to the cave.

His fingers itched with the magic inside him, as if it

couldn't wait to get out. Just as he couldn't wait to release it. He'd always loved using magic. He'd felt more alive, more powerful . . . more everything with his magic.

Ramsey took a deep breath and slowly released it as he lifted his hands to the invisible barrier that blocked his way.

He tried spell after spell, but nothing worked to weaken the barrier. Each time he used his magic it became more and more difficult to pull it back.

How many more times could he use it before he was taken completely? The idea of it didn't frighten him as much as it had before, which told him he was fast losing control.

Ramsey bent over at the waist and rested his hands upon his knees. His head ached from trying to hold back his magic as well as from all the spells running amok inside his brain.

He held his head with both hands and let out a roar of fury.

The sound of footsteps rushing up the hill had Ramsey whirling around to face his friends. "Nay!" he bellowed.

Galen's brows shot up. "It's just me, old friend."

"Get back."

"Look at yourself," Fallon said.

Ramsey glanced at his hands to see his skin flickering from normal to bronze and his claws out. He could well imagine his eyes had transformed as well.

He squeezed his eyes shut and shook his head. "Get back," he repeated. "Please."

Thankfully, Fallon and Galen did as he requested. Ramsey didn't waste another moment before he faced the cave again. He swallowed and searched his mind until he found the spell he'd hoped not to have to use.

As soon as the words began to fall from his lips his magic expanded inside him so that he thought his skin would explode from the force of it.

The magic grew and grew until it came into contact with the barrier of the cave. Every time his magic pushed against it, it pushed back.

Ramsey peeled back his lips with a growl and dropped

his guard so that all of his magic could be used. With a roar, he gave a final shove against the invisible wall. It crumbled beneath the weight of his magic, but by then it was too late.

The magic had taken him.

CHAPTER
THIRTY-FIVE

Tara hated that Ramsey was gone. It seemed her entire world dimmed when he wasn't around.

"Stop being such a imbecile," she mumbled to herself. "One night doesn't make him yours for life."

Odd how that thought made her almost giddy. If only all she had to worry about was what was going on between her and Ramsey, but Declan was never far from her thoughts.

And to her chagrin, neither was her mother now that Ramsey had told her she was dying. Despite everything her mother had done, even killing her grandmother, Tara still wanted to see her.

Tara started when she realized Marcail and Saffron were standing next to her. "I'm sorry. I was lost in my thoughts."

"We were just making sure you were all right," Marcail said.

Saffron smiled and nodded to Tara's hands. "You touched Ramsey and the ribbons of magic didn't show. Can you turn them on and off so easily?"

Tara lifted her hand and rubbed her thumb over her fingers. "I'm not the one controlling it. I never thought I was, and how it began and then halted, I have no idea."

"I do," Reaghan said as she walked up, a kind smile on her face. "I saw Ramsey the other morning on his way to the tower."

Tara knew if she were the kind of woman to blush her face would be flaming. "Oh," was all she could manage.

"There's no need to be embarrassed." Marcail grinned, her turquoise eyes sliding to Quinn. "These Warriors are certainly difficult to resist."

"Difficult?" Saffron asked on a choked laugh. "More like impossible."

Reaghan nodded in agreement. "Impossible is right. They don't stop until they get what they want, and sometimes we have to show them what they want."

Tara licked her lips as she listened to the banter of the women. It was so easy to fit in at the castle with the welcome she'd received. It was no wonder they had all stayed through the centuries.

"What I'm trying to say is that I think after you and Ramsey were together it might have prevented us from seeing the white tendrils," Reaghan said.

"Ramsey said the same thing," Tara said before she thought better of it.

Saffron chuckled and shared a glance with Marcail. "I think we've all shared our Warriors' beds before they officially laid claim to us."

"That's true. So, no one will look twice at what is growing between you and Ramsey," Reaghan said.

Marcail cleared her throat. "What we really came to you for was to talk about your magic. Ramsey said you don't use it because it's unpredictable."

"That's an understatement," Tara said and let loose a long breath. "My magic has always been hit or miss, but the older I got the more it seemed I couldn't do the simplest things. Every time I tried to make a plant grow it died instead because too much magic went into it."

"Have you meditated?" Saffron asked.

Reaghan asked, "Or found what helps to strengthen your magic?"

"No and no," Tara said. She shook her head. "What do you mean, what strengthens my magic?"

Reaghan shrugged and tucked a strand of curly auburn

hair behind her ear. "For me it's water, but the loch not the sea."

"For me it's fire," Saffron said with a glance toward the hearth.

Marcail shifted from one foot to the other and adjusted the watch on her wrist. "And mine is being underground."

"I've never heard of this," Tara admitted. "I wouldn't even know where to begin."

A moment later she was being dragged all over the castle to try and discover what would help strengthen her magic. The interest the women were taking in her only made her smile. So she didn't complain when they tried place after place after place.

Declan stood in the middle of the room he kept in the basement. Shelves were filled with an array of different books pertaining to magic and Druids. He'd devoured them as a child, and learned many interesting facts about magic.

And spells. Oh, the spells he had learned.

He'd woken from a fitful sleep with the remnants of a spell lingering in his mind. Though Declan couldn't recall exactly what the spell was for or the words, he knew that somehow it pertained to Tara.

She was at the center of his thoughts. He had to find her, had to turn her *drough*.

Declan walked to one of the bookshelves and looked at each book before moving to the next shelf and then the next.

At the bottom of the third shelf he found the small red leather-bound book. He pulled it from the others and smiled as he recalled finding it on his twentieth birthday at a small bookstore in London.

The owner hadn't realized how much the book was worth. Declan had paid the twenty-five pounds and left the store with a wealth of spells in his hand.

Declan thumbed through the pages twice before he found the spell toward the back of the book. " 'A Connection Spell,' " he said, reading the title.

He'd already used one form of a connection spell, but this

one allowed him to enter into Tara's mind when she slept so he could see her thoughts.

For the first time in days he truly smiled as he sank into his chair and began to chant the simple, but brilliant, spell.

Tara was about to think there was nothing in or near the castle that would strengthen her magic. And then the clouds broke and a ray of sunlight hit her through the window.

She immediately turned toward it, and a moment later she heard Saffron gasp.

"I think we found it," Reaghan said.

Tara looked at the women and frowned. "Why? Because I turned to the sun in the middle of January?"

"No," Marcail said with a laugh. "Because that was the smallest ray of sun I've ever seen, but your entire face lit up. You're drawn to it."

"I've always been drawn to the sun," Tara said with a shrug.

Reaghan pulled Tara down onto the floor. "Just try it."

Tara crossed her legs and looked at Reaghan. "Now what do I do? Just sit here?"

"Close your eyes," Saffron urged.

Tara did as she was told.

Marcail leaned her hands on Tara's shoulders from behind and whispered into her ear, "Now think of your magic. Search for it and let it fill you. All of you. Don't stop, Tara. Concentrate on the magic."

The more Marcail spoke the more distant her voice became until it faded altogether. Tara seemed to be floating, but she wasn't alone. There was something there, just out of reach, something she knew and recognized.

Her magic.

She smiled as she called to it and it came closer. When she embraced it as she'd never done before, it suddenly swarmed her until she could feel it everywhere all at once.

And then she heard the drums.

They were like a distant echo. She didn't think more about them as she instead concentrated on her magic. It was as if it were spinning around her and through her. As if it were testing her.

That thought surprised her, but then again, she hadn't used her magic much since her grandmother's death. She'd been too afraid. Her grandmother had been trying to teach her to control it.

Tara let all thoughts leave her mind as she floated along with her magic. It was heavenly and peaceful. A place where nothing mattered and nothing could harm her.

The drums sounded again, this time louder and closer. The beat was hypnotic and it lured her toward the sound. She wasn't afraid of what she would find. It wasn't just the music either, but the chanting she heard as well.

If the music was captivating, the chanting was enthralling. Tara couldn't understand the chants, but it didn't matter. For once, everything felt as if it were as it should be. As if she'd finally found a place where she could be a part of her magic and not fear harming someone.

She smiled at the ancients around her. How she knew that's who was chanting she had no idea. Only that the knowledge was there and she readily accepted it.

They urged her to become one with her magic, to accept it. Or there could be dire consequences. Tara wanted to know what those consequences could be, but they refused to answer her.

She eventually gave up asking and did as they requested. It was as if she could control her magic properly in this wonderful new place she'd found. And she would worry about how to do that when she woke later.

Tara was so lost in her magic that it took her a moment to realize the chanting and drums were fading again. She wasn't ready to leave them or to wake.

"*Careful,*" she heard a voice near her ear whisper.

What could the voice mean? She was safe with the ancients. They had told her so.

"Hello, Tara," Declan's voice said from behind her.

She turned and found him in shadows with a light behind him showing her nothing but his silhouette. "You're not here."

"Oh, but I am. I've warned you before that I'm capable of just about anything. It appears I can even invade your mind while you sleep. Except you are no' sleeping now, are you? Nay, you're . . . meditating, which lowered your defenses even more."

Tara took a step away from him. "You can't harm me here."

Declan threw back his head and laughed. "No' physically, nay. But there is so much more I could do. For instance, by the time I'm through with your mind, you'll do whatever I want. Including killing the Warriors." He paused. "And becoming *drough*."

"Never!"

"You should know better than to say never, Tara. You said I'd never find you. Yet I have. Twice."

"Ramsey will kill you yet. He hurt you, didn't he?" she asked with a smile. "I know he did."

"I think I'll have you kill this Ramsey first since he means so much to you."

Tara grabbed her head and shook it. "Get out! Get out of my head!"

She desperately wanted to believe it was all just a dream, a fear that manifested itself in her mind. But even her magic was telling her that Declan was all too real.

Strong fingers bit into her upper arms as he gave her a vicious yank. "There's no escaping me now," he said through clenched teeth.

CHAPTER
THIRTY-SIX

"Goddammit, Ramsey, open your eyes!"

Ramsey inwardly winced at the way Galen bellowed in his ear. "No' so loud!"

"About damn time," Fallon muttered on the other side of Ramsey.

Alarm swept through Ramsey then. There was only one reason for his friends to be worried. He cracked open his eyes to find that they were inside the cave with only the light filtering in through the entrance, but with their enhanced vision, they could all see as easily in the dark as in daylight.

Galen dropped his chin to his chest and raked a hand through his hair. "You bastard. Doona ever scare me like that again."

Ramsey slowly sat up to find Fallon watching him with hooded eyes. "Do I want to know what happened?"

"Besides you glowing?" Fallon asked.

"Glowing?" Ramsey repeated.

Galen snorted loudly. "Aye, my friend. You were fucking glowing. And you were no' answering us."

"We had to knock you unconscious." Fallon said it with a wry twist of his lips.

Which let Ramsey know it had been a much greater affair than either of the Warriors wanted to admit. "And then?"

"Then you wouldna wake up!" Galen got to his feet and

began to pace. "And your magic. My God, Ramsey. I thought Isla and Reaghan had powerful magic. Yours exceeds that by—"

"Anything we could comprehend," Fallon finished.

Ramsey scrubbed a hand down his face and climbed to his feet. "Thank you. Both of you."

"Are you sure you're all right?" Fallon asked.

Ramsey nodded. "I've wasted enough hours already. We need to start searching."

"What are we looking for?" Galen asked, but he didn't seem as interested in discovering it as he had before Ramsey had . . . glowed.

Ramsey still couldn't imagine himself glowing. It wasn't something he'd ever done before. Why now? He inwardly shook his head and focused on the cave.

The walls were covered with the writing of his people and Celtic symbols, some small, some large.

"If anything was left behind it would be here," he said.

Since the cave was relatively small, with a large opening in the middle where the six elders probably stood, and ended shortly after the entrance, they didn't have much area to search. There were multiple scrolls that had been encased in magic to prevent them from succumbing to the elements, but none were important enough to put a hiding spell on the cave.

"Ramsey," Galen called.

He rushed to his friend to find Galen looking at an elaborate Celtic circle knot.

"I've seen this before," he said as he placed his right hand on the symbol.

A panel below the symbol moved to reveal a small opening with one scroll inside.

For a moment, Ramsey simply stared at it. Then he reached inside and took it. Ramsey held the ancient scroll gingerly in his fingers and slowly turned it over until he found the seal.

"What's that?" Fallon asked from beside him.

Ramsey ran his thumb over the mixed red-and-gold seal.

"It's magic mixed with blood. It was only used for the most sacred of documents. Magic is mixed in so only the person who was meant to open it is able to do so."

Galen leaned over his shoulder for a closer look. "How? Just by breaking the seal?"

"You can no' just break the seal. Because blood was used to create the seal, it takes blood to break it."

"Ah. A sacrifice," Galen said with a nod.

"No wonder the rumors of Druids performing sacrifices spilled over the land," Fallon said with a frown.

"We didna sacrifice lives. Just a little blood. And no' all Druids had the ability to create seals of this kind," Ramsey added.

Galen nudged him. "Can you open it?"

Ramsey ran his thumb once more over the red-and-gold-colored seal with the image of a skull in the wax, a sadness settling into his soul. "This was my father's seal. He was most likely the last one to enter the cave."

"That's a skull, Ramsey," Galen said.

Ramsey smiled. "There are knotwork designs in it as well. For a family to be given the skull as its symbol was highly prized with my people. It meant the family was no' only important but incredibly strong with magic as well as having physical strength."

"None of which surprises me since we know what a strong Warrior you are. So the scroll is for you?" Fallon asked.

Ramsey shrugged. "He probably thought me dead, so nay. Yet . . . if what I read in the pages from the book Galen found are true then maybe."

"You have to try." Galen shrugged when Ramsey looked at him. "I would."

Fallon nodded slowly. "I agree with Galen. You have to try."

Ramsey carefully set the scroll on the ground. He lengthened one of his claws from his right hand and cut across his left forearm.

Blood welled quickly, and Ramsey moved his arm over

the seal so it would catch each drop. All too soon the wound mended. And the seal didn't break.

"It was no' meant for me," Ramsey murmured more to himself than the others.

Once more he lifted the scroll in his hands. He was in the process of replacing it in the slot when there was a loud crack and the red-and-gold seal broke in two.

"It looks as if it was meant for you," Fallon said, his voice filled with wonder and curiosity.

Galen rubbed his chin thoughtfully. "Maybe since you are now a Warrior, it took more time to recognize that it was you."

None of that mattered to Ramsey now, not when he wanted to know what was inside the scroll. What was so important that his father had not only hidden the scroll, but had put the seal on it as well?

"How long after I was taken did my people disappear?" Ramsey asked.

Galen glanced at the ground. "It's estimated between sixty and eighty years."

The scroll had been hidden even while other Torrachilty Druids remained. His father had always been selective in what he'd told Ramsey, but never this secretive.

Ramsey gently unrolled the scroll, and read the first words aloud. " 'Ramsey, my son . . .' "

The pain of those words slammed into Ramsey like a hammer. His breath locked in his lungs and his eyes refused to focus. He lowered the scroll and walked to the edge of the cave. "He did know what happened to me," he said. "My father knew what Deirdre did to me."

Fallon placed a hand on Ramsey's shoulder. "He also knew you would come through it or else he wouldna have left a message for you."

Ramsey knew Fallon was right, but the knowledge that his father had known he was in Cairn Toul and had sent men to rescue him left him with a crushing weight that would never leave.

But he had to know what his father had wanted to tell

him. Ramsey began to read again, this time to himself, and the more he read the more concerned he became.

"Shite," he muttered when he'd read about half of it.

Galen was at his side in an instant. "What?"

"No' all of my people died in Deirdre's attack. There were a few who were bidden to go out and find a new place in the world. Men who were destined to keep our line going in some small way."

"That's good, aye?" Fallon asked.

Ramsey shook his head. "No' exactly. It would eventually dilute our magic, but even then I'm no' sure it would be enough for any female to be able to use it and no' go daft."

Galen asked, "How many men were sent out?"

"It just says a handful." Ramsey looked at the scroll and shook his head. "This idea came into being after I was taken and the first few sets of Druids sent out didna kill Deirdre. This plan was in place for decades."

"What else does it say?" Fallon asked.

Ramsey swallowed as he looked at the scroll and his father's bold handwriting. He took a moment to read the next few paragraphs, his stomach falling to his feet with a thud.

His gaze snapped to Fallon. "Get us back to MacLeod Castle. Now!"

Without a word, Fallon placed a hand on both Ramsey and Galen. The next moment they stood in the castle's great hall. Which was empty.

A sick feeling filled Ramsey. "Tara!" he called.

Larena appeared at the top of the stairs. "You three better get up here now."

Ramsey took the stairs four at a time, his heart beating with a low, thunderous pounding in his chest. When he turned the corner and saw Larena walking down the corridor to the right, he knew she was going into Tara's chamber.

He ran to Tara's doorway, and stopped short when he found her lying in the bed with the Druids surrounding her, their magic filling the room.

"What the hell?" Fallon said from beside him.

Ramsey shouldered his way into the room and knelt beside

the bed. He rested his hand atop her forehead and looked up at Sonya. "What happened?"

"We were teaching her how to strengthen her magic," Marcail said.

Saffron nodded. "We discovered that it's sunlight that she's drawn to."

Reaghan met Ramsey's gaze. "She went to the ancients, Ramsey. She should have been safe."

He clenched his jaw, the scroll clutched in his other hand. "How long has she been like this?"

"A few hours," Sonya replied. "We tried to call on Fallon's mobile, but he never answered."

Dani cleared her throat, but couldn't meet Ramsey's gaze. "I . . . I know what happened."

"What?" Ramsey demanded, afraid to find out by using his own magic after what had happened at the cave.

Dani exchanged a glance with Ian. "It's Declan. Saffron felt him, and I used my magic to search Tara's mind. He's not just taken over as he has with others. This is different."

"As if he's in Tara's thoughts and not just telling her what to do," Saffron said.

Dani nodded, and the knot inside Ramsey tightened. For long moments he simply stared at Tara lying so still upon the bed. He didn't know how to reach her, or if he even could.

"What did you read in the scroll?" Galen asked.

Ramsey blinked and glanced at the scroll in his left hand before he looked at Galen. "The plan to send a handful of men out into the world wasn't the only thing they had done. It seems there was a Seer who foretold of one family who would take in a Torrachilty Druid. It was a *drough* family."

Every eye shifted to Tara.

"It was Tara's family," Ramsey finished.

"Holy hell," Quinn said as he rubbed a hand over his chin. "No wonder she can no' control her magic."

Broc held out a hand. "Wait. I thought you said no woman could withstand the magic, that it drove them insane."

"Aye. A full dose of our magic would," Ramsey said. "But it's been diluted many times over the centuries."

Lucan leaned against the wall, his face thoughtful. "What does this mean for Tara?"

"It means if she can ever control her magic, she's likely to be as powerful as Isla and Reaghan," Ramsey said. "But first, I have to get her free of Declan."

Camdyn grunted. "At least now we know why Declan wants her so desperately."

"I'm no' so sure," Charon said. "I doona think Declan knows what she holds inside her."

Ramsey slowly stood. "If he didna before, he does now. If he's inside her mind, he has access to all her thoughts. He'll be able to look deep into her consciousness for things she doesna remember."

"What do you need from us?" Sonya asked.

Ramsey rolled up the scroll and handed it to Fallon. "Keep this for me."

"What are you going to do?" Logan asked.

Ramsey smiled, but it was filled with malice and vengeance. "I'm going to get Declan out of her head."

"I don't think that's a good idea," Gwynn said, her lips pinched with worry.

But Ramsey wasn't deterred. "I'm no' leaving her like this. There's no telling what he's doing to her."

"And what if he takes you?" Broc asked.

"He's going to die by my hands one way or another." But Ramsey heard their concern and understood it.

There was a lot at stake in trying to go into Tara's mind, but he was willing to do it. He would do anything for her.

That thought brought him up short.

He had felt that for the other Warriors, but never for a woman. Not once in all his centuries of living had anyone ever captivated him as Tara did.

Something touched his arm and he looked down to find Dani's hand. Her emerald eyes clouded with worry.

"I barely got into her mind," Dani said. "As soon as I did a wall went up, blocking me from going further. And it wasn't Declan who put the wall up."

"You're suggesting it was Tara?"

"I'm saying it was Tara," Dani said. "I'm sorry, Ramsey, but I think he already has her."

"Nay. Nay," Ramsey said again, more forcefully. He wouldn't believe it until he saw it with his own eyes, and even then he would fight for Tara.

Ian moved behind Dani and wrapped her in his arms. "My wife knows what she saw and felt, Ramsey. You need to prepare yourself."

He gave a curt nod. "I'm prepared. Now you all need to leave."

"But—" Reaghan started to say.

It was Galen who took his wife's hand and pulled her to the door. "Ramsey is right. Everyone needs to get out."

Fallon motioned his hand to the door for everyone to leave. "The sooner we get out the sooner Ramsey can reach Tara."

One by one the Warriors and Druids left the chamber until only Fallon, Ramsey, and Tara remained. Ramsey watched the eldest MacLeod closely. Fallon felt responsible for everyone within the castle walls, and he wanted to protect them all.

"Will you be all right?" Fallon asked.

Ramsey shrugged. "I can no' answer for sure."

"I know you want to save Tara. We all do, Ramsey, but if we're going to defeat Declan we're going to need you. Especially after what I saw today."

"My glowing?" Ramsey asked with raised brows.

"It wasna just that, my friend. It was the magic I felt as well. You've hidden it from us, and I doona want you to do that any longer. We need you as a Warrior and as a Druid."

Ramsey didn't have words to respond. Instead, he held out his arm, and with a wry smile, Fallon clasped his forearm.

"Be safe," Fallon whispered before he left the chamber and closed the door behind him.

Ramsey took a deep breath and faced Tara. Now that he was alone with her, he let the distress show in his face. "Hold on, Tara. I'm coming for you."

He climbed in bed beside her and took her hand in his. Then he closed his eyes and gave himself up to his magic. The drums and chanting soon filled his ears. He moved toward it, seeking the only connection he had to reach Tara.

If the ancients couldn't help him, he didn't know what he could do.

"He has her," their whispered voices echoed around him.

The fact that they knew Declan was in Tara's mind was good. If they could reach Tara, then he could as well.

"She doesn't hear us," the ancients wailed.

What little hope Ramsey had disappeared with their words, but still he tried to cross over to Tara. He concentrated all his magic as he meditated deeper, searching, seeking Tara.

And with an ease that raised an internal alarm, he was suddenly inside Tara's mind,

But the Tara he saw wasn't the one he had made love to the night before. The Tara looking at him had cuts down her wrists, signaling she was a *drough*.

CHAPTER
THIRTY-SEVEN

Declan knew the instant someone entered Tara's mind. Not that he cared. It had taken him longer than he'd thought, but Tara was his.

The torture he could dole out physically was nothing compared to what he could do to a person's mind. Tara had withstood a lot, which impressed him.

He had only been in her mind a few hours, but to her it had been months. Her mind wasn't nearly as fragile as he'd always believed. She was strong in mind and in body. And her magic . . . Declan smiled as he relished her potent magic.

If he'd known ten years ago what kind of magic she held within her, he'd never have taken his eyes off her. He wasn't sure how she'd gotten such powerful magic when it wasn't evident anywhere else in her family, but he wasn't going to complain.

With her magic added to his, nothing and no one would be able to stand in their way. And unlike Deirdre, Tara would never think to go against him. Not now, at least.

Declan knew he couldn't stay in her mind much longer. It was wearing on him, and the pain from the magic tearing at his insides was making it more difficult to keep his concentration.

If Tara had only lasted a little while longer she would have bested him. But Declan was effective when it came to knowing how to torture a person. The fact that he enjoyed it only made it more pleasurable.

Just as Declan was about to leave Tara's mind, he felt the presence of a Warrior. Things couldn't have gone better had he planned them himself.

"Kill him," Declan ordered Tara.

Ramsey's eyes flew open as he heard an furious scream in his ear. He saw a dagger come at him, and instantly he lifted his arms to stop the attack.

"Tara?" he whispered as he looked at his attacker.

And just like what he had seen inside her mind, this wasn't the Tara he knew. Her blue-green eyes were filled with malice. And her strength. He had no idea how she'd suddenly developed the strength of four men, but even that couldn't compare to the might of a Warrior.

Ramsey's first thought was to toss her off him, but he didn't wish to hurt her. Whatever had happened to her he knew it was Declan's doing. This wasn't his Tara.

"You have to die," she said through clenched teeth.

Her voice, laced with hate, startled him enough that his arm slackened and the dagger she held drove into his chest.

Ramsey roared, not in pain, but in anger over what Declan had done. Ramsey pulled the dagger from his chest and plunged it into the stones in the wall. Then he flipped Tara onto her back and held each of her arms in his hands.

He straddled her, and the way she bucked against him reminded him all too well of her silky body as he'd made love to her the night before.

"Fight whatever Declan has done," he urged.

Tara began to chuckle, and it grew into a laugh that echoed off the walls of the chamber. "You have no idea what Declan can do. Or what he's done to me. He's freed me from the restraint I had on myself. Now the magic I feared is mine to use as I wish."

"If you doona fight Declan and the evil he has planted inside you, Tara, you'll be lost to me forever. The magic and Declan will see to that."

"Maybe I was never meant to be yours. If not for you I wouldn't have come to MacLeod Castle," she said as she eyed the blood seeping from the wound that was even now closing. "If not for you I wouldn't have been befriended by the Druids and learned how to seek out the ancients. Declan wouldn't have found me, and I wouldn't have access to my magic."

"Tara . . . please, fight this," Ramsey begged.

She smiled. "He told me to kill you. I won't stop until it's done."

Ramsey closed his eyes, the knowledge that Tara was beyond his help too much to take. His chest felt split open, a hole too dark and too deep to imagine threatening to swallow him whole.

His magic swelled inside him as he called to it. He let it move freely from him into Tara. She stiffened as if it hurt her before she began screaming and bucking against him.

But Ramsey didn't relent. When he opened his eyes and locked gazes with her, he said one word, *"Cadal."*

Instantly she fell asleep.

"Do I even want to know?" Charon asked from the doorway.

Ramsey gently wiped the locks of hair from Tara's face, his heart shattered by the realization that the beautiful woman who had lain beside him in his bed had been replaced by someone who despised him.

"Declan got to her. The spell I used will cause her to sleep, but I doona know for how long. We need to put her somewhere she can no' escape."

"The dungeon," Lucan said.

Ramsey wiped the emotion from his face. The others didn't need to know how greatly Tara's change affected him. If they knew, they wouldn't let him carry out his plans. And even if he had to lock all of them in the dungeon, he was going after Declan.

He jumped from the bed and lifted Tara in his arms. When he turned to the door he found everyone watching him.

Arran looked from the dagger embedded in the stone to the blood on Ramsey's shirt. "She stabbed you?"

"Aye."

Phelan's lips twisted in confusion. "I doona know whether to ask how she stabbed you or where she got the dagger."

"She stabbed me because she caught me by surprise," Ramsey answered. "As for the dagger, I doona know."

Ian walked into the chamber and yanked the blanket off the bed before he tucked it under his arm. "The girls have gone below to begin a spell on one of the cells in the dungeon so Tara can no' get out."

Ramsey gave a nod of thanks as he walked from the room. With each step his anger grew, and the need for revenge filled him. He would have to control the vengeance if he was going to use his magic, because revenge could turn a good person to evil quickly.

And though Ramsey knew he wasn't without his faults and bad deeds, he didn't consider himself evil. Yet the god inside him was.

It was a constant battle he fought against his god, and the first time Ethexia found a way to overtake Ramsey, he would.

Ramsey didn't say a word as he walked down to the dungeon. Below the castle, the dungeon was dark and dank, with only a few torches to light the way for the Druids.

As he walked down the middle of the cells Druids lined the aisle. A small cot had been brought into the square, iron-barred prison. Ramsey gently placed Tara on the cot before he straightened and walked out.

He pulled the door closed behind him. After another look at her, he put his hand on the iron and bound the prison with magic. He also allowed the magic to penetrate deep within the ground so no one would be able to free her except those within the castle.

Ramsey lowered his hand as he saw Tara begin to move. Her eyes flew open as she pinned him with a lethal stare.

"I know what you did to me," she said as she sat up. "I know how you bound my magic because you feared I had too much."

Ramsey inwardly winced at her words. "None of that is true."

"It is! Declan told me all of it. He opened my eyes!"

"He's brainwashed you," Ramsey replied calmly when all he wanted to do was bash his hand into the stones to release some of the anger inside him. "Do you no' recall the friends you made here?"

Her lips lifted in a sneer as she took in the others. "Every one of you used me. And I'll have my vengeance."

Ramsey didn't know what pained him more, that Tara actually believed the words she was saying or that Declan had harmed her in the process of turning her to his side. Because Ramsey knew Tara may not show physical harm, but Declan had hurt her. Ramsey would stake his life on it.

"Think what you want," Ramsey said before anyone else could reply. "You claim it is the truth you have now. Do you remember before? Running from Declan because he's evil?"

Tara laughed. "It was you and the rest of the Warriors I was running from. I remember the maroon Warrior in Edinburgh." Tara then looked to Isla, Larena, Fallon, and Broc. "I remember all of you chasing me."

Isla started to respond, but Ramsey held up a hand to stop her.

He turned back to Tara. "Think what you will. For now, you'll stay in here. There will be food brought to you, and anything else you might need."

"I need out."

"Except that," Ramsey said, and released a breath.

Tara folded her arms over her chest. "So you plan on keeping me here forever? Wasn't it enough that you made me think my family evil so I would run from them? Wasn't it enough that I spent ten years looking over my shoulder and running from everything I considered a threat?"

Ramsey didn't reply. He knew there was nothing he could say to Tara that would change her mind. And getting inside her mind to try and alter whatever Declan had done wasn't an option now that Tara had effectively locked everyone out.

It took everything Ramsey had to turn and walk away

from her, especially when all he wanted to do was take her in his arms. Had he finally found a woman who fit in his world and touched his soul only to lose her?

It wasn't until Ramsey was back in the great hall that he noticed how his fellow Warriors surrounded him, the Druids standing in a larger circle around his brethren. He saw the worry and concern etched onto the Warriors' faces.

"Say something," Larena urged.

Ramsey had learned early on that as the only female Warrior, Larena could hold her own against any of them. Anyone that underestimated her quickly realized their mistake.

"What do you want me to say?" Ramsey asked. "Declan has effectively altered Tara's mind by some form of torture. I have no idea how deep Declan has gone, or if it can be reversed."

Camdyn crossed his arms over his chest. "Or if we should."

There was that, but Ramsey didn't want to think that far ahead. He wasn't ready to give up all hope just yet.

"What's your plan?" Broc asked.

Ramsey wasn't surprised Broc would know he'd already begun forming a plan. While in Deirdre's mountain they had formed countless strategies for every conceivable option.

"I'm going after Declan." The announcement didn't seem to alarm everyone as Ramsey had expected.

Logan nodded, his face thoughtful. "When do you leave?"

"Now."

It was Fallon who shook his head and said, "Nay, Ramsey. Give it some time. Think about this."

"For once I'm no' going to think. For once I'm going to act. Declan used Tara. He would have her kill us all and go to him. The first chance she gets she's going to escape," Ramsey said, realizing his voice had risen.

He took a breath and looked at the faces around him. "I beg each of you, doona let your guard down with Tara. She thinks we're the ones who have harmed her. She's like a cornered animal now, and she'll strike at any of us."

"I hear you," Lucan said. "But I agree with Fallon. Give it a day, Ramsey. Let us plan."

"Us?" he repeated and smiled wryly. "There is no 'us.' By the time I'm finished with Declan I may no' even be here. I doona want any of you near his mansion because of it."

Hayden snorted and raised a blond brow. "If you think I'm going to allow you to go to that evil place alone, then you'd better lock me in the dungeon as well."

"Hayden's right," Arran said. "Declan's forces might have outnumbered us in the north, but we nearly got him."

Ramsey raked a hand through his hair. "That was on neutral ground. At his mansion there will be spells and wards preventing anyone from gaining accesses."

"Unless you're a Druid," Larena said as she looked pointedly at Ramsey.

Charon chuckled. "She's got a point. Think what we could do if Declan believes only Ramsey has come for him. Think of how easily we could take out his forces."

Ramsey couldn't believe everyone didn't understand how important it was that he go alone. Even Galen and Fallon who had witnessed him supposedly glowing, and Arran whom he'd nearly killed agreed that they should all attack.

"I know I'm no' one of you, but I've listened to all this with interest."

Ramsey turned to find Phelan behind him leaning against the wall, one foot braced on the stones. "And?" Ramsey asked.

Phelan's blue-gray eyes met his. "If we're going to take this son of a bitch out, then it needs to be done with all of us. And aye, before you say something sarcastic, Camdyn, I'm including myself in this."

"Then it's settled," Quinn said.

Ramsey knew he couldn't talk them out of coming, but he'd be damned if he would allow himself to harm them.

"This is shite, just so you know. But if any of you come, make sure you're far away when I use my magic."

"I agree," Fallon said. "I saw enough earlier to know that it's better for everyone."

Isla pushed her way past Hayden's form and glared first at Hayden then at Ramsey with her ice blue eyes. "If you think you're leaving us Druids out of this fight, you need to re-think things."

"Over my dead body!" Hayden shouted.

Soon Arran, Charon, and Phelan were standing with Ramsey as they watched the couples argue about whether the women were going or not. It didn't take long for the women to claim a victory.

Ramsey looked at everyone as the hall quieted down. "All right. But someone must stay here to make sure Tara doesna leave."

"That will be me," Fiona said.

Since she had very little magic they agreed to allow her to stay.

"Do you have a plan?" Broc asked Ramsey again.

Ramsey's smile was slow. "Oh, aye. I do."

CHAPTER
THIRTY-EIGHT

Declan tapped his finger on the arm of the leather sofa in his office as he sipped his whisky. Things couldn't have gone better with Tara.

The Warriors of MacLeod Castle had a habit of getting in the way, but Declan had found a way around them. Now nothing they could try would change what he'd done.

"When will she arrive?" Robbie asked as he refilled his glass with whisky.

Declan shrugged. "It doesna matter when Tara will arrive. She will. And that's all that matters."

"The MacLeods might try to keep her."

"They can certainly try."

Robbie turned and leaned against the sideboard while he swirled the whisky. "What did you do to Tara exactly?"

"Ah, that's the brilliant part, cousin." Declan leaned forward, wincing slightly as his body protested the sudden movement. "I wish I'd thought of this sooner. All these years wasted on trying to find Tara. Just think if I had had both her and Deirdre."

Robbie chuckled before he drained the whisky in one swallow. "Now that would have been something."

"Tara was strong, but with the right torture, I managed to break through her defenses in her mind and alter her perceptions of everything. Instead of fearing me, she now fears all the Warriors."

"That was brilliant. So she's now truly ours?"

Declan's gaze narrowed and he slowly sat back on the couch. "She's mine, aye. Mine to command."

"Of course," Robbie said hastily.

Declan took a swallow of whisky and asked, "Have you found more men?"

"I've got another three coming in tomorrow from South Africa. Do you really think the MacLeods would be stupid enough to attack?"

"I think they'll try." Declan wiped his mouth with his hand and thought again of the Warrior who had tried to gain access to Tara's mind. "There could be a Warrior who has grown attached to her."

"I'd say it was the one from Dunnoth Tower, but he's dead."

Declan made a sound in the back of his throat. "Aye. He should be. There's something that still bothers me about that entire event, cousin. Where was the Druid who sent that blast of magic?"

"I've no idea," Robbie replied with a slight shrug.

"Warriors can no' be Druids, right? There's nothing that would suggest that, yet . . ."

"You think there might be one?"

Declan clenched his jaw as pain radiated throughout his body when he gained his feet. He walked to his desk and sank into the high-backed black leather chair. After he set aside his glass he opened his laptop and pulled up the files he'd stored there on Druids.

"In all my years and all my research on Druids I doona remember anything that would suggest that any of us became Warriors."

Robbie walked around behind Declan and looked at the screen. "Surely if there was a Warrior who was also part Druid, he would have attacked Deirdre well before she grew too powerful."

A laugh escaped Declan, and he closed the computer. "You're right. I just can no' stop thinking of that Warrior or the magic that was sent at me." Magic that was even now eating at him, agonizingly slowly, but eating just the same.

"But think about it. If they had someone who was half Druid, half Warrior, he'd have already come to battle you."

"And no one will be able to defeat me, even if they try." Declan was smiling as he braced his hands on his desk and stood. "I think it's time for dinner, Robbie."

Declan didn't think any more about the MacLeods as he made his way into the dining room to the food that awaited him.

Ramsey, Broc, Isla, and Phelan were the first ones Fallon jumped to Declan's mansion. Within minutes everyone, including Fiona's son, Braden, and Marcail and Quinn's son, Aiden, were at Declan's.

Twenty-four pairs of eyes looked at Ramsey from their hiding spot about three hundred yards from Declan's mansion.

"I count only four guards patrolling," Camdyn whispered.

Broc grunted. "Aye, but I feel layers upon layers of magic."

"His spells," Ramsey said with a nod. "Declan wanted to make sure if we ever returned that we wouldna be getting into his house."

Logan's smile was huge when he said, "Because we scare the hell out of him."

Hayden elbowed Logan, but smiled just the same. "So what is the plan, Ramsey?"

Ramsey looked at Larena. "I'm going inside, but I willna be alone."

"Wait," Fallon said when he understood Ramsey's meaning. "Larena is a Warrior. She willna be able to get through those wards."

"By the time I'm through, you'll all be able to get in."

Larena placed a calming hand atop Fallon's and looked at Ramsey. "What do you want me to do?"

Ramsey looked past Larena's shoulder to the lights coming from the mansion. Dark was falling, and it needed to be deep into the night for Ramsey's plan to work, besides it would take him awhile to get through the spells.

"I want you to enter his house while invisible. Find Declan's room or wherever he keeps his spells. There will be a book or two full of them. I need them destroyed."

Quinn frowned. "Why? They're just spells, and he's probably memorized them by now."

"No, my love," Marcail said. "There are thousands of spells. We can't remember them all, which is why so many Druids write them down. It's why we have three books full of them at the castle."

Ian shifted in the snow. "Quinn's right. Why destroy them? Bring them back to the castle. There could be something in those spells that our Druids can use."

"Those books are full of black magic spells," Ramsey pointed out. "I doona think bringing them into MacLeod Castle would be ideal."

"I agree," Fallon said.

Isla caught Ramsey's gaze. "Wait. Not that I'm advocating the use of black magic, but not all the spells are evil. You know as well as I, Ramsey, that it depends on the Druid using it whether the spell is good or evil."

"If somehow Declan survives this, I doona want him to have anything to turn to," Ramsey said.

Hayden growled deep within his throat. "He willna survive this, my friend."

"Hayden's right," Broc said. "I know your plans, Ramsey. He willna survive."

Ramsey rubbed his jaw, his thoughts turning to Tara for a moment. "We need to wait until it's fully dark. I want each Warrior with a Druid wife to set up a circle around the mansion. No one gets out."

"I'm liking this," Gwynn said as she rubbed her gloved hands together.

He saw the anger in the Druids' eyes. All of them had been ready to battle Deirdre, but Gwynn, Dani, and Saffron hadn't really known who Deirdre was. But they knew Declan all too well.

They had also seen what he'd done to Tara.

"What then?" Logan asked.

"You stay there," Ramsey said. "No matter what you see, you stay there and fight, because once I'm inside, it willna take long for the others to try to leave."

Charon asked, "What about us who doona have women?"

Ramsey looked at Fallon. "Fallon, Larena will be inside, but I need you to stay with the others. As soon as Larena gets out with the books, I want both of you to remain outside the mansion."

"Done," Fallon said.

Ramsey then looked to the three who weren't mated. "Phelan, Charon, and Arran, when you feel the magic drop from around the mansion I need the three of you to get inside and make sure he's no' holding any more Druids. If he is, then free them."

"And if we happen to run into any of his mercenaries?" Phelan asked.

Ramsey smiled. "Do what you will."

"Is that all?" Arran's eyes were hard, his jaw locked as he prepared for the upcoming battle.

"Nay." Ramsey fisted his hands beside him and looked around at the group of people he called family. "Declan is mine. When we begin our battle I need all of you to keep a safe distance away from the mansion. I doona know how far my magic will reach when I unleash it all, but I'm no' going to stop until Declan is dead."

Hayden's lips flattened as he let out a long sigh. "I doona like that part of the plan, Ramsey. You said you've kept your magic at bay since you can no' control it because of your god."

"That's true. And being a Warrior only adds more to my magic. I can kill Declan, but I need to know that none of you will be harmed."

Galen swallowed hard and replied, "You have our word."

It was enough for Ramsey. He gave a nod and looked away.

"You heard Ramsey," Fallon said. "Everyone take their positions. I know it's cold, lasses, but your Warriors will keep you warm. Everyone, stay vigilant. This bastard has done enough to us already."

The others crept off among the shadows to take their positions around the mansion. Ramsey remained with Fallon, Larena, Phelan, Charon, and Arran.

"I'm finding it rather difficult to tarry when I know the arsehole is waiting to die," Arran said.

Charon looked at him and smiled. "You feel the need for another battle so soon, Arran?"

"Who doesna like killing evil?" Phelan asked.

Ramsey looked at the moon, tracking its ascent into the sky. It wouldn't be long now.

Tara thought she'd known real fear, but she hadn't truly experienced it until she'd woken to find herself locked in a dungeon.

A freaking medieval dungeon!

She tried to stay calm, but her heart was racing and the blood pounding in her ears was so loud it drowned out everything else.

Tara had to find a way out of the dungeon. She still couldn't believe she'd been fooled so completely by Ramsey and the others.

What hurt the worst was that she had fallen for him. Hook, line, and sinker. She should have known he was too good to be true.

"Oh," she gasped, and clutched her head as another headache slammed into her.

It felt as if a battering ram were being jabbed into the base of her neck and up into her skull. The pain made her see spots before her eyes, but she refused to black out. She had to stay awake, to stay focused and alive.

Tears gathered in her eyes as she realized who Ramsey

and the other Warriors really were. How they and the Druids she had thought were her friends had worked alongside Deirdre to bring evil into the world.

It sickened Tara to know she had lived among such evil, that she had considered making MacLeod Castle her home.

It also proved how strong the magic of the Druids at the castle really was. Not only could they hide the castle and prevent people from aging, but they could also make someone believe a lie as if they'd known it their entire life.

Tara wiped at a tear that escaped and sniffed. She wasn't going to cry. She'd been in tight situations before. No matter what, she'd get out of this one.

She thought again of Ramsey standing on the other side of the bars, pretending to be upset at her words. But there was no more pretending with her. She knew the real him, the real monster that he was.

There had to be some way to get out of the dungeon. There was an overwhelming urge for her to get out of the castle as fast as she could. The castle had gone eerily quiet, but she knew they wouldn't have left her all alone. There was someone at the castle. But who?

She wasn't left to wonder for long as the door to the dungeon creaked open and the sound of light footsteps could be heard descending the stairs from the great hall.

Tara watched Fiona as she came into view carrying a tray of food. She had once thought Fiona one of the kindest people she'd ever met. But that was before Tara knew the truth, before she knew how evil they all truly were.

"Are you hungry?" Fiona asked.

Tara just glared at her. "Why are you doing this? I've never harmed you."

"We're doing this for your own good."

Tara snorted in response. "My own good? Is that so? So is it for my own good that I'm locked in this medieval dungeon? Is it for my own good that you all tricked me?"

"We didn't trick you."

For a split second Fiona's face switched from gleeful cruelty to one of confusion and worry, her kind eyes full of concern.

Tara shook her head and squeezed her eyes closed. The movement caused the pain to slice through her mind again, but she refused to show Fiona any emotion save anger.

"Enough!" Tara shouted. "I'm tired of the lies."

"You don't know what you're saying."

Tara's eyes snapped open. "I know exactly what I'm saying. I'm going to get out of here, Fiona, and God help you if you try to stand in my way."

Fiona slowly set the tray down next to the iron bars. She straightened and dusted her hands off on her khaki pants. "You can try, but I'm afraid you won't leave this cell until the others return."

If there was one thing Tara had never been able to ignore, it was a challenge of any sort. And she'd heard exactly that in Fiona's voice.

Tara rose from the narrow cot and walked to the door so that she stood directly across from Fiona, only the iron bars separating them. "I have to leave. And I will."

Just saying the words sent a zing of magic shooting through her center outward to each arm and leg, down to her fingers and toes. The magic vibrated with potency inside her, urging her to use it, to feel its power.

"Get out of my way, Fiona," Tara warned.

Fiona shook her head and sighed. "There's no use in even trying. You'll only hurt yourself."

But Tara wasn't listening. No more would she hear the lies spoken from the lips of people she thought were her friends, people she thought were protecting her. Instead, they wanted to use her, to hurt her.

To kill her.

"No," Tara said more to the idea of anyone laying a hand on her rather than Fiona's comment. "I'm leaving this damned castle and never returning."

Fiona took a step back. "Tara, please. We're only trying to help."

A thrill went through Tara at the fear she saw in Fiona's

eyes. That added with her magic was all she needed. She reached for the bars and wrapped her hands around the iron.

The magic sizzled through her skin and into the metal. When she spotted a tendril of white smoke move from her to the bars, her breath caught in her throat as a memory flashed in her mind of seeing magic like that before.

But who had it wound around? It was a man, Tara was sure. But who?

She was jerked back to the present when the loud click of the door unlocking sounded in the silence. Tara swung the door open and cocked her head at Fiona.

"I told you I was leaving."

Fiona's mouth was hanging open, her eyes huge. "You . . . there's no way you should have been able to open the door. There was magic preventing it."

"Ineffective magic," she replied. But she recalled the single ribbon of magic and wondered.

Tara turned and started for the stairs. The quicker she was out of the castle, the easier she could breathe. But she had only taken two steps when Fiona grabbed her from behind.

They fell forward, Tara taking the impact of the fall. All the fear she'd been keeping inside erupted in that moment. She lashed out with her hands—and her magic—as she struggled to get away.

Her magic flew from her hands with a force that caused her heart to skip a beat, but she didn't think about it. Not even when she heard a strangled cry or when Fiona's body went limp did Tara stop to question it.

She shoved Fiona off her and ran up the stairs to the great hall. Tara stumbled as she pushed open the door and looked around the huge expanse of the hall.

Then she saw her coat hanging near the door and she rushed to it. She jerked it on and ran outside. Only to slide to a halt as she looked at the cars before her.

She smiled and rushed to the Land Rover. The Warriors never locked the vehicles, and always left the keys inside. Because who would dare to steal what they all shared?

Tara didn't care why they did what they did, only that she now had transportation to get away from MacLeod Castle. She slid into the seat and shut the door. The keys were in the ignition, and she wasted no time in starting the SUV.

She put the vehicle in reverse and pressed the gas as she buckled her seat belt. The SUV took a moment to move through the snow, and then she had it in gear and gunned it with both hands on the wheel.

The huge wooden gate was closed, and Tara thought she might have to ram through it, then she glanced up and saw a little remote hooked to the visor. She pushed the button. And to her delight, the gate began to open.

It wasn't until Tara was through Isla's barrier hiding the castle and on the main road that she felt relatively safe. She had no idea where she was going, only that she was putting more and more distance between her and the evil that had taken her.

A tear slid down her cheek, and then another and another.

She sniffed and wiped at the hated moisture. How could she have been so foolish as to believe they were the ones who would help her? How could she have been so naïve as to tell them all that she knew?

How could she have been so stupid as to fall in love with a monster?

That's what hurt the worst. Not that they had tricked her, but that she had believed Ramsey's words and his sweet caresses. She had thought he was someone special. The one.

The man she had been hoping to find for years.

Tara shook her head. "No. No more will I think of him. His memory and everything that happened between us was a lie. He's wiped from my mind."

If only that were the truth. But Tara knew better than anyone that if you told yourself something enough times, you'd eventually believe it.

She turned up the radio, blaring Godsmack as she drove. It wasn't until she pulled over to grab something to eat that she realized where she was headed.

"Declan," she whispered.

* * *

Malcolm tossed the remainder of his food in the trash. How he missed the taste of the food at MacLeod Castle. He was sure most of the food he ate in this modern world wasn't real. Processed. Everything was processed.

He rolled his eyes and stepped out into the clear night sky. After weeks of snow, the sky had finally cleared.

Malcolm glared at the café behind him, wishing he'd eaten at the restaurant he'd seen up the block, but he hadn't wanted to sit in a restaurant and have everyone stare at him because of his scars.

Now he wished he had, because at least then his stomach would be full.

Malcolm stepped off the curb and began to walk when Druid magic slammed into him, the force of it making him take a step back.

He looked around and spotted a black Land Rover drive past him. As soon as his gaze connected with the woman driving, he knew she was a Druid.

With just a second's hesitation, Malcolm turned around and watched the SUV pull into the same café he'd just left. He hid behind a car and watched the woman get out and walk into the café.

There was no doubt she was a Druid, but her magic was a curious mix of *mie* and *drough*, as if she didn't know what she was.

By the time the woman returned, Malcolm had climbed atop the Land Rover.

CHAPTER
THIRTY-NINE

Declan poured another glass of single-malt whisky into his glass. It didn't seem to matter how much he drank, nothing helped to dull the agony inside him.

The magic had slowed considerably, but still the black marks worked their way up and over his face, as well as his body.

His entire left arm and shoulder were covered with long, jagged black marks that reminded him of lightning that forked across a sky.

Declan held the glass up to his forehead and closed his eyes. He sighed wearily. The pain was manageable, and even if his looks were never restored properly, he could fix it with his magic.

Everything would be righted once he had Tara.

He opened his eyes with a smile as he caressed the small leather-bound book that had given him the spell he needed to access Tara's mind. Of all his spell books, this was the one he would treasure most.

Declan laid his hand flat over the book. A hiding spell fell from his lips that would keep the book hidden from his enemies.

Because no matter how many wards and spells he put around his home, or how many mercenaries Robbie hired, Declan knew the Warriors would come for him.

And he wanted them to.

Their interference would end as soon as they attacked. And Declan knew it wouldn't be long. Not after what he'd done to Tara.

He chuckled, marveling at his own cleverness. To make Tara think her friends were her enemies, and her enemies her friends. It was priceless, and she'd never know the difference.

There was no need to convince her to come to him. Not now at least. She thought he was her savior, so she would come on her own. And once at the mansion she would willingly become *drough*—thinking all the while she was doing good magic.

How different things would be had he done this ten years ago. The Warriors of MacLeod Castle would have been the first thing Declan got rid of.

"Soon," he murmured, and rose to replace the spell book behind two larger ones on the bookshelf.

Declan resumed his seat and reclined back in his chair with his ankles crossed and resting on his desk. This room was one that no one was allowed into except Robbie. This was his room where he did nearly all his spells.

The room where he had honed his magic over the years.

And the room where he had first encountered the Devil.

That day had forever changed his life. Because of it, this small room, sparsely furnished with only the bare minimum, was the place he came to dwell upon his magic.

Unlike his office, which was more for show than anything else. His office displayed his power and his wealth, and when he conducted business in it, it proved to his business associates that he wasn't someone to be trifled with.

Declan turned the ruby cuff link and clasped his hands over his stomach while he imagined how he would rule the world.

Tara slowed and then stopped the Land Rover as she neared Declan's mansion. Even in the dark and through the trees she could see the tall structure that lit up the night.

She'd left him when he had offered her sanctuary. Had run from him repeatedly, and feared him like no other. Would he see her? And more importantly, would he forgive her?

With a long sigh, she eased her foot on the gas pedal and drove into Declan's drive. The large metal gates blocked her entrance, but before she could lower the window and press the intercom, the gates opened.

Tara leaned forward and looked out the windshield. "Here goes nothing," she whispered.

She maneuvered the car around the massive fountain situated in the circular drive and parked at the front steps. Tara put the SUV in park and turned it off.

For just a moment she sat there, rehearsing how she would greet Declan. The all-too-familiar pain stabbed into her at the base of her skull.

Tara grabbed her head and gritted her teeth as the agony sliced through her. Images of people flashed in her mind like snapshots, but one repeated over and over.

It was Ramsey.

She slammed her hand against the steering wheel. "No. No!"

Instantly, the pain and the images stopped.

With a shaky breath she lifted her head. It was now or never. Tara opened the door of the Land Rover and stepped into the snow.

And waiting for her on the steps was Declan.

"I didna think you'd ever return to me," he said with a welcoming smile. "I'm glad to have you home, Tara."

When he spread his arms, she eagerly walked into them. "I'm so sorry for running from you," she said.

"Think nothing of it, lass."

Tara pulled back, and frowned when she saw the black marks over the left side of his face and down his neck. The marks weren't an elaborate tattoo.

"What happened?"

Declan shrugged. "It's nothing I can no' handle. Let's get you inside where it's warm. I have your old room waiting. And I did some shopping for you. I think you'll enjoy the clothes."

Tara didn't care about the designer clothes. All she wanted was to find a home, a place where she could feel safe and happy.

An image of MacLeod Castle flashed in her mind, but she pushed it away and smiled at Declan.

"What the hell?" Fallon murmured.

Phelan shook his head in confusion. "That's—"

"Tara," Ramsey finished for him.

Arran said, "I doona understand how she got free. I saw you put those spells on the prison, Ramsey."

Ramsey couldn't take his eyes off her. He clenched his hands when he saw Declan wrap his arms around her. A growl sounded deep in Ramsey's throat, the need for blood—Declan's blood—was fierce.

"Calm down," Charon said from beside him. "You willna do her any good if you lose control."

Ramsey didn't look away until Tara was inside the mansion and the door closed behind her. Then he raked a hand through his hair and paced behind the trees that blocked them from view.

"She shouldna have been able to get free," he said.

Fallon stood from beside Larena. "I'm going to return to the castle and see what happened. I'll be back soon. Doona start without me," he warned.

"We willna," Arran said.

Just seconds after Fallon teleported away, all five of them turned at once to the sound of approaching footsteps. And in a blink, they all released their god.

"Easy," Malcolm whispered when he came into view, his hands held up in front of him.

Larena gasped and tamped down her god. "Malcolm," she said, and ran to her cousin and hugged him.

Ramsey met Malcolm's gaze, and knew it hadn't been coincidence that brought Malcolm to Declan's estate.

"What are you doing here?" Larena asked him when she stepped back.

Malcolm glanced at Declan's mansion. "I felt a Druid, but no' just any Druid. The magic was . . . off."

"How so?" Ramsey asked.

Malcolm rubbed his chin thoughtfully. "Like her magic couldna decide if it was *mie* or *drough*. While she was in the café, I climbed atop the Land Rover to see who she was. Imagine my surprise when we arrived here. And I sensed other Druids."

"Her name is Tara," Larena said. "Tara Kincaid. We've been sheltering her from Declan."

One of Malcolm's brows lifted. "She didna appear afraid of him after what I just saw."

"That's because Declan switched her memories," Ramsey said. "She thinks the people who are her friends are now her enemies and vice versa."

"Damn," Malcolm murmured.

Phelan grunted. "That's putting it mildly, mate."

Malcolm sent him a flat look before turning back to Ramsey. "I'd have thought precautions would have been taken to ensure she didna leave the castle."

"They were," Arran answered.

Fallon appeared beside Larena, his face twisted with grief.

"What is it?" Larena asked. "What happened?"

But Ramsey knew the moment Fallon's gaze met his.

"Fiona is dead. By magic," Fallon said.

Larena covered her mouth with her hand and bent over at the waist, her tears as silent as the scream she kept locked within her.

Ramsey knew this because he felt the same way. What was worse was that he knew who was responsible for Fiona's death.

"This doesna mean Tara did it," Charon said.

Ramsey shook his head and looked at the mansion. "Declan turned her against us, and in doing so, made sure she would do whatever it took to get free."

"You think she killed Fiona?" Phelan asked.

Ramsey shrugged. "I'd have to feel the magic used on Fiona to know, but I think she did. No' on purpose though. Regardless of what Declan did to Tara, its no' in her to kill."

"I agree," Arran said.

Ramsey looked at Fallon to find him comforting Larena, their arms locked around each other. Yet, for all his talk, it wasn't just Declan who was responsible for Fiona's death. It was also himself.

He'd been the one to spell the prison. He'd been the one to make sure someone was left behind with Tara.

He'd been the one who was overconfident that Tara wouldn't be able to leave.

"Carrying the weight of the dead is a heavy burden," Malcolm whispered.

Ramsey looked into his blue eyes and nodded. "I'll have to tell Braden."

"Nay." Larena finally spoke as she wiped at her tears. "I'll do it. You feel responsible, Ramsey, but you aren't to blame."

Fallon stopped Larena when she started to walk away. "Let's wait until after the battle. Braden doesna need to be thinking of that when he needs to stay safe."

Larena nodded in agreement, but her tears didn't slow.

Malcolm stuck his hands in the front pockets of his jeans and looked at Ramsey. "So. What's the plan, and how can I help?"

CHAPTER
FORTY

The moon was high in the sky when Ramsey stepped out from behind the trees and made his way to the front door of the mansion. Declan's wards and spells didn't stop the Warriors from venturing onto his property, just the house.

Once again, Declan's arrogance was going to cost him. And if Ramsey had any say in it, the cost would be Declan's life.

Ramsey tried not to think of Tara as she had been at the castle when she tried to kill him or when he locked her in the dungeon. He tried not to think of her in Declan's arms, or the fact that she'd killed Fiona.

Instead, he remembered Tara as they had been the night before. Her smiles, her sighs. Her body sliding sensuously against him. The way she whispered his name as they lay wrapped in each other's arms after making love.

He would fight to return Tara to the woman she had been. If it came down to it, Ramsey was willing to die in order to gain her freedom from Declan.

It was then he realized just how deep his feelings went for Tara. Feelings deeper and stronger than he'd ever had for anyone.

Or ever would.

Ramsey paused beside the Land Rover and glanced inside it. To his right his enhanced hearing picked up a grunt that came from one of the mercenaries as his plan went into effect.

He waited as, one by one, the guards were killed.

"Ramsey?" Larena whispered from behind him.

She was already invisible, waiting for him to finish getting through the wards so she could carry out her part.

"Stay behind me," Ramsey said with a small shift of his head to the side. "You'll feel when the magic begins to fade. When I start toward the steps, you'll be able to get in. Doona wait on me. Get inside as quickly as you can."

"All right," came her soft reply.

Ramsey knew Larena would be safe. It was the only reason he had bid her to gain entrance. As long as she stayed invisible no one would even know she was there.

Anger that Ramsey had kept at bay rose within him like a tidal wave. It thundered, gaining momentum as it poured through him. And he didn't stop it.

He welcomed it, urged it. Embraced it.

Ethexia roared inside Ramsey, encouraging him to find Declan and rip his heart out. His god wanted blood and death, and for once Ramsey felt the same.

They had thought Declan wasn't the adversary Deirdre had been. They had been wrong, so very wrong. But it was time to right things, to mete out justice as only a Warrior and Druid could.

Ramsey called to his magic. His lips tilted up slightly as the magic eagerly answered him. It filled him, diminishing his anger so he could focus properly. A balance had somehow been struck, and it was all Ramsey needed to proceed.

He lifted his hands, palms out, toward the mansion. Because of his gift of being able to determine what kind of magic or spell was used, after just one touch of the wards around the mansion Ramsey knew how to remove them.

The words from the first spell his father had taught him tumbled from his lips. It wasn't a reversal spell so much as one that—if a Druid had enough magic—could destroy whatever magic stood in the way.

As the last word was spoken, Ramsey's smile grew when

the wards shattered. They couldn't be seen, but the magic could be felt as it melted away into nothing.

"You did it," Larena whispered.

But Ramsey didn't have time to answer her. The door to the mansion flew open to reveal Declan.

"I knew a Warrior would come to claim Tara," Declan said carefully as he took a step out of his home.

Ramsey didn't respond, allowing Declan to move farther and farther from the house. Ramsey wanted him as far from Tara as he could get him.

"Does he know the wards are gone?" Larena asked softly.

Without moving his lips, Ramsey said, "Nay."

"You should be dead," Declan continued. "We put several X90 bullets into you, Warrior."

Ramsey lifted his lips in a sneer. "I thought you knew, *drough*. Warriors are notoriously difficult to kill."

"No' if I sever your head," Declan spat angrily.

Ramsey laughed. It didn't take much to incense Declan. Which was just what Ramsey needed to know. "You can certainly try. I think you'll find it harder than you think. Tell me, how are you feeling?"

Declan's eyes narrowed. "I'm no' dead."

"No' yet. I can remedy that."

"Tara is mine, Warrior. Leave now, and I willna kill you."

Ramsey smirked. "I thought you knew us better than that. We doona walk away from what is ours. Hand her over to me now and fix whatever you've done to her, and I willna make you suffer before I kill you."

"You'll never get near me. I've warded the house with powerful spells," Declan taunted.

Ramsey lifted a brow. "Are you sure?"

"You willna be able to rest a foot on these steps."

Without another word Ramsey closed the gap between them and stood upon the bottom step. "You were saying?"

"How?" Declan murmured, his mouth gaping and his eyes bulging with confusion.

"I thought you knew of the Torrachilty Druids. If you did, you'd know that I was one."

"Nay," Declan said with a shake of his head.

"Oh, aye."

Ramsey sent a jolt of magic toward Declan which knocked him backward so that he tumbled inside the house. Something brushed past Ramsey, and he knew it was Larena.

"Robbie!" Declan shouted.

Ramsey slowly walked up the steps and into the mansion. "Your mercenaries are otherwise engaged."

"Robbie!"

"Keep shouting for help. There's no one to aid you now."

Out of the corner of Ramsey's eye he saw movement a second before Tara walked from a side room and into his line of vision to stand between him and Declan.

"There's me," she said.

Ramsey looked into her blue-green eyes and steeled himself for what was to come. "Get out of the way, Tara."

"I won't allow you to hurt him. He's done nothing."

"He's done more than you know!" Ramsey bellowed, unable to hold back the anger. "He held Saffron prisoner for three years, torturing her and blinding her to use her Seer abilities."

Tara shook her head. "You lie."

"He tried to take Gwynn as well. Logan nearly died saving her. Believe what you will about me or the other Warriors, but know what he's told you about the Druids is wrong."

Her gaze never wavered. "Are you done talking?"

Ramsey had just one more try before he knew he would have to take action. "What kind of man allows a woman to stand between him and death?"

Her brows knit and her gaze lowered for a moment.

"If Declan really opened his home to protect you, he'd have you safely away from this battle," Ramsey said, pressing the issue. He'd seen an opening, and he was going to do whatever it took to turn Tara.

"I didna ask you to step in the middle of this," Declan said as he gained his feet. "You did it, Tara, because you know how powerful you really are."

Her eyes lifted to Ramsey once more, though there was a hint of uncertainty in them.

"I've come for Declan," Ramsey said. "He's hurt too many people, including you. He needs to pay for his crimes."

Declan's laughter rang out in the foyer. "Tara knows the truth. She knows it's the Warriors who have done the killing."

"I admit I've killed," Ramsey said as he looked into Tara's eyes. "I've killed Deirdre, hundreds of her wyrran, and anyone who sought to harm innocents. It's my duty as a Warrior."

Ramsey fisted his hands as his magic burned, ready to be released upon Declan. He didn't want to have to move Tara aside, but unless he could convince her, he'd have no choice.

"Tara, remember," he urged. "Remember our time at the castle. Our nights. Remember the magic that flowed between us."

Tara had never been so uncertain of anything in her life. Ramsey's words made sense, yet every time she began to believe him, horrific images of him would fill her mind.

But amid those images she saw him smiling down at her, his silver eyes full of desire and tenderness.

She had the ability to read people, yet no matter how many times she tried to do that with Ramsey the pain at the base of her skull would explode.

It was all she could do to keep herself standing still as she listened to Declan and Ramsey. She didn't speak because she couldn't, not with the pain so intense and her confusion so thick.

Declan moved up behind her and put his hands on her shoulders. "He forced you, Tara. He took you without your consent. He just wants to make you believe there was something between the two of you. Look at him. Look at the monster he is."

Before Tara's eyes Ramsey, with his gray gaze and black,

wavy locks, suddenly became a monster with blood staining his hands. She blinked and Ramsey was once more the handsome man she recognized, though his gaze had shifted to Declan and in their gray depths Tara saw hatred so deep that she knew Ramsey would stop at nothing to kill Declan.

"You want to see a monster?" Ramsey asked. "I'll show you a monster."

Tara had witnessed Ramsey shift to his Warrior form, but seeing the deep bronze color penetrate his skin didn't frighten her as it should have. Neither did his long bronze claws or the fangs she saw when he peeled back his lips in a sneer.

It was the metallic bronze that bled into his eyes from corner to corner, overtaking the gray eyes she knew so well, that gave her pause.

She didn't know what to do. Did she stand before Ramsey to save Declan who had opened her eyes to who she really was? Or did she move aside because of the images she continued to see of the nights she'd spent in Ramsey's arms?

Which was the truth, and which the lie?

Who did she trust?

It was obvious one of them was lying, but Tara couldn't tell. She didn't want to be responsible for someone's death, but neither did she want to be the one who allowed evil to live.

She wanted to just back away, to pretend that she didn't know either of the men. But no amount of wishing could change the situation she was in.

"Last chance, Tara," Ramsey said. "Get out of my way, or I'll move you myself."

Could a man with a god inside him have loved her tenderly? Could a man who was immortal and had slain so many people be the one on the side of good?

Or was it the man hiding behind her? The one who used his money to buy whatever and whoever he wanted?

Who was the evil?

Tara met Ramsey's gaze, and she heard him say, "I love you," right before magic enveloped her.

Ramsey watched Tara crumple to the floor. He clenched his jaw, praying he hadn't killed her. But he knew how strong her magic was. He had to ensure that he got her out of the way for however long it took him to kill Declan.

"That was a nice touch," Declan said as he eyed Tara. "I doona appreciate you killing her."

"It's better than her falling into your evil hands. But doona worry, you slimy arse, your end comes tonight."

Declan gave a bark of laughter. "My end. Oh, I think no'."

Ramsey heard the retort of the gun a second before the bullet slammed into his heart. Three more followed in quick succession.

The bullets stung, but it was the *drough* blood leaking from the bullets that caused the real pain.

Ramsey lifted his gaze to the stairway above him to find Declan's cousin, Robbie, with the gun still aimed at him. When Robbie fired another two shots, Ramsey was able to move quickly enough to avert them.

And while he did, he made his way up the stairs to Robbie.

Robbie gasped when he realized Ramsey was beside him. He tried to turn the gun on Ramsey, but Ramsey reached out and gripped his arm.

"Why do you even try?" Ramsey said.

With a slight squeeze he broke Robbie's arm in two. The man cried out, clutching his arm. Ramsey lifted his hand, his claws out to sink into Robbie's chest, when he was thrown against the wall by a gust of magic.

Ramsey bellowed as he rolled to his knees and stabbed Robbie in the heart with his claws. He didn't look down to see if Robbie was dead. He knew he was.

Ramsey then leaped over the banister and landed in the foyer in front of Declan. "I've been looking forward to this moment a long time."

"The moment you die?" Declan said with a sneer.

"You really think you're going to come out of this the victor? I'm no' alone. All the Druids and Warriors are here.

They've taken out your men and invaded your home. You're all that's left."

Declan merely smiled. "If you knew the power I was given, you wouldna dare to challenge me."

"There willna be a challenge," Ramsey said as he leaped into the air and flipped over Declan as he sent a huge wave of debilitating magic into him.

CHAPTER
FORTY-ONE

Malcolm stood next to Phelan as the inside of Declan's mansion began to light up. The flood of magic that poured from the house was so forceful that Malcolm could feel it prickling his skin while they were still in the driveway.

"Ready?" Phelan asked.

Malcolm glanced at the gold Warrior and gave a single nod. "Let's go."

The two rushed into the mansion, dodging magic as they headed to where Tara lay. Phelan scooped the Druid into his arms and ran back out of the house.

But Malcolm remained.

He grinned as he saw the damage Ramsey had dealt Declan, but the grin faded when Malcolm took in the blood pouring down Ramsey's chest. It soaked his black shirt, making the tee look slick and sticky as it clung to Ramsey.

Malcolm was still behind Declan. He winced, but remained standing, when a couple of Ramsey's shots of magic missed Declan and landed on Malcolm. The magic coming from Ramsey was unlike anything Malcolm had ever experienced.

It was more powerful than Deirdre's and Declan's put together. And Declan had yet to realize it.

Malcolm understood then that Ramsey had been toying

with Declan up until that point. He hadn't wanted anyone in the house when he let loose his magic on Declan.

"Malcolm," a voice whispered next to him. "I need help."

He recognized Larena's voice. "What do you need?"

"I can't carry all the books Ramsey has requested."

Malcolm cursed beneath his breath. He caught Ramsey's gaze to let him know they weren't clear yet. With a sigh, he spun on his heel and raced to the stairway that led to Declan's dungeon and his private office.

Quinn stood side by side with his wife as they battled the mercenaries who tried to attack them from the house. On the other side of him was his son, Aiden.

And next to Aiden was Braden. Both were young men now, and Quinn hated that they were seeing so much death and evil. But the simple fact was that they needed all the Druids, no matter how much magic they had.

A bullet richoeted off a tree and grazed Aiden's arm.

"Careful, son," Quinn said.

The words weren't out of his mouth before Braden's body jerked backward and he fell into the snow.

"No!" Marcail screamed before she turned and sent a blast of magic to the merc who had dared to fire upon them.

Quinn rushed to Braden and gathered him in his arms. He'd watched him grow from a small boy into the man he was.

"Dad?" Aiden asked.

"He's gone, son. I'm sorry."

Aiden ducked his head to hide his sorrow. Quinn looked around at the Warriors and Druids fighting before he felt Marcail reach his side.

There had been so much death, so many innocents killed.

"This stops tonight," Quinn said.

He gained his feet and let out a bellow as he rushed to a mercenary who had come out of the mansion. Quinn raised his claws, his lips pulled back over his fangs.

* * *

Ramsey grimaced when he glimpsed Malcolm rushing below the house to the dungeon. The X90 bullets were doing their job, more slowly because he was half Druid, but they were beginning to affect him.

It was all he could do to keep from releasing all his magic on Declan as he longed to do. Only Tara had kept him from losing what little control he had.

When Phelan had left with her in his arms, Ramsey thought it would finally be over. How wrong he was.

He managed to block several of Declan's blasts of magic to keep the *drough* off balance. Even the use of his claws on Declan had had the intended effect and left him reeling.

But it hadn't been enough.

Ramsey had hoped and prayed he'd be able to overtake Declan without releasing all his magic, but somewhere deep inside him he'd known the truth. It was going to take it all to destroy evil such as Declan.

With a spin, Ramsey avoided another hit of Declan's magic full on, but he got a brunt of it that sent him staggering backward.

"I thought you were a Torrachilty Druid?" Declan shouted then lifted his lips in scorn. "You're nothing."

Ramsey felt his magic rise up, ready to answer Declan once and for all. He nearly lost control, but somehow he managed to yank his magic back.

"What? Do you no' like how my magic has altered your appearance?" Ramsey mocked as he motioned to the black veins that covered Declan while they circled each other.

"A minor inconvenience."

"Liar. You should be dead from it by now."

Declan laughed. "Ah, it depends on whether you have friends in high places. And I have the highest. Satan stopped the progression."

"Another lie," Ramsey said with a tsk. "He didna stop it. He slowed it. I know because if he'd stopped it, it wouldna have reached your face. Tell me, if he's so mighty and you're his favorite, why didna he heal you?"

Declan bellowed his fury and sent three short shots of magic at him.

Ramsey took each of them. He had no choice. His body wouldn't move as he told it to do, so there was no time to get out of the way.

Suddenly, Malcolm was once more in the foyer. He gave a nod to Ramsey and was gone. Ramsey didn't know how Larena had gotten out, only that she had.

Now that the house was clear, he didn't have to hold back any longer. The only problem was, he wasn't sure if he had enough strength to finish Declan.

He'd used so much of his force just to remain standing that he could feel himself fading. And quickly. There was no doubt now. Ramsey knew he wouldn't live after he released his magic.

It took incredible control and strength to pull back his magic, and he had neither at this point.

He was saddened deeply to be leaving Tara. His only hope was that the others could somehow, someway undo what Declan had done to her.

And that she remembered him in the years to come. For she would always be with him. In this life or the next, she was meant for him. He wished he had understood it sooner so they could have spent more time together.

At least he could free her of one evil.

Ramsey smiled and began laughing as he unleashed his magic and his god. If he was going to go out, he was going to make sure it was spectacular.

"What are you laughing at?"

Ramsey glanced at his hands that he held out to his sides. He saw them begin to glow over his bronzed skin, and soon the glow took over his entire body.

"Are you ready to die?" Ramsey asked.

Understanding dawned in Declan's blue eyes. "You were toying with me."

"Nothing of yours will survive this night. The evil inside you that affected all those around you will be wiped clean," Ramsey spoke calmly as he walked toward Declan.

"Nay. Please. I beg you. I'm no' ready to die."

"Neither were the ones you killed."

"Please!" Declan screamed and fell upon his knees.

But Ramsey ceased to hear him. He thought of Tara, of the love that had begun to blossom in his heart. Then he closed his eyes and poured all his magic into Declan.

It was the screams, the terrible, blood-curdling screams, that pulled Tara to consciousness. She opened her eyes to find herself lying upon a patch of ground that had been cleared of snow.

All around her were the Druids and Warriors from Mac-Leod Castle, their gazes locked on something. The men's faces were held in anguish, the women crying, some softly, some racked with pain.

Tara blinked, confused as to why she was outside and with those she thought of as her enemies. Yet, none of them had bound her or even watched her to make sure she didn't escape.

She turned to the house and her breath caught in her chest. Something was glowing so brightly she had to shield her eyes just to see. The light from the glow penetrated every window on the first floor, flooding the night with light.

The screams, she realized belatedly, were Declan's. They had faded away, but the glowing hadn't stopped.

"He's injured," Malcolm said into the silence.

Fallon's head snapped to the Warrior. "How badly?"

"I'm no' certain. There was blood. Lots of it."

"I heard gunshots while I was below," Larena said as she lifted her face from Fallon's chest.

I love you. Ramsey's words echoed in Tara's head from earlier.

Evil men didn't know they were evil. They thought they were in the right, which was why they always fought so hard against those who opposed them. And evil men could love.

The images of hatred in her mind about Ramsey were in stark contrast to the ones that remained of their nights together.

Regardless, Declan was dead. And Ramsey was soon to follow. Could she allow it? Could she live with herself?

Tara silently climbed to her feet and licked her lips. She recalled how much Ramsey hadn't wanted to use his magic for fear it would harm innocents.

Where that thought had been earlier, she didn't know. It had just suddenly appeared. The truth of that memory was undeniable.

She felt the gaze of someone and turned her head to find Charon staring at her. His eyes were inscrutable in the dark, but she could feel his anger and resentment.

Tara turned back to the house. Ramsey had yet to come out, and she had a sinking feeling he wasn't going to. If he was the evil Declan claimed him to be, why would that bother her so much?

Was she evil?

One moment she thought she knew who she was and who her friends were, and the next it got jumbled with memories of feelings of security and love while at MacLeod Castle.

Declan had claimed it was their magic convincing her of that, but now Tara didn't know what to believe.

"Why is Ramsey no' coming out?" Broc asked, his voice thick with emotion.

Tara looked down at her hands. A memory came to her, distant and so vague that she wasn't sure if it was a memory or a dream or a fantasy, but there had been white ribbons of magic swirling around her and through her.

That magic had been strong and true. That magic had been incredible.

That magic had come from Ramsey.

She jerked her eyes to the mansion and suddenly knew what she had to do. Tara ran as fast as she could to the front door, plodding through the thick snow. But she didn't slow. Not when the snow tripped her, and not when the others called for her to come back.

Not even when Gwynn's voice begged her to return because Ramsey wouldn't want her hurt.

Tara burst through the front door to find Ramsey still in

the foyer but with his back to her. She could see him, but his skin glowed, and the ribbons of magic she had remembered wound around him fast and thick.

"Ramsey," she said as she neared him.

The force of his magic made her take a step back, but it wasn't until she stood before him and saw his bronze Warrior eyes glowing that she knew he was lost to her.

She tried to touch him, but his magic burned her it was so fierce. "Ramsey," she said louder, and tried once more to touch him.

Her skin sizzled from his magic, but she didn't relent as she pushed through the glow and touched his bronze skin. Blood coated his front, and continued to seep from the four wounds in his chest.

She gasped when she saw one had entered his heart.

"Ramsey? Can you hear me? I need you to hear me."

Tara swallowed, the pain becoming unbearable. "I don't know who I am. I don't know what to believe. I need you to help me, Ramsey. I need you."

To her horror, Ramsey's magic continued to grow and spread. It swallowed her, the agony causing her to clench her teeth together to keep from crying out.

No wonder he had been so adamant about everyone staying clear of him. His magic was more than she could have ever imagined or dreamed of.

Tara wrapped her arms around his thick shoulders and buried her head in his neck. His breaths were uneven, ragged, as he struggled to draw in the next breath.

She could feel her skin burning, and knew if she didn't do something she would die soon. So Tara did the only thing she knew, she called to her magic.

It swarmed her, and instead of pushing against Ramsey's, it meshed with his. The pain began to ebb soon after. She wasn't given long to celebrate, however, as Ramsey fell to his knees and then onto his back.

Tara never released him. She braced her hands on the floor and leaned over him as she saw the tendrils of magic slow and move between the two of them.

She knew then, in that instant, that Ramsey wasn't her enemy. The feeling inside her, the love that had somehow been hidden, burst through at the moment the ribbon of magic touched Ramsey then her.

No amount of tricks or spells could hide what was between them. Everything in her mind began to right itself, but she didn't care. Her attention was on Ramsey as his life faded before her very eyes.

"Ramsey!" she yelled and touched his cheek. "Hear me. You have to return to me. Please."

His bronze skin vanished, and with it his claws, fangs, and his metallic bronze eyes. He blinked and his gray gaze focused on her.

"Ramsey?" she asked hopefully.

He lifted a shaky hand to her face and softly stroked her cheek. Then his eyes closed and his hand dropped to the floor.

"Ramsey!"

A large hand touched her shoulder, and she lifted her head to find Phelan.

"Let me," he said.

Tara looked back at Ramsey.

"You took his magic into yourself," Dani said from beside her. "You saved him. Now let Phelan do the rest."

Tara climbed off Ramsey and watched as Phelan cut away Ramsey's shirt with a claw. After a quick swipe of that same claw of his arm, Phelan let a few drops of his blood enter into each wound.

As soon as Phelan was done, Tara once more leaned over Ramsey. She smoothed Ramsey's wet hair away from his face and waited for him to open his eyes.

"Please," she begged Ramsey and God. She rested her forehead against his and did nothing to stop the tears that fell. "Please don't let me lose him."

"Why?" said a deep voice she knew all too well.

Tara heard someone gasp as she opened her eyes and looked into gray ones. "Because he said he loved me. Because he didn't give up on me. And . . . because I love him with all my heart."

"Is it really you?" Ramsey asked.

Tara nodded. "I'm back. I don't know how exactly, but somehow our magic reversed whatever Declan did."

His arms wrapped around her and held her tight. "I thought I'd lost you."

"Never," she whispered.

Ramsey rolled her onto her back and leaned up to look at her. "I'm no' going to waste another moment without you. I want you beside me always, Tara Kincaid. Will you marry me?"

Joy so brilliant and bright shone through Tara she thought she would burst from it. In all her dreams she had never thought to be so happy, and like Ramsey, she wasn't going to let go of it.

"Yes. Of course!"

Amid Ramsey's laughter and smiles she heard the others cheering, but she only had eyes for her man. Her Warrior.

Her Highlander.

EPILOGUE

Spring had come early to MacLeod Castle. The sun was bright in a clear, blue sky, and the castle was filled with happiness.

Tara smoothed her hand down the front of her Versace silk dress that was decorated with hand-sewn beads and pearls. She stared at a woman she had thought would never be in the full-length mirror.

Not just happy, but confident. And loved.

"Are you sure you're happy with your hair?" Saffron asked for the third time as she walked into Tara's room.

Tara laughed and locked eyes with Saffron in the mirror. "You flew one of the premier hairstylists in all of London to the castle blindfolded. Five times. Just so we could get the hairstyle right. It couldn't be more perfect."

And that wasn't all Saffron had done. She and the others had spent the last two months shopping for a wedding dress with her, finding the right makeup, jewelry, and shoes.

All the women had bonded so well, that she knew nothing would ever pull them apart.

Saffron came up behind her and rearranged the long sheer veil that fell to the floor and flowed behind Tara's white silk gown. "You look radiant. Are you ready?"

"I've been ready."

"Good, because Ramsey is about to come get you himself," she said with a laugh.

But Tara knew she wasn't joking. Ramsey had told Tara she could have whatever kind of wedding she wanted, and when she'd told him a traditional one in a church, he hadn't batted an eye. He just hadn't anticipated having to wait two months for the ceremony. But that was the quickest they could have the dress made.

With one last look at herself, Tara followed Saffron out of the chamber and down to the great hall. A small bouquet of pale yellow and lavender roses awaited her. She lifted the flowers to her nose and inhaled their scent.

When she spotted the two white roses she had requested in the middle for Fiona and Braden, she had to blink back tears.

Braden had never known she had been the one to kill his mother, and it was a weight Tara would carry with her until the day she died.

Saffron took her elbow, and together they walked from the castle into the bailey and then to the small chapel where all the Warriors had married.

"Oh," Tara murmured when she saw all the yellow and lavender roses and tulips decorating not just the outside of the chapel, but inside as well.

Saffron gave her arm a small squeeze before she hurried into the chapel to stand next to Camdyn.

Tara's gaze was drawn to the front of the chapel where Ramsey stood in a dark green, red, and navy kilt, his gaze locked on hers. She knew her smile was as big as her face, but she didn't care.

The music began and Tara made herself take slow, measured steps down the small aisle to Ramsey instead of running to his side as she wanted to do.

And when she finally reached him, he took her hand and said, "You look stunning."

"As do you." She knew he had been born in a time when they didn't wear kilts, but a clan's plaid had still been important. "I think you should wear your kilt all the time."

The voice of the pastor, who had also been flown in blind-folded, filled the chapel.

"I love you," Ramsey said.

She smiled. "And I love you."

Malcolm stood at the back of the church. Declan was dead, and though he hadn't been the one to kill him, at least the evil was gone.

But now what was he to do?

It had been the need to end the evil that had kept Malcolm going. Where was he to go now?

He should have known that staying at MacLeod Castle for any length of time would get him caught up somehow with something Fallon wanted him to do.

Just as they left the church for the celebration in the castle Fallon said, "I have need of you, Malcolm."

"You have others."

"Aye, but if you doona do this, Larena will."

Malcolm stopped walking and faced his cousin's husband. "Doona use Larena."

"She's my wife. I want to protect her."

"She's a Warrior, Fallon. She can take care of herself."

"One day, you'll find a woman who will seep into your heart and soul. Then you'll understand my position."

Malcolm ran a hand down his face. "What do you want of me?"

"I need you to go to London. See if you can find anything about articles that were taken from Edinburgh Castle in 1132."

"You think this spell you are looking for is in London?"

"We doona know. There were three shipments. Two by land, one by water. One by land and the one by water reached London. One went missing. We need to know if the spell is in the one that went missing."

Malcolm nodded. "I'll do this."

"Good." Fallon clapped him on the back. "Now come and have some cake and whisky."

Malcolm was slow in following Fallon. He wasn't sure

how he felt about the assignment. Part of him was relieved to have something to do, but another part of him feared that he would become the monster he knew he was if he left Mac-Leod Castle.

Jason Wallace shifted uncomfortably in his chair. He'd come at the request of a Mr. MacCray, who was most insistent.

Jason wasn't the type who stayed out of trouble with the law; the request had been . . . worrisome. When he hadn't shown up to two of the meetings, he'd woken this morning to find four men at his flat who had brought him to this posh office.

The door to the office opened, and a man walked in. He wore a dark suit, perfectly tailored. He had a full head of hair that was more silver than black, but his brown eyes were sharp, intelligent, as they landed on him.

"Well, Mr. Wallace, I'm glad to finally have you in my office."

"Mr. MacCray," Jason said as he scooted to the edge of his seat.

MacCray held up a hand. "Before you start, let me interrupt you. It seems, Mr. Wallace, that you are the surviving member of the Wallace family. I'm sure you saw the headlines that Declan Wallace was killed in the fire that destroyed his home?"

"Aye."

"Since you are the next in line to the family's fortune, I'm pleased to tell you that you've inherited everything that was Declan Wallace's."

Jason licked his lips, already mentally spending the money on trips and suits. "Everything?"

"That's right." MacCray slid a piece of paper across his desk to Jason. "Just sign here, Mr. Wallace, and you'll be leaving my offices wealthier than most in the UK."

Jason didn't hesitate to sign the papers. All he could think about was the money and paying off his gambling debts. Of being an important man so that people couldn't ignore him anymore.

He set down the pen and slid the paper back to MacCray. "Was the mansion completely destroyed?"

"No' all of it."

"Good. I visited there often as a lad. I'm anxious to make it my home. And everything inside is mine?"

"Everything."

Jason left the office with his head held high. There would be no returning to his roach-infested flat. He was going to his mansion.

Read on for an excerpt from

MIDNIGHT'S KISS

—the next Dark Warriors epic from
Donna Grant and St. Martin's Paperbacks!

Arran parked the Range Rover and looked through the windshield at the chaos before him. A sizzle of magic rushed over him. He was definitely in the right place.

He'd been told by Saffron that the excavation site was run by Dr. Ronnie Reid, who was one of the best archeologists to ever come out of the field.

Arran had also been warned that Dr. Reid ran a tight operation, so he'd have to be careful while he searched for any clues to the missing spell.

Not that Arran was concerned about this Dr. Reid. He would put himself in the good graces of the man, and make sure Reid saw him was a good worker. Once that was established, then Reid would leave him alone.

Thereby giving Arran the time he needed to look around.

He sighed. He'd thought this mission would be a quick one, but as he watched the dozens of people moving back and forth from the dig sites hauling away dirt, while others were prone on the ground dusting possible finds with what looked like paint brushes, Arran realized this was going to be anything but simple.

In all likelihood he'd been here several weeks.

Not that he was upset about it. With no more evil to fight, Arran had been bored. It wasn't that he wanted evil around, it was just that the god inside him craved battle, yearned for bloodshed.

Demanded death.

What better way to appease his god than by battling evil?

Arran let out a long sigh. There would be no clashes at the dig site, which meant he would have to find another way to work off some of the pent-up energy he felt thrumming through his body.

Exerting his muscles with physical labor was just the thing.

Arran opened the door and got out of the Range Rover. The wind was howling across the land, and a glance at the evening sky showed that rain was on the way.

He closed his door and quickly opened the back passenger door to grab his duffle and backpack. Saffron had assured him that lodgings would be made available to him. In a way Arran was hoping there wasn't anything. It had been a very long time since he'd slept under the stars as he'd used to four hundred years ago.

After adjusting the bags on his shoulders, he shut the door and looked at the site once more. The summer sky was still light despite it being past nine in the evening. It wouldn't get truly dark until well after midnight, yet lights standing tall around the dig had already been turned on.

"Here we go," Arran said and started toward the site, the feel of magic growing with each step he took.

He'd barely gotten ten steps in before he was dodging people who assumed he'd get out of the way. Since there was a possibility they were carrying magical ancient items, they were right.

But still, a low growl sounded deep within his throat.

He was a Warrior, a man used to being feared. It didn't set well that he was dismissed as easily as he was.

Arran made his way to a man with thin, windblown white-blond hair and glasses he kept shoving up his nose. The man was bony, his shoulders already hunching forward despite his being as young as the mid-thirties, if Arran guessed right.

"Excuse me," Arran said as he reached the man.

For several moments Arran was ignored. The man glanced up from the clipboard in his hand as he scribbled something on the papers with his pencil.

Arran raised a brow when the man seemed to look right through him.

Then, a double-take later, the man took a step back, his blue eyes wide. "Dude. How long have you been standing there?" he demanded, his American accent thick.

"Longer than I'd like," Arran replied, giving just enough inflection in his voice to tell the man his irritation was rising.

"Oh. Yeah. Sorry 'bout that. I tend to get involved with my work. I'm Andy Simmons, the site manager."

"Arran MacCarrick," he said and held out his hand.

Andy shook it with a grip that was much stronger than he appeared. "You arrived earlier than I expected. I was just told a few hours ago that you'd be helping out."

"I was eager to get here," Arran said with a smile.

"We're glad to have you. Anyone connected to Ms. Fletcher . . . er . . . Mrs. MacKenna, is a friend of ours. Sorry. I'm still getting used to the fact that Saffron is married."

"Aye. To a verra good friend of mine. Saffron knows how interested I am in the history of my land, and when she told me about the dig, I wasna about to let the opportunity pass." Arran wondered if he'd layered on the lie a little too thick, but Andy just nodded as if he understood.

"You either love archeology or you don't." Andy shoved his glasses up his nose again and jabbed the pencil behind his ear. "Everyone seems to think it'll be like the *Indiana Jones* movies."

Arran just chuckled along with Andy since he hadn't watched those movies and had no idea what Andy was referring to.

"Can you point me to Dr. Ronnie Reid? I'd like to get acquainted," Arran said.

There was a loud pop followed by static and someone's disembodied voice yelling Andy's name. Andy jumped and reached for the walkie-talkie strapped to his waist.

"Dr. Reid is there," Andy pointed over his shoulder before

he clicked the walkie-talkie and began a conversation while walking away.

Summarily dismissed, Arran let his gaze wander the site. Since he didn't know what Dr. Reid looked like, he began to search for someone who appeared to be in charge.

His gaze paused when he found himself looking at the nicest bum he'd seen in a long time. The woman wore tight, faded jeans that looked well worn, as if they were her favorite.

The wind paused, allowing the back of her tan jacket to fall into place, instantly hiding her backside from his view. Arran frowned. He'd liked what he'd seen, though he wasn't there to flirt.

Just before he looked away, the man beside the woman caught his attention. The man was older, his full beard more gray than black. A wide-brimmed, khaki-colored hat rested upon his head. He was speaking while the woman nodded her head of wheat-colored hair pulled back in a low, loose bun.

Arran knew he'd found Dr. Reid. Without hesitation he walked to the duo. His curiosity about what the woman looked like caused him to change course so that he came up from her right side instead of from behind her.

His gaze slid over her at his leisure, and it was too bad he couldn't give her the attention he wanted to. Her face was a golden bronze from her time in the sun. Her boots were muddied and as well worn as her jeans, proving she didn't mind getting dirty.

The long-sleeve plaid shirt he glimpsed under her jacket was tucked into her jeans and showed off her breasts. But it was the gold chain with the trinity knot dangling just above her cleavage that intrigued him.

It wasn't just any piece of jewelry. It was ancient, and Arran would bet his immortality that she had unearthed it herself on some dig.

Where, he'd like to know.

There was another crackle of magic, and for an instant Arran thought it might come from the woman. It could be coming from the pendant, yet he wasn't taking any chances.

The magic was *mie* magic, or good magic. The *mie*s were the ones who used the magic nature gave them to heal and to help things grow. They were the ones who had counseled the leaders of the clans, the ones who had educated the young.

Had he felt *drough* magic, black magic, he would have sought the source immediately and ended it. Because *drough*s were evil. They gave their souls to Satan in order to use black magic.

The feel of their magic was cloying, sickening, whereas the feel of *mie* magic was calming to a Warrior.

As far as he knew, only Warriors could sense or feel the magic of the Druids. It had saved his brethren more times than he wanted to count.

The woman glanced at him, her hazel eyes barely giving him a second's notice as she went back to her conversation.

A smile pulled at Arran's lips. It was too bad he didn't have time to pursue the woman, because he loved a good challenge, and that's exactly what she'd be.

"Dr. Reid," Arran said to the older man as he walked up.

Except it wasn't the man who answered, "Yes?"

Arran looked at the woman to his left and narrowed his gaze. He jerked his gaze back to the man. "Ronnie Reid?"

There was a long suffering sigh before he heard, "Right here, imbecile," to his left.

Arran's eyes jerked to the woman. "You?"

"Yes," she said with a roll of her eyes. "Why is everyone so surprised?"

"Maybe because you use 'Ronnie' as your name."

The older man chuckled, but kept quiet when Ronnie sent him a scorching glare.

"Listen, I don't know who you are, but let's get this straight once and for all. I'm Dr. Veronica Reid, also known as Ronnie. Understood?"

"There's no need to get riled, lass," Arran said to calm her. By the way her hazel eyes blazed, he knew he'd said the wrong thing.

"Really? No need?" Ronnie asked, her American accent

getting higher the more irritated she got. "How would you like everyone questioning who you were?"

"Ronnie," the man said as he tried—and failed—to hide his smile. "Give him a break. He can't know you've had a bad day."

Ronnie closed her eyes and took a deep breath. When she looked at Arran again, all her anger was gone. "Forgive me. As Pete so wisely put it, you can't know about the day I've had. I had no right to get riled, as you put it."

"No harm done. I'm Arran MacCarrick."

She winced when she heard his name. "Saffron said you were coming. I know first impressions are important, Mr. MacCarrick, but I hope you'll forget mine."

Arran had no such plans, but he didn't tell her that. Besides, he liked what he'd seen. Maybe a little too much. But the fact she was *Dr.* Reid definitely put the brakes on any kind of flirting he might have thought of doing.

"Doona think twice about it, Dr. Reid."

"Please," she said as she held out her hand. "Call me Ronnie. Any friend of Saffron's is a friend of mine."

Arran took her small hand in his. As soon as he was alone he was going to call Saffron and let her know her little jest about keeping Ronnie's identity as a female a secret hadn't been a funny one.

He'd wondered why she had intentionally left out what Ronnie had looked like. At first he thought she was just preoccupied with the baby, but now he knew the real cause.

Yet, for all the reasons he was irritated with Saffron, Arran was more than pleased with what he saw of Ronnie.

Her wheat-colored hair and hazel eyes stood out against the dark bronze of her skin. She wore no make-up, but then again she didn't need it. She had perfect skin, marred only by a small scar on her chin.

With almond-shaped eyes, high cheekbones, pert nose, and wide, full lips, there wasn't anything about Ronnie that wasn't feminine and altogether too alluring.

She was the kind of woman who would look great whether dressed in a formal gown, or as she was with jeans, shirt, and coat dusted with dirt and mud.

She was the kind of woman Arran liked. The kind that he'd never been able to find.

The irony didn't go unnoticed by him. "Call me Arran, please."

"I'm Pete Thornton."

Arran reluctantly released Ronnie's hand and shook Pete's. "How do you factor in this dig?"

Pete looked at Ronnie and they both laughed, but it was Pete who answered. "I was Ronnie's professor at Stanford. She had a love for archeology I'd never seen before. And her knack for finding things is unparalleled."

"Is that so?" Arran grew more intrigued about Ronnie Reid the more he discovered about her.

"Enough, Pete," Ronnie said with a smile. "You know sometimes we get lucky in our digs, and sometimes we don't."

"Ah, but you're luckier than most."

"Come, I'll show you to your tent," Ronnie said to Arran.

With a wave to Pete, Arran followed her as they walked across the roped-off area that allowed them to dig, while keeping others out.

Thousands of conversations, shouts, the sound of shovels plunging into the ground, and even that of hammers striking rocks filled the air.

As if reading his mind, Ronnie smiled. "No one ever realizes how loud dig sites can be."

"Aye. I wasna expecting this. The noise, nor the sheer amount of people."

"We could use about a dozen more. So this is your first archeological dig?"

"It is. I willna be a hindrance though."

Arran didn't miss the way she looked him up and down once they reached the set of tents that stood in a semi-circle in front of dozens of caravans.

"No, I don't expect you will be. Why my dig though?"

"It's my country. I want to see what the past holds."

She gave a small nod of acceptance. "This is your tent. You'll be sharing it with Pete for a few nights before he returns to the States for business."

Arran ducked into tent through the zippered opening. He saw two cots, one on either side. It wasn't optimal since he'd have to share, but it could have been worse.

"This will do fine," he said over his shoulder before he tossed his two bags on the freshly-made cot.

Ronnie tried not to look at his ass, she really did. But she'd never seen a man fill out a pair of jeans the way Arran MacCarrick did.

In one word, he was yummy.

From his wide shoulders and muscular chest, to the way that chest narrowed, to jeans resting low on slim hips and encasing long legs. Ronnie would bet that beneath that black tee were abs so defined she'd be able to count every single one of them.

The newest member of her team was friendly enough, but she didn't miss the way his gaze moved around the site as if trying to study everything without being seen.

Saffron had funded many of Ronnie's digs, so Ronnie wasn't about to say no to Saffron when she asked if a friend could help on the site. Yet now Ronnie had the urge to call Saffron and learn all she could about the man.

It wasn't just his rugged good looks that set her off-kilter. It was the gleam in his golden eyes, the way he stood, as if he was ready for battle.

Which was silly, because there was nothing to fight.

Ronnie chuckled to herself.

"What is it?" Arran asked when he straightened.

She shook her head and grinned. "Every time I come to Scotland I find myself thinking I'll see men with swords strapped to them, ready for battle."

He didn't laugh as she had expected. Instead, he gazed at her with his amazing golden eyes, an intensity about them that made it difficult for her to draw breath.

Dark brows slashed over those eyes amid a high forehead. A wealth of hair so dark a brown that it almost appeared black was kept long and hung around just to his shoulder. He had impossibly long, thick eyelashes, and the dark stubble on his chiseled cheeks and square jaw only added to his appeal.

Then there were his wide lips, which were fuller than a man's ought to be. They made her think of kissing, of long, sensual kisses where she'd forget everything but the man touching her.

As a total package, Arran was the kind of man who drew heads wherever he went. Women wanted him, and men wanted to be him.

Ronnie knew what came with having a man like Arran around. Every instinct told her to have him leave, but she needed extra hands around. And she couldn't refuse Saffron's request.

"You're no' off the mark," he finally said, drawing her out of her thoughts. "My land has seen countless battles as men fought to rule us."

"You speak as if you've lived here from the beginning of time."

He shrugged. "Maybe I have, in a past life."

Ronnie normally dismissed such inane sayings, but somehow, she believed it when Arran said it. Maybe not that he'd lived another life, but that he was much more than he appeared to be.

He was dangerous. Of that she was sure.

Dangerous to her psyche. Dangerous to her capacity to forget him as she had done so many other men.

He was captivating, charming, and entirely too interesting.

"Why do I get the feeling, lass, that you doona want me here?" Arran asked.

"Because men like you—"

"Men like me?" he interrupted.

"Yes, good-looking men who come to the digs distract the women. They flirt and get involved instead of focusing on the dig. People can get injured, artifacts lost, broken or even stolen, and any number of things when people aren't concentrating on their tasks."

"So, you think I'm handsome," he said with a crooked grin.

Ronnie sighed and rolled her eyes. She had the urge to

return his smile, but she had learned her lesson long ago with such dangerous, gorgeous men.

"What I think is beside the point. You're here because Saffron requested it. I know her. There's a reason you're here, and if you're her friend, I just want to ask that you remember that when the women begin to take notice of you."

His smile disappeared and his gaze narrowed on her. "I know my duty. You willna have a problem with me sniffing around any of the women. I canno' help if they come to me, but I give you my word I will dissuade them."

This Ronnie hadn't expected. "Uh . . . thank you."

"I'm many things, Ronnie, but I wouldna think of compromising this dig, or you."

She shifted from foot to foot feeling like an ass for saying all those things to him. "I just needed you to understand."

"And you did, lass. Doona fret over it anymore. My hide is thicker than most, so it'll take more than your honest words to rile me."

"I'd almost like to see that," she said with a grin. Though as soon as the words were out she wasn't sure where they had come from.

She cleared her throat. "Why don't you take the rest of the evening to look around? We're wrapping things up for the night, and Andy and Pete are around if you need anything. First thing in the morning, I'll give you your duties."

"Sounds good. Only, you might want to think of covering that," Arran said as he pointed to the twelve-foot-by-four-foot section that was being excavated. "There's about to be a downpour."

"They said not until sometime tomorrow."

"Scottish weather is as fickle as I've seen. You canno' trust what weathermen say. You have to learn to read the weather yourself, lass."

Ronnie looked at the section. They'd dug just four inches, but already they had found bits of broken pottery. If it rained, there was no telling what would get washed away.

Yet, if they covered it now, it would put them behind schedule.

The other six sections they had been digging on for over a month were already covered to shield ninety percent of the rain.

Ronnie glanced at the sky before she looked at the new section. There was something important underneath all that dirt. She knew it in her soul.

She felt it.

It wasn't something she told anyone, but that same feeling was what had led her to so many finds on her past digs.

"Andy," she called. "Cover the new section ASAP. Rain is coming!"

Andy gave a nod, and instantly the diggers moved while others hurried to cover the section. Ronnie was surprised when Arran rushed to help.

So surprised that it took her a moment before she followed suit. As they all struggled with the bright blue tarp the wind howled around them, trying its best to jerk the canvas out of their hands.

It wasn't until the tarp was staked securely in the ground that Ronnie looked up. And found golden eyes watching her.

A heartbeat later, the first fat raindrop landed on her cheek. Before she could gain her feet the heavens had unleashed a rainstorm like none she had ever seen.

While everyone rushed to get out of the driving rain, Ronnie checked the stakes one more time before she moved on to the other tent-like structures that had been erected over the sites.

The rain soaked through her jeans, but her jacket, which was waterproof, helped to keep her upper body mostly dry. The way the wind lashed the rain couldn't stop all of it.

And the droplets running down her face and head and into the neck of her shirt were quickly drenching her.

As she checked on the ropes of one structure covering a dig, another came loose and began to flap wildly in the wind.

Ronnie jumped for it, but it seemed to flap higher, as if teasing her. Suddenly, a shadow loomed behind her as a large hand grabbed the rope.

She jerked around to find Arran. He blinked the rain out

of his eyes, and with a nod, knelt to retie the knot. She didn't watch him or the way the wet tee clung to his back so his muscles moved and bunched as he worked.

At least she tried not to notice.

It was difficult when he so big. She wasn't a tiny person, but he made her feel that way.

With both of them checking the rest of the structures, Ronnie was done in half the time. She motioned Arran to follow her as she ran to her tent, her boots splashing water with each step.

It wasn't until she was inside her shelter and had turned to watch Arran dip his wet head to step inside that she wondered what had compelled her to invite him in.

No matter how handsome he was, dangerous was dangerous. Despite how much she argued with herself, she was intrigued by Arran.

It was a precarious and perilous game she played, but she was confident she wouldn't make the same mistakes she'd made before.

That was, until Arran's golden eyes fastened on her, then dropped to her breasts, which were outlined by her impossibly wet shirt and tank. . . .